PRAISE

"Author Lara Bernhardt creates a downright spooky tale that successfully captures and melds elements of a campfire, Halloween chiller with the drama and intrigue of the X-Files."—certified Amazon reviewer

"This is by far the best book I've read all year."—Tamara Hanks Grantham, author of the award-winning Fairy World MD series

"I know people say this a lot but it is very rarely true for me - I couldn't put this book down. This author brings a freshness to this novel that makes it far more than a haunted house/ghost story." James R. Ludwig, author of The Maui Mysteries series

"Riveting thriller! Absolutely loved it!"—certified Amazon reviewer

"*The Wantland Files* is such a unique premise, Lara Bernhardt has an imagination and a way with words that will entrance readers, take them on journeys through spirit worlds, and introduce them to characters they will not soon forget."—certified Amazon reviewer

"*The Wantland Files* is . . . the most enjoyable paranormal-themed book I have ever read."—John Biggs, author of *Shiners*

"I look forward to reading the next installment of the adventures of Kimberly, Sterling and their crew! I hope this is the first of a long and successful series."—Betty Ridge, author of *Deadlines*

THE HAUNTING OF CRESCENT HOTEL

The Wantland Files Book 2

LARA BERNHARDT

ADMISSION PRESS

The Haunting of Crescent Hotel

© 2018 Lara Bernhardt

Print and eBook editions published by Admission Press

All rights reserved.

This is a work of fiction. Names, characters, organizations, places, events, and incidents are either products of the author's imagination or are used fictitiously. Any resemblance to actual persons, living or dead, or actual events is purely coincidental.

No part of this book may be reproduced, or stored in a retrieval system, or transmitted in any form or by any means, electronic, mechanical, photocopying, recording, or otherwise, without written permission of the publisher.

Cover design by BEAUTeBOOK

To Mom and Dad, with wholehearted gratitude and thanks for your unflagging support and encouragement. I'm enormously proud of our family.

THE WANTLAND FILES

THE HAUNTING OF CRESCENT HOTEL

BY LARA BERNHARDT

ADMISSION PRESS

PROLOGUE

CLARA SMOOTHED the comforter and fluffed the pillows, wondering if Ms. Theodora would show herself today. The bed could have no wrinkles, no creases. She continued working until the pillows, evenly plumped, rested equidistant from the edges of the bed. The comforter hung impeccably, the edges level. Perfect.

She scrutinized the room. Vacuumed, dusted, and scrubbed, it was nearly ready for the next occupants. Nothing out of place. Which was the only acceptable state for this particular room. Though she wanted every room spotless for every hotel guest, she knew Ms. Theodora wouldn't settle for less than perfect in room 419.

She grabbed a stack of clean towels from her cart and carried them to the bathroom. Folding them lengthwise exactly in thirds, she hung them on the towel rack so that the edges aligned perfectly.

When she heard movement behind her, she whirled around, eyes darting, searching for the source of the sound.

The tiny toiletries she'd stocked a few minutes ago had shifted. She stepped closer to the sink and inspected the small shelf above it. The little bottles she'd clustered in a bunch on one side of the shelf now sat in a perfect row exactly in the center. But no one else was in the room. At least not anyone still living.

She laughed. "Okay, Ms. Theodora, have it your way. I thought it looked pretty nice the other way, but it's your room."

She sang as she gathered her cleaning cart and locked room 419 behind her, ready for the next guests. Dirty sheets and towels filled her linen bag so she pushed her cart to the elevator. She needed to detour to the laundry room in the basement before moving on to the next room on her cleaning schedule.

She greeted each guest along the way and gave the young men manning the industrial washers, Adam and Joe, a huge smile. Sudsy water swirled in the doors of the front-load machines already in use while Adam pushed a load into an empty machine. Joe pulled laundry from a completed cycle and transferred it into a waiting dryer.

"You know," she said, "someone on the other side of that wall is enjoying a massage."

"Yeah, yeah. And we wash their robes," Adam said. "You don't have to remind us every day. I don't go in for massages anyway. Who wants some stranger's hands all over you?"

She laughed. "Glad you're content. Got another bag for you."

She grasped the edges of the linen bag and tugged. It didn't move. "Strange." She gripped tighter and pulled harder. The bag did not move.

She heard a voice in her ear as though someone stood directly behind her and whispered over her shoulder. She gasped and spun around.

No one stood near her. Both Adam and Joe remained across the room.

"Did one of you say something?"

"Nope. Just shifting this load to the dryer," Joe answered.

"No, ma'am."

She turned her attention back to the linen bag, which lifted easily. *Must've been snagged on something.* She dropped the dirty linens into a hamper and selected a clean replacement bag, which she hung on her cart.

Grasping the handle, she turned to tell the boys goodbye and caught her reflection in a washing machine door.

A man stood directly behind her, one arm raised above her head.

She caught her breath and spun around, cringing in anticipation of the expected blow.

No one stood behind her. She whirled again and looked for her reflection in the washing machine. Nothing stared back but her own panic-stricken face. She leaned on her cart, taking deep breaths.

"You okay, Miss Clara?" Adam asked. Both of them watched her, concern etched in their faces, laundry forgotten.

She forced a smile and took a deep breath. "I thought I saw . . . never mind. I'm fine. We should all get back to work." She grasped her cleaning cart firmly and, chiding herself for letting her imagination get the better of her, pushed it toward the exit. Wouldn't her son laugh if he knew? "See you two next load."

The laundry room door creaked and slammed shut.

Joe turned from his machine. "Did you close that?"

"No," she whispered, unable to take her eyes off the door.

"Weird. Must've blown shut."

She heard her own pulse whooshing in her ears, the blood pounding a warning. "I don't think so."

"Well, just prop it open again when you leave. It gets too hot in here when it's closed."

Something loomed behind her, she knew without a doubt, daring her to open the door. To move one muscle.

"Seriously, Miss Clara. It's getting stuffy already. Open the door."

Open the door.

She heard the whisper over her shoulder as clearly as she heard the boys' voices. A man's voice. Ugly. Mean. Deep with malice.

Her grip on the cart tightened until she shook. The temperature around her plummeted, yet a drop of sweat trickled from her temple.

Ragged breathing whispered against the back of her neck. She couldn't move. Didn't dare turn. Could barely breathe.

"For crying out loud." Adam passed her, arm extended to open the door.

Every washing machine slammed shut and whirred to life. Water gushed and sloshed against the doors.

Adam spun on his heel. "What the hell?"

"I don't know," Joe cried. "They all closed and started at the exact same time."

"Well, turn them off." Adam ran to help.

"They won't turn off. Look." He pressed buttons to demonstrate.

Pulse racing, she willed her feet to carry her forward, praying the door would open when she pushed on it.

The space around her grew colder still. Her breath fogged in little clouds as she gasped for air.

A man appeared in front of her, or what must have once been a man. This thing appeared to have crawled out of a grave. The same decaying face and hollow eyes she'd seen reflected in the washing machine door. She knew he meant her harm.

She opened her mouth to call for help but produced no sound. She heard the boys behind her, distracted with the bewitched washing machines.

She let go of the cart and raced to the door, dodging the translucent form in her path. She threw her shoulder against the door. Nothing happened.

The ghostly corpse crossed the room and stood in front of her, dark eyes peering into hers. He extended one arm.

"What do you want?" she managed, her words barely audible.

He rested his hand on her arm. Cold. So cold. She couldn't move. Why hadn't she hugged her son the last time he came home from college to visit? Would she ever have the chance again?

"What do you want?" she whispered, trembling.

He dug his nails into her forearm and raked them along the flesh, drawing three crimson lines.

When she screamed, he opened his mouth and uttered a single word.

"Revenge."

CHAPTER ONE

KIMBERLY ADMIRED the limestone hotel built on a flat plain on the top of a mountain. The structure had survived numerous changes of ownership, abandonment, a devastating fire, renovations, and a brush with demolition. But here it still stood, persisting since its 1886 completion, with a beautiful exterior and a scandalous history. And apparently a collection of previous occupants who never moved out.

"What a gorgeous old building," Rosie declared. "Not at all what I imagined."

"Just what I was thinking. Not what you think of when someone says 'haunted house.' Or hotel, in this case."

A photographer snapped shots of a wedding party in the lush garden, pausing only to adjust the bride and groom on the arching wooden bridge.

Rosie nudged her with an elbow. "Giving you ideas? Taking notes?"

"What? No. Why would you ask me that? I'm not even dating anyone."

Rosie raised one eyebrow. "Speaking of Sterling."

"We weren't talking about Sterling."

"Have you seen him yet?"

"I have not seen Sterling since we wrapped last season. Didn't see him at headquarters. Didn't see him while I dragged my butt on a promotional tour. I take that back. I believe I saw him in a photo he snapped of himself lying on a beach surrounded by an assortment of women wearing very tiny bikinis."

"You checked him out on Twitter? You stalker, you."

"I wasn't—" She gave up, knowing arguing was pointless. Nothing stopped Rosie once she got going. And maybe she had peeked at Twitter a few times to see what he was up to. Rosie didn't need to know that. "And I didn't see him the past couple of weeks during pre-season prep."

"I heard that he went on his own promotional tour. That Mr. Hoffmeier opted for a divide-and-conquer approach to maximize publicity."

"That's what Michael told me, too. Yet Sterling's promo landed him on beaches with hot girls while mine left me in lonely hotel rooms." So what if she didn't want to sit on the beach anyway? If Sterling had been along with her for the publicity tour, she would have had an excuse to see him. Maybe this was better. Work and relationships should be separate. At least, that's what she'd heard.

"You need your hematite to ground you and some soothing tea to ease that jealousy right out of you."

"I'm not jealous."

"You sound a little jealous. But you shouldn't be. Remember, you get me."

She relaxed her face into a smile. "You're right. And no other personal assistant could compare. So I win no matter what. The day you quit is the day this show ends."

Rosie tipped her head. "I'll remember that the next time my contract is up for renewal. Anything happen at your house while we were in Albuquerque?"

"Not really. Wish I could spend more time there. But Angela will let me know if anything happens."

"She seems like a solid house sitter. That's reassuring. How's the renovation going on The Ronald McDonald House? I know you're funding that, even though you're trying to keep it on the down low."

"How did you . . . ? I didn't tell anyone about that! It was an anonymous donation."

"The same way I know you're the one who granted several wishes through Make-A-Wish this summer."

"Are you sure you're not the psychic around here? Seriously, how did you figure that out?"

Rosie hugged her. "I know you. We've been best friends for too many years. I know you will do anything for anyone. And you have a soft spot for kids."

"I don't have any of my own, so I thought I could help other families. Nothing worse than children facing medical issues. And families who don't have the financial resources to handle them. I wish I could do even more."

"I don't really understand why you try to keep it quiet. Maybe Tweet about it a little. You'd probably be surprised how people would respond. I saw that your school supplies drive was a huge success. And the food pantry drive. I suspect you made donations to them as well, but when you share your involvement with the public, they respond."

"Other people shared my involvement, not me. I don't get involved for attention or praise. People would think I was bragging."

Rosie raised an eyebrow. "Or maybe they would join in with support. That would be a simple way to do more."

Perhaps Rosie was right. The thought of sharing her personal life with strangers made her skin crawl. And sharing that she'd donated to charities seemed like a blatant play for attention and praise. Asking people to part with their hard-earned money didn't appeal to her. And frankly she was still surprised that people cared what she did. But maybe she needed to think of the greater good and encourage other people to donate.

The Wantland Files van pulled into the parking lot, the graphic wrap of her face and logo announcing her presence. Guests and tourists turned their cameras from the landmark hotel to the van. Then they spotted her.

A small group gathered in front of the hotel, watching her. They hovered at a distance until a brave woman crossed the parking lot and walked right up to her. The woman's chakras spun brightly.

"Ms. Wantland? Hi. I'm Kerry. I'm a huge fan. Are you investigating here?"

She shook the woman's outstretched hand, overcome by the energy radiating off her. "Yes. Yes, we are."

"Oh my God. I'm staying here!" the woman squealed. "I can't believe I'm staying someplace Kimberly Wantland is investigating. *While* she's investigating!"

Rosie took her by the arm. "Okay, Kimberly, we need to—"

"Hey, Susie! Come over!" Kerry waved to the group milling in front of the hotel. Another woman scurried to join her.

She clutched her quartz crystal and breathed in and out, in and out. She wasn't allowed to be her normally shy, withdrawn self anymore. Since her show skyrocketed in popularity, everyone recognized her and behaved as though they were friends. She could do this.

"Hi, Ms. Wantland," Suzie breathed, clutching her hands to her chest. Her eyes widened. "You're wearing the necklace Sterling gave you."

Kerry chimed in. "Oh my God, that was the sweetest thing I've ever seen in my whole life."

Both women fanned their faces, eyes tearing.

"Yes, very sweet," she allowed. Of course, she'd immediately offered him a job, but jewelry was nice.

"Okay," Rosie tried again, "Ms. Wantland needs to—"

"Where *is* Sterling? He's on the show now too, right?"

Suzie clutched her chest again. "God, he's gorgeous. How do you work with him?"

The women stood on tiptoe and craned their necks.

She sighed. "Actually I was wondering exactly the same thing."

The door to the van opened and Michael hopped out. "Kimmy! There's my girl."

Her fans dropped on their heels and wrinkled their noses. "Oh, it's that guy," Kerry said. "Who is he exactly?"

"Ugh. He's still calling you Kimmy, huh? Sorry." Suzie patted her arm.

She gritted her teeth. Since Sterling caused a fuss over her nickname in the season finale, she'd heard and read a lot of comments about it. So many people making her business theirs. She would never presume to weigh in on someone's personal life. Why did everyone think they could comment on hers?

"He's my—"

A roaring engine interrupted her. Every head turned toward the approaching car as it whipped around the curved road and into the parking lot. A steel gray sports car cruised past the onlookers, wide and low to the ground, and slid into a parking space. Neon blue accents curved over the bumper and swept over the wheel wells. The engine rumbled to a stop.

"If Doc Brown steps out of that car, I'm out of here," she said.

"I'll go with him!" Rosie said.

"That's not a DeLorean, Kimmy. It's a BMW i8. Though they do have butterfly doors. If I hadn't bought the New York City flat, I might have splurged on a sports car like that."

"Since when have you been into sports cars?"

"Since I found out my ex is driving one. Besides, that's a sweet ride."

The driver's side door lifted. Sterling stepped from the sports car, dressed in his signature all black, dark sunglasses covering his eyes.

"There he is! There's Sterling!" Kerry pointed while Suzie gripped her arm.

"Oh my God, he's gorgeous!"

Her rapturous fans ditched her, drawn to her new cohost. The loitering onlookers buzzed from their clustered mob. Hotel guests clamored down the stairs from the lobby. Even the wedding party and photographer stared and whispered.

Sterling spread his arms wide, smiling from ear to ear as women descended on him. "Who's ready to bust some ghosts?"

"And there he is," she said, pressing her fingertips to her temples.

"Well, you wanted the spotlight off you," Rosie said. "Now we can go to your trailer and settle in. I know you need some tea and meditation to hone your energy before facing spirits. And steal yourself for crowds of people."

She should go. Nothing about watching her fans flock to Sterling would make her feel better. But like a gawker at a crash site, she couldn't look away.

"If you scowl too long, your face will freeze like that," Rosie whispered in her ear. "Come on. Let's go settle you in your trailer."

She nodded and allowed her stylist to guide her toward the trailer, noting a second trailer set up in the lot as well.

"Kimberly!" Sterling called, waving an arm. "Come here and join us!"

She shook her head.

"You gotta come be in some pics. It's not the same without the star!"

Michael gestured her toward Sterling. "Publicity. Part of the job."

"Go on," Rosie said and pushed her. "It'll be good for you."

Star? The zealous fans hanging all over him didn't seem to consider her the star. When Michael raised his eyebrows, she plodded across the parking lot to join Sterling, stomach quivering. She hadn't seen him in months. What should she say? He'd admitted to liking her when the show wrapped last season—and then disappeared all summer. Did he change his mind?

12

Decide he liked the company of scantily clad beach bunnies better?

He stepped away from his adoring fans and curled an arm around her shoulders, squeezing her close. "Hey."

She swallowed hard. "Hi." She sought his eyes, but he wouldn't look at her.

He returned his attention to the women. "Okay, Suzie. Now we're ready. After all, we're a team."

Suzie, Kerry, and the other women looked vaguely disappointed they could no longer cozy up to Sterling. He kept her tucked against his side as one after another of the waiting group pressed in beside them. Michael offered to handle cameras and then coached her to raise or lower her chin, tip her head a certain way, or smile bigger. Rosie dashed in to rearrange her hair when the wind blew it askew.

Sterling never dropped his arm from her waist. And any time a male fan approached, Sterling pulled her even closer while angling to keep the guy away from her. His warm body against hers sent her heart thumping and made coherent thought difficult. She found the attention of her fans much easier to handle with him by her side. Despite the annoyance she'd experienced only moments ago, she appreciated that Sterling ran interference and didn't let strangers press up against her.

Finally, Michael cleared the crowd. "Thank you all for your interest in the show. Be sure to watch this fall so you can see Kimberly's investigation. We need to get started now."

Sterling dropped his arm, removed his sunglasses, and turned to face her. His dark eyes searched hers. "How was your summer?"

Her heart pounded even harder. "Not as good as yours, I think."

"I thought I might hear from you. A text or something."

Hear from her? She'd been waiting to hear from him. "You know how to reach me if you want to. And you looked pretty busy hanging out with women on beaches."

"That was a publicity stunt. Hoffmeier's idea." He smirked. "You sound a bit jealous. Is that why you didn't text?"

"I'm not jealous. And not contacting you wasn't a conscious decision. I was busy. Besides, you didn't text me. What's your excuse?"

He rubbed the back of his neck. "Scared, I guess?"

"Of me?" When he shrugged, her stomach quivered. What in the world could scare Sterling Wakefield? Not sure what to say, she looked anywhere but his piercing gaze. Why would this self-assured guy be scared of her? His car caught her attention. She gladly changed the subject. "Were you driving that last season? I don't remember it."

His face lit up. "Heck, no! I bought that with my signing bonus. Well, part of it, anyway. Do you like it?"

No one had mentioned Sterling got a signing bonus. Shouldn't someone have at least told her, if not consulted her? How much did a car like that cost? "That's some signing bonus." She imagined the impact a donation of that magnitude could make to one of her favorite charities. And he'd blown it on a car.

Michael finished dispersing the onlookers and joined them. "Let's go inside, shall we? The ghosts await. Time to start this investigation."

CHAPTER TWO

KIMBERLY WALKED with Michael and Rosie as the crew entered the magnificent old hotel.

"Did you hear Sterling say he bought that luxury car with his signing bonus?" she asked.

"I didn't hear that, no," Michael said.

"Did you know he was paid a bonus? And his salary is probably nothing to sneeze at either."

"Sweetie, as many viewers as he drew to the finale, the network doubled the cost of advertising spots during your show. And this season is still selling out. So, yes, they're probably paying him well for being here."

"I didn't get a bonus or a salary increase. If ad prices doubled, shouldn't I be getting some of that?"

"You admitted to being on Twitter over the summer," Rosie said. "I'm sure you saw something about inequality of women's salaries compared to men's. Shouldn't be that big of a surprise."

But it's my show. She remembered the years she worked long hours at two jobs to support herself while investigating paranormal disturbances at night. She had more than paid her dues, sleep deprived and barely scraping by. But Sterling? "We built this show from nothing, Michael. Turned our side project into an empire. And he waltzes in and gets handed a bonus and a huge salary. I assume you didn't get a raise either. Surely that has to bother you a bit."

Michael shrugged. "I like my job, want to keep it, and Sterling brought a new dynamic. People like you two together."

Rosie nodded. "He's right, Kimberly. People are shipping the two of you. Hard."

"People are what?"

"Shipping you. Online. It means they want to see you in a relation*ship*. So they *ship* you. Your celebrity name is Kimberling. It's been trending since the finale. Instant hit."

"Kimber*ling*?"

"Your names mashed together. I love it. Much better than Sterberly."

"Ugh. I'll never get used to total strangers involving themselves in my personal life."

"Relax," Rosie said. "They think you're cute together. Not that anyone would object if you were a thing. And your name does come first."

"I know, I know. Price of success." She considered for a moment. "It is kind of a cute nickname, even if we're not really together."

They climbed the steps and entered the lobby.

"Oh, this is beautiful," Rosie breathed.

Kimberly took in the burgundy walls, a sharp contrast to the dark wood and gold accents of the curved front desk that stretched across one side of the lobby. A small gift shop sat opposite the entryway and an old-fashioned ice cream parlor offered "confectionary delights" in the corner.

Stan, the show's lead camera operator, set down his cases and looked around. "Hope the wiring has been replaced and can support our equipment."

"Solid Internet will be imperative to ongoing research during the investigation," Elise, her researcher, said.

Sterling clutched his phone. "The Wi-Fi is good. I uploaded some pics to Twitter."

Her phone pinged. Her Twitter app notified her Sterling had tagged her in a tweet—a photo in front of the hotel.

Season 4 Ep 1 Investigation starts today. Let's bust some spooks! #crescenthotel #EurekaSprings #aminvestigating @KWantland

He had already uploaded additional photos with her and their fans. While she watched, he leaned his back against the front desk, snapped a selfie with the desk attendant, and uploaded that too.

She wormed her way across the lobby, past gawks, whispers, and pointing fingers, and nudged Sterling. Keeping a smile firmly in place, she whispered, "Stop tweeting exactly where we are. You are inviting trouble."

He waved and smiled at a swooning fan. "You know I want you to be happy, but no can do. I'm contractually obligated to fulfill a minimum number of tweets and posts every day. I'm your social media expert now. You didn't think they handed me that signing bonus for nothing, did you?"

Actually that was exactly what she thought. But the tweet requirement was news to her. Social media expert? She was last to know everything on her show anymore. She smoothed her expression to mask her surprise. "You need to upload photos and videos and snarky comments, fine. Upload to your heart's content. I'm asking you to be cryptic about our exact location."

"The town of Eureka Springs boasts a total population of twenty-five hundred people max. And I'm positive they all have better things to do than come follow you around."

"I'm sure you're right. But don't underestimate the lengths a stalker will go to—"

Sterling scoffed. "Stalker? How many stalkers do you have?"

"I've been lucky. I haven't dealt with many. But I've been *careful*. And you're not."

"You tell yourself that. Personally, I think it's more likely because no one cares that much."

She sucked in a breath, remembering how she'd helped him deal with a stalker last investigation. Apparently it was not appreciated and the same thoughtfulness would not be extended to her in return. "I will refrain from attempting to help you any further. Should Amber show up, however, I cannot promise I won't say, 'I told you so.' You're on your own."

She spun on her heel and into the outstretched hand of a smiling older woman.

"Ms. Wantland. Welcome to Crescent Hotel. I'm Selma Reddick."

She shook the woman's hand. Selma Reddick. The hotel owner. "Ms. Reddick. Nice to meet you. Your hotel is beautiful."

"Call me Selma. And thank you for coming. We need you."

"Glad to be here."

"We've never experienced anything like this before. I really want to see it resolved quickly. Let's get you settled into your rooms." Selma led them to the front desk. "Marcus, let's get this crew some keys and help with their bags and equipment."

"Yes, Ms. Reddick. Right away."

Selma turned back to Kimberly. "I was able to give you some of the most-requested rooms for your crew—rooms where the most activity occurs. Normally we have wait lists for them, but the current activity is affecting our reservations. We've had lots of cancellations. I've put you in Ms. Theodora's room, Kimberly. She's one of our most-reported apparitions. I'm hoping she'll interact with you. Sterling can stay in Jack's room and try his darndest to pretend ghosts don't exist."

Sterling crossed his arms and smiled at the older woman who stood only as tall as his shoulder. "Whose room?"

"Jack." Selma rubbed her palms together. "Oh, Jack is going to have so much fun with you."

"I hope so," Sterling laughed. "Kimberly will protect me, I'm sure."

"Jack may give even her a run for the money. He's ornery as all get out."

"I'm sure I'll enjoy our stay here in your lovely hotel."

Selma laid a hand on Kimberly's arm. "I hope you don't underestimate the disturbance. Don't get cocky with this one, Kimberly. I'm not sure you've come up against anything so dangerous before."

The woman's concern seemed to imply doubt. She'd never once failed. That wasn't cockiness. She knew to approach with caution. "I appreciate your concern. I always assume an entity to be potentially dangerous until proven otherwise."

Sterling raised a hand. "And I always assume an entity to be completely nonexistent until proven otherwise. And not once has that happened."

"I think this might be the one to change your mind," Selma said.

"What's behind your ear?" Sterling frowned and peered at the side of Selma's head. He reached out, passed his hand behind her ear, and presented a flower in front of her.

Selma laughed. "Clever. I almost forgot you started as a magician."

"Illusionist, please. I also have a PhD in Physics but no one cares about that."

Selma laughed. "Let me get out of your hair and let you all settle in. You might want to try the Sky Bar on the fourth floor for dinner. And rest tonight as best you can. You're going to need it. I'll leave you in Marcus' very capable hands." She left them to check in.

Sterling leaned against the front desk, both elbows behind him. "She's adorable."

"I agree. But you're the one she should've warned not to get cocky."

One eyebrow shot upward and his mouth twisted into a devilish grin. "What exactly are you suggesting?"

She flushed from her neck to her cheeks. How did he do that? He could bend anything into a double entendre. "That's not... I meant—"

Rosie looped one arm into hers. "Girl, stop. You'll only make it worse."

The sultry look Sterling gave her definitely made it worse. What a rake. Though in truth, she'd never seen him look at anyone else that way. Not even Amber. But she'd spent so little time with him she couldn't judge. She had to stop thinking that way. Otherwise she'd spend this entire week in the trailer trying to relax and focus.

At least her trailer was all hers again. She'd noted a second trailer in the parking lot. Though she hadn't noticed a new stylist for Sterling. *Huh.*

"Hey, Michael? Where's Sterling's stylist? I saw his trailer, but—"

The look exchanged between Michael, Sterling, and Rosie stopped her.

Rosie clicked her tongue. "You didn't tell her?"

Sterling rubbed the back of his neck. "I thought Michael was going to tell her."

"Uh-uh! Don't try that. I specifically said I was *not* going to tell her."

The three of them had a conversation she knew nothing about? She narrowed her eyes. "Tell me what?"

Michael sighed. "Sterling accepted the trailer but declined an additional stylist. The two of you will continue to share Rosie."

"What? I need Rosie! He doesn't. Rosie is my personal assistant, trained to keep me in top shape for the show. Anybody can dust a little powder on his face."

"I don't want just anybody." Sterling looked insulted. "I want the best. And as you always say, Rosie is the best."

Rosie put an arm around her. "You'll always be my top priority, girl. You know that. Like the finale. I barely spent any time with him."

"I don't agree with this. Find someone else for him, Michael."

"Sweetie, it's too late. You'll just have to accept it. And really, do we want the added expense of a whole other person to apply a dab of makeup to him? How can I justify that to RandMeier?"

Michael knew how frugal she was. He knew how to get to her. She clenched her fists and gritted her teeth and fought the urge to stomp her foot like a child. This was her show. *Her show.* How did Sterling keep making changes without her approval?

Before she could come up with an answer that didn't leave her sounding like a whining brat, a woman stepped to the counter and banged the bell even though Marcus stood directly in front of her.

"Young man, I've had enough."

Marcus' hands fumbled with his jacket. He stood taller and gave the woman his complete attention. "I'm sorry, ma'am. What's the problem?"

"My room is far too cold. I cannot tolerate it any longer."

"Yes, ma'am. I'll send someone to adjust your thermostat right away."

"No. I'm not an idiot. I've adjusted the thermostat and nothing happens. Either the thermostat is just there for show or housekeeping is cranking it down when I leave."

Marcus took a deep breath. "Ma'am, we—"

"And don't give me any nonsense about ghosts. I know you claim this is the most haunted hotel on the planet, but I've been on this earth a long time and never seen a ghost. I don't believe in such foolishness."

Sterling leaned to the side and held a fist in front of the woman. "Fight the good fight, sister."

The woman scowled at him over her glasses.

He retracted his fist. "No? Okay."

She rounded on Marcus again. "Instruct housekeeping not to attempt to enhance my experience by making my room unbearably cold. Or I will find another hotel."

Kimberly heard the woman muttering about "ghost nonsense" and "young people these days" as she left the lobby.

Marcus shook his head. "I promise we don't do anything like

what that woman suggested. We don't need to. Here are your keys. Ms. Wantland, you'll be in four nineteen. Sterling, two eighteen. I have a Rosie and Elise in three twelve. Stan and TJ, we'll put you next to them in three eleven. And field producer Michael Thompson, you'll be in the penthouse suite."

Michael beamed. "No one ever calls me field producer."

Kimberly threw an arm around his shoulder. "Sweetie, you've been directing me since our college days. One acts. Student-written plays. Your senior project. You'll always be my director."

"You romantic, you." Michael snapped up his key. "Penthouse? I like the sound of that."

"Selma thought it would give you plenty of space for the equipment and computers during footage review. And since Norman Baker lived there, it gets plenty of activity."

Michael gulped. "Norman Baker? The quack doctor responsible for an untold number of deaths?"

"He was really more con man than quack doctor, since he wasn't a doctor at all," Elise said. "You are correct, however, that we have no idea how many people died from his cancer 'cure,' since all records were destroyed when the authorities moved to prosecute him. No wonder the suite has so much reported activity."

"On second thought, a suite seems like so much space for one guy. Anyone want to trade?"

CHAPTER THREE

KIMBERLY SCANNED the Sky Bar menu. The restaurant on the fourth floor of the Crescent was known for pizza, so salad options were few. The view, however, could not be beat. She and her crew sat on the balcony, overlooking the beautiful rolling forested hills. Elise, TJ, and Stan, together after summer hiatus, chattered about summer vacations and caught up on each others' lives. She closed her menu and peered over the rail at the immaculate hotel grounds, green and lush.

Sterling leaned close. "Did you decide already? And if you say 'just a salad' I might stage a revolt. We're at a pizza place, for heaven's sake."

If only her immediate surroundings were as serene as the hotel grounds. Rosie had maneuvered so Kimberly and Sterling sat together—and then batted her eyelids in mock innocence. She still seethed over being forced to share Rosie with him and the seat beside him was the last place she wanted to be.

She spoke through gritted teeth. "Yes, I'm going to get salad. And I'll gladly share."

Sterling wrinkled his nose. "Ick. I'm getting pepperoni. And I'll gladly share."

Michael closed his menu. "The pizzas come one size here—huge. We will order several and all share."

Sterling grinned at her. "There ya go. No excuse not to have a slice of pepperoni with me."

She turned away. "I don't eat processed meat. But thanks."

"Well, I'm not eating salad pizza." Sterling elbowed her.

She frowned and pulled her arm out of reach. "No one is ordering salad pizza. That's not even a thing."

Rosie rested a hand on her arm. "Relax. Have fun tonight. Why are you so edgy?"

She shook her head, unwilling to admit how much Sterling frustrated her, particularly with him listening for her response. Something else bothered her though. It wasn't simply Sterling. "I don't know. Something about this place. High energy. I feel the air pulsing around me. I'm not even inviting a connection, but I feel drained."

"Sounds like you're hungry to me," Sterling said. "Have a couple slices of pizza. That'll energize you."

She grasped her quartz, now on a necklace he'd given her, and breathed deeply. In. *Deep down, I like Sterling.* Out. *His presence doesn't make me want to crawl out of my skin.*

Rosie patted her hand. "Wish I'd made some sage tea."

"Thanks, but I'll need my abilities tonight during the Ghost Tour. I don't want to dull them."

Michael glanced over his shoulder. "Isn't the fourth floor where the young woman jumped from?"

Elise switched from her conversation with the camera operators and corrected Michael. "Third floor."

TJ peered over the railing and shuddered. "That's a long way down, even from one floor lower. Who jumped?"

"A student named Sarah Hawthorne," Elise said. "When this was an all-girls boarding school back in the early nineteen hundreds. But she may not have jumped. She may have been pushed. It was quite a scandal. The autopsy revealed she was pregnant."

Michael grimaced. "That's grisly."

"Seriously, what a downer," Sterling said.

"I'm sure we'll hear all about it tonight during the Ghost Tour. Many guests over the years have reported seeing a young woman in a nightgown on the third-floor balcony. A few of them claim they saw the figure fall to the ground. It resulted in some frantic phone calls."

Kimberly shivered and wrapped her arms around herself. This location held so much history and experienced so much activity. No wonder she felt on edge. And Sterling sent her right over it.

"We will definitely want a camera out here," Stan said. "Would be awesome to record an apparition like that. Maybe we can find out where it manifests so we can determine best camera angle. This is a big place. Impossible to be everywhere. But we can set up a few sta-cams and some GoPros."

"Well, here's our waiter, thank goodness," Sterling said. "I definitely need a beer after that buzz kill." He gave her an am-I-right look.

She scowled. "Sorry. No beer. No alcohol at all. Not during shoot week."

Sterling rolled his eyes. "We're not working tonight."

"Yes we are. The Ghost Tour will function as our walk-through."

"Come on. It's one beer. What happens in Eureka Springs, stays in Eureka Springs, right?"

"Not while we're working."

"Michael?"

"Sorry, Sterling." Michael shook his head. "I'm afraid we have to enforce this one. We cut you a little slack last season as a guest. But it's in our contracts. No alcohol while investigating locations."

"Sorry," Kimberly said. "Price of celebrity. But I'm sure you had plenty of tropical cocktails on the beach this summer."

Sterling's brows knitted together, then he shrugged. "Fine. Who cares? So let's order food."

Michael selected an assortment of pizzas and a large salad to share. As the waiter finished taking down everyone's drink orders, Selma appeared at their table. She placed a hand on the waiter's arm.

"Kimberly Wantland and her crew are my guests. This check will be on me."

Michael looked stunned. "That's not necessary at all, Ms. Reddick. The show covers our meal expenses."

"I understand. And you can pick up the rest of the meals. But your first dinner is my welcome and thank you."

"Really, it isn't necessary," Michael persisted.

"If you refuse to let me pay, you will break a seventy-five-year-old woman's heart. And most people, me included, believe my late husband still resides here. Chivalrous man, he was. Don't think he'd allow a slight like that go by unnoticed." Selma tapped the side of her nose and pointed to him. "Now, here are the Ghost Tour tickets for everyone tonight. You'll have the majority of spots in your group, but it is open to others as well. Enjoy dinner and the tour."

"See you tomorrow for the interview," Kimberly called as Selma waved good-bye and left them to eat.

Michael blinked at her. "Did she just threaten me with revenge at the hands of her husband's ghost?"

"I believe she did," she answered.

Sterling leaned back in his chair, arms crossed. He muttered a "thank you" when the waiter placed his glass of water in front of him. But continued to look miffed about the moratorium on beer.

Good. About time someone told him no.

Michael leaned onto his arms and looked around the table. "Everyone get settled in? Rooms okay? No one wants to take me up on the offer to trade? The suite is huge. And gorgeous."

Sterling laughed. "Surely you're not really worried. You're a ghost exterminator. Anyone actually experience anything yet? Kimberly?"

"I was in my room all of ten minutes. So, no, not yet. I'll be interested in the laundry room. Apparently that's where the first manifestation and interaction with this entity took place."

Stan shook his head. "There is no way we can completely cover every room with cameras. I think we will need as many of the crew as possible carrying handhelds. I'll set up stationary cameras in the hotspots Kimberly identifies, but this place is too big to cover every square inch."

Michael waved away the concern. "You'll handle it. We always manage. I believe you have some news to share, Stan?"

She sat forward and narrowed her eyes at her director and supposed close friend. Why was she not in on whatever news caused Michael to grin like the Cheshire Cat?

Michael held his hands up in defense. "Don't look at me like that. I was sworn to secrecy."

Stan brimmed with a delight she'd never seen on his face before. "My wife and I are expecting."

The crew exploded into congratulations, uplifting their glasses of water, tea, and soda to toast the health of the new baby.

Rosie leaned close and whispered. "Spend a little time with that baby and you'll be wanting one of your own."

She shook her head. "You never quit, do you? The very idea causes an anxiety attack."

Rosie leaned forward. "How do you feel about children, Sterling?"

"In general? They're absolutely necessary for the continuation of the species."

"What about more specifically?"

He squirmed. "I haven't really given it much thought."

She felt his red chakra flare with fear. Finally, something they agreed on.

The food arrived. Kimberly ate salad before taking a slice of cheese pizza, trailing cheese from the pan to her plate. The thick, chewy crust supported the weight of the sauce and cheese to perfection.

They ate in silence, and she had to admit, the food helped her feel a bit better. Of course, she'd never admit it to Sterling. She leaned back and sighed after swallowing her last bite of crust.

"Nice to see you eat some real food for a change," Sterling remarked as he reached for his third slice of pepperoni. "You'll feel better in no time."

She shook her head. "I eat real food. You'll see. I just prefer to focus on healthy options most of the time."

"So can we have dinner tomorrow night? I'll take you someplace nice for some real food."

She did a double take and reached for her water glass to stall for time. Her heart hammered. That sounded like a date. Did he mean for it to be a date? Or was she reading too much into something meant to be a casual meal between coworkers? When had life become so complicated? Oh, right. When Sterling Wakefield walked into it. Rosie dug an elbow into her ribs.

"I . . . we can probably . . . I'm sure we'll have dinner plenty of times."

"Does that mean yes?"

She gathered her purse. "If you'll excuse me. I need to relax and freshen up. I don't want to be late for the Ghost Tour."

Michael noticed her leaving. "Yes, everyone be sure to arrive early for the Ghost Tour. This will function as our walk-through, so come prepared."

"Rosie, I'll meet you for makeup in the trailer."

Sterling jumped to his feet. "Don't run off. Maybe we can grab ice cream cones downstairs at that confectionary."

"That's a great idea," Michael said. "Dinner didn't cost anything. Why don't we go support the hotel by enjoying ice cream cones?"

"I'll pass. But I'll wait for Rosie in the makeup trailer."

Most of the crew pressed into the elevator, but Kimberly took the stairs.

Sterling seemed to deliberate a moment before he followed her down the staircase.

"Kimberly, you didn't really answer me about dinner. Will you let me take you?"

She avoided his eyes. She couldn't think clearly when he turned the full force of their warmth on her. Which he seemed to do regularly. She wasn't sure if it was because he realized what that look did to women and was hoping to gain something from it . . . or if it was something else. "I'm not sure—"

He wrapped a hand around her arm, pulling gently until she stopped descending. "Have I done something? Upset you or made you angry? I didn't mean to if I did."

She lifted her eyes to meet his and instantly regretted it. Her anger dissipated and her stomach turned a cartwheel. His gorgeous eyes conveyed genuine concern. He went where Rand-Meier sent him, just as she did. It wasn't his fault he got beach duty. Or that the producers offered him a signing bonus. And honestly, she was acting like a spoiled brat over sharing Rosie with him. Michael was right. Why pay for another stylist? Rosie could throw a little makeup on him in no time. She swallowed. "No. You haven't. We can have dinner. That would be lovely."

The smile that lit his face sent her stomach cartwheeling the opposite direction. Good thing she didn't want ice cream. What was she thinking when she invited him to stay on her show permanently?

As she crossed the lobby, she noticed Marcus behind the desk staring at her. The desk phone rang and rang. His hand reached for it but he didn't take his eyes off her. The young man hadn't behaved like a star struck fan when he helped them check in. What caused this?

The elevator opened and spilled her crew into the lobby.

She stopped at the desk instead of going straight to her trailer. "Everything okay?"

"Ms. Wantland," Marcus stammered as he picked up the phone. He sounded scared. "Hello?" His eyes widened and he slammed the phone.

"Everything okay?" she repeated.

"Is someone in your room right now?"

"No. I'm right here. Locked the door behind me before we went to dinner."

"Someone keeps calling me from your room."

"My room? You're sure? What do they say?"

"That can't be right," Sterling said, hovering close beside her. "You must be confused. The room is empty."

Stan brought out a camera and began recording. TJ and Elise joined her by the desk, enormous ice cream cones in hand.

The phone rang. Marcus looked back and forth between her and the phone. "Not again."

"May I?" She took the handset. "Front desk."

A garbled voice whispered from the earpiece. *Hello*. Static buzzed in her ear followed by a hissing noise. She strained to catch words in the metallic whirring sounds. "Hello? Can I help you?"

More static. She thought she heard another *hello*. And maybe *Help me*. Michael stepped forward but she held up a hand. She closed her eyes and opened her senses, inviting the entity to communicate. Many presences pressed in on her. Too many at once, all eager to connect. Overwhelmed, she grasped her quartz pendant and tried to filter them. *Tell me how I can help you.* More static. Then a dial tone.

She held the phone back out to Marcus. "Whoever it was, she hung up." Was it Theodora? Or another spiritual entity, a remnant of another guest from another time? Was it the entity she was here to exterminate for Selma?

"What do you mean? Did someone talk to you?" Sterling asked.

"I heard a voice, yes."

Marcus accepted the phone tentatively, as if it might bite him.

"Don't worry," she said. "I think it's merely a remnant. A residual haunting, stuck in a loop. Not something intelligent. Has this happened before?"

"No. Never. At least not for me. It started today, after you arrived."

So much for the loop theory. Something was reaching out to her.

Marcus glanced about, leaned forward, and whispered, "Don't tell Selma. I adore her. She's so sweet. But I'm looking for another job. This place creeps me out. I never believed in ghosts when I started working here. Thought it was just stories and a way to attract people to the hotel. I've seen things though. I don't know what to believe anymore."

Sterling smiled. "It's easy to get swept up in something when everyone around you believes in it. If you can't remain objective while working here, you're probably much better off finding a new job."

Kimberly scowled at him. "Sterling, don't encourage him to quit. Fear of what we don't understand is normal. But ghosts can't hurt you, Marcus. You don't need to be afraid of anything you see or hear. You can even ask them to leave you alone, and if the disturbance is intelligent, it will understand. And if it's a loop, well, it's only like watching television or listening to the radio. It can't interact with you." She offered a comforting smile.

Marcus relaxed. "That helps to know. Thanks, Ms. Wantland." He smiled back at her.

Michael looped an arm around her waist and directed her toward the confectionary. "What did you hear? Was it cognizant?"

"I'm not certain. Maybe 'Hello' and 'Help me.' I'm worried though by how much interference we may have with this investigation. When I reached out to connect, I couldn't control anything. The incoming energy was too much. This is going to be challenging."

"You can do it," Michael assured her. "I know you can."

She wished she was as confident as her director.

CHAPTER FOUR

THE GHOST TOUR began in a lounge across from the Sky Bar. Kimberly presented her ticket to a costumed woman clad in a long skirt, high necked, long-sleeved blouse, and a shawl. A wide-brimmed hat perched atop the woman's head.

"Enjoy the tour, Ms. Wantland. We're all counting on you to get rid of Jasper, the Unfriendly Ghost."

Kimberly, already headed into the room, did a double take and returned. "Who?"

"Jasper. That's what all us employees call him. Sometimes we joke that Casper the Friendly Ghost lives here. But this one isn't friendly so we call him Jasper."

Kimberly nodded. "And you feel certain this is a new manifestation? And the ghost of a male?" If the new disturbance was male, who had reached out to her over the phone?

"Clara saw him. She saw a man. No reason not to believe her. And none of our ghosts hurt people. They're respectful to our guests."

"Nothing worse than a disrespectful ghost," Sterling said, holding out his ticket.

The woman's face pinched. "Mr. Wakefield."

He rolled his eyes. "Not Mr. Wakefield again. You make me sound so old."

"Talk to me when you leave. People come skeptics and leave believers." The woman sniffed.

"I'll believe it when I see it. I'd love nothing more."

"Then you're in the right place. Enjoy the tour."

Rosie held out her ticket as the costumed woman muttered, "I hope one of the ghosts pokes him."

Kimberly and Sterling wandered the room as the remainder of the crew and other tour participants checked in. Eerie music played. Newspaper articles papered the walls with stories about the hotel's history and some of the people who had lived there.

Rosie gripped her arm. Kimberly recognized the look on her face and followed her gaze. Rosie had spotted the tour guide, tall and thin with dark hair. Like the woman who took their tickets, he was costumed, though in slacks, a dress shirt, a vest and bow tie, and a straw cap.

Without taking her eyes off the man, Rosie ran her fingers through her hair. "If you'll excuse me, I need to go snag a seat front row center, smack dab in front of that tour guide."

Kimberly watched her stylist scamper to the front row and shook her head. "That's my Rosie." She smiled at Sterling who grinned back at her.

"Oh my God!" a high-pitched voice squealed. "I can't believe we're in the same tour as Kimberly Wantland and Sterling Wakefield!"

Kerry and Suzie crossed the room, huge smiles stretched across their faces.

"Hello again, ladies," Sterling greeted them.

Both women giggled and pressed closer. Kimberly realized she would have to get used to middle-aged women deteriorating into schoolgirl fits around Sterling. And to Sterling's evident satisfaction with his effect on women. A burst of jealousy wicked from her heart and pulsed through her.

She looked for Rosie and spotted her deep in conversation with the tour guide. *Great. Abandoned while she flirts.*

Sterling rested a hand on her lower back and leaned so close his lips brushed her ear. "Let's talk after the tour, okay?"

His touch sent an electric jolt up her spine. She shivered and nodded. And suspected no one could resist Sterling Wakefield. Did that make her as pathetic as the two women trailing after him? His smile sent a warm and fuzzy tingle through her abdomen.

She moved to the front of the room and settled into the front row center seat Rosie had mentioned wanting. Though they stood not even two feet from her, neither Rosie nor the tour guide gave any indication they noticed her.

When her watch read 7:00 and other tour participants had also settled into chairs, she cleared her throat. Loudly.

No response. She kicked Rosie, but her stylist merely waved a hand at her as if to shoo her away.

At 7:05, Sterling flopped into the seat beside her. "Whew. Didn't think I'd ever shake those two."

A brief flare of jealousy was soused by the satisfaction he'd left them behind to sit with her. She found his presence soothing. And irritating. But mostly soothing.

Sterling glanced at his watch. "Can we get this thing going? I can't think of a bigger waste of time than a ghost tour. But I can think of a dozen other ways I'd rather be spending my evening."

His attitude regarding the ghost tour didn't surprise her, but she agreed with getting things started. She kicked the tour guide.

The man jumped and checked his watch. "Oh, my! Let's get started. I'm sorry for the delay."

Rosie shot daggers at her but sat down.

"I'm Lorenzo," the tour guide said. He adjusted his vest and smoothed his dark hair. "We normally start by finding out where everyone is from. Today we have *The Wasteland Files* crew, as I'm sure you've noticed. Everyone from Albuquerque, New Mexico?"

While Kimberly and the others smiled and nodded, Sterling

raised his hand. "Not me. I'm from Santa Monica, California. Though I'm thinking about moving to Albuquerque. The commute's a killer."

The room erupted in laughter. She didn't know Sterling lived in California. She hadn't thought about where he lived. No wonder so many of his Twitter pics were on the beach. Was he really thinking about moving? Behind the amusement at his own joke, she saw a question in his eyes. He wondered how she felt about that.

Lorenzo circled the room, allowing everyone to introduce themselves. Kerry and Suzie, she learned, were sisters who lived only about an hour away from Eureka Springs but had wanted to visit the haunted hotel for years and were finally fulfilling that dream. "And we still can't believe our luck that *The Wantland Files* is here while we are!"

"Glad you're all here today," Lorenzo said when everyone had shared where they were from. "We're going to start here on the fourth floor and work our way down to the morgue in the basement."

At the mention of the morgue, the tour participants shifted and murmured.

"That's correct," Lorenzo said. "The morgue used by Norman Baker during the cancer cure treatment days."

"Nineteen thirty-seven to nineteen thirty-nine," Elise murmured, pen poised over a legal pad, ready to jot down notes.

"I like to begin with a brief history of the area and the hotel," Lorenzo continued. "And I assure you that we tour guides adhere strictly to historical facts and reported phenomena. I do not attempt to convince non-believers."

Rosie raised her hand. "Are you a believer?"

Lorenzo smiled broadly. "I believe you may be an angel sent from heaven, beautiful."

Rosie ducked her head and giggled.

Kimberly couldn't resist. "A fallen angel, maybe."

Sterling and the crowd laughed while Rosie gave her the look. She batted her eyelids in mock innocence at her stylist.

Lorenzo didn't miss a beat. "That's my favorite kind."

Rosie met his gaze, eyes blazing. Kimberly knew that look. Lorenzo would "get some" soon.

Lorenzo cleared his throat. "Let's start the tour."

CHAPTER FIVE

"Follow me, please, across the hall to the balcony beside the Sky Bar. We've had numerous reports over the years of ghostly apparitions below on the hotel grounds. Go ahead and take pictures. You never know what—or who—might show up in the photos."

Kimberly held back. Her crew would capture any manifestations out for an evening stroll. She felt no ripples, no disturbances, and doubted anyone would capture anything.

Kerry and Suzie wiggled their way through the crowd and pressed themselves against the balcony railing, cell phones extended.

Sterling crossed his arms. "If you'd let me have a few drinks with dinner, I'd probably see ghostly apparitions wandering the grounds."

She gave him a look and shook her head.

"I'm just saying. Is it really a coincidence that so many sightings are reported near the hotel bar?"

Since she couldn't think of a clever retort, she said nothing. Some day something unusual would happen and wipe that self-satisfied look off his face. She hoped she was there to see it.

Kerry and Suzie flipped through their photos. "Nope. Nope.

Nope. Nope. No orbs or shapes or anything." They looked at Kimberly.

She shook her head. "I'm not detecting anything here."

"There's nothing here. Let's move on," Suzie instructed Lorenzo.

If Lorenzo heard her, he gave no indication. He withdrew a laminated, enlarged photograph. "One of the best photos ever taken in this part of the hotel seems to capture the image of a young woman. I'll pass this around. Make of it what you will."

He handed the photograph to Kimberly. She took in the image of a young man gulping a beer while a ghostly figure lurked behind him.

Sterling rested his chin on her shoulder. "How'd you like to be that man? Remembered forever as the beer guzzling guy in the ghost picture?"

She allowed him to remain on her shoulder and laughed. "I hadn't thought of that."

Rosie pressed against her for a look. "What do you think?"

"I'm not getting anything from the photo itself." She took a deep breath and closed her eyes. Her crew fell silent. She grasped her crystal.

"She's reaching out to the spirit world," Kerry whispered.

"I'm getting goose bumps," Suzie enthused.

She blocked out the excited whispers and focused on her indigo chakra, imagining it whirling faster and faster, growing to envelop her entire being. Opening her senses to input from displaced entities, she sent out a beacon. She envisioned herself as a lighthouse, a guiding light in a stormy blackness.

Something bumped her.

Her breath hitched. Whatever considered engaging drifted away. She reined in her excitement. She couldn't force a connection, only offer.

"Kimmy?" Michael wanted to know if she was okay. She held off answering and focused on her lighthouse beacon.

A hand rested on her arm. She nearly shook off the presumed

overly concerned crew member. Then, as if two puzzle pieces clicked into place, she shared her presence with another.

Darkness enshrouded her, but pinpricks of light shone above. She clutched a railing in her hands. Somehow she knew she stood on a balcony overlooking the hotel grounds. Worry consumed her, so much her heart raced. One thought ran through her mind. *Must tell... must tell... must tell...*

Footsteps behind her sent a new flush of panic coursing through her. She whirled to meet the approaching person. A man. She saw no features, only a dim outline, but she knew it was a man.

Must tell. Must tell. Must tell.

Anger. Red flashes. Furious words.

Something grabbed her arms and shook her. The man. The man was shaking her. He was angry. So angry he couldn't think, only feel. She tried to pull away but his grip tightened.

Her back banged against the iron railing. She had to get away. Had to get back inside. Needed help. She leaned backwards to avoid his advances. One more shove threw her off balance. Unable to right herself, she pinwheeled her freed arms, grasping for the railing. She missed, and gravity held firm, coaxing her, tipping the balance against her. Her toes lifted off the balcony. Her final brief scrabble to regain footing accomplished nothing. Her feet flipped over her head and she fell.

A hand grabbed her arm, jerking her to a halt. Hope sprouted. All was not yet lost. Straining to reach with her other hand, she willed herself to hold on. She had to tell him. She kicked her feet, though nothing offered support as she dangled above the ground so far below.

She slipped. Her fingers brushed against his. He clawed at the air, trying to regain a grip. She saw his eyes as he realized it wasn't meant to be.

Only one thought crossed her mind in the final moments of terrifying descent, a plummet of loss and sadness.

I never got to tell him.

CHAPTER SIX

Kimberly fell backward, directly into Sterling's arms.
"Has anyone checked her blood sugar?" Sterling asked. "Maybe she's hypoglycemic. Look how tiny she is. And she barely ate any dinner. She's probably hypoglycemic."
"I appreciate the concern, Sterling, but this is unrelated to blood sugar issues." Michael peered in her eyes. "You okay, dollface?"
She nodded. "I'm fine."
"You passed out," Sterling said. "All of a sudden fell backward. Lucky for you I was right next to you and caught you. Otherwise you'd probably have a concussion right now."
Season Four was off to a bang—Sterling catching her as if she needed saving.
"She didn't pass out," Michael insisted.
"This is what a vegetarian diet will do to you," Sterling continued as if Michael hadn't spoken. "You're probably anemic and have low blood sugar." He pulled her eyelid up and stared at her eyeball. "What does anemia look like?"
He leaned entirely too close for comfort. His face close enough to kiss her was more than she could handle. She swatted

his hand away. "Stop that. Did I miss the part where you earned a medical degree? You don't know what you're talking about."

"What did you see?" Michael asked.

"I spiritually co-existed with someone. A young woman, I believe. I fell off a balcony. Backwards. I was pushed backwards off a balcony."

Lorenzo's eyes widened. "This is incredible. Many believe the spirit in the photo I just passed around is—"

"Sarah Hawthorne," Elise interrupted. "The pregnant girl who fell from the balcony while the hotel was the Crescent College and Conservatory for Young Women. We talked about it briefly at dinner."

"Yes! See how the image appears to be cradling an infant?"

The crew circled around her as she studied the image a second time.

"I see it," TJ breathed.

Sterling sighed. "Of course you see it now, after someone suggested the idea. Not one person said, 'Hey! That ghost looks like it's holding a baby,' when we first looked at it. And I'll bet you conveniently didn't catch anything on camera either."

"I did," Stan said, an edge to his tone. "You think I'd miss an opportunity like that?"

TJ hung his head. "My batteries went dead. I don't know what I got before my camera cut out. I . . . I was so worried about Ms. Wantland, I didn't notice."

"Didn't see you recording anything, Sterling," Stan said.

Sterling whirled on the camera operator. "Recording is your responsibility."

"Just saying, if you think you can do better, take your best shot."

Lorenzo cleared his throat. "Shall we proceed?"

Michael raised his eyebrows at her. "Kimmy?"

"I'm fine. Lead on."

The group fell into a silent jumble behind Lorenzo.

Kimberly felt a hand on her arm and turned to see Suzie's eyes full of sympathy.

"I see why you hate Kimmy so much. It's truly dreadful." The woman jockeyed her way through the crowd and planted herself firmly beside Sterling.

Rosie gripped her forearm. "Breathe in. Breathe out. In. Out."

She obeyed until she caught Stan's eye. "What was that?"

He grinned. "Just a little hashtag Wantland drama for your fans to post. Every one of them had a phone out. Thought maybe I wouldn't let the new guy orchestrate all the drama."

"Brilliant." Her crew was incredible. But she knew that already.

He winked at her then caught up to TJ and palmed him new batteries. "Happens to everybody at some point. Man up and quit moping."

Lorenzo continued the tour. "Also here on the fourth floor we have Ms. Theodora's room. One of our most requested rooms as we have consistent activity here. Ms. Theodora served as a nurse while Norman Baker operated a cancer treatment center out of the hotel. She appears as a full-bodied apparition and speaks and interacts with guests. We believe she is a sentient haunting. She is also a compulsive neat freak and will not tolerate a messy room. Some people believe she chooses to remain here, possibly to continue helping others who find themselves left behind and unable to move on. Once a nurse, always a caregiver perhaps. Notice the lack of doorknob on the door. I'm afraid visitors attempt to enter the room without permission rather than respecting the privacy of the occupants. So you can only get inside with a key. And of course Ms. Wantland is staying in it. Has she moved around your belongings yet?"

Kimberly shook her head. "I haven't been back since I left my things when we checked in. But I think she may have called the front desk and spoken to me over the phone."

"Or maybe there was a really bad connection and what you

thought was a ghost was an actual person sounding garbled and ethereal," Sterling said.

"Marcus said the phone call was from my empty room. You saw how spooked he was."

"There you have it, folks. Undeniable evidence of ghosts. Marcus looked spooked."

TJ spoke up. "Dude! The call came from her empty room! You're ignoring that completely."

"Stop calling me dude, kid."

"I'm not a kid! You make me crazy. I swear, one of these days . . ." He stopped before he shared what he intended to do to Sterling.

"Anytime, kid. Empty threats don't scare me."

"Please!" Kimberly squeezed her temples. Would they continue this all week? Every week? She couldn't handle this sort of constant tension. It clogged up her chakras and made reading paranormal activity difficult.

"Better watch him, Michael," Sterling said. "He obviously has a huge crush on Kimberly."

TJ shoved his camera into Stan's hands and rushed at Sterling, fists balled. "I do not! Don't you dare talk about Ms. Wantland that way!"

Michael stepped forward and caught TJ. "Come on, you two. This isn't helping anything. Keep it professional or I can't let you work on the investigation. This stops now."

"I think he proved my point," Sterling gloated.

"Sterling, shut it!" Michael raised his voice uncharacteristically. She'd never heard him sound so miffed.

Sterling crossed his arms and shrugged, delighted smirk plastered across his face. TJ continued to seethe, but retrieved his camera from Stan, kicking the floor once.

"Don't let him goad you like that," Stan murmured to TJ. "You can't let him get to you. Best revenge is great footage so rise above it."

The others in the tour group looked stunned or amused.

Most of them had phones up, presumably recording the altercation. Her show was totally out of control. Sterling acted like a child and irritated everyone involved. Except women. They continued to fawn over him no matter how much of an ass he made of himself. She felt ill. What had she done? Inviting Sterling to co-host was supposed to take the show to the next level, not drag it down to reality television brawling.

Lorenzo cleared his throat. "Before we move on, gather around and notice the bannister railing around our stairs. Notice how low the top of the railing is and how wide the space between the slats. Our railing does not meet current OSHA safety requirements. However, our designation as a historical building means we cannot make any significant changes to the hotel. We preserve as much as possible."

Elise lifted a hand. "Several people have fallen over it, haven't they?"

"Yes, sadly. Most notably the young daughter of a nurse who lived here during Norman Baker's years. She was so small, she slipped through the slats. Many people report seeing her skipping down the hall. We suggest taking lots of picture here and on the landing at the bottom." Lorenzo peered at his watch. "We should move along. These tours run every hour and we don't want the next group to catch up to us."

"Then why did you spend the first ten minutes flirting?" Sterling and TJ said together.

"Jinx! You can't talk until I give you permission," Sterling declared.

"Bullsh—"

"TJ!" Kimberly shook her head and scowled.

He huffed and crossed his arms. "He's not even doing it right. It's supposed to be, 'Jinx, you owe me a soda.'"

Sterling rubbed his chin. "I think I prefer your silence to a soda. I can buy myself a soda. I can't buy your silence. I can only win it in a jinx."

"Dude. You can't stop me from talking."

Sterling raised his eyebrows and shrugged. "Jinx rules."

"That's not the rule. You're doing it wrong."

"This way, please. Down to the third floor," Lorenzo called, raising his voice to be heard.

"Well, what if I buy you a soda? Then will you be quiet?" Sterling asked as they walked away.

Thankfully, she couldn't hear TJ's reply.

Rosie stepped in front of her, eyeing her critically. "You sure you're okay?"

"Yes, I'm fine." Rosie's mere presence and concern lifted her spirits and recharged her as they always did. A surge of gratitude filled her. The attention Sterling garnered as the new guy bothered her more than she wanted to admit.

"Good. Then I'm off to move closer. I can't hear a thing."

Kimberly knew exactly what her stylist intended to move closer to as she watched the woman worm her way through the crowd. "Et tu, Rosé?"

"Aw, let her have some fun," Michael said. "You know she gets irritable and unbearable if she goes too long without being hit on."

"Indeed I do. What about you? Did you meet anyone special this summer up in New York?"

"Nah. Saw some terrific shows though."

"Didn't hook up at all? Come on. Dish! We've always shared our darkest secrets."

"Alas, I've nothing to share. I think I'm getting too old to hook up. I'm ready for something more meaningful in my life."

She clutched her chest, staggered a few steps, and gasped. "What?"

"Stop it, you brat. I never got around that much and you know it."

She hooked an arm through his and leaned against his shoulder. "I do know it. But I rather resent the use of the phrase 'too old' considering we're the same age."

He laughed. "Fair enough, honey. Let's say I've finally matured emotionally to your level."

"Accepted. I never got around at all though, so I guess I matured early."

"Nothing wrong with that. Except it left your unguarded heart easy to break."

In the silence that followed, he must have realized he'd picked a scab off the wound because he switched subjects. "What about you? Did you have any luck with the house?"

"No. Nothing yet. If I had any sense, I'd let it go."

"Now, Kimmy—"

"No, it's true. Any other place I would've deemed no manifestation by now. Why do I do this to myself?"

He pulled her head to his shoulder. "I know why, honey."

As they rounded the landing onto the third floor, Kerry called out to her. "Kimberly! Come quick!"

CHAPTER SEVEN

As soon as she joined the group, Kimberly felt the excitement radiating from the participants. And something else. Something pulled at her, demanding her attention, wanting to share. She felt a sharp pain and closed herself off from the connection.

Kerry and Suzie raced to her side. "Look! Look at the orbs we caught!" They thrust their phones in her face. She took one and focused on the image. Three balls of light glowed in the hallway, a halo radiating from each.

A piercing pain shot through Kimberly's brain. She returned the phone and squeezed her temples. "Yes, those appear to be orbs."

Rosie broke away from Lorenzo. "Kimberly?"

She reached for Rosie, gulping breath after breath as the pain increased.

"Kimmy, what is it?" Michael joined them.

She shook her head and sat on the hall floor. Closing herself against this bombardment didn't stop the onslaught. She felt dozens of ethereal hands pulling at her, clinging to her, eager to connect. It was too much. "I can't . . . block it." The edges of her vision blurred, closing in to a circle of light.

She felt Rosie ease her onto her back and heard her stylist

direct everyone to circle around. "That's it. Nice and close. Shoulder to shoulder. Everyone that can fit."

She heard Rosie open a case and then felt chakra stones placed strategically on her body.

"Everyone take one of these," Rosie said.

"Twigs?" Sterling asked.

"Sprigs of sage. Kimberly's psychic energy is depleted and needs to recharge. She's being overwhelmed by all the presences in the hotel. We need to create a safe place for her while she recovers. So make a circle of sage. Surround her with positive energy. Hold the spirits at bay."

"We're helping Kimberly Wantland," Kerry whispered in an awed hush. A strangled cry, presumably of excitement, escaped Suzie.

"Sterling?" Rosie said.

"I'm not going to stand here like a fool clutching a useless piece of seasoning. You know this won't do a thing, right? When will you call for the medical intervention she so clearly needs?"

"If we all encircle her with sage, it will block the spirits from draining her. You'll see. She'll be back to new in no time."

"Jeez, Sterling. We thought you wanted to be part of the show," Kerry said. "Way to support your coworker."

"You are such a douche," TJ said. "You're breaking the circle. Get out of it and let someone else in. Someone who actually cares about Ms. Wantland."

"I don't see you in here," Sterling said.

"I'm recording! This is integral to the show. I may catch evidence of the spirits attacking her."

"Attacking—oh, for Pete's sake. Give me the stupid plant. This is asinine."

"You're asinine," TJ muttered.

"Do you even know what that word means?"

"Well, I knew Ms. Wantland would be upset if I said you're an ass, so . . ."

Even drained and fighting for consciousness, Kimberly wanted to yell at them to be quiet.

Rosie's voice took command. "Everyone needs to focus on happy thoughts and surround her with positive energy. Create a circle of loving protection."

Finally silence descended. She breathed a bit easier. The energy current reversed, flowing to her rather than draining away.

The hands withdrew. The piercing pain ebbed. The stones radiated energy into her chakras. She relaxed and breathed deeply. She opened her eyes.

"Much better. Thank you all. Something about this floor. I felt so much pain."

Rosie collected the sage and thanked the participants, then removed the chakra stones.

Lorenzo's face appeared above her as the circle disbanded. "Are you certain you don't need me to call someone?"

She sat up. "I'm much better now, thank you. Rosie is all the help I needed."

"That was a quick recovery," Sterling commented with an eye roll.

"Rosie knows her stuff." Her personal assistant didn't comment but smiled as she packed away her supplies.

Lorenzo twisted his hands together, guilt radiating from his aura. "I should have warned you. This floor figured prominently during the cancer hospital years when Norman Baker owned it. Are you sure you can continue the tour?"

"Absolutely." Rosie and Michael helped her to her feet. "We have to press on. I can't solve a disturbance until I know exactly what I'm dealing with."

The tour participants clapped a little when she rallied and thanked them all for their help.

"Oh, please," Sterling said. "No one recovers that quickly from a serious issue. She obviously faked an 'episode' for attention and sympathy or to invent some danger."

No one out-right booed him, but she delighted in the ugly looks they shot him. And she noticed Kerry and Suzie hovered near her, not him.

Lorenzo continued the tour. "Now we come to the portion of the tour where we discuss Norman Baker."

The crowd quieted, a thrill of excitement settling over the group. Elise flipped pages of her notebook.

"Though history remembers him for his infamous cons, the man was actually quite brilliant, if also unscrupulous. Or perhaps not. Perhaps he truly believed he could help people. He invented a calliope as a young man and made a million dollars on the patent. He later developed a vaudeville act as a mind reader. But he's best remembered for his cancer treatment center here at the Crescent. Baker heard about and acquired—"

"'Secret recipe number five,'" Elise blurted. "Purported to cure cancer."

Kimberly bit back a smile. Her lead researcher couldn't help herself when she got excited about something.

"Yes, that's right," Lorenzo picked back up. "Baker purchased Crescent Hotel for next to nothing during the Great Depression and opened his cancer treatment center. He advertised a pain-free, one-hundred-percent-guaranteed cure. Lured in by his promises, desperate families brought their sick relatives to be cured. Baker paid local residents to stand out front and profess to having been cured. We now know the secret formula was—"

"A mixture of antioxidants, crushed up watermelon seeds, clover, and carbolic acid!" Elise said.

Lorenzo darted a glance at Elise. Kimberly couldn't tell if he was impressed or annoyed. "Someone has done their research. That's correct. And of course carbolic acid, also known as phenol, is a chemical that should never enter the human body. In fact, Nazis used injections of phenol during World War Two as a method of extermination. Cancer patients of Baker received injections directly to their tumors seven times a day. These were extremely painful injections, and no pain medications were administered. No real doctors were on staff either. His patients only grew sicker as they suffered, since the cancer continued to spread and further sicken them. To keep the patients screaming and crying in pain from scaring the touring potential patients, and from exposing his pain-free promises as a lie, Baker transformed the servant's quarters here on the third floor into what was known as the psych ward. He installed heavy metal doors across this hallway leading to the ward to isolate the screaming patients so no one could hear them as they cried out for help."

Most of the tour participants shuddered at this news. They raised phones and snapped photos of the hallway. No wonder Kerry and Suzie caught orbs. Any place experiencing so much pain and death would inevitably be haunted by some of the spirits.

Michael nudged her. "Seems like the place to start your investigation. If I'd been duped and tortured, I think I'd be out for revenge too."

She nodded. "Does seem the logical place to start."

"This portion of the hotel is now where you'll find our honeymoon suites," Lorenzo informed them, laughing at his own joke. "From psych ward to honeymoon suites. Seems logical doesn't it? And we receive a lot of reports of activity consistently. Anyone with the *Wantland* crew staying on the third floor?"

Rosie, Elise, Stan, and TJ raised their hands.

"Well, perhaps you'll experience the nurse pushing a gurney down the hall from the psych ward to the elevator that a number of our guests have reported seeing. This usually occurs around three in the morning, and the nurse does not respond to anyone who attempts to engage her. Previous investigators determined she is a residual haunting. This elevator was the only way to transport the deceased patients from the psych ward to the morgue in the basement back then. Let's go down another flight to the second floor."

Sterling plodded beside her, without his two fans. "Be honest.

You at least faked the last one. I personally think your researcher gives you information on the reported 'ghosts' and you invent encounters with them based on that info. But at least that last one. You bounced right back from that."

Tired of arguing with him, she didn't answer. How could she make him understand the sensation of wispy fingers dragging against her arms, tugging at her clothing, and pulling for her attention? Or the drain on her psychic energies when a spirit latched onto her and tried to manifest? She couldn't. He wouldn't be convinced of anything he didn't experience himself. And he didn't possess the same abilities so he dismissed them.

"Come on." He rested a hand on her arm. "I get scared when you pass out. I'm pretty sure you need a doctor. Unless it's fake. Please tell me it's fake so I can stop worrying. Your partner should know what's happening."

She met his gaze and was taken aback by the real concern there. For the first time since he'd joined her last season, he seemed not to be trying to prove a hoax. He seemed genuinely concerned.

"You're sweet to worry. Really. I appreciate that. But I've told you before I'm not faking. I know you refuse to accept what you don't understand. You'll just have to trust me. All of this is real and I don't need a doctor."

As she turned to continue with the group, she heard Michael say, "One of you please tell me you caught that emotional exchange. That is *so* our first sneak look at season four."

She spun on her heel. "Are you kidding me right now? That was all for the cameras? Every time I start to think you're a nice guy . . ." She fought the urge to shove Sterling. "Stay away from me. You're the real fake. Not me."

She stormed away but he ran after her. "No! It wasn't. I was only talking to you because I'm worried. I didn't know— Which of you had a camera on us?"

TJ raised his hand.

"Tell her. Tell her it wasn't planned. I didn't orchestrate anything."

TJ shrugged. "You know Sterling. He's all about that hashtag drama."

Sterling blinked once, then dove for TJ. "You little shit!"

CHAPTER EIGHT

M‍ICHAEL THREW HIMSELF BETWEEN THEM, this time catching Sterling and holding him back.

Kerry and Suzie squealed and covered their mouths.

Kimberly caught her breath and stepped backward, hit by a powerful surge of red chakra energy flowing from Sterling.

He's furious. Huh. He really didn't plan that moment for publicity. Which meant he was sincerely concerned about her.

TJ struggled against Stan, trying to take a swing at Sterling, who still fought against Michael, who looked like he wouldn't last much longer.

She strode to Sterling and grabbed his arm, situating herself in front of him. She placed one hand on each side of his face and forced eye contact. "Stop it right now. This is ridiculous!"

"Not until he admits we didn't plan anything."

TJ tried again to break free from Stan. "Not happening, dude."

"I'm not lying," Sterling said.

"I know," she told him.

"I didn't—" He shook his head and focused on her. "Wait. What?"

"I know. I can tell."

"But . . . how?"

"My sixth sense."

"You believe me?"

"You're telling the truth."

Sterling relaxed. Michael let go but continued to eye him warily.

She crossed her arms. "I'm disappointed, TJ. Remember, just like your mom, I always know when you're lying."

Sterling laughed. "Yeah, TJ. Don't lie to Mom."

TJ pounced at him. Both Stan and Michael restrained him.

Sterling raised a fist but held back and only pointed at TJ. "And you're still a little shit."

TJ looked next to tears, his frustration so intense. "You don't even believe in her sixth sense. You're an asshole and you don't belong on our show."

"*Our* show? It's her show."

"I was here before you, dude! I've been here, supporting her, helping. I would've stood in the circle holding sage and protected her. I sure as hell won't let you hurt her. Or the show." He stormed away.

"TJ!" She started to follow him but Michael looped an arm around her waist and spun her around.

"No, sweetie. Let him go."

"Yeah," Stan chimed in. "Let him cool off."

"But what on earth? I've never seen TJ behave that way."

Sterling looked stunned. "He definitely has a raging crush on you. Worse than I realized. Comparing yourself to his mom really upset him."

She turned to him, incredulous. "No. You really upset him."

"The guy was lying to make me look bad in front of you. That's something guys do when they have feelings for a girl."

"Not TJ. No way. He must be at least ten years younger than me."

Sterling hummed a few bars of "Puppy Love."

She suppressed the urge to punch him. "Leave TJ alone. I'm serious. You two are more than I can handle."

Lorenzo raised his voice. "Here we are at room two eighteen. We call this Jack's room, and I believe Sterling is staying here."

"Yep. Didn't see a ghost though."

"Give it time. This is our most active room after Ms. Theodora's. Jack was only seventeen years old and worked on a construction crew building the hotel. Apparently the young man loved the ladies. He was balanced on a scaffold when he caught sight of a pretty girl in the garden. He fell trying to get her attention and didn't survive. Room two eighteen is the spot where he fell and passed away. Women have reported the shower curtain opening suddenly while they showered. Men report a foot on the back pushing them out of the bed. Lights flip on and off. Sometimes the water turns on in the middle of the night. He seems very much to still be interested in the ladies and still behaves rather like a teenage prankster."

"We're definitely going to need cameras in this room," Kimberly whispered to Michael and Stan. She noticed TJ had rejoined the group and resumed recording.

"I think I should have a say in whether or not my room has cameras in it," Sterling said.

Lorenzo held out an arm, directing them to the stairs. "Let's move to the lowest floor, the basement, and finish out the tour in the morgue. At the bottom of the staircase, I invite you to take more pictures of the area where the little girl plummeted to her death."

Kimberly held back, hoping for a private word with TJ. Her younger camera operator scurried past, however, giving her a wide berth and refusing eye contact. She considered reading his spectrum but opted to give him privacy.

Sterling joined her though. "Told you. He has a crush on you."

She glared sideways at him but held her tongue.

"So dinner tomorrow night?"

She felt a hand on her back and jerked away, thinking he was getting entirely too friendly, too fast.

Then she realized she could see both of his hands.

She glanced over her shoulder. The staircase behind them was empty.

"What's wrong?" Sterling asked.

"TJ! FLIR! Behind me!" she cried, as two hands planted firmly against her back.

A shove sent her tumbling down the remaining flight of stairs.

CHAPTER NINE

She landed flat on her back. Hard. Conscious, but unable to breathe. No matter how she gasped, her lungs refused to draw air. Her limbs thrashed as panic set in.

Rosie and Michael knelt on either side of her.

Sterling stated the obvious. "She can't breathe."

"We see that," Michael replied.

"Does she have asthma?"

"No. I think the fall knocked the air out of her. Relax, sweetie."

Rosie rubbed her temples. "Easy. You'll be okay. It's scary, but you'll be okay. Relax."

Easy advice to give but difficult to follow when she was suffocating. Her lungs had never before refused to work. No matter how hard she pulled at the air around her, she couldn't take a breath. She clawed at her throat. She needed air.

Stan approached. "I used to play sports. Can I help?"

Michael stood and made room for him.

"Kimberly, your diaphragm is spasming. Breathe in through your nose and out through your mouth." He lifted her knees and drew them to her chest. "This will help it relax."

Her attempts at breaths remained shallow and ineffectual.

But then, slowly, she drew in air. And then more. Her chest began to inflate again, replacing the paralysis that had so terrified her. And in a few minutes her breathing had returned to normal.

She lowered her legs and sat up. "Thank you, Stan. Seriously. That was awful."

Michael squatted beside her. "Can you tell me what happened? I heard you yell. Did you trip?"

"I was pushed."

All heads swiveled to stare at Sterling.

He held up his hands. "Whoa! I didn't push her. You don't seriously think I pushed her."

"Did you see what happened?"

"It's pretty obvious. She fell down the stairs."

"No, I was pushed. I am aware none of our group was behind me. But I felt hands on me. Something pushed me. Hopefully, TJ managed to capture something on the FLIR."

Now all heads swiveled to TJ, who looked startled.

"Oh. I did get the camera on you before you fell. For a moment or two anyway." He fumbled with the thermal recording device. "I'll run it back and see if I caught something."

He stared intently at the screen. His face lit up. "I see something. A figure right behind her."

The crew clustered around him while he ran it back and replayed it for them.

"I'll be damned," Stan said. "There is something behind her. Right before she pitches forward."

Michael's brow furrowed. "This is quite alarming, sweetie. It certainly appears to be an intentional, hostile act."

Rosie cringed as she watched the footage again. "You could have been seriously injured. Asshole ghost!"

Sterling pressed through the group. "Asshole ghost? Really? Can I take a look?"

"Asshole cohost," TJ muttered.

"I heard that." Sterling scowled.

For a moment Kimberly feared another skirmish. Though they scowled, neither moved toward the other.

"Go ahead and replay it, TJ," Michael directed.

Sterling watched but appeared unimpressed. *Big surprise.*

"That 'image' you're calling a ghost is simply her heat footprint trailing behind her on the recording. Like a shadow. Not some aggressive entity trying to hurt her. Everyone needs to rein in their imaginations."

"Where is your heat shadow, then?" TJ asked.

Sterling watched the footage again. "I guess I'm not as hot as Kimberly." He flashed a grin at her, but no one laughed.

"You're theory doesn't hold up if it doesn't apply to both of you," TJ said.

"I have to side with TJ on this," Michael said.

Sterling opened his mouth to respond. Kimberly felt another argument coming on and decided to end it before it started. She attempted to push herself to her feet. "Let's finish the tour. We can review this tomorrow and argue about it then. After I've had some rest and caught my breath."

"Take it easy," Michael said. "I think you've endured enough tour."

"But I haven't seen the morgue yet."

"Stan and TJ will film. Elise knows how to operate the EMF and assist with voice sessions. She's helped us before. Let's get you back to the room."

"I'll take her," Sterling offered. "I don't add anything to the tour anyway. I can't operate the equipment and I won't encounter a ghost either. I guarantee it."

"It's moot because I won't miss the morgue. I need to be there to read the space for energy."

"You need to be in top shape for the investigation tomorrow. I'm afraid I have to insist. We can't risk jeopardizing your health any further."

She scowled at her director.

"You can make all the ugly faces at me you want, I won't budge on this."

She tried to stand but nearly toppled over. "I'm a little woozy."

Before she knew what was happening, Sterling scooped her up in his arms.

"Hey! Put me down. You'll hurt yourself!"

He laughed. "Please. Do you even weigh a hundred pounds? I could bench press you."

Michael pushed the button to summon the elevator.

"I will take the elevator, though. Don't want to risk tripping carrying you up the stairs. But I could carry you."

The last thing she saw as the elevator doors closed with Sterling cradling her against him, was Rosie, face alight, giving her two thumbs up, and calling, "Enjoy your evening."

CHAPTER TEN

STERLING OPENED the door for Kimberly and ushered her inside, helping her sit on the bed. He filled a glass with water from the bathroom sink and hovered while she drank it.

"I'm okay," she reassured him.

"Then why are you shaking?"

"I'll be okay. I'm not hurt. Thank you."

"I'm not convinced. That was a hard fall. You couldn't breathe for several minutes."

"Just knocked the wind out of me. Nothing hurts. Much. You can check me out if you'd like."

He cocked an eyebrow at her. "I'll remember you said that."

"Not what I meant and you know it."

Sterling stared around her room. "See anything out of the ordinary? Your luggage looks untouched."

"Well, that fruit arrangement wasn't here earlier."

"You don't seriously believe a ghost left a fruit arrangement for you, do you?"

She glowered at him and crossed to the dresser. Skewers of berries, pineapple chunks, and grapes mimicked flowers, clustered together in a green vase. "This is almost too beautiful to eat." But she lifted a fruit "flower" and savored the sweet end to a rough day.

Sterling joined her. "No card or tag? Maybe you shouldn't dive in when you don't know who sent it."

She swallowed a bite of pineapple "petal" and turned the arrangement. "No card at all? Well, it's probably from Selma." She bit into a juicy strawberry center.

Sterling shook his head. "Selma already paid for our pizza. I'm not convinced she sent this."

"Want some?"

"Not when I don't know where it came from."

"You're too suspicious." She shrugged and went to rinse her face and fingers in the bathroom sink. One look at her toiletries and her heart raced. She smiled. "Sterling. Looks like Ms. Theodora has been busy in here. Come see."

He joined her and took in the tiny shelf above the sink. "See what? Nothing looks weird to me."

"No, not weird. But all the things I unpacked have been rearranged in order of shortest to longest and are spaced equidistant from each other. I just tossed them on the shelf." She hoped her use of equidistant wasn't lost on him. She knew plenty of science-y words too.

He leaned closer, then cocked one eyebrow at her. "Really? This is the best you have?"

"Things moved while I was gone. Proof."

"Proof housekeeping came in here and straightened up after you."

"Housekeeping? We just settled in a few hours ago. There is no way housekeeping came by in the evening immediately after we checked in."

"It's part of the act, then."

"I don't have any cameras in here. Why would I be acting without a camera?"

"You can always make a big to-do about it tomorrow when you are filming. 'Report' the ghostly activity."

Her face hardened into a scowl and she crossed her arms. "You are so negative. Suspicious of my fruit gift and not even willing to consider any idea not your own."

"I'm not negative at all. I'm actually very positive. Completely positive that no ghost moved your belongings."

She stood and walked to the telephone on the nightstand, lifted the receiver, and dialed the front desk. "Hi, Marcus. This is Kimberly Wantland in four nineteen. Yes, really. No, not another prank ghost call. I want to request no housekeeping services at any time during my stay. Okay? Right. No knob to hang a Do Not Disturb sign on, so can you make a note somewhere for me? It's for research. Great. Thank you." She hung up and gave Sterling her most triumphant look.

"Why in the world did you do that?"

"Now you can't claim anyone from the staff is moving things around my room. And I vow to be a complete slob. Let's see what happens."

"You'll have a filthy room, that's what will happen. So what do we do tomorrow?"

"Right. This will be your first full episode. In the morning we will have an interview with the woman who first encountered the ghost we're here to investigate."

"First encountered?"

"Yes, it's continued to harass staff and guests since then. You'd know that if you attended the pre-show meeting at our headquarters in Albuquerque. After the interview we will determine where to place cameras—"

"Where you find hot spots."

"Right. The locations we decide are most likely—"

"See? I remembered."

"Good job. Then the crew sets up. We have a lot of area to cover in a place this big with so much consistent activity. So set up will take a while."

"What do you do during set up?"

"Not a lot, truth be told. Until I meet Rosie in the makeup trailer for relaxation and preparation."

"Why don't I schedule a massage for you at the spa downstairs during set up? You can still have time for Rosie to do her thing"—he waved his hand in front of her face and torso—"before we get going. I don't need much time anyway. I'm naturally beautiful." He posed with a hand on his cheek.

She couldn't help laughing when he batted his eyes. "You don't have to do that."

"I know you're annoyed I asked for Rosie instead of getting my own stylist. Let me make it up to you a bit. Least I can do for my partner."

Partner? That word used to cause butterflies. Why did it now make her cringe? Could a person who disagreed with everything you believed in and stood for ever truly be a partner?

CHAPTER ELEVEN

KIMBERLY TRIED and failed to stifle a yawn. Footage review never held her enthralled, but today she found paying attention particularly difficult.

She'd been excited to explore Norman Baker's penthouse. After all, Selma had confided that her dog refused to cross the threshold into the stairwell that led to the isolated suite. Baker had apparently grown paranoid during his stay at Crescent, when it was his cancer hospital. He'd acquired several German shepherds to protect himself. Current hotel guests reported hearing scratching at the door inside the stairwell, "like dogs wanting to be let in," only to find the stairwell empty when they investigated.

This knowledge led her to expect a potentially exciting experience in his previous residence. Dogs were known to be sensitive to entities most people couldn't detect. If Baker haunted his previous home, however, she detected no evidence of it. She tried again and again to make contact but nothing responded.

On top of that disappointment, footage review thus far produced no images, sounds, or any inexplicable phenomena. Which left Sterling full of himself and gloating.

Her right hand absently reached for a cup of coffee, which

she reminded herself wasn't there. The hotel didn't serve breakfast and Ms. Theodora's room wasn't equipped with a coffee maker.

She yawned again and checked her watch. 9:00 a.m. Nine o'clock in the morning and she hadn't had a drop of coffee.

Michael removed his headphones. "You okay, Kimmy?"

"Yeah, I'm fine." She pressed her fingers to her temples.

"Anything yet?"

"The room is silent. I'm not getting anything. What about you?"

"Not much. Stan recorded you falling backward by the lounge on four. But we don't see anything around you when it happens. Cameras caught some orbs on three and at the bottom of the staircase. TJ's image on the stairs is the most promising thing we got last night."

Sterling stood and stretched. "That's pretty impressive. A place this haunted and you can't catch one single ghost on camera. You guys are doing my work for me."

She really couldn't handle Sterling without coffee. "You still need me, Michael, or can I go get ready for the interview?"

"Go ahead. I think we're finished for now. Maybe try one last attempt to detect Baker."

As frustrated as she was, she doubted she could successfully direct her psychic energy. But she clasped her quartz, took several deep breaths, and opened herself to input. She heard only static.

"Nothing. I'm going to go find Rosie."

"Wait a minute," Sterling said. "No one has said anything about a new opening segment. When can we talk about that?"

She narrowed her eyes. "What do you mean?"

"I'm cohost now. I should be in the opening sequence. When are we going to record it?"

"I don't see any need for that," she said. "It's my show, my name is on it—"

"For now," Sterling said. "We should be thinking about changing that too."

She crossed her arms. "No way. You're more of a junior cohost. We're not changing the name of my show."

"Junior cohost? That's not in the contract anywhere. I never would've signed on to be someone's junior anything. We're equal partners."

"Your contract is for this season only. A trial basis to see how it works out. I will not even consider changing the name of the show that I built—"

"Kimmy, relax," Michael said. "The show will always be *The Wantland Files*. No question. But Sterling has a point. New season, new intro. It makes sense. And it makes sense that Sterling should be included now."

She scowled at Sterling. "We could have filmed a new intro and discussed creative changes to the show over the summer. If you hadn't disappeared. To the beach, apparently."

"My contract started season four, day one. And here I am."

"You could have been with me, promoting the show and preparing for the new season."

"I promote this show all over the place. More than you do."

"No one promotes this show more than I do. You didn't attend one interview or one convention—"

"I tweeted about the show every day. I tweet even more now that I'm here. That draws viewers."

"That draws stalkers. I never leak where exactly I am while I'm there. You might want to pay attention and learn something."

"Yeah, Michael, I can see why you stay single. What I can't see is how you put up with the nagging day in and day out."

"Nagging? Preserving the integrity of my show and my personal safety—"

Michael spoke up. "Actually, I agree with her. We're wasting time hammering out details that should've been sorted out over the summer."

Sterling looked annoyed that Michael sided with her. "Let's film a new intro here. World's most haunted hotel, right?"

"*America's* most haunted hotel. And then the intro would be site specific. We filmed the last intro at our Albuquerque headquarters. Which you haven't bothered to visit."

"Set up a green screen or something. You can add whatever generic background you want later."

"Michael, would you please—"

"Both of you calm down. Kimmy, you know I have to run this past RandMeier first anyway. We can't make any big changes without his approval. And Sterling, now you know. I'll talk to him later. For now, go get ready for the interview. And focus more on the investigation and less on each other."

She turned on her heel and stormed from the room. She would gladly focus less on Sterling, if only he wasn't there every time she turned around.

CHAPTER TWELVE

Kimberly stormed into her trailer, stooping so low as to slam the door behind her. How childish. And yet she couldn't stop herself. Sterling always managed to bring out the worst in her.

Rosie pressed a cup of hot tea into her hands, humming.

"You're in a good mood," she noted, accepting the tea.

"And you're not." Rosie's forehead furrowed. "It's awfully early in the morning to be this annoyed already. What happened?"

"Sterling. The same thing that always happens. He wants to change the show name and the opening sequence. He can't just walk in here and take over my show. Who does he think he is?" She balled her fist and stifled a growl of frustration.

Rosie guided her to the chair. "Sit. Relax. Put this out of your mind. You have an investigation to focus on."

She followed instructions while Rosie lifted bottles of essential oils, considering each, returning some. "Lavender, obviously, for relaxation. Not the sandalwood, that could make you too sleepy. Bergamot. And I think a little patchouli."

"I can't stop thinking about him, Rosie. He makes me crazy."

Rosie combined a few drops of each of the selected oils and

rubbed it into her hands. "Breathe deeply. You have to relax. I don't believe anyone will approve changing the name, so don't waste energy worrying about that. And if you record a new opening sequence, is it really the end of the world? How bad would it be? You need to allow for a slightly different dynamic now that Sterling is here. Things won't be exactly the same."

"He acts so entitled. He makes me crazy. He didn't come to our pre-season meetings. He didn't ask nicely how I'd feel about making some changes. He just demanded to know when we will record a new opening."

Rosie massaged her temples. "I can tell his attitude bothers you. Let's work on letting it go for the time being. You can speak with Michael about your concerns later."

"At least this year I don't have to worry about him barging into my trailer."

Rosie moved to her shoulders and rubbed out some of the tension. "There we go. That's better. Some of those knots are relaxing."

"Why are you in such a good mood? I don't think I've ever heard you hum before." She suspected she knew the answer.

"Lorenzo took me to a late dinner last night after the ghost tour. He gave me that rose on the counter. Because my name is Rosie."

"No one has ever thought of that before?"

"No one ever gave me a rose before. Here, get dressed."

She eyed her stylist, who still hummed and practically danced around the trailer while handing her an outfit and plugging in the curling wand. "So I guess dinner was very nice?"

"It was so nice. Lorenzo is completely classy. What a gentleman."

"You're practically swooning!" She cracked a smile, despite her bad mood. Rosie's delight seeped into her psyche. She slid out of her T-shirt and into the blouse Rosie had selected for her.

"Sorry. I'll try to be quiet."

"No, I love seeing you this happy. Tell me about it!"

"You're sure you don't mind?"

"I feel better just being around you. Let's hear it!"

"We went to this quiet little restaurant right outside of town. Everything they serve is produced locally and organically. It's owned by a town resident. And it was amazing! We had candles on the table, a gourmet meal, and Lorenzo asked me where I'm from and wanted to get to know me. I've never been treated so well. Sit. Let's do your make-up."

"That's wonderful! I'm really happy for you. So I guess after dinner . . . " She raised her eyebrows as Rosie began applying foundation.

"Nope. We didn't. He kissed me goodnight and that was it."

"No way."

"I'm serious. I told you he's a total gentleman. Close your eyes." Rosie traced her eyes with liner and dusted shadow on her lids.

"Wow. This really is a new experience for you."

"And I'm loving it. Open your eyes and look up."

As Rosie began brushing her eyelashes with mascara, the door to the trailer opened and Sterling waltzed in. Her improved mood evaporated.

"You have your own trailer. Don't barge into mine."

"Michael sent me to get you. Jeez. Why are you such a grouch? Someone add whole milk to your coffee this morning?"

"I haven't had coffee yet, if you must butt into my business."

"Rosie? You didn't get her coffee?"

"I . . . I didn't know she didn't . . . I was a little distracted this morning. I'm sorry, Kimberly."

"I'm not complaining. I'm fine."

Sterling looked around the trailer. "Why the heck doesn't a coffee addict like you have a coffee machine in here? You're Kimberly freakin' Wantland. You could have anything you asked for."

"You just don't get it. We started out with a budget of zero dollars. Michael and I bought all our own equipment. Maxed out credit cards to fund our company. We never expected it to blow up into a prime-time television series."

"That was then. Now you do have a budget. And celebrity. You can ask for things."

"I built the show from nothing and have no idea how long it will last. I won't waste money on frivolous things."

"It's a coffee maker. And for you it's a necessity, not frivolous. You don't need to make yourself suffer. Or make those of us around you suffer."

"I don't expect you to understand. I don't think you've ever gone without in your life. I can go without coffee for a few days. Will you please do me the courtesy of using your own trailer and staying out of mine? I need to finish getting ready for the interview."

Sterling gave her a hard stare and left, declaring, "I can't work like this."

She heard his i8 roar to life and jumped from her makeup chair in time to see him skid out of the parking lot.

CHAPTER THIRTEEN

Rosie finished applying mascara, neither of them speaking. They completed relaxation exercises, but she found focusing difficult after the spat with Sterling. Rosie checked her hair for fly-aways and the two of them went inside for the interview. The crew congregated in the lobby, waiting for the action to begin. Michael spotted them and threaded his way to her.

"You look fabulous, dah-ling," he said. "Now what's happened to Sterling? He was supposed to return with you, not disappear."

She and Rosie exchanged a glance. Neither spoke. Rosie held up her hands and shook her head.

Michael's brow furrowed. "What? What happened?"

"He drove away. I think he might have been mad." Her stomach churned with guilt. Her head pounded, though probably from caffeine withdrawals.

"Why was he mad? He was in a fantastic mood when I sent him after you." Michael narrowed his eyes. "What did you do?"

"I didn't . . . I asked him to use his own trailer."

"Terrific. The way last season ended, I thought you two were on good terms."

"I thought so, too," she mumbled. "Something about him gets under my skin."

Rosie nudged her. "I think you'd feel a lot better if you really let him get under your skin."

"Absolutely not. Stop that before someone hears you!"

Michael stared out the front door before speaking. "Well, let's get on with the interview I guess. Maybe he'll cool off and come back." He gave Kimberly the look and she knew he was not happy with her. "You need to rein in whatever personal issues you have with him and keep it professional."

"You're right. I know." She gestured to Rosie. "You both keep telling me the same thing and I agree. And yet he opens his mouth and rubs me the wrong way and I react poorly. I'll do better."

Rosie cocked an eyebrow at her. "I really think you should let him open his mouth and rub you the right way. That will fix all your issues."

"No, that would open up a whole new set of issues. Seriously, Rosie. Stop. Sterling and I are not a thing."

"You would be if you gave him half a chance."

Her stomach quivered, but she squelched that. Michael was right. She had to put everything else aside and keep her relationship with Sterling nothing but professional. And Rosie was right, too. The show would not be the same. And apparently, not the way she'd imagined it either. She would have to accept it and deal with the consequences. After all, bringing him on board had been her idea. She couldn't even blame anyone else.

A roaring engine announced Sterling's return before he ripped back into the parking lot. A quiver of nerves jolted her as she watched him slam the door and trudge back inside. She would have to apologize whether she liked it or not. For the good of her show, she had to find a way to get along with her cohost.

Sterling walked right up to her. She took a deep breath, but before she could say a word, he thrust a cup at her. "Mud Street Café. Excellent reviews online and only five minutes from here. I got the biggest size and the strongest brew they had. And of course skim milk."

She did a double take. "What?"

"Coffee. Best in Eureka Springs, apparently." His eyes twinkled as he reached into a paper bag and extracted an enormous cinnamon roll wrapped in foil. He peeled back the wrapping and bit into the pastry. "Mmmmmm. Now that's how every cinnamon roll should taste. Want a bite?"

She stared at the coffee cup, mouth watering as the aroma reached her. "I don't know what to . . . thank you for this."

"You didn't think I'd let you go without coffee, did you? It's our first full show together. You need to be on top of your game. Can't have people saying the show's going downhill now that I'm here. Seriously, try this cinnamon roll." He took another huge bite then held it out to her.

Michael cleared his throat. "Umm, there are other people in this crew. None of us knew the most amazeballs cinnamon rolls in the world were a short five-minute drive away."

Sterling handed Michael a bag. "I got plenty for everyone. Give one to Kimberly to keep her blood sugar up."

Kimberly sipped the coffee, then took a long drink. She felt better immediately. "This really is good coffee. Thank you so much."

"Now try a cinnamon roll," Sterling suggested.

"Though cinnamon is a fantastic addition to any healthy diet, the rest of the roll is white flour, sugar, and saturated fat. No thank you." She drank deeply from the coffee, feeling a bit like an addict and not caring.

"You have got to lighten up a little. This thing is amazing and you're missing out. One bite won't kill you."

"I haven't had fruit or anything with antioxidants to counterbalance the negative impact of—"

"One bite."

She stared at the gooey sugar and cinnamon oozing from the folds of the roll, the sugar glaze coating the top. When was the last time she had indulged in anything so decadent? Her mouth watered.

He seemed to know her resolve wavered. "Look at it this way. You'll be saving me from eating every single bite of this massive breakfast confection you seem to consider a heart attack waiting to happen. You'd basically be throwing yourself on a grenade for me. At least, I think that's about how you see it."

She reached out and pulled off a bite. Warm and delicious, it melted away in her mouth.

Rosie gasped and muttered, "She ate refined sugar."

The crew blinked, silently exchanging glances.

Sterling grinned. "Wasn't that worth it?"

She allowed a smile. "You're going to be a terrible influence on me. I can tell already."

"I certainly hope so."

CHAPTER FOURTEEN

KIMBERLY STOOD beside Selma and her employee, Clara, in the hotel laundry room. Two young men, Adam and Joe according to Michael, stood waiting their turn in front of the camera currently focused on the three women.

"Clara has worked here at Crescent for five years now," Selma said. "She's a terrific employee."

Kimberly allowed her brow to furrow with concern over the gravity of the situation. "Clara, can you tell us what happened that day?" She rested a hand on the woman's arm.

Clara nodded. "I had just brought a full load of laundry down here. I had a little trouble lifting my laundry bag. It felt like something was pulling on it. But I finally got it out of my hamper and put it there, in the laundry bin. I got a fresh bag and turned to leave. That's when I saw his reflection in the washing machine door."

"Whose reflection, Clara? What did you see?"

"A man. I saw the face of a man reflected there in that door. See how it acts like a mirror? Looked like he was standing behind me." The woman shivered at the memory.

Kimberly rested her chin on her fist. "What did you do then?"

"I spun around, but no one was behind me."

She heard Sterling mumble, "Shocking," and shot daggers at him. Michael had instructed him not to upset the witnesses. Sterling had promptly scoffed at using the word "witnesses" to describe them.

"What happened then?" she pressed Clara.

"I assumed I had imagined it and tried to leave."

"What do you mean, *tried* to leave?"

"The door slammed shut. And the ghost stood in front of me. I was so scared, I couldn't move. He looked angry."

"And did the boys see the apparition too?" she asked, knowing they hadn't. Leading the conversation the direction they wanted it to go was part of her job.

"No. They didn't. They were distracted."

"By what?"

"All the washing machines slammed closed and started running."

"All of them? At the same time?"

"Yes."

"Adam, Joe. Would you join us, please?"

Adam and Joe moved into the shot and shifted awkwardly as if they didn't know what to do with their hands and feet.

"You were both present during this experience?"

"Yes, ma'am," Adam said.

"And did you witness all the machines turn on at once?"

The boys nodded.

"All of them," Joe agreed. "Never seen anything like it."

"I was going to open the laundry room door," Adam said. "So I didn't see the doors all slam shut. But I heard them."

"I saw them." Joe shivered. "All the doors. All of them slammed shut."

"I ran back to try to turn them off," Adam said. "They wouldn't switch off, they wouldn't open. We were going to pull the cords, but Miss Clara screamed and we went to help her."

She turned to Clara. "Why did you scream? What happened while they were busy with the washing machines?"

"I was so scared, at first I just stood there. Then the ghost appeared again, right in front of me. He touched my arm and he was so cold. So cold. Then he scraped my arm. Scratched it right open. That's when I screamed." Clara held out her arm.

"I don't see anything," Sterling said. "Not even a scar."

"They weren't deep wounds. They've healed now, of course," Clara said. "This happened months ago. I took pictures though." The woman withdrew her cell phone and brought up photos.

Stan stepped closer, presumably to zoom in on the cell phone images.

Kimberly took the phone and shook her head. "This must have been horrifying. Only a powerful spirit could inflict a wound like that. I haven't seen this very often."

Sterling tipped the phone and stared at it. "They look like scratches. That could've been caused by anything."

Clara nodded. "Sure. Could've been. But they weren't. I didn't bump into anything or brush against anything. I watched the apparition scrape my arm."

Sterling smirked. "Or do you simply remember it that way? It's easy to convince ourselves after the fact, remember things a little differently than they happened. Especially when we're caught up in excitement."

Clara gave Sterling a hard stare. "Young man, do I appear hysterical or overwrought?"

"Well, no, but—"

"I'm not afraid of ghosts. I talk to them all the time while I'm working. They don't disturb me. When you've been around as long as I have, you see a lot. Some things you can't explain. But what I encountered that night was mean. Vicious. This one scared me."

"What do you think it wanted?"

"I think it wanted to hurt me."

"Why? Why you?"

"That I can't answer. He said he wanted revenge. I can't imagine he meant against me."

Kimberly placed a hand over Clara's while glaring at Sterling. "The manifestation has continued to appear and harass other staff and guests. I don't believe the attack was personal against you. Whatever grudge the ghost seeks revenge for, he appears to be randomly lashing out. Perhaps he's the entity who pushed me down the stairs last night."

"I certainly hope it was the same ghost who pushed you," Selma said. "I hate to think what could happen if the hostile spirit's behavior rubs off on our other residents."

"I doubt that will happen," Kimberly reassured her. "But we're here to help."

"And I invited you because you're the best," Selma said. "Please don't disturb the rest of our resident ghosts. We welcome and enjoy them. I don't want to inadvertently displace one or scare them off. I believe you can pinpoint the disturbance and resolve it with as little disruption as possible. We're normally at capacity, but word of this is getting out. Sure, some thrill seekers are still coming hoping to get scratched by a ghost. But we've had some families cancel on us. Even lost a few wedding party bookings over it. We want to get back to normal as quickly as possible."

"That's why we're here," she assured her. "Thank you, Clara. Thank you, Adam and Joe. I appreciate you reliving your harrowing experiences with us today." She faced the camera. "Crescent Hotel is known as the Most Haunted Hotel in America. The owner and staff welcome their spiritual residents. Many guests come hoping for a glimpse of or encounter with a ghost. What has upset the normal routine, causing one of the entities to lash out? Join us tonight as we isolate the angry presence from the harmless occupants and exorcise it from the hotel."

CHAPTER FIFTEEN

"AND CUT," Michael said. "Okay, do we want to break for a quick lunch before we get this place set up for investigation tonight?"

Selma shook Kimberly's hand before she could respond to Michael. "I'm so grateful for this. Let me know if you need anything else while you're here."

"My pleasure. And we will."

Sterling closed in on her. "Where do you want to get lunch?"

"One moment, Sterling." She turned to Michael. "I'm really bothered I didn't tour the morgue last night. Did anything happen?"

"We haven't thoroughly analyzed footage yet, but nothing we noticed. Lorenzo used an EMF detector that blipped a few times, seemingly on cue. But who knows. That's part of his routine."

Sterling leaned between them. "Do I detect . . . sarcasm?"

She ignored Sterling. "We must be near the morgue, right? It's somewhere in the basement."

Selma remained close by and spoke up. "It's down the hall here. You're welcome to have a look right now if you'd like."

"You don't mind?" Kimberly asked. "I've never missed an area on a walk-through and it bothers me I didn't get through the entire tour."

"Don't mind in the slightest. No one is in it right now anyway. Why not?"

Rosie grabbed her arm. "I don't think that's a good idea. You were completely drained last night, we didn't prepare you for a confrontation with hostiles—"

Sterling patted his chest, eyes wide. "Should I be wearing a Kevlar vest?"

"Dude, can you ever be serious?" TJ's harsh tone startled her. She had to do something about those two. Soon.

Michael sighed heavily. "Everyone calm down. Sterling . . . " He raised a palm in a "stop" gesture.

Sterling shook his head. "*Me* stop?"

Michael turned to TJ. "And TJ . . . " He held up a palm to the camera operator. "Both of you. Just stop. You've rendered me speechless. We've never had any problems like this before."

TJ crossed his arms. "Exactly."

Michael held up a finger, shushed TJ, and glared at both offenders as if daring them to speak.

Kimberly took a deep breath. "I appreciate the concern, albeit excessive, but would really like to take Selma's offer and walk through the morgue. I'll be careful. You'll all be here. I'll be fine."

Before anyone voiced further concerns, she gestured to Selma to lead the way. The older woman winked and headed down the hall.

Kimberly quickened her steps and caught up to the woman. "By the way, thank you for the fruit arrangement. It was delicious."

Selma's brow furrowed. "I didn't send a fruit basket."

"Not a basket. An arrangement. Fruit made to look like flowers in a vase."

Selma shook her head. "It wasn't me. Sounds like you have a secret admirer."

Sterling had caught up with her. "She didn't send it? See? I told you not to assume."

"I survived," she grumbled, wishing he hadn't heard Selma. If Selma hadn't sent the fruit, who did? She hated to think maybe she should have listened to Sterling.

"Did you get any sleep last night, Sterling?" Selma asked. "Or did Jack keep you up all night?"

"Not a single disturbance," Sterling gloated. "Slept like a baby."

"That's what Jack does," Selma said. "He lures you in and then he strikes."

"I'll be on alert tonight, then," Sterling said, the smirk on his face communicating his true thoughts.

"Here we are," Selma said, opening a door into an empty, square room. Mostly empty, as it turned out. "This is the original autopsy table from the cancer hospital. Drained into the floor there. And this"—she swung open a large metal door, revealing a smaller room—"was the freezer where the bodies were stored, kept cold by huge blocks of ice. The room is below ground, of course, which also helps regulate the temperature year round."

Her crew didn't make a sound. She stepped softly, unwilling to disturb the unnatural silence in the space. An onslaught of fractured images rushed at her without any encouragement. Quick bits and pieces flashed through her mind. Still frames of stacked iced bodies, cadavers on the table, scalpel opening grayed flesh, hands lifting lifeless organs from exposed cavities. She saw a face, eyes feverish with delight. Delighted by discovery? Knowledge? Education? Or the mere act of dismemberment?

She staggered backward and covered her face as if to block the images.

Rosie clicked her tongue. "Girl, you know I'm perfectly happy to say I told you so."

"I'm okay," she told her stylist. She took a deep breath and clasped her quartz crystal.

"I gave her that necklace," Sterling told Selma.

Selma patted his arm. "I know, dear. I saw."

"Did you connect with something?" Michael asked.

"No. I thought maybe the entity that attacked Clara might be lurking here in the morgue. It's so close to the laundry room. But I don't sense a presence. I experienced visions, not a connection. Though what I saw could leave someone wanting revenge. Elise, do you happen to have a picture of Norman Baker?"

"Of course." Elise rifled through papers in a folder and produced a black and white photo. "That's him."

The eyes in the photo were relaxed, not the manic eyes she'd seen in her vision. Still, she was certain. "I saw that man in the visions. And he didn't hold a medical degree?"

"Correct. He was an entertainer, an inventor, a radio station founder, and a charlatan. But he never attended so much as a day of medical school."

Kimberly grimaced. The visions left her stomach sour. "According to my visions, he considered himself qualified to perform autopsies. Or at least dissections."

"Disgusting," Rosie said.

Michael shook his head. "That's grisly. What did he possibly hope to gain by cutting open his patients' bodies?"

Sterling raised a hand. "If I could interject the obvious here. Again. By her own admission, Kimberly saw visions. In her mind. Most probably products of her imagination and influenced by our current surroundings. Nothing more substantial than a dream. Do any records indicate Baker performed amateur autopsies?"

Elise returned the photograph to her research folder. "No. As I said before, we don't have any records from the cancer hospital. The staff destroyed all records when the authorities arrested Baker. Destroyed them on Baker's orders."

"Pretty incriminating. Sounds like he had something to hide," TJ said.

"Of course he had something to hide," Sterling said. "He

opened a cancer treatment center without a medical license, lured in desperate, vulnerable people, and inflicted terrible pain by subjecting them to injections of what amounted to poison. His own test subjects died one after another, yet he published an article detailing their miraculous recoveries and declaring he'd cured cancer. And that was before he even opened the hospital here."

Every jaw dropped.

"You researched him?" Elise asked.

"Of course I did my research. I'm not defending this guy. I'm just saying there is no proof that Kimberly's visions of him slicing people open are founded in actual occurrences."

"Ew Sterling! Gross."

"She had the visions. Not me."

Selma laughed. "I love watching young minds work out problems. And you haven't even seen the specimen room yet. Come this way."

Rosie's eyebrows shot up. "Specimen room? I think I'll pass. I'm going to peruse products at the salon. Let me know if you need me." With a wave, she exited the morgue.

Kimberly followed Selma, pretty sure Rosie was off to peruse Lorenzo. She hoped this fling ran its course quickly and that Rosie didn't wind up devastated by it. Then again, Rosie's description of their first date didn't sound much like a fling.

The specimen room sent a shiver down her spine. An old wheelchair sat in one corner of the small room. Shelves lined one wall, covered with sealed jars of dark liquid. Each jar held a shadowy lump.

"He stored and saved bits and pieces," Selma told them. "Tumors, organs, that sort of thing. No one knows why. But it seems a shame to destroy these relics of the hospital. Without records, the specimen room preserves some memory of the people who lost their lives here."

Michael held a handkerchief over his nose and mouth. "Kimmy? Getting anything here?"

She reached out, but nothing answered. "No. No spirits at all. Which would make sense really. No one died here. The bodies were stored in the morgue, and these pieces were saved after death. Any spirits left behind most likely remained near the place of death. You okay?"

Michael shook his head. "You know I don't do well with dead things. Break for lunch everyone. Then come back ready to hustle. We have a lot of hotel to cover. Set up will be intense." He hurried from the room.

"Squeamish group you've got," Selma commented as the crew filed out of the morgue.

"In some ways," she agreed, working her way toward the exit. "And in other ways, they're the toughest people you'll ever find."

"I'll get back to work myself," Selma excused herself. "But let me know if you need anything at all."

"Thank you, Selma. We will."

Michael stood outside the spa as she and Sterling passed it. "Didn't Rosie say she was coming down here? I don't see her."

"I suspect she went to find Lorenzo," she said. "Doubt this was her destination at all."

"Where do you want to start your investigation tonight?" Michael asked.

She hadn't thought about that. "Good question. Why don't I start in Ms. Theodora's room? I noticed a little activity. We might be able to make contact. She seems like a live one. You didn't send me a fruit arrangement, did you?"

"No, sweetie. I didn't. We might consider breaking into groups to cover more hotel each night."

"Good idea. Let's see how things go tonight. And we can break into groups as needed."

"Want to grab lunch?" Sterling asked.

"I think I'll relax in my trailer for now. I'm not hungry at the moment. But thanks."

Sterling's face showed his disappointment. "Okay. Well, don't forget your massage. I scheduled it for two o'clock and they said to be there fifteen minutes early. I'm starving. Gonna grab some food. See you later." He hesitated and almost looked like he wanted a hug. He patted her arm before leaving.

Michael raised an eyebrow.

"What? He offered to book a massage for me. So what?"

"I didn't say anything."

"He's just being nice."

"Mm-hmm."

"He felt guilty about making me share Rosie. He's trying to make it up to me."

"I'm sure."

"Stop judging me."

"I haven't said a word."

"But you're judging. I can feel it. You're judging so hard right now."

"I'm really not, sweetie. I think it's cute. But I also think you must be feeling guilty."

"It's just a massage. At the spa. I mean, it's not like he's giving me a massage himself." She laughed far too hard at the feeble joke. "What would I feel guilty about?"

"Sweetie, you feel guilty whenever you make time for yourself or do something you consider extravagant. Relax and enjoy it. Besides, I wouldn't blame you a bit if you've developed some feelings for Sterling. He's very attractive and a nice guy. Not at all my type, of course. But a nice guy."

"He's not my type either."

Michael slung an arm over her shoulders and started down the hall. "I know. At least I know that's what you think. Enjoy the massage he's arranged for you in a totally platonic gesture of friendship and nothing more."

CHAPTER SIXTEEN

SOOTHING birdsong and trickling water greeted Kimberly when she arrived for her massage, fifteen minutes early as instructed. She relished the botanical fragrances pervading the air, sure she detected lavender. Breathing deeply, she felt a layer of stress melt away.

"Ms. Wantland. Hello," an attendant at the desk greeted her. "Welcome. Mr. Wakefield said you prefer hot tea. This has been steeping for five minutes and should be the perfect temperature."

"Thank you. That was thoughtful of him. And you." She accepted the cup of tea and held it to her face, enjoying the fragrant vapor. Another layer of stress melted away. *Okay, so some of Sterling's ideas are actually pretty good.*

"We have a form we ask all first-time guests to complete prior to treatment. You can sit anywhere. And please let me know if you need more tea or anything else. Chance will be taking care of you today. She will be out to get you shortly."

She accepted the clipboard and paperwork, then settled into a seat, taking another sip of tea before resting the cup on a table beside her. The babbling brook continued to trickle and birds twittered while she completed the form, verifying she did not suffer from any medical conditions and indicating where she would like her therapist to focus today.

She remembered Sterling's comment about liking to spoil girlfriends while they were filming last season's finale. Did this fall under spoiling? Surely he didn't consider her that way. They were cohosts and nothing more. This was a generous gesture, though, from one coworker to another.

"Ms. Wantland?"

A young woman, blonde hair in a cute pixie-cut, smiled at her from the desk.

"Yes." She jumped up from her seat and returned the smile.

The woman approached and extended a hand. "I'm Chance. I'll be taking care of you today. I'm a big fan of your show so I'm really happy I have the opportunity to work with you."

"Thank you. I'm always glad to meet a fan of the show."

"I think it's awesome how you help people. I know there are ghosts and it's so nice to see someone pay attention instead of say it's crazy."

"No one likes to be called crazy. I know that. I hear it myself plenty."

"Would you like to wait or go ahead and get started?"

Why would I want to wait? Did I look that comfortable and relaxed? "Let's go ahead and start."

"This way, then." Chance led her down a narrow hallway and into a room with two massage beds. *Odd.* Perhaps it was the only massage room they had open when Sterling scheduled. This was rather last minute.

"Is this your first massage?" Chance asked.

"My first massage here, but not my first massage ever. I've had a few. Usually my personal assistant keeps me relaxed for the show and she utilizes some massage."

"I'm glad you're here today. Here are some towelettes to remove your makeup and some hair ties to pull back your hair. I'll let you undress. Slide under the sheet on your back and relax. I'll be back in a moment."

Sounds of rolling waves and seagulls filled the dimly lit room. Candles burned, issuing a gentle fragrance. She wiped away her makeup, pulled back her hair, undressed, and slid under the sheet. A moment later a light knock on the door preceded Chance.

"Come in," she said.

"All set?" Chance asked. "Great. Mr. Wakefield said you don't like to be cold, so I've brought a warmed towel for you."

Chance arranged a round pillow under her knees and draped the warm towel over her. "Comfortable?"

"Yes. That feels amazing." Heat suffused her limbs. If she relaxed any more she might melt away. She closed her eyes and cleared her mind, allowing her senses to simply enjoy. Sterling certainly paid attention and took note. She didn't remember telling him she didn't like to be cold. She heard Chance adjusting things behind her.

"Breathe deeply," Chance instructed. "This is some warmed essential oils, a blend designed to help you relax."

She followed the instructions, the musky scent reminding her momentarily of Sterling, though she wasn't sure why and quickly pushed the thought of him away. That would not help her relax.

"How much pressure do you prefer?" Chance asked in a hushed tone. "Gentle? Deep tissue?"

"Can you start medium and I'll let you know—"

The door opened and she heard voices. She tensed, waiting for the expected, "I'm so sorry!" from the intruders. Chance said nothing and merely continued to massage her shoulders and neck.

"Sorry I'm late. My facial ran over a little. Glad you went ahead and started."

Sterling.

She lifted her head and propped herself on her elbows. "What are you doing here?"

"I got a couples massage. This was the only room available

last minute." He looked at her intently. "You look tired. I should've booked a couples facial too."

She scowled at him.

"We don't have a space for couples facials," Chance said. "Sorry."

"I was joking," Sterling said. He wore a robe. Which he dropped before she could look away.

She averted her eyes and lay back down, staring carefully at the ceiling as her heart raced. But she'd gotten a good look at his broad chest and shoulders. And those abs that somehow seemed only more defined since her last inadvertent glimpse of them. His honey skin proved he'd spent time on the beach this summer. Thank God he was in boxers. She heard the sheet rustle as he settled onto his massage table.

"I forgot about your Puritan sensibilities. So easily offended." He laughed softly.

"I'm not a prude just because I don't think it's appropriate to come in here and disrobe in front of me."

"I'm sorry," Chance said. "I thought you two were together."

"We are," Sterling said. "We're partners."

"We are partners on my show. Cohosts. Not romantic partners."

"Meh. Close enough. What's the difference?"

"What's the—" She sat up, clutching the edge of the sheet to her chest. "The difference is we work together. We aren't intimate."

Sterling sat up and met her eye, smirk crooked across his face. The sheet fell just above his waist. "You've seen me in nothing but a towel before."

"Not intentionally!" *Those abs.* He needed to cover those up.

"If you'd been on the beach with me this summer, would you have been offended to see me in my swimsuit?"

"That's different."

"How? You didn't see anything now you wouldn't have seen on the beach."

"I . . . well, I wasn't at the beach. I was busy working."

He grinned, his eyes laughing at her. Until they drifted lower, to her bare arms, shoulders, and décolletage. "I wish you had been there. Wouldn't mind seeing you on a beach."

Not prepared for the heat radiating from his dark eyes, she tucked her sheet closer while butterflies danced in her stomach. "We're supposed to be relaxing and getting ready for the investigation tonight."

She settled back onto her table. Her therapist returned to her shoulders and neck. Sterling's periodic moans indicated his therapist was working on him too. She gritted her teeth, determined not to say anything lest he tease her again about her "Puritan sensibilities."

Chance's soothing massage oil calmed her. The soft sounds of waves and gulls over classical music lulled her. Why didn't she have relaxing music in her trailer? Or the coffee maker Sterling thought she ought to have? *You're Kimberly freakin' Wantland. You can have whatever you want.* What did she want? She'd never thought about that. Never even thought to ask. Life was good. But now Sterling complicated it. He struck her as generally flirty and friendly. But his behavior toward her was different. Rosie remained convinced he liked her. She wasn't blind. She saw how he acted around her. But did she want a relationship? They'd never ended well for her.

She stopped worrying about Sterling and gave herself over to the massage. No one topped Rosie, but Chance knew her stuff. She found knots and tight muscles and gently worked them out. Chance quietly instructed her to turn to her stomach, removed the pillow propping her knees, and adjusted the sheet. She situated her face into the doughnut-shaped face prop.

Chance worked on her back, then her legs. The foot rub was too much. She relaxed completely, drifting into a semi-conscious state.

Something ugly and menacing reached out to her. Cold. Angry. Hostile.

Revenge.

She jumped, rising off the massage table with a gasp.

Chance pulled away. "I'm sorry? Too much pressure?"

"Did you hear that?" Kimberly asked.

"Hear what?"

"That voice."

Sterling lifted his head and eyed her with a smile. "I think you dozed off. Sign of an excellent massage. You were so relaxed you fell asleep."

"No. I was awake. The massage is great," she assured Chance, "but I didn't fall asleep. And I heard a voice say 'Revenge.' Like Clara heard."

Sterling raised up on his forearms. She couldn't help but notice how his biceps flexed. And how bronze his chest was. He tilted his head. "I think you fell asleep and dreamed you heard a voice. And you were influenced by the interview this morning."

"I know I was awake. Whatever entity scared Clara is now reaching out to me. And it wants revenge."

She heard nothing more for the duration of the massage. When it ended, the two masseuses quietly left them to dress. Sterling popped off his table, camera in hand.

Where did that come from? He didn't have any pockets. He barely wore any clothing.

She sat up, clutching the sheet to herself. He stood next to her, leaned entirely too close, and held his camera up.

"Massage selfie," he said, snapping a picture before she realized what he was doing.

"No! No pictures! I have no make up on. And no clothing for that matter."

"Posting natural selfies is big among celebs now. It'll be brave of you."

"Do not post that! I don't want people jumping to conclusions about us."

"What? People online jumping to conclusions?" He rolled his

eyes and laughed. "Let them jump. As long as they watch the show."

She saw him bring up his Twitter app. "I'm serious. Don't post it."

"You don't need makeup. But with the right filter . . . voilà! Look at that face."

He'd filtered it to black and white, and adjusted the lighting in such a way that her eyes popped and nearly glowed. She appeared thoughtful and actually the lack of makeup wasn't a bad thing. And of course Sterling looked as incredible as always.

"See? Just our faces. Can't even tell you're undressed," Sterling said. "Like I'd let other guys ogle you on Twitter. It'll be our secret."

"As long as you don't label it a massage selfie."

"You have to take the fun out of everything, don't you?" He sighed but altered the comment. "And it's called a hashtag, not a label."

"I don't think I'll ever remember that. And I don't need to. That's what I keep a media expert around for."

"Damn. Thank goodness I have some useable skills to make myself desirable."

The emphasis he placed on the word desirable set her heart hammering.

"Actually, I'm not ready for a natural photo. Please don't share it online."

He pursed his lips and pocketed the phone. "So, excited for dinner?"

She pulled the sheet higher and clutched it tighter. "I think I might just relax after all. So how are we going to get dressed? Will you be a gentleman and step out of the room?"

"Hold on. Aren't you thoroughly relaxed after the massage?"

"Oh. Well, yes. But I need to get dressed for the investigation tonight. And have Rosie reapply my makeup."

"That can't take long. You have to eat. Come on. Don't bail."

How could she explain without hurting his feelings? She

couldn't handle the fluttering in her stomach every time he leaned close or grinned at her with that look in his eyes or twisted her words into a double entendre.

Or worse, what if she tried to explain and he reacted with shock? Or laughed at her for developing feelings for him?

Feelings? No. She did not have feelings for Sterling Wakefield.

"I'm not feeling well. Can we push dinner to tomorrow?"

He searched her eyes, a slight furrow on his brow. "Sure. If that's what you want."

CHAPTER SEVENTEEN

KIMBERLY STOOD in the hotel lobby, drawing deep, cleansing breaths to hold her nerves at bay. Rosie had selected a dark blue outfit with a paisley print from a boutique in town for her to wear. The light fabric fluttered when they went outside to review camera placement on the grounds.

The voice she'd heard in the spa unnerved her. Michael had seemed inclined to believe Sterling's theory that she fell asleep. "Come on, Kimmy," he'd said. "You're chronically sleep deprived. We understand if you nodded off." But she knew she hadn't fallen asleep. She didn't jolt awake when she heard the voice. It startled her. And scared her. But it hadn't woken her.

She, Sterling, and Michael had walked through the opening for the first night investigation before breaking for dinner. She knew what she needed to do. So why was she so nervous?

Surely it had nothing to do with the look on Sterling's face as he walked away for dinner break.

The elevator pinged and Sterling arrived in the lobby, offering a half-hearted smile, clearly still disappointed with her.

"Hey," she greeted him. "Did you have a nice dinner?"

He shrugged and looked away. "I had a pizza delivered. Going out alone is no fun."

"Pizza again? I thought you wanted steak."

"I do want a steak. When we go to dinner together."

"I'm sorry. I needed time for makeup and to prepare myself. And going out to eat with my stomach out of sorts wouldn't be fun. I didn't feel up to—"

"You don't have to make excuses. It's fine."

"No, really. Tomorrow night we'll have dinner for sure. I promise."

Sterling shrugged again and bent to study a binder of photographs collected over the years by guests who believed they'd captured ghostly images on camera. He flipped a few pages and then wandered to the gift shop.

Rosie joined her to smooth her hair again and powder her face one last time. "That was about the saddest thing I've ever seen. He must have really been looking forward to taking you to dinner."

"More likely he's simply used to getting his way and doesn't know how to handle being told no."

Rosie glanced over her shoulder. "Look at that face. You did that."

"I see him. He's moping."

"After he went and got coffee for you this morning. And booked a massage for you, too." Rosie clicked her tongue.

"Okay. I feel like a total heel. I didn't know he'd take it so hard. I didn't cancel completely. I only asked if we could go tomorrow instead. I wasn't hungry and I felt very drained and needed some time to not be on and not have anyone pulling at me."

Michael clapped his hands once. "Let's get started. Ready, Kimmy?"

The crew moved to the back patio, overlooking the hotel grounds. Rosie smoothed her hair and fussed with her clothes. She gestured to still-moping Sterling to join her.

"You don't really need me here," he mumbled as he took his place beside her.

"Of course I do. We're partners. Not starting without you." She grabbed his arm and pulled him closer.

The corners of his mouth turned up and a little of the typical sparkle returned to his eyes. She marveled at how much his emotional state impacted her. Seeing his little boy smile lifted her spirits. *Why?* Why should she be so affected by someone who annoyed her so much?

Stan and TJ hoisted cameras and aimed them at the two of them. Rosie scurried out of the frame. Michael counted her in.

She gestured behind her. "We have cameras in the back lawn where guests have reported seeing a young woman in a white nightgown fall from the third floor balcony. *Did* she fall? Or was she pushed? If she appears tonight, we will catch it on camera."

The group shifted inside where Michael oversaw recording as she and Sterling climbed the stairs together to the second floor. She spoke over her shoulder, negotiating the stairs at an angle. "An entity known as Jack, believed to be the ghost of a seventeen-year-old construction worker who died on site, is well known as a mischievous haunting. Has something set him off? Could he be seeking revenge for the loss of his life at such a young age?"

She and Sterling continued up the stairs before stopping in front of the psych ward. "We've left recording devices around the third floor honeymoon suites that once functioned as the pain management ward for cancer patients slowly dying agonizing deaths under the care of Norman Baker. Could one of them want revenge for the lies and pain Norman Baker subjected them to?"

One more flight of stairs brought her back to the room she was staying in. "I'm staying in room four nineteen, where already I've noticed personal belongings moved around the room. Ms. Theodora, once a nurse, is believed to remain here in the room that belonged to her when she cared for Norman Baker's cancer patients. She has appeared to hotel guests as a fully corporeal, interactive apparition. Since Ms. Theodora is willing to communicate and make her presence known, I'm starting my investigation here tonight to see what she might be able to tell us."

"This ought to be over quick," Sterling said.

"And because she interacts so readily, I'm going to ask her specific questions and offer her the means to answer directly."

Elise handed two flashlights to her. She switched them on and loosened the tops so that the batteries barely made contact with the connectors. The bulbs went dark though the switches remained in the "On" position.

"I'll be using two flashlights during our question and answer session. Ms. Theodora will be able to manipulate the electrical connections to answer yes and no."

She placed the flashlights on the dresser and rotated them so that the switches would inhibit rolling. "The flashlights are unlit but switched on. If the bulbs light in response to questions, we can assume Ms. Theodora, or someone, is choosing to speak with us from another plane."

"Oh, boy," Sterling said. "While you said 'assume' I think you actually intend to take this as factual evidence and I must object."

"Wait and see, Sterling," Michael whispered.

She settled onto the bed and worked to clear her mind.

Sterling didn't cooperate. "Flickering lights do not prove the existence of ghosts. They prove a faulty connection you've manipulated to create."

"Dude, stop interfering," TJ said. "FLIR is ready, Ms. Wantland."

"For the last time, stop calling me 'dude!'"

Michael sighed, forcefully and loudly. "Sterling and TJ, you must stop. Kimmy requires concentration and focus and you two make enough racket to wake the dead. And while we are trying to communicate with the dead, you're not helping."

"Sorry, Ms. Wantland." TJ stared at the floor.

Sterling eyed the flashlights and shook his head but said nothing.

In the contrite silence that followed, she grasped her quartz, and focused all her energy out and beyond, until she barely noticed her surroundings. She opened her eyes and stared at the tiny bulbs in the flashlights, imagining herself as a conduit from the spiritual realm into the physical. *Use me, draw my energy.*

She felt a nudge, a presence, letting her know it was near and willing. "Someone has joined us," she told her crew, then addressed the entity. "My name is Kimberly. We'd like to ask you a few questions. You can answer us with the two flashlights on the dresser. Light one bulb for yes and both bulbs for no."

"This is ridiculous," Sterling muttered.

"Save it, Sterling," Michael admonished.

She waited for silence and took a deep breath. "Do you see the flashlights?"

Both bulbs remained unlit.

"If you see the flashlights, can you light one of the bulbs to let me know you understand?"

Nothing.

"Can you light—"

One of the bulbs glowed in the dark of the room.

The crew shifted and a few of them murmured excited "ooohs."

She smiled. "Thank you. I'm very glad you chose to speak to us tonight. Are you Theodora?"

One bulb lit again.

"Thank you. Was this your room when you lived here?"

One flash.

"Have you been straightening my room?"

One flash.

"Did you know Norman Baker?"

One bulb illuminated again.

"Thank you. We're here because someone has been disturbing guests. Someone has been hurting people—"

A long flash this time.

Rosie clapped her hands softly and Elise giggled at the interruption.

"She says yes. Okay. She is aware of the scratching."

Sterling took a few steps closer to the dresser. "So far only one flashlight has lit up. The same one. This does not prove communication."

She continued her question session despite the interruption. "Have you been scratching them?"

Both bulbs illuminated.

"No. Of course not. We didn't think it was you. You're always nice to staff and guests."

One flash.

The crew laughed.

"She agrees with that," Rosie said.

"You were saying, Sterling?" TJ said. "This is awesome. I've never seen something respond so clearly with the flashlights before."

"I feel like the guy dragged out of the cave and then forced to go back inside in Plato's *Allegory of the Cave*. You're all entertained by shadows and made up nonsense," Sterling said.

Though hot words bubbled to her lips, she fought to remain calm and maintain the connection with the spirit. "Do you know who has been scratching guests?"

One long, bright flash.

"So who is it?" Sterling asked.

Neither flashlight lit up.

TJ scoffed. "That's not a yes or no question, brah."

"Can you please stop using juvenile nicknames to refer to me? Mr. Wakefield is the appropriate way for you to address me."

"Whatever, dude."

"What the hell is your problem?"

She gritted her teeth until she couldn't stand it any longer. "Stop bickering or I will ask Michael to eject you from the room. I cannot work like this."

Sterling didn't attempt to mask the disgust in his voice. "Then rein in your little lap dog. His yapping is out of control."

"Do not respond, TJ," she instructed her camera operator. "This ends now."

"Sorry, Ms. Wantland. For the record, I hate him now more than ever. But for you, I'll behave."

"We all suffer for our art, TJ. Can we please return to the investigation?"

She closed her eyes, focused inward, and imagined all the stress from the interruption evaporating from her body. She took a few deep breaths and tried to remember what more she'd intended to ask Ms. Theodora.

"Is Norman Baker's ghost the entity disturbing guests?"

No response.

She shifted on her sit bones and gripped her quartz. "Is one of the cancer patients who died here angry and seeking revenge? Perhaps one of the patients you treated?"

Both bulbs remained unlit.

She reached out, searching for a presence.

The door to the room creaked, opening several inches.

Furious at yet another interruption, she opened her eyes, ready to yell at the nosy busybody disrupting her investigation.

Then she remembered there was no knob on the outside of the door. She stood, eyeing the shaft of light from the hallway.

"Michael?"

Her director peered into the hallway. He shook his head. "No one there."

She tried to cross to him, wanting to see for herself, but tripped on something. "What the—"

"I'm turning the light on," Michael warned before he flipped the switch.

"You sure fall down a lot," Sterling noted.

She glared at him from the floor. "I tripped."

"Maybe you shouldn't leave your suitcase in the middle of the room?" he suggested.

She stared at it. "I didn't. And you know I didn't. Every one of us would have tripped on it when we walked in here."

Sterling scowled. "Who the heck moved the suitcase? That's not funny. Kimberly could've been seriously injured."

"I'm the only one who's been on this side of the room, Sterling," Michael said. "And don't dare suggest I would resort to such a cheap stunt."

"Someone snuck over and moved it then."

Kimberly flipped the suitcase open. "Next are you going to suggest someone in the crew also managed to sneakily pack the suitcase?"

"What?"

"Look. All my clothes are folded in here. The dirty ones I left on the floor as well as the clean ones I left sitting on that chair. I told you I intended to be messy."

She pushed herself off the floor and inspected the door. "No one could have opened this from the hall. Michael was the only one in the room near the door." She looked at the suitcase. "Ms. Theodora packed my bag and opened the door. I believe we're being asked to leave."

"Of course," Elise said. "Ms. Theodora doesn't like bickering."

Rosie steepled her fingers over her mouth.

Michael hung his head.

"Thanks, guys," she said, glowering at Sterling and TJ. "Way to derail my investigation."

TJ looked like he might cry but said nothing.

Sterling rested his hands on his hips. "Seriously? Your flashlights stopped randomly connecting and lighting up so you're going to blame me? How can you even call this an investigation? That isn't evidence."

"It is so evidence. And she was cooperating nicely until you two irritated her."

"There is no she. Just loose connections on flashlights that probably became so loose they can't accidentally connect anymore."

"I know she was here. I could feel her presence. I might've even learned who's been scratching hotel guests if you hadn't interfered."

Sterling balled his fists. "You can still figure it out. You were making things up anyway. Pick a ghost, any ghost. That can be your culprit. It's all fabricated."

"Clara showed us pictures. How can you dismiss everyone's experiences?"

"I haven't seen one shred of evidence, that's how. Clara could have scratched herself on anything."

"What about the washing machines?" TJ asked.

"You shut up, you punk!"

Kimberly crossed her arms. "How do you explain that, Sterling?"

"No one saw it other than the three employees, probably collaborating to build a little publicity for the hotel. There is no evidence anything inexplicable happened."

"Enough," Michael said. "We're wasting time going around in circles. We know you don't believe anything you don't see or experience, Sterling. But we have a job we're being paid to do and fans expecting a show."

"And I'm doing my part. So tell this kid to get off my back." Sterling stormed from the room.

She watched him leave, mouth agape. "Wow. Okay. Didn't expect that."

Michael rubbed his temples. "I told him no diva fits."

"I'm not a kid," TJ insisted.

"You're certainly acting like one," Michael said. "Do not speak to Sterling again if you have nothing productive to say. No more goading him. Period."

"Fine." He kicked at the floor. "Still hate that guy."

"Kimmy, do you want to try again?"

She looked around the room, frustration building. "No. It

will be a waste of time. Ms. Theodora made her opinion of us clear. And I don't sense her presence anymore. It would be fruitless. Maybe another night."

"Where to now?" Michael asked.

"Let's do what you suggested. We can split up and walk the halls and see if we can get anyone to talk to us."

"Maybe you should go see Sterling," Michael suggested.

"Not a chance. I'm not rewarding what amounts to a temper tantrum with attention."

"Something needs to give. He and TJ keep bickering. The two of you set each other off. I had high expectations for the two of you together."

"Me too."

"You're going to have to swallow your pride and soothe his hurt feelings. We can't have a repeat of this. I just hope we can salvage tonight."

She nodded. For the good of her show, she had to make peace with Sterling.

CHAPTER EIGHTEEN

KIMBERLY SAT in her makeup chair while Rosie twirled her hair around the curling wand, leaving long, loose waves cascading around her face. Exhaustion combined with dismal disappointment, resulting in a foul mood. The first night investigation had not picked up after Sterling disrupted it. Unless they found something during footage review, they had basically wasted a night. Terrific. Kimberly freakin' Wantland, indeed.

She also hadn't been able to bring herself to seek out Sterling, even though she'd walked right past his room in the night. Three times. She dreaded seeing him today, not knowing how he would behave or what she should say to make things better. And Rosie wouldn't stop chattering about Lorenzo.

"He brought me two roses last night when he picked me up for dinner," Rosie enthused as she lifted another lock. "Did I mention that?"

"Yes." She had listened to how wonderful Lorenzo was since she walked into the trailer. She needed caffeine. Sterling's idea of keeping a coffee maker sounded better and better. Why hadn't she ever thought of that?

Her head throbbed as Rosie prattled on.

"Dinner was amazing. He took me to this little Italian bistro.

And he actually paid! He didn't start patting his pockets when the check came and pretend like he dropped his wallet somewhere like Donald used to do. Remember that guy? Ick. What a sleeze."

"I remember. That guy always gave me the creeps. Although you'd think after he pulled that stunt twice, you might have realized he was scamming you."

"Yeah. I really am a sucker, aren't I?"

"Nah. You're just so sweet and honest, you can't believe anyone could be as awful as some guys are. You just can't see it."

"I think the word you're searching for is 'gullible.'" Rosie sprayed her hair to fix the loose curls in place and picked up eyeliner. "Close."

She closed her eyes and tried to be happy her stylist seemed to have attracted the attention of a decent guy. But Sterling storming from the room last night kept replaying in her mind.

"Then," Rosie continued, "after our early dinner, he took me to a matinee of an illusionist. It was the coolest show I think I've ever seen. I wish you'd been there. If I didn't have to race back here after the show for the investigation, I would have gone back to Lorenzo's place with him. If he asked. He hasn't asked yet. He keeps saying good things are worth waiting for. Do you think he's gay? He's so hot. Why doesn't he want to sleep with me?"

"I don't know."

Rosie spun her chair around. "What's up? You're barely talking and I know I've been going on and on about Lorenzo but you're very quiet. It's not like you to pass on an opportunity to make smart remarks about my current guy."

"I'm fine. And no, I don't think Lorenzo is gay. He sounds like a nice guy. I'm happy for you."

"You're not happy. I can always tell. What's bothering you?"

"Sterling."

"I knew it! Come on. Vent. You'll feel better."

"Things aren't going the way I expected. I don't know. The way we ended last season's finale, I sort of thought he liked me.

Then he spent all summer on beaches and I didn't hear a word from him. He doesn't seem that interested in the show. He ruined my session last night. He won't stop bickering with TJ. What have I done?"

"You can't reform a guy. He's either right for you or he isn't. You have to take him as is or not take him at all."

"I'm taking advice from a woman who once dashed off in the middle of the night to meet a guy she discovered online. I'm lucky you're alive."

Rosie lifted one eyebrow. "Do we need to declare the trailer a judge-free zone at each location or . . . ?"

"I'm sorry. As usual, you're right. That's what's really bothering me. I invited him here. I made it happen. I brought it on myself and now I'm afraid I made a huge mistake."

"Girl, you must have known he'd keep right on trying to disprove ghosts and all paranormal activity. That's his thing. It's what he does."

"I thought we'd be partners. Then I didn't hear a word from him all summer. He strutted in here like it's his show now. He wants to change the opening sequence. And he isn't cooperating at all."

"But he did run to town for coffee for you and book a massage. Those are good things. He's trying."

"That was a couples massage, by the way. He booked it for him too. I can't figure him out."

Rosie bobbled the makeup brush as her jaw dropped. "And you didn't bother telling me? You saw him . . . what, completely naked? Or how naked? Dish, girl!"

"No! Stop. You're making me blush. And I don't mean with the powder."

Rosie stared at her in the mirror, eyes scrunched into tiny slits.

She caved. "Not completely. Boxers."

Rosie squealed. "And?"

"And what? He looks as amazing as you're imagining. But the

point isn't how hot he is. The point is I can't figure him out and he's driving me crazy."

Rosie clicked her tongue and shrugged. "No way to figure out guys. Especially when they like you. They do crazy things when they like you. But you don't seriously believe Sterling booked a couple's massage with someone he hates, do you? Come on. I know guys are horn dogs, but no one wants to get naked with someone they don't like."

She flushed at the memory of Sterling eyeing her bare skin during the massage. And felt herself respond to the memory of him undressing. "If he likes me, why does he disagree with everything I say and do? Why is he trying to take over the show?"

Rosie finished her eye shadow and sponged on some foundation. "I think you two just have different ideas about how to make the show better. He may be trying to show you he cares in ways that aren't registering with you. For example." Rosie picked up her phone and brought up Twitter. "You two are being shipped hard. Have you seen some of his latest tweets? He has women drooling and so jealous of you. Look."

@KWantland agreed to a dinner date with me. Awesome start to season 4 of #WantlandFiles

@KWantland and me after our awesome massage #WantlandFiles

She snatched Rosie's phone. "I explicitly told him not to label that picture as a massage photo. I look disgusting!"

"You couldn't look disgusting if you tried and Sterling knows it. Look how many likes these posts are getting. Meanwhile, someone uploaded a video from the ghost tour when TJ and Sterling were fighting over you. Look."

#Wantlanddrama Sterling making his feelings for Kimberly quite clear #Kimberling

She watched the repeating clip of Sterling attempting to break free from Michael to get at TJ. "But they weren't fighting over me. Sterling was mad because TJ suggested he was lying. It wasn't about me."

Rosie gave her the look. "Girl, that was so about you. Stop playing. He likes you. The question now is, do you like him?"

She mulled the question while Rosie dusted her face with powder and blushed her cheeks. "Sometimes I think I do. And then sometimes he makes me crazy. But I don't know if I'm ready for an actual relationship. Especially with someone who works on the show."

"It can work if you want it to. Other people manage fine. And after all, you're 'Kimberly freakin' Wantland.' Ta-da!"

Her stylist twirled her around to face the mirror for approval. The door opened and Sterling barged in carrying a large box.

Had she just been thinking about how much she liked this guy? "Will you never learn to knock?"

"Sorry."

She narrowed her eyes at his smiling face. He didn't look one bit sorry. "Seriously. I change in here. You could open the door and waltz in while I'm undressed."

He frowned. "You know that's not really a threat, right?"

She opened her mouth to further chastise him, then realized what he meant. Rendered mute, she flushed. How did he always do this to her?

He shrugged. "Honestly more of an encouragement than—"

"What's in the box?" Rosie asked.

He placed it on the floor and waved his hands over it. "I call this a Kimberly Care Package and from it I will produce the most amazing treasure trove of delights our fearless leader could ever desire. May I have an assistant from the audience, please?" He drew his hands across his face and lifted an eyebrow.

Rosie laughed and raised her hand.

"Yes, you. The beautiful vixen with the mocha skin. If you would please." He gestured beside him. "You can see this is a plain, ordinary box. Yes?"

"Just a cardboard box that says Amazon priority—"

"A plain, ordinary, cardboard box. Thank you, my dear." He opened the top flaps and extracted a coffee maker. "Voilà!"

"Wonderful! It's exactly what she needs," Rosie said.

"What, you couldn't make it appear from behind my ear?" Kimberly mumbled.

He reached behind her ear and flourished an envelope of plain oatmeal. "You mean like that?"

Rosie clapped. "That's amazing! You're as good as the illusionist I saw yesterday afternoon."

Sterling dropped his act and stage voice. "What illusionist? Here in town?"

"Yes. He has an assistant who hears spirits. At the end of the show, he moves through the audience and takes objects people offer him and even though she's blindfolded, she will know what he's holding every time."

Sterling smirked. "That's Houdini's old trick."

Kimberly narrowed her eyes. "The assistant hears spirits?"

Sterling cocked his head at her. "Doth mine ears deceive me? Do I detect skepticism that another fair maiden possesses the same skill you doth claim to possess?"

"I'm aware this field is plagued with frauds."

"Interesting. We should go see the show."

"We won't have time. The investigation is our priority."

Sterling shrugged. "Just different types of shows, really. Why begrudge them? You're far more successful and don't need to feel threatened."

"I am not remotely threatened. I know my abilities are legitimate—"

"This coffee maker is awesome, Sterling," Rosie interrupted, staring intently at Kimberly. "It's exactly what we needed in here."

Accepting gifts wasn't easy for her. In her experience, people only gave you something if they wanted something in return. Or wanted to make you feel guilty by reminding you of the gift. She took a deep breath. "Yes. Thank you for the coffee maker. You didn't have to do that. Where did you even get it?"

"I ordered it from Amazon, natch. Priority overnight shipping. I'll still run to Mud Street Café for you if you'd rather. But the coffee maker seemed like a good idea. Rosie keeps an electric tea kettle and a vast assortment of teas. But no coffee."

"The teas help regulate moods and boost her chakra energies. She always gets coffee at the hotel," Rosie said. "I've never had to worry about it."

Sterling thrust the coffee maker at Rosie. "You still don't have to worry about it. Ta-da!"

"I'll set it up and try it out right now. Oh. I guess we need to get some coffee first."

Sterling's eyes sparkled. He dove into the box and withdrew packages of assorted coffee pods, individual cups of skim milk, and a sleeve of coffee cups with lids.

"You thought of everything," Kimberly said.

"But wait! There's more!" He reached into the box and extracted a value-sized container of plain oatmeal packets, paper bowls, a box of plastic spoons, a bag of dried fruit and nuts, a bottle of cinnamon. "And finally . . . a honey bear!"

Rosie laughed. "It's like Mary Poppins' bag. You keep bringing out more goodies."

"Sterling, I . . . I don't know what to say. You shouldn't have done this. Priority overnight shipping is outrageously expensive. We'll only be here a few days. A week at most. I could've managed."

"Now you don't have to manage. You can surround yourself with all the things that make you happy." He searched her eyes.

A warm rush ran through her. "But I—"

"I know. You've gotten along all this time on your own—"

Rosie cleared her throat.

"With Rosie's help, of course. But I want you to know I'm a true partner. You gave me a job when I needed one. I'm here to support you, not take anything away from you. As for the expense . . . "—he stepped closer and pulled a penny from behind her ear—"You're worth every penny."

She melted. What had she been upset about earlier?

"Besides, I got a sweet sports car out of this deal. I think you at least deserve some coffee and oatmeal."

And there he was. Glib, flashy Sterling. The other half of the coin.

"Make some coffee and let's go look at blobs and shadows from last night," Sterling said. "Rosie, can you do my makeup in here?"

"Uhhhh . . . " Rosie looked at her for direction.

"What's wrong with your trailer?" she asked.

"You're not in it."

CHAPTER NINETEEN

SHE STEPPED out of her trailer, coffee in hand, and crossed the parking lot for the hotel. Were her feet connecting with the ground? Something felt different. A giggle escaped her. Maybe she should take Rosie's advice. Perhaps she could make a relationship work.

"Kimmy?"

She stopped in her tracks, jarred out of her the short-lived euphoria and rooted firmly back on the ground.

That voice didn't belong to Michael. It belonged to the only other person in the world who ever called her Kimmy.

The person who gave her the nickname.

No. He couldn't be here.

"Kimmy!"

No mistaking that voice. She turned slowly, eyes scanning the small group of people clustered in the parking lot watching her.

"Hey!"

Someone poked her in the ribs. She whirled on Sterling. "Don't scare me like that."

"Why'd you stop? Miss me already? My makeup is done." He tried to curl an arm around her waist but she maneuvered sideways, searching the crowd.

"No. I heard—"

"Kimmy!" A waving hand caught her attention.

Sterling's head whipped around, eyes zeroing in on the owner of the voice. "That's not Michael. Who is that guy?"

She felt Sterling's red chakra flair as the guy approached.

He stopped in front of her. "Hi, Kimmy."

"Kimmy?" Sterling edged closer to her.

"Hi, Jason." She started to offer a hand, almost went for a hug, then decided to wait and see what he did.

Jason grabbed her hand and shook. His eyes drank her in. "Wow. You look great. I mean, you've always looked great, but you haven't aged a day in six years."

"Has it been six years? Wow. Doesn't seem that long." She noticed gray hairs speckling his temples and searched for something positive to say in return. "You've lost some weight. You look good."

He patted his abs. "Finally started taking some of your advice. Better late than never, right?"

Sterling thrust a hand forward. "Sterling Wakefield. And you are?"

Sterling's rough tone startled her. She hurried to introduce them. "Sterling, this is Jason. Jason, Sterling Wakefield."

Jason gripped Sterling's hand. "Nice to meet you. Love your show. Never missed an episode and sorry to hear it's ended."

She threw her head back and laughed. "You *would* love *Spook-Busters*."

Jason grinned sheepishly. "You know me."

Sterling looked back and forth between them, brow furrowed, apparently not sure if that was a compliment or an insult.

"Sterling," she said. "Jason is my ex-fiancé."

Sterling stepped backwards. "You never mentioned you'd been engaged."

Jason waved a hand. "I'm ancient history."

"Still." Sterling turned a questioning gaze on her and seemed to be seeking answers.

"You never asked," she said. "We know little about each other's personal lives."

He nodded. "You have a point. We can fix that over dinner tonight."

Michael appeared on the hotel stairs. "What is the hold up, you two?"

She knew the moment he spotted Jason because his eyes bulged and his jaw fell nearly to his sternum.

"Oh, dear. Come on. Might as well come say hello to Michael."

"You know Michael too?" Sterling asked.

"We go way back," Jason told him.

She led the two men across the parking lot and up the stairs, one on each side.

"Jason," Michael greeted him, eyeing her as if expecting her to explode. "This is a huge surprise."

"I'm sorry, Michael. I won't disrupt things. I only wanted to say hi to Kimmy."

Michael blinked, then stared at her. "Kimmy. Right. Yes. Of course. What brings you to the Crescent, Jason?"

"Sterling, really. I've wanted a chance to talk with Kimmy for a couple of years now. In person, I mean. I figured she would ignore any message I sent. So when Sterling tweeted you guys were here in Eureka Springs, I went for it. Wasn't sure when I'd get another chance. Although maybe Sterling plans to post your location every week. I don't know." He laughed.

She turned to Sterling, eyes narrowed. He held up a hand and shook his head. Michael stood as if transfixed, resting his chin on one hand, palm pressed to his cheek.

"Did you get the fruit flower arrangement?" Jason asked.

"*You* sent it. The mystery is solved. I did, thank you."

"I remember you don't like cut flowers because you hate to watch them wilt and die. A live plant on the road seemed like a bad idea. But fruit. You always loved fruit. And from the look of you, that hasn't changed. I can't get over how great you look."

Her cheeks grew warm and she dropped her gaze. "Thank you. That's very sweet. I did enjoy the fruit. So, thank you."

Michael blew out a long breath. "Well, this has been a surprise reunion. But we have work to do. And you probably have a job to get back to."

"I took the whole week off, "Jason beamed. "I had some vacation time saved up. Kimmy, I don't suppose you'd have dinner with me tonight?"

Sterling pressed against her side and took her hand in his. "Kimberly and I are having dinner together tonight."

Jason stared at their clasped hands and nodded. "Oh, right. You two are—"

"Just having dinner," she said. "I mean, we already made dinner plans." An enormous cloud of sadness rolled off of Sterling. Guilt squeezed her insides. But why should she feel guilty?

Rosie trotted up the steps. "Hey, Kimberly, do you mind if I skip footage review? Lorenzo and I—" Her gaze swept over their faces and landed on her hand clasped in Sterling's. "Why does everyone look freaked out? What's happening?"

"This is my ex-fiancé."

"This is Jason?" Rosie shook his hand.

Jason's face lit up. "I guess you haven't completely forgotten about me, Kimmy."

"Kimberly and I talk." Rosie stared pointedly at her and Sterling's hands and lifted an eyebrow. "And I'll be back for prep before the show. Lorenzo and I are going to lunch."

She dislodged her hand from Sterling's and smiled at Jason. "Maybe lunch or dinner tomorrow?"

Jason beamed. "Name the time. I'll be here."

"Let's go, you two," Michael said. "Jason, it was . . . interesting to see you again."

Jason gave her a smile and a wave before she turned to leave. "I'm in room two seventeen," he called after them.

"You're right by Sterling," she called over her shoulder.

"Why would you care what room he's in?" Sterling asked as they stepped into the lobby.

"I don't."

Michael looped an arm through hers and veered for the elevator. "How did I not remember that loser started the nickname Kimmy?"

"It's not important."

"And how did you listen to it all these years? Every single time I called you Kimmy must have reminded you of that jerkwad."

"I try not to think about him. It was a long time ago."

Sterling leaned closer. "I told you she didn't like it."

She scowled at Sterling. "I told you to stay out of it. You didn't even know for sure. You guessed."

"I could tell something about it bothered you. My emotional intelligence is quite astute."

"Why didn't you tell me, Kimmy?" Michael asked. "Oh, goodness. Now it's a habit. This could take some time to break."

"I didn't ask you to stop," she said. "You've called me Kimmy since college. Don't worry about it."

A raised voice at the desk drew Kimberly's attention. The woman who had previously complained about the temperature of her room stood at the counter, arm outstretched, suitcase on the floor beside her. Marcus appeared quite alarmed.

She crossed to the desk. "Everything okay?"

Marcus turned to her. "She says someone inflicted a wound on her arm and she's leaving."

She turned to the woman. "Who hurt you?"

The woman peered over her glasses. "Who are you?"

She extended her hand. "Kimberly Wantland. I'm a paranormal investigator. My show *The Wantland Files* is here investigating a disturbance."

"Thought you looked familiar. Well, I don't know who scratched me. But look."

She stared at the woman's arm. "Michael. Do we have a camera nearby?"

Michael and Sterling joined her.

"The cameras are all upstairs for footage review. I can call one of the guys to come down if you want. What's up?" Michael asked.

"Look at her arm. This scratch pattern looks exactly the same as the scratches on Clara's arm."

"And like every other scratch on every other arm in the history of scratches on arms," Sterling said. "What are you implying?"

She ignored Sterling and turned her attention back to the woman. "Can you tell me what happened? Did you see someone? Hear anything?"

"Brush your arm against something ragged and sharp?" Sterling asked.

"Let her talk," she admonished him.

The woman went pale. "You'll think I'm crazy. *I* think I'm crazy."

"I won't," Kimberly assured her. "You can confide in me."

The woman licked her lips and glanced around the lobby. "No cameras?"

"Not if you don't want them," she said. She would prefer to record this exchange but would take the evidence off camera rather than not hear it at all.

"Let me start by saying I stayed in this old hotel because I'm a history buff. I don't believe in ghosts," the woman said.

"Smart woman," Sterling said.

"But I think there was something in my room last night. I kept waking up. I swear I would hear something and wake up, but when I listened, nothing. Then I woke up and my arm hurt. And I think when I woke up . . . I saw . . ."

"What did you see?"

The woman shook her head. "I thought someone was standing over me. I jumped. Sat up. It was still there. I blinked and shook my head and opened and closed my eyes. Nothing made it go away."

"What happened?"

"I turned on the lamp, fully expecting to see a man standing in my room. I tell you, my heart was racing. At my age, that's not healthy."

"But there wasn't a man?" Sterling asked.

"No. I turned on the lamp and there was no one in my room. But I do have these scratches on my arm."

Kimberly reached for the woman's arm. "May I?"

The woman nodded.

She wrapped her hands gently around the woman's forearm, closed her eyes, and felt for any residual electrostatic charge a spirit might leave behind. Her hands tingled. Not exactly an electric shock, but something prickled her skin. She also felt a moment of vertigo, as if standing atop a high ledge or falling.

"What are you getting, Kimmy? Anything?"

She opened her eyes. "Which room are you staying in?"

"Three thirteen. Why?"

"Michael, will you ask Selma if we may look into it?"

Michael's fingers flew over his phone screen as he typed a note to himself.

The woman's brow furrowed. "Do you think someone was in my room?"

Sterling shook his head. "Don't you think maybe you simply scratched yourself at some point in the night?"

"No. I don't. I've never done any such thing in my life."

"You had a rough night. You tossed and turned and didn't sleep well. Your arm got scratched."

"Then how do you explain the figure standing over me?"

"That is a common phenomenon. We get caught between sleep and wakefulness. We think we're fully awake but aren't quite there yet. So we see things our minds project. It happens."

"Does that happen to you, Sterling?" Kimberly asked.

"Sure. Happens to everyone."

"Interesting."

"Nope. Not interesting. Common. Happens to everyone."

The woman picked up her suitcase. "I don't know what happened but I'm moving to a lovely bed and breakfast in town. I'll leave you two to sort out this place."

Marcus watched her leave. "Poor Ms. Reddick. This place is usually completely booked. Now we have empty rooms and people walking out. I really hope you can get rid of that ghost, Ms. Wantland."

"Me too, Marcus. Me too."

CHAPTER TWENTY

GRAY SCALE IMAGES glowed from the computer monitors as the crew reviewed footage. Kimberly circled the screens, alert for tidbits of information, eager for any excited response from her crew.

Sterling fidgeted, adding to her growing anxiety. The most haunted hotel in America and still they had not succeeded in capturing anything impressive on camera.

She sipped her coffee and noticed one of Sterling's legs began to bounce. Expecting a comment about lack of evidence, she held her tongue, unwilling to provoke him.

The silence unnerved her. Rosie should be here pressing cups of tea into her hand. At least the headphoned crew had the audio from last night in their ears. She had only silence. Correction—now she also had the jangling of change in Sterling's pocket as he jiggled his leg. Wasn't like him to be quiet. Where were his smart remarks?

Jason. What a shock Jason had appeared out of nowhere. What could he possibly want? His chakras had glowed predominantly green and blue, the heart and throat. Friendship and communication. He probably came seeking resolution. She sensed no jealousy or lust from him.

She held the jade stone on her chakra necklace, pinching it between thumb and forefinger. Perhaps Rosie was right. Maybe she should open her heart and try to balance work and a relationship.

"How's the coffee?" Sterling asked.

She pulled herself out of her thoughts and focused on him. "Perfect. Thank you."

"What were you thinking about? How good the coffee is and how eternally grateful you are to your partner who gave you the coffee maker?"

"You've been hiding your psychic abilities," she teased. "That is exactly what I was thinking."

He lifted his hands to his temples like a stage psychic reading someone's mind. "Except I've never seen you go all moony-eyed over a cup of coffee. I think something else put that dreamy look on your face."

Michael yanked off his headphones. "You two know we're listening to sensitive recordings over here, right?"

"Sorry," she mumbled.

Sterling waved away Michael's complaint and stared at the table.

She circled the room, watching over shoulders, hoping for a glimpse of something helpful on the screens.

What sort of resolution could Jason want? After all these years, why now?

Sterling drummed his fingers on the table. Every head in the room swiveled to glare at him.

He stood, hands on his hips. "I'm sorry. Fiancé?"

Her brow furrowed. Why was he bringing up Jason again? "Ex-fiancé. I haven't seen him in years."

"Until today?"

"Right."

"Doesn't it strike anyone else as curious that she canceled dinner with me last night and today we learn her old flame is in town?"

"I didn't—is that why you're uptight? I didn't see him last night if that's what you're implying. He surprised me this morning. I assume he just got here."

"Really? Because you were eating his fruit last night." He pressed the heels of his hands into his eyes. "Gross. Not what I meant. No one say a word."

The crew stifled giggles.

Except TJ. "What is your problem? She said she didn't see him last night."

Stan waved her over. "I have something."

"Good," Michael said. "Because I finished footage from the grounds and saw nothing. Not so much as a shadow or an orb."

"That's discouraging. What did you find, Stan?" She crossed to peer over his shoulder.

"I watched the flashlight session frame by frame. I can assure you there is no stray or random flickering. Response time from the moment your question ends to the moment the bulb or bulbs illuminate is the same from question to question. I can also confirm the batteries tested completely dead following the session, which supports your theory that Ms. Theodora opened the door. Watch this."

He clicked "Play" and advanced the recording slowly.

"You got the door in the shot. Excellent." She patted his shoulder.

"Notice Michael is about two feet from the door. His hands are clasped in front of him. No one else is near him."

She heard a click followed by a squeak as the door swung open.

"And no doorknob on the exterior of the door. So no one in the hallway opened it."

Sterling pressed his hand to his forehead. "None of you are looking at this objectively. The simplest explanation is that the door latch wasn't fully engaged and the door either blew open, jostled free and swung open, or was pushed open by someone walking by who happened to notice it wasn't closed. Everyone in the hotel is aware we're here."

"Thanks to your tweets," she reminded him. "Though you tried to convince me no one cared."

"I said no one wanted to stalk you, not that no one cares about the show. I think your graphic-wrapped van alerted the hotel guests to our presence. And they were already here."

She crossed her arms and raised an eyebrow. "Not all of them."

He opened his mouth but closed it before he said anything.

"Ms. Wantland," TJ said. "The cameras we left in the psych ward captured a lot of activity. Orbs passing in and out of the walls. At one point one of the cameras shakes—"

"I want to see these orbs," Sterling said, pushing himself out of the chair. "And a real live person could have bumped the camera and jostled it."

"No," TJ said. "The mike would've captured someone bumping into it. No audio. The camera simply shakes."

"You could've erased the audio," Sterling said.

Kimberly rested a hand on TJ's shoulder. "He wouldn't do that. We're here to tease out the truth. We can't do that if our evidence is tampered with."

"We have different definitions of truth."

She noticed an uptick in her pulse. Irritation coursed through her, causing an unwelcome queasiness in her stomach. She grasped her quartz and took a deep breath. "I'm well aware of that."

"Orbs are so easily explained. Every time. They're smudges on a camera lens or reflections of a flash or a nearby light source."

"Not when they move," TJ said.

"I guarantee I can discern the true source of every orb on that recording," Sterling said.

"Whoa. What the—" TJ clicked his mouse several times, then sat back in his chair. He blinked at the screen and shook his head. "I thought I saw something in the mirror at the end of the hall, so I zoomed in and enlarged it. This is wild."

She'd never seen TJ appear shaken. Evidence of activity normally excited him.

He rubbed a hand down his face and shook his head, as if to clear it. "Kinda sorry we can't drink during investigations. This one gets to me."

Sterling threw his arms wide. "See? Even the kid agrees with me."

When TJ didn't leap to his feet and yell, "I'm not a kid," she knew he was truly bothered by whatever he saw. She bent over his screen.

A pale, gauzy image of a woman in a loose hospital gown reflected from the mirror, though the hall in front of the mirror was empty. Hollow eyes stared from a gaunt face above a skeletal frame, mouth pulled back in a tortured grimace. She shuddered at the pain obvious in the face silently screaming at them.

"She's only there for a moment," TJ said. "Next frame she's gone. I happened to notice a blip and zoomed in on it."

"Good work," she praised him.

Sterling glanced at the image. "I think I've seen that same picture used in at least three ghost movies. Nice photo manipulation, though. It looks seamless."

"Dude, I didn't manipulate anything. That's a real image of a real spiritual remnant. Look at her."

"Activity on the third floor confirmed, Michael," she said. "We definitely need to devote some time there tonight. I can't help but think a patient of Norman Baker seems a likely candidate for someone seeking revenge. The hospital gown would suggest this was a patient."

"Third floor tonight, definitely," Michael said. "And I agree. Who wouldn't want revenge on this guy? Painful treatment and no pain meds. Did he get off on torturing people?"

She stared at the image. "This is a woman though. The entity seeking revenge and scratching guests has been described consistently as male. And I know I heard a male voice during my massage. Still, this seems a promising starting point. Elise, can you try to dig more into Norman Baker's later years? Find out if he ever came back. And I know you said all records were destroyed, but maybe you can find something about some of the patients treated here. Maybe personal accounts or testimony. I don't know. Research is your thing."

Elise jotted notes on her pad of paper. "I'm on it."

"Why now? What's changed? The cancer treatment center was shut down in nineteen thirty-seven. We need to determine who has been roused and why."

"Kimberly," Stan said, "Check this out. I noticed something on the doorknob and went in for a closer look. You're gonna love this."

She tore her gaze from the disturbing young woman in the hospital gown and hurried to see what Stan had found.

"I noticed kind of a cloudiness over the doorknob. Look what happens when I zoom in for a closer look." He clicked his mouse, zooming in on the cropped doorknob.

Translucent fingers curled around the knob.

Stan sat back and crossed his arms over his chest, a satisfied smile on his face. "Those are fingers. Something opened that door."

"Wow. Well, we didn't really find answers to our mysterious revenge seeker, but we captured some incredible images. I feel convinced my theory was correct. Ms. Theodora had enough of us and not-so-subtly asked us to leave. She's done things like this before."

Elise giggled. "According to one well known account, a couple here to be married were staying in room four nineteen and squabbled with each other. Probably wedding nerves or stress. But they came back to find their bags packed and ready to go. Ms. Theodora is no-nonsense."

"I agree."

"I'm still freaked out," TJ said. "The woman in the mirror

looks like she hurts so bad. I don't want to see her again, Ms. Wantland. Or maybe I do. I don't know."

"Her image is a reminder of a disturbing time in the hotel's past, I know. But remember, she's gone. What we're seeing is a memory. She doesn't hurt anymore and hasn't for some time."

"How can you know that?" TJ asked. "Her face . . . she looks like she still hurts. It looks like she's trapped here suffering forever. If her soul is stuck here, will you help her move on to the next life so she won't hurt anymore?"

She hesitated. "Selma was pretty clear that she only wanted us to find the spirit who's scratching her guests and leave all the others alone. I think the image you caught is probably simply an imprint. She didn't interact with us. She appeared and then was gone. Let's try to focus on the haunting we were asked to solve."

"Okay," TJ agreed, though his downcast face let her know he wasn't satisfied with her answer.

Michael cleared his throat. "We will start in the psych ward tonight. Anywhere else you'd like to try, Kimmy? Kimberly, I mean." He drew out the second syllable as if it was awkward in his mouth.

She opted not to comment on the name issue. They could sort that out later. "Let's see what happens on the third floor. I think I want to try an EVP session in the laundry room as well, if we have time. That's where the spirit first manifested."

"And if we don't have time tonight, we can start there tomorrow," Michael said.

"Sounds like a plan."

"Everyone try to get some rest. I think we're in for a long night tonight," Michael advised. "See you back here at dusk."

Sterling maneuvered to catch her before she could reach the door. "I made dinner reservations for five o'clock. I hope I don't have to cancel them again." His intense gaze sought hers.

"I'm planning on dinner. If you still want to."

"Yes, of course. I don't know if I can handle rejection two nights in a row." He offered a smile.

He had just sat there ridiculing her interpretations and disagreeing at every turn. But apparently he still expected to have dinner. She didn't think she could ever figure this guy out. "I didn't . . . never mind. What time should I meet you? How far away is the restaurant?" In truth, she wouldn't mind taking a ride in that new car of his.

"Meet me in the lobby about five minutes to five."

Didn't sound like she was getting that ride after all. "See you then." *Rosie better turn up in time for makeup.* She wanted to look good for this dinner. And in case she bumped into Jason. If he didn't regret letting her go, he would by the end of the week.

CHAPTER TWENTY-ONE

"How was your lunch with Lorenzo?" Kimberly asked Rosie.

Rosie swept mascara onto her eyelashes as she answered. "Absolutely fantastic. Which is how you look right now, girl. You need to smell just right, too."

Her stylist lifted bottles of essential oils, contemplating each before returning it to its spot or squeezing a few drops into a bowl, until she held one bottle in each hand and appeared to be debating between them.

"Patchouli or sandalwood? I can't decide." Rosie sniffed the contents of each bottle, then held them out. "Which one smells like sex?"

"I'm having dinner with Sterling, not trying to lure him to bed."

"I don't think you'd have to try very hard. Alluring, that's what we want." After smelling each one more time, she made her choice. "Patchouli. It has a nice earthy scent and will mix well with the vanilla and cinnamon that will subconsciously make him think of home and comfort. This will put him in a fantastic mood."

She held out her wrists for Rosie's scent blend, then pulled her hair back to let her dab some behind the ears.

Rosie spun her around to face the mirror, fluffing her long curls. "There you go. You're ready to knock him dead in his tracks. Wish I could see his face. Let's adjust this."

Rosie tugged her shirt lower around her cleavage. She swatted her stylist's hand away, laughing.

"Stop that. I will never be in good shape for the investigation tonight at this rate. I'm excited and I feel silly. And you're not helping! I need to relax."

"You can relax later. After dinner. Maybe after a little dessert." Rosie lifted her eyebrows. "A little *dessert* always relaxes me."

"You're incorrigible! It's only dinner."

"Does Sterling know it's only dinner?"

A knock on the door startled them both.

Rosie opened the door to a smiling Sterling.

"Is she dressed?" He peered around Rosie and waved. "I knocked first."

"Thank you. I appreciate that."

He took the steps in one long stride and held out a bundle of flowers. "I heard what Jason said about you not liking cut flowers, but these made me think of you. And I thought maybe things have changed since he knew you."

She didn't miss the hope in his expression as she accepted the bouquet of lilies and carnations and breathed deeply. "These are some of my favorite. Thank you. They brighten up the trailer and smell wonderful. I thought I was going to meet you."

"I got nervous. Scared you'd bail on me again. Thought I'd come meet you just in case."

He had changed from his usual black denim and black T-shirt, wearing instead dark slacks, a dress shirt, and a jacket. She also detected cologne. Perhaps he was trying Rosie's approach. He definitely had made an effort. Even his unruly hair seemed more intentionally disheveled. Maybe even gelled.

"I wasn't going to bail. You look nice."

"Thanks. You look incredible. And smell great."

A warm flush crept up her neck and spread into her cheeks while Rosie nudged her. "Thank you."

She didn't know where to look or what to say. Rosie came to her rescue.

"Let me take those flowers, girl. I'll get these into a vase of water and you two can go to dinner. I'm going to grab a quick bite with Lorenzo but I'll be back to prep before the investigation."

She nodded her thanks and looked to Sterling.

"Rosie," he said, "be sure to toss the bouquet before they wilt and die."

Rosie winked at him. "I doubt I'll be the first of us to toss a bouquet. But I know what you mean." Possibly knowing her comment warranted a stomp on the foot, Rosie ducked out of reach and did her best to look innocent. "Now where would we keep a vase in here?"

He crooked his arm at her. "Shall we?"

She looped an arm through his and waved to Rosie.

"You two have fun," Rosie called after them.

"And you and Lorenzo," she called back.

Sterling led her into the hotel lobby. "I made reservations for us at the Crystal Dining Room. It looked really nice. And it's close, so we'll be right here for the investigation. Don't need to stress about getting back."

"Good thinking."

"They open at five. That was the earliest I could schedule dinner. Wanted us to be able to relax and talk."

The maître d brightened as they approached. "Mr. Wakefield. Table for two at five? Secluded but with a view of the grounds."

"Thank you," Sterling said, palming him a bill.

"This way, please."

They crossed the wooden floor to a table tucked away in the corner. Floor to ceiling windows allowed the evening light to fill the room. Sterling held her chair for her as she settled into her seat.

Before taking his own seat, he bent low, instructed her to smile, and snapped a selfie. He inspected the photo and smiled. "Perfect. Let me upload this."

Her phone buzzed with what she knew would be a Twitter notification. She glanced at it.

Out to dinner with @KWantland #Kimberling #WantlandFiles #datenight

"That ought to blow up Twitter," he grinned. "The shippers will go crazy over this."

"So this is a publicity stunt? A way to get attention?"

"No. Not just for publicity." He offered his trademark smirk, which she found more annoying and less endearing than she had earlier.

She opened her menu quickly and stared at the choices without really reading them. Rosie was so wrong. Sterling had no feelings for her. What was she thinking? How could she have let herself listen?

"After all, when you look as fabulous as you look tonight, you ought to share it with the world."

"You seem to share everything with the world. I noticed you labeled the massage pic I requested you keep to yourself."

"Did you also notice how well received it was? People love you."

Unable to think of a reply, she scanned her menu and quickly honed in on the grilled salmon with avocado risotto. And a harvest salad. She closed the menu and looked up to find him eyeing her quizzically.

"You okay?"

"Yep. And I've decided so we can order anytime."

"No rush." His brow furrowed. "Sure you're okay?"

"Yeah, I'm fine."

"Well, I already know I'm ordering a steak. Any way I can convince you to okay a glass of wine each?"

She shook her head. "I really can't drink when I'm investigating. It interferes terribly with my sensitivity. Even a single glass dulls my senses."

He nodded. "I understand. I mean, I wasn't trying to get you tipsy or anything."

"If you want a glass, I won't say anything. Limit it to one though, please. I don't want to put either of us in an awkward situation."

"Thanks!" He raised a finger at the waiter who hurried to their table. "I'll have the filet mignon and garlic mashed potatoes and a glass of merlot, please. And I'm betting she wants the salmon."

She laughed in spite of herself. "Seriously, I'm starting to think you're a true psychic. Yes, the salmon with risotto, and a harvest salad, dressing on the side, please."

"Any wine for you, ma'am?" the waiter asked.

"Not tonight. Thank you."

Sterling watched the waiter scurry away and then reached across the table, extending his hand. "I think perhaps I said something to offend you again. I didn't intend to. I've really been looking forward to the chance to get to know you better."

His phone beeped repeatedly, each time resulting in a smile. "I knew it. We're a hit. Likes and retweets are starting already. People love you."

"I'd rather not everyone know all the details of my personal life, though. Did you have to post we're having dinner? Or is dinner for the attention?"

Kerry and Suzie walked by on their way to a table, yanking out phones when they spotted them. "Oh, my gosh! You guys are having dinner! Suzie, I told you not to give up on Kimberling! It's a thing."

Sterling beamed. "Mind if I use that? '*Kimberling. It's a thing.*' I love it."

"Take it! It's yours to use," Kerry said.

"We're not actually a thing though," Kimberly said.

Suzie snapped a picture, then bent low to take a selfie with them in the background.

"Be sure to hashtag that," Sterling said.

"Are you kidding? I wouldn't miss being in a Kimberling pic for anything. Of course I'm hashtagging it. Kerry, look at their dinner pic! I'm retweeting that."

The two women finally followed the flustered maître d they'd left standing alone in the middle of the restaurant.

Sterling spread his arms wide. "Ta-da. We're a hit. I promised more publicity and I delivered. I'm a man of my word."

"I'd prefer a quiet dinner with no interruptions."

"You're a celebrity, like it or not. You'll have to learn to tolerate some of the side effects."

"Easier said than done for some of us. Unlike you, who thrives on the attention."

"Why not? In this business, attention means we have a job. So tell me about yourself. Other than you don't really like attention, which I already deduced."

"What do you want to know?"

"Tell me about your summer."

"Nothing to tell, other than what I mentioned before. Interviews, appearances, a couple of conventions."

"You must have had a few days off."

"A couple."

"Did you go somewhere? You must have done something."

"I spent my days off in the house I lived in as a child."

The waiter brought her water and Sterling's merlot. Sterling nodded his thanks and sipped his wine.

"You own your childhood home?"

"I do. Waited a long time for it to come on the market." She lifted her water glass, mouth suddenly dry. The water didn't quench her thirst. "Got it not too long ago."

"So you snapped it up, what, for nostalgia sake?"

"Something like that. Sure. Nostalgia."

The waiter placed her salad in front of her. "And dressing on the side. Anything else? Cracked pepper?"

"Yes, please."

He twisted the grinder over her salad until she held up a hand. "Let me know if you need anything else."

"We will. Thanks," Sterling dismissed him. He propped his chin on his fist. "I suspect there's more to that home purchase than nostalgia."

She drizzled dressing over her salad and mixed it in. When he continued piercing her with his intense gaze, she shrugged. "Not really."

"Kimmy! Hi!"

Jason.

CHAPTER TWENTY-TWO

She watched Jason cross to their table, leaving the maître d in his wake and once again flummoxed.

"Secluded table, my ass," Sterling muttered. He gulped his merlot.

"What's wrong, Mr. Personality? I thought you liked the attention."

"Not from your exes."

"Snap a picture of us and stir up some real *Wantland* drama."

"That's not the kind of drama I'm interested in." He jumped to his feet. "Jason! What a surprise."

"Right? I figured you two would find some intimate little corner in town."

Sterling's jaw clenched. "This was more practical since we're, you know, working here."

"Right, right. Cool, cool, cool."

A wave of jealousy rolled off Sterling and washed over her. His red chakra flared.

Jason extracted a phone from his pocket. "Kimmy, could I maybe get a picture with you?"

Sterling held out a hand. "Hey, pal? She's eating. Do you mind?"

"Oh, sure. Sure. Maybe I could pull up a chair and join you two."

"We're discussing work," Sterling said. "That would be inappropriate. Confidential and all."

"Ooooh. This is a work dinner. Gotcha. Thought it was social." Jason wiggled his eyebrows at her. She'd forgotten that habit of his.

Sterling's jaw tightened and she thought she heard teeth grinding.

"We'll catch up, Jason," she said. "I promise. But Sterling and I do need to prepare for tonight."

Jason held up both hands. "No problem. Totally understand. I was sorry, though, to hear about your father's passing."

Her stomach clenched. She rested her fork on the salad and nodded.

"Sorry if I shouldn't have brought it up. I wanted so badly to reach out to you at the time. I didn't know how."

"Yes, well, thank you."

"Did you two ever . . ."

"No. But I made my peace with that."

Sterling scowled. "How did you know about her father?"

Jason blushed. "I read all the news on Kimmy. And, truth be told, she never unfriended me on Facebook, so . . ."

"So you creep on her page?"

"I've watched her success skyrocket with great pride. We were engaged, after all. Curiosity gets the better of me from time to time. I'm truly happy for you, Kimmy."

"Thank you."

The waiter approached with their food.

Jason pointed at him. "I'm in your way. Talk to you tomorrow, Kimmy. Oh! And glad to hear you got your house back. Maybe you'll finally find some closure on your mom. Good luck tonight."

Sterling took his seat, watched Jason depart, and finished his wine in one swallow.

The waiter served their meals and left them in silence.

Sterling lifted his fork, but paused, squinting at her. "How did he know you bought your old house?"

"Maybe there was something in the paper? I don't know."

"How did he know about your dad?"

"I don't know. Everything I do winds up online somewhere."

"Does he still live in Albuquerque?"

She shrugged as she dove back into her salad, eager to finish it and move onto the main course. "No idea. This salmon smells incredible. Look at that risotto."

Sterling sliced a bite of his steak. "The guy is a stalker. He creeps on your Facebook page. Searches for articles about you online. That's a stalker."

"Well, you brought him right to me."

"I thought you didn't post on Facebook."

"Private information I share on my personal page. Not on my fan page."

"You need to go unfriend and block him. You should have when you dumped him."

About to take another bite, she stopped, fork in midair. "I didn't dump him. He called it off."

"What? You've got to be joking. You are so far out of his league. What did you ever see in him to begin with?"

Out of his league? Hardly. "It was a long time ago."

"So what happened?"

"I really don't want to talk about it. Can we focus on something else? How's your steak?"

He turned his attention to the still uneaten bite of steak on his fork and opted to lay it on the plate. "I'll wait for you to finish your salad."

She shoved mixed greens in her mouth and chewed, wondering if lettuce always crunched this loudly. The crouton sounded like a jackhammer on concrete in the silence. She waved her fork at his plate. "Go ahead and eat."

"No. I'll have my entrée with you. Try to pretend your ex-jerk didn't interrupt."

She chewed another bite, staring out the window and feeling even more on display than normal.

Sterling twiddled his thumbs. "He, uh, seems to know a lot about you. Your mom and dad even."

"Well, we were engaged. He wasn't exactly a stranger."

"How long?"

"What?"

"How long were you engaged?"

"Two years."

"Two years? Was he not serious? Or were you dragging your feet? Which would be understandable."

"I don't know. I guess we wanted to establish our careers first. But then some issues came to light. We wanted to work through them."

"What career? What does he do? And what sort of issues?"

"Can we please not talk about him? It's ruining my appetite."

Sterling's face brightened. "Sure. I thought you were kinda glad to see him. I mean, you did agree to meet him for lunch tomorrow. But yeah, screw him."

"I won't deny how much I enjoyed hearing him acknowledge my success. That's quite gratifying. He broke my heart."

His face clouded. "I'm sorry."

She finished the last bite of salad and pushed the plate away, replacing it with the salmon and risotto. "This looks amazing."

Sterling finally tried his steak, nodding his approval as he chewed. "Excellent. How's the salmon?"

She pressed the tines of her fork against the fish, which was so tender it flaked away with no effort. Grilled to perfection and only lightly seasoned, she savored the bite. "Fantastic. And the risotto is so good. Creamy and perfect. Want to try a bite?"

Sterling's mouth curled into a half smile. "Careful. Sharing dinner is a couples thing."

"I just thought you'd like to try it."

"I do. Especially since Jason keeps glancing over here watching us. Let him see us eating from each other's plates." He reached across the table and took a bite of salmon. "That is delicious! Here, try the filet mignon and the garlic potatoes." He pushed his plate toward her as he tasted the risotto from hers.

She shook her head. "I haven't eaten red meat in almost a decade."

"One bite won't kill you. It's really good. And the idea is we share each other's food."

"It's not part of my diet anymore. I'm careful about what I eat so I'll hopefully enjoy better health and a longer life."

"Whatever you do clearly works. You look fantastic."

She felt her face flush at his compliment. "Thank you."

"But living well sometimes means splurging a bit," he went on. "You don't want to look back some day and regret letting opportunity pass you by."

She laughed. "I can't imagine lamenting a bite of steak as a lost opportunity."

"Nothing is promised in life. I could get hit by a bus tomorrow and then who would harass you to try this incredible steak that you will never again have the chance to taste? This particular steak will cease to exist in the very near future."

He cocked an eyebrow at her and nudged his plate closer. "If you don't like steak, that's another story altogether. But if you're denying yourself like you denied yourself a coffee maker and you deny yourself general frivolity and pleasure, then come on. Let go a little bit."

The steak did in fact look amazing. And he was right that one bite wouldn't negatively impact her health. She stretched her fork across the table and stabbed the bite he'd cut for her, surprised by how good it tasted. "Wonderful. Absolutely delicious."

"Awesome. Glad you tried it."

"This restaurant was an excellent choice. And my dad would adore you for convincing me to eat a bite of steak. That was his favorite food and my decision to restrict it from my diet infuriated him. He took it personally, as if I stopped eating red meat simply to spite him. One more disappointment to add to the list."

"Hard to imagine a parent being disappointed with a child who achieved such success."

"He disapproved of the way I achieved success. Had I been a doctor or a lawyer, he would've been proud. But a paranormal investigator? He considered it nonsense. Never believed in my abilities and never supported my endeavors."

Sterling had stopped eating and shifted a bit in his seat. She saw a glimmer of understanding in his eyes. "My parents didn't exactly appreciate my magic tricks. I have a degree in physics they'd brag about, but not once did they tell anyone I was the most successful illusionist in the nation. I wish they'd seen *Spook-Busters* though. I like to think they finally would've been impressed."

"I'm sorry they didn't." She hadn't known his parents were gone but didn't feel comfortable asking what had happened. "A successful television show never impressed my dad. He called it nonsense. I receive thousands of pleas for help every day. People I've helped send me letters of thanks. I've had homeowners collapse on my shoulder in tears, sobbing gratitude for believing them and clearing disturbances so they can live in peace. I'm proud of what I do. I offer assistance to people shunned and turned away. And he was embarrassed of me."

"I'm sorry. I know it hurts."

The compassion in his eyes dissipated the frustration the dredged up memories had stirred back to life. Her heart softened. He seemed to realize something shifted and smiled, his dark eyes intense. She dropped her gaze.

"Sorry," Sterling said, his tone teasing once again. "Did we almost have a moment there?"

She managed a laugh, unwilling to admit how glad she was for his company. "I think we did. We better finish dinner. I'll need time for touchups and relaxation before we start the investigation tonight."

"You look incredible. You don't need a bit of touching up. But whatever you need to feel better about tonight."

That look again. She attempted to rein in her emotions as her heart fluttered and her stomach quivered. If she wasn't careful with him, he could sneak past her carefully constructed barricades. And the last thing she needed was another Jason.

CHAPTER TWENTY-THREE

KIMBERLY STOOD in the third floor hallway, Stan's camera trained on her. "We've left the stationary cameras throughout the building and grounds. I'm starting tonight's investigation here on the third floor, the psych ward used by Norman Baker to hide his patients in the advanced stages of cancer, crying out in pain and misery. Any place wrought with so much agony and death carries the residual energy left behind by the tortured souls. Could one of these patients now be back for revenge?"

She turned and crossed over the threshold that used to be a heavy steel door and into the hallway. Hand clasping her quartz, she breathed deeply.

Blips. Everywhere. From the hallway, the rooms . . . this space teemed with spiritual residue. All of it foul.

She closed her hand around the quartz on her necklace and opened her senses to presences. "Will someone talk to me tonight?"

Silence.

"Are you angry? Have you been hurting the guests here?"

She felt the presences the way you might see something out of the corner of your eye. When she attempted to focus, they eluded her.

A knocking drew her attention. She followed the sound. Rhythmic and even, a steady rapping seemed to originate on the other side of the wall at the end of the hall—directly beside the full-length oval mirror the ghost had appeared in the previous night.

The honeymoon suites in this wing were all occupied. She could not gain access to them. "Can anyone else hear that sound?"

"What kind of sound?" Michael asked.

"A thumping or knocking sound." She raised her fist and mimed striking the wall in time to the pounding.

They spoke in whispers, aware of the sleeping guests.

Approaching the wall, she reached out, opening herself to the spirit attempting to communicate. She only cracked the proverbial door open, however, with so many entities swirling around the space. Too many spirits would drain her completely.

She pressed her forehead against the wall, the sound directly on the other side. In her mind, she could see the image of a man opposite her, pale and translucent, banging his head against the wall, over and over.

Hey, now, stop. Don't do that.

The pounding paused for a moment but resumed.

Bang. Bang. Bang.

Again and again he bashed his head against the wall, until her ears rang with the sound and her head throbbed.

"Stop!" She pressed both hands against the wall and sent as much positive energy toward him as she could.

The sound stopped. She had his attention. Opening herself more to the spiritual link, she encouraged him to connect with her. Like drawing back a curtain between this world and the spirit realm, she revealed herself more fully, coaxing him closer. She couldn't bear the tortured head pounding.

He stepped through the wall, joining her in the hall.

"Directly in front of me," she whispered, her breathing rapid. "Keep the cameras in this area."

"What is it, Kimmy? Er, Kimberly."

"Just make sure they keep recording."

TJ moved closer. "I don't see anything on the FLIR."

In her peripheral vision, she noticed Stan shift as well and hoped one of the cameras caught something.

"EMF climbing," Elise said. "Currently seventy and rising, but slowly."

"Kimmy?" Michael tried again. "I mean Kimberly. Ugh. What are we dealing with?"

"Full body, corporeal manifestation. Appears to be male. The thumping sound I detected was him beating his head against the wall. He is directly in front of me but not attempting to interact. No cold spot as yet."

"Ambient room temperature stable," Michael said.

"So is this Mr. Revenge?" Stan asked.

"Unclear," she said. She moved a step to the right. The spirit's head swiveled to follow.

She stepped to her left. The spirit turned its head in reaction. "He's not attempting to communicate, but he is responsive."

"EMF has leveled off, fluctuating between seventy, seventy-five," Elise said.

Kimberly stepped to her right again, fascinated with the spirit's interaction. Clearly, this was a cognizant entity. Drifting to follow her movements a single instance could be explained as coincidence. But this one seemed to be playing a game with her. She couldn't help smiling as the ghost continued to follow along. She encouraged the connection, hoping to learn something valuable from the entity.

Kimberly stepped to the side again. The ghost's arm shot forward, curling around her waist like an icy belt. She gasped. The previously blank face came within an inch of hers, emanating malice. Was it aimed at her? Or someone else? Pretty sure she could escape the grip if she wanted to, she allowed the encounter to continue.

What is it? What do you want to tell me?

The spirit drifted sideways, his cold arm coaxing her.

"Talk to me, Kimmy," Michael said. "What's happening?"

"He's trying to tell me or show me something." Her voice quivered and her teeth chattered. "His arm is around my waist. Cold."

"KII confirms temp plummeting around you," Michael confirmed. "Thermal imagining still good, TJ?"

"Batteries at eighty percent. Fully charged replacements in my pocket. And another set in my bag."

"Atta boy," Stan said.

"EMF nudging higher at one hundred. One hundred and five," Elise said.

The entity stopped her in front of the mirror. She saw herself and the crew reflected back. But nothing else.

What do you want me to see?

She knew Sterling had moved beside her even before she saw him in her peripheral vision because the ghost's translucent head whipped around to face him.

"Why are her teeth chattering? I'm standing right here and feel no temperature fluxuation—"

The ghost pressed a hand to Sterling's chest.

Sterling drew in a breath as though caught in a gale-force wind.

"Go back," she told him. "He doesn't like you this close."

"What the hell?" Sterling asked. "How are you doing that? Am I under a vent?" His head angled back, searching for a source he couldn't see.

"I'm not doing it. And this hotel doesn't have central heat and air. It's the entity. Please step back."

For once, Sterling listened to her.

She returned her attention to the ghost. He seemed unable to communicate further. Offering more energy might enable further interaction. Or it might only result in draining her. This was the first breakthrough they'd had on this case. She wasn't going to stop now.

She pushed more energy to the spirit. *What do you want me to know?*

Feeding off her energy, the ghostly image pulled into sharper focus. He gestured to the mirror.

The young woman from TJ's footage stared from the glossy surface, face contorted in agony.

Pulling her closer to the mirror, the ghost tightened his grip around her waist.

The young woman's arms extended from the mirror. Her pain-stricken face lowered, stretching to escape the glass, the wild gaze locked onto her.

Kimberly tried to pull away, struggling to step backwards. But the entity kept his arm firmly around her waist and thrust her forward toward the woman in the mirror.

The woman's hands closed around her upper arms.

The sudden energy drain left her woozy. She stumbled but the arm around her waist and the hands clutching her upper arms held her in place.

The woman in the mirror reached out with her psyche and connected. In her weakened state, Kimberly was powerless to stop it.

She felt herself drawn into a spiritual coexistence, pulled along with the woman in the mirror who took her to relive a powerful moment in her life. She lay in a bed experiencing the moment in time as the woman in the mirror once had. Pain pulsed through every muscle in her body. A nurse approached, smiling, syringe poised in her hand. She thrashed her head and cried, "No," stunned by the feeble croak she produced.

The nurse lifted her gown though she struggled to hold it over her torso. Glancing down, she saw a rounded bulge over her lower belly. She knew no baby grew within her, but rather a cancerous tumor ate away at her body.

She grasped the nurse's arm, protesting the approaching needle. "No. No more," she whispered. "Let me go home."

"You must take your medicine so you can get well," the nurse scolded, easily breaking her feeble grasp. "Then you can go home."

"No one goes home," she gasped. "Especially not from the third floor."

The nurse only smiled and sat on her arm to hold it in place on the bed. "Cooperate. We want you to get well."

The needle plunged into her belly. Burning liquid gurgled into her. She felt every drop. Tears welled. "Oh, God! It hurts! It burns! Stop. Please." She thrashed but her puny limbs were no match for the healthy nurse.

She looked closer at the smiling face. Something struck her as familiar.

Ms. Theodora. Nurse Theodora.

With a gasp, she severed the connection and found herself back in the hall. The young woman's reflection peered at her from the mirror. The grimacing mouth moved. *Help me.*

"Help," the male ghost said.

Arms stretched toward her from the mirror, the walls, the air around her.

"Help," voices repeated over and over as fingers plucked at her, pulling at her clothing, her hair, her necklace.

Help.

Help.

Help.

They sucked away her energy, every happy thought, every ounce of strength, and every flicker of warmth, leaving an empty, dismal void and no will to live.

Unable to take any more, she felt her knees buckle and saw the floor rush to meet her.

CHAPTER TWENTY-FOUR

KIMBERLY REGAINED CONSCIOUSNESS, lying on her back, staring up at the ceiling and somewhat confused. Her head pounded. A moment later she remembered where she was. Sterling crouched over her. A crowd of people clustered about. Kerry and Suzie were among the onlookers. They both held cell phones, snapping pictures or perhaps recording.

Sterling glared up at them. "Can all of you please step back and give her some air? I mean it. Get back." He held up an arm as if to hold them off.

"We want to see a ghost," Kerry said. "This is so exciting!"

"We all want to see ghosts. I didn't see one. I saw Kimberly pass out and fall over. Can you please show a little concern and give us some space?"

No one moved.

"She obviously experienced a psychic connection that drained her," Kerry said, continuing to snap pictures. "The ghost could still be here."

"Well, do you want the same thing to happen to you?"

"Oh, my God! That would be awesome!" Suzie said.

Sterling glanced down and saw her eyes open. He waved an

arm at the crowd. "Get back. Go away, you vultures. Michael? A little help here?"

Kerry continued to hold out a phone while backing away at Michael's insistence. "Look at him protect her. I told you they're together. Or he at least has the hots for her."

Kimberly no longer saw Suzie but heard her agree. "Isn't it the sweetest thing? I'm posting this on Twitter. Kimberling is totally a thing."

Rosie pressed through the crowd, her hand gripping what looked like a smoking bundle of grass. "There. I burned some sage to temporarily clear the area of spirits. Chakra stones in place. Wanted to make sure you were okay before I left to make tea. You recharging? Feeling better?"

She breathed deeply and took stock. "Weak limbs. Massive headache. But I don't think anything is broken or short-circuited."

"I'll go make tea while you recharge. Don't get up. Sterling, massage this lemon oil into her hands." Rosie bent down and checked the placement of the chakra stones before she turned and raced for the stairs.

Michael leaned over her. "You sure you're okay? You appeared to be . . . convulsing. Maybe we should follow Sterling's advice and take you to a doctor this time."

"Not tonight. Not now. I need to finish here." She tried to sit up.

Michael and Sterling both pushed her back down.

"Rosie said don't get up." Sterling lifted her hand and massaged gently.

"But you don't understand. I was wrong about—" Sterling's thumb rubbing circles in her palm distracted her thoughts. Lemon always calmed and rejuvenated her. But Sterling's warm, caressing hands roused her more than the essential oil. His delicate attention to each finger, the warm strokes over the back of her hand, had her wide awake. Rosie had massaged her hands plenty of times and it never felt like this.

"I'm fine. Thank you." She pulled her hand away, trying to remember what she'd been saying.

Sterling helped himself to the other hand. "Rosie said hands. Plural. Both of them."

She met his gaze, expecting to find mirth and self-satisfaction, but saw only concern as his fingers tenderly kneaded her hand.

"Is that okay?" he asked. "Too much pressure?"

She reveled in the soothing circles his thumb traced on her palm. No one had ever massaged her hands but Rosie. Her face flushed. "No, that's . . . fine. It's nice."

TJ cleared his throat, "You wanted me, Ms. Wantland?"

She couldn't help but notice the scowl TJ sent toward the sight of Sterling rubbing her hand.

She tried to sit up, but Michael and Sterling again insisted she remain prone.

"I know this isn't a blood sugar issue this time," Sterling said. "I took her to dinner. She ate. Something else is causing these fainting spells."

"I didn't faint. Never mind. You're not going to be convinced. TJ, I'm sorry. I was wrong earlier when I told you not to worry about the woman in the mirror. She isn't a recording. She's stuck here, reliving her last painful days over and over."

TJ's face paled. "I thought so. Something about the image . . . I had a feeling, you know?"

"Your feeling was absolutely correct. Michael, we need to talk to Selma. She needs to know how many spirits are trapped in the psych ward."

"I don't know, Kimmy. Selma was quite clear about leaving all the ghosts alone but the one terrorizing the guests."

"But she doesn't know. She can't possibly. No one would intentionally leave these poor souls to suffer endlessly. They deserve to be freed. I can help them cross over and end the torment."

Michael looked skeptical. "I think she considers all the ghosts part of the hotel. I rather doubt she will okay this."

"If we tell her, she will be appalled. She only knows about the ghosts who appear happy to stay on site. Not these miserable people."

Sterling shook his head, smirk in place. "People? Come on. The cameras aren't on you right now. You can let it go."

"You know what I mean. They're what's left of people. You felt one tonight. You can't deny it. We have to help them."

"I felt a cold breeze. That I can't deny. I do not, however, extrapolate—"

Michael held up a hand and shook his head. "I'll talk to her, Kimmy. You relax."

Rosie returned with a steaming mug of tea, gathered the chakra stones, and peered into her eyes. "You look better. Feeling better? Here. Drink your tea."

She gladly removed her hand from Sterling's and sat up to accept the warm cup. His touch sent electric quivers through her she didn't want to deal with right now. "Let's move on. I suggest the laundry room next."

"Oh, no, sweetie. You're done for the night," Michael said.

"No, I'm just getting started."

"The sight of you convulsing was more than I can take. I'm not going to send you into harm's way depleted and psychically exhausted."

"Michael, I haven't made a bit of progress on the main focus of the investigation. I found spirits needing to be freed, but we have no clue what's causing the recent problems here."

"And one more day isn't going to bring about the end of the world. This isn't the usual domestic investigation where a family's life is being disrupted."

"I suspect Selma would disagree with you. The quicker her problem is solved, the happier she will be."

Rosie placed a hand on her head. "I agree with Michael. Whatever happened really took it out of you. You're still ice cold. Let's call it a night. Get plenty of rest tonight and start up again tomorrow."

"This is a waste of time and I strongly object," she said.

"But I'm the boss." Michael shrugged. "Okay, crew. We're calling it a night. Can I get a tech check, please? Make sure the stationary cameras and recording devices are functioning."

"Michael, please—"

"Kimmy, I said no. You're no good to us if you can't function. No sense blowing out your senses before we even get started here. You've been knocked out and knocked down more times in one day of this investigation than you normally are in a week. I'm putting the brakes on."

"I think that's smart," Sterling said. "And I still strongly urge a trip to a clinic."

"Forget it. I know when I need a doctor. And I don't." She pushed herself to her feet, woozier than she would let any of them know. She held herself completely still, didn't wobble once. "See? I'm fine. I also know when I can keep going with an investigation. Which I could. But since you're calling it, I'll go to my room. And attempt to engage Ms. Theodora if nothing else. She was there in the vision."

Rosie touched her arm. "You're sure you're okay? You don't need me?"

"I'm perfect."

"Do you mind if I go on another ghost tour? It's early enough I could catch the last one."

"I don't mind if you go see Lorenzo, Rosie. Have fun."

"Seriously, though, girl. Take it easy and rest. Don't try to engage anything."

She watched her stylist dash for the stairs leading to the lounge and her beau. She'd never seen Rosie quite like this. And she hadn't even heard any crazy schemes or requests for outrageous sums of cash from Lorenzo. The guy seemed to be treating her pretty well. Unusual for Rosie. But a nice change.

"I'll walk you to your room," Sterling said. "Make sure you're okay."

"I'm fine," she insisted.

"I was going to walk you back, Kimmy. I don't want you alone right now. But I'll let Sterling take you tonight."

Sterling stifled a laugh. "Slow down, there, Michael. We've only been on one date."

"To your room!" Michael said. "Take you to your room."

CHAPTER TWENTY-FIVE

STERLING WALKED her to the door of her room, but she closed it after a terse, "Thank you. Goodnight." Her hands were beginning to shake and he was observant enough he would notice. After stalking away self-righteously, she couldn't stand for anyone to realize Michael might have been right to call it after all.

She sank onto the bed, her wobbly legs threatening to stop supporting her weight, and focused on not passing out. A deep emptiness yawned in her stomach, a chasm of exhaustion threatening to engulf all of her like a black hole.

The psych ward spirits had completely drained her. Not just psychically but physically, too. Yet no one had scratched her. And she had only sensed pleas for help, desperation for relief, desire to be freed. They were trapped and miserable and wanted her to send them on. She hadn't sensed revenge. Perhaps she'd been too overwhelmed to detect a lone vengeful spirit.

A noise in the bathroom drew her attention. Not a typical creak or settling sound. Something moved. She tried out her legs, found they would support her weight, and cautiously crossed the room.

She peered into the bathroom. "Ms. Theodora?"

Another sound.

Pushing the door further open, she ventured one step inside. Nothing on the floor. The bathtub appeared as she'd left it. Toilet lid down. She moved further into the space.

Her toothbrush and travel lotion lay in the sink.

She'd left the toothbrush on the edge of the counter. Perhaps it had simply fallen in somehow. But the small bottle of body lotion had been on the shelf above the sink, well back from the edge. How to explain that one? She saw no way it simply fell in. In her current state, a mob of ghosts could hold a rave in her room and she wouldn't be able to sense them.

Hands shaking, she retrieved the items and put them away again. Who was knocking her things into the sink? Knowing it was probably fruitless, she closed her eyes and grasped her quartz.

Hello? Who is with me?

The door slammed shut.

Something or someone was here with her. And her psychic energy was too depleted to connect. Or defend herself.

Heart pounding, she wrenched the door open.

Her pajamas lay on the bed.

She knew with utter certainty she'd dropped her pajamas in a heap on the floor that morning. As she'd promised Sterling she would, she left her room cluttered and messy. She'd just sat on the bed, for Pete's sake. She would've noticed.

Come to think of it, who'd made the bed? She hadn't. Housekeeping wasn't cleaning.

"Ms. Theodora?" she whispered. But of course she couldn't sense a response if the spirit offered one.

Someone was playing with her. What if it wasn't Ms. Theodora?

She needed to alert someone from her crew. *Michael. Call Michael.* She snatched her phone from the dresser. Once it was in her hands, she was torn between documenting the activity and summoning backup. The paranormal investigator in her won the struggle. She tapped the camera app, selected "video," and began recording.

Another sound from the bathroom. She turned the camera on the door.

"I hope you can hear that on the recording. The bathtub faucet just turned on."

Phone in front of her, she crept to the bathroom and raised a hand to push the door open.

Her phone screen went black, the battery as drained as she was.

"Are you kidding me right now?" Considering how many years she'd been doing this, how did drained batteries continue to irritate her so badly? Probably because spiritual entities always seemed to drain them at the worst possible moment. Now she could neither record evidence nor call for help.

She rushed to plug in the phone, knowing it would take time to recharge. Worst case scenario, she'd simply leave the room.

Water continued to splash into the tub. She returned to the bathroom door, listening intently. Poltergeist? The moving objects weren't flying around violently as she typically saw with a poltergeist. Something seemed to be toying with her.

She pushed the door open a crack, enough to view the bathtub faucet. Considering how much steam filled the bathroom, she assumed the hot water ran—full blast.

The urge to take a hot bath consumed her. She closed the bathroom door, white cotton robe swinging on a hook. She moved to the tub and pressed the stopper in place to fill it rather than waste the water.

She sat heavily on the toilet, exhaustion drooping her eyelids. The bathrobe fell from its hook onto the floor.

She jumped to her feet. Still nothing in the space she could see. Or sense. No wonder she was so jumpy. The temporary loss of her extra senses left her vulnerable.

Steam condensed on the mirror, coating it heavily. Except for four letters traced on the glass.

BATH

She turned in the space. Toothbrush, lavender lotion, pajamas, robe, hot water running. And the written command. Someone seemed to be encouraging her to take a bath and go to bed.

"Ms. Theodora?"

She remembered the young nurse from the vision, while she coexisted spiritually with the female patient. Perhaps Theodora still attempted to practice her craft in the afterlife. Granted her methods were no longer the same if that were the case. A hot bath sounded much better than burning shots.

A soft sound sent her spinning. The scrunchy she used to pull back her hair had fallen into the sink.

The steam soothed. The hot water enticed. She was overwhelmed by the desire to submerge her body in hot water.

She twirled her hair into a bundle on top of her head and dropped her clothes on the floor. Dipping a toe into the water, she found it the perfect temperature and lowered herself into the luxurious cocoon of hot water that soothed her sore muscles and aching head. Breathing in the steam, she could have sworn she detected eucalyptus. But that made no sense. She washed the makeup off her face and leaned back.

Weariness pulled at her. Her eyelids drooped.

And then a voice whispered in her ear, "Get well so you can go home."

CHAPTER TWENTY-SIX

KIMBERLY JERKED AWAKE, splashing water out of the tub.

Why am I in a bath?

She sat up and blinked several times before she remembered. Had she imagined the voice telling her to get well?

Her lavender lotion sat on the edge of the tub. *Did I move that from the shelf?*

Disoriented, she noted the water was still warm and concluded she must not have been out very long. Odd she actually nodded off. She yawned and stretched, strangely rested after a catnap.

A knock on her door startled her. *Who in the world...?*

She assumed they would go away if ignored but vacated the bath and toweled dry anyway. Time for bed so she could be ready for some serious work tomorrow. She squirted some lotion into her hands and rubbed it into her arms and legs. Her skin drank up the moisturizer. The scent soothed her.

The knocking returned, more insistent. Then bordered on pounding.

She snatched up her robe. No amount of lavender lotion could counteract the annoyance of someone disturbing her precious few hours of downtime.

She thrust her arms into the sleeves, yanked the tie closed around her waist, and peered through the peephole.

Sterling.

Seriously? Shaking her head, she cracked the door.

He leaned against it with all his weight and burst into the room, slamming the door behind him.

"What are you—"

"There's something in my room," he gasped. She noticed he panted as though he'd run the entire way. "Or there was. I saw something. I think." He pressed his hands to his eyes.

"So you ran to my room shirtless?" She lifted an eyebrow. And couldn't avert her eyes from his broad chest. Biceps that flexed as he fisted and stretched his hands. And those abs above his loosely tied plaid pajama bottoms. Bare feet she imagined curled around her own. She shivered a little and drew her robe tighter.

"I felt . . . I saw a . . . I saw something in my room. I didn't stop to grab a shirt."

She narrowed her eyes. "I need sleep. If this is a joke—"

"No, I swear. This isn't a joke. I'm here asking for your help. I saw . . . "

She waited until it was obvious he wasn't going to complete the sentence. "You saw what? A ghost?"

"Yes. No. Maybe. I don't know. But I saw something. Can you come check my room?"

"Sterling Wakefield is asking me to check under his bed for monsters? Sure. No way am I falling for this. I don't know who you've recruited to record your prank, but it's not going to work."

"And who do you think would help me prank you? Stan? He's asleep for sure. TJ? That kid hates me."

"Valid point." She crossed her arms and reconsidered. He did seem shaken about something. No one could fake the beads of sweat on his forehead. Or the genuine fear in his eyes. She waved him toward a chair but he sat on her bed.

"I thought you were going to sleep and be rested."

She followed his gaze and noticed her bed was made and would pass military muster. "I haven't been to bed yet."

"Why are you in a robe? Did I interrupt something?"

"No. I took a quick bath to—"

"At three in the morning?"

"Of course not. Just now. Right after you left me here." Her stomach dropped and her feet went cold. "Are you suggesting it's three a.m.?"

Without waiting for a reply, she retrieved her phone from the dresser. Completely recharged, the screen read 3:20 a.m.

"What time did you think it was?" he asked.

She stared at him, mouth gaping, then at the bathroom, then her phone. "This is not possible. The bath is still warm."

She crossed to the bathroom and plunged her hand into the water.

Ice cold.

And her towel hung neatly from the rack, and all her toiletries sat aligned on the little shelf, shortest to tallest.

She stepped back into the room and closed the door behind her. "I'll deal with that later. We definitely have activity here."

"What's in there?"

"Don't worry about it. Let's focus on your experience. Tell me what happened."

He blew out a breath and ran a hand through his hair. "I woke up after feeling someone pushing on my back. I know it sounds crazy, but I swear someone was pushing on my back."

"That doesn't sound crazy at all. Remember Selma warned you Jack would probably mess with you. And he's known for tormenting men and flirting with women."

He shook his head. "I don't know what it was. Maybe I dreamed it. But I do know that after I woke up, I looked around to see what poked me and I saw a woman in a white gown walking across the room. I was awake. Fully awake. I didn't dream this. I even thought for a second that you were in my room."

"Why would you think that?"

"Wishful thinking, I guess. I said your name but the woman didn't answer. I stood up and that's about when I realized there was no way it was you. Her hair was all wrong and done up in little ribbons all over her head. So I said, 'Excuse me, can I help you?' She turned and looked at me and gasped. She looked surprised and dashed into the bathroom. At that point I was really disturbed that some strange woman was in my room so I went to see who the heck had gone into my bathroom." He turned his intense gaze on her. "It was empty."

"Do you think you saw a ghost?"

"I don't know. No. I don't know what happened."

"But you're okay? Nothing attacked you?"

"Yeah, I'm fine, except I think I might have just had a psychotic moment. Am I going crazy?"

"Not at all. You witnessed a spirit moving past you."

"But that's crazy."

"That's what people said when Columbus first postulated the world is round and not flat. I understand you're scared of things you don't understand. But your flat little world is starting to curve on the edges. Open your mind to new ideas."

"I'm always open to new *quantifiable* ideas. Ghosts and spirits are not quantifiable."

"Sounds like you've already sorted it out for yourself. Can I go to bed now?"

His face fell and he stood. "I'm sorry. I shouldn't have disturbed you. I feel like a fool. I can't believe I thought I saw a ghost."

What did he want? He seemed alarmed and yet he dismissed her queries and suggestions of paranormal activity as he always did. Still he lingered. He must be hoping for something. "You sure you don't want me to check your room? You looked pretty shaken."

"I'm fine now. I don't know what I was thinking. It's just . . . you told me before to keep a diary of weird things that happened at three in the morning. And you said you'd help me figure out what was causing these weird dreams that feel so real."

Indeed she had. Promised him he could reach out at any time of night and she would be there for him. And here he was asking for help and she tried to send him away. "You're right. I did. Nothing happened all summer? This was your first experience since?"

He nodded, eyes wide.

"Let's go to your room. I'll get an EMF reading. High levels could affect your nervous system. Staggeringly high levels can result in hallucinations."

"There. Now you're talking my language. Quantifiable readings. Thank you."

"Let me get dressed."

"The halls are empty. No one is out here. If something is in my room, I don't want to miss it."

"I think I've already missed it. Personally, I think you probably saw a residual image. Nothing to worry about."

"No offense, but that's what you told TJ about his woman in the mirror and then she nearly strangled you this evening. And that's the problem with unquantifiable data. No one else can confirm it and it's completely dependent on your interpretation."

"That's not what happened. Look, nothing is going to strangle you. Listen to you, talking like ghosts are real." She couldn't help but smile. Was he finally opening his mind to the existence of spirits?

He flushed and stared at the ground.

Piano music played from somewhere in the hotel.

She opened the door and cocked an ear, listening. "I thought you said no one was awake right now."

"Right. The place is dead. Let's go."

"Then who's playing the piano?"

He tilted his head and furrowed his brow. He joined her at

the door, his body directly behind her as he listened. He looked down at her. "What are you talking about?"

Those eyes of his peered at her intently, the smooth skin of his bare chest so close she could feel the heat radiating from him. She'd never been so physically affected by near proximity to any other man. "The piano. Someone is playing it."

He smirked as if she teased him. "Come on. Don't mess with me. I'm already freaked out by what happened in my room. Are you trying to take advantage of me?"

Though her pulse pounded and she couldn't ignore that bare chest of his, she needed to determine if the piano music in the wee morning hours was due to an inconsiderate jerk or something more sinister. "Of course not. You can't hear that? Be honest."

"There's no music." He stepped closer.

"Maybe your hearing isn't very good." She turned away from his pecs and crept into the hall. The music grew louder. She cocked an eyebrow at him before continuing.

He followed her all the way to the stop of the stairs and even leaned over the bannister. He shook his head.

"You can't expect me to believe you don't hear that," she whispered.

"Hear what? I'm a little concerned about you hearing things."

The notes were loud enough that she recognized the melody. "It's *Für Elise*. You have to hear that unless you're completely deaf." Whoever played the tune missed a note and went back several measures for a second try.

Sterling's brow furrowed. He grasped her arms and looked her directly in the eye. "You're not joking? You hear music right now?"

She broke away from his grip and scowled. "Yes. And I'm going to see who's playing it."

She scurried quietly down the stairs, Sterling close on her heels.

"There's no music," he insisted. "It's completely quiet."

"You'll see." She turned the corner around the second landing. And ran into Kerry and Suzie. She stopped so abruptly Sterling bumped into the back of her, encircling her waist with an arm to catch his balance.

"Sorry," he murmured in her ear.

The two women gasped. Kerry, quickest with her cell, snapped a picture of them intertwined.

Suzie giggled. "We wanted to try to catch some ghosts. But we caught something better."

Sterling withdrew his arm and stepped away. She adjusted her robe.

"We're pursuing a lead in the investigation," she told the women. "Nothing more."

"Seriously, this isn't what it looks like," Sterling said.

"Right," Kerry said. "You two are barely dressed and appear to be returning from a tryst somewhere."

"Yeah, that's what it looks like. But that's not what it is."

"Kimberling is a thing," Suzie said, fists around her beaming face in gleeful excitement.

"No, it isn't," Kimberly said. "If you'll excuse me." *That stupid name.* She tried to press past her admirers.

"We're actually pursuing a lead," Sterling whispered, eyebrows high as if he was sharing forbidden information. He gestured to Kimberly to continue downstairs. "She needs quiet so she can concentrate. Why don't you two go ahead and see if you can catch the ghosts you were hunting? You might find something we missed earlier up on the third floor."

The women's eyes widened. "Are we helping Kimberly Wantland with an investigation?" Kerry asked.

"Oh. My. Gosh." Suzie squealed.

Sterling hushed them. "Quiet is important. You don't want to disturb the other guests. Or the ghosts."

Kerry and Suzie nodded. "Got it. We'll be quiet."

"Report in tomorrow," Sterling said.

Kimberly watched the women scamper upstairs, eyes wide

and cells held out like shields. She grinned at her partner. "That was a stroke of brilliance. I think they even forgot about Kimberling."

Sterling struck a pose and intoned his best Elvis. "Uh, thank you! Thank you very much!"

She giggled. "That was a terrible impression. Don't quit your day job."

"I don't intend to." His husky voice told her exactly why he didn't intend to leave and she knew it had nothing to do with ghosts. His face shifted, a thoughtful expression in his eyes. "So why exactly did you want to buy your parents' old house? Why did Jason say he hoped you'd get closure?"

"You don't want to know about all that." She rested a hand on the railing and headed for the lobby.

"I do. Wouldn't have asked otherwise."

"It's really nothing. Not important."

"It must be for you to go to all that effort and expense. And it's important to me regardless," he insisted, halting her progress with a hand to her arm. "Besides, Jason knows. Seems like if your ex-beau knows this intimate information, your partner ought to know."

Ah. Was that jealousy she heard, though he did his best to sound casual? "Jason knows intimate information about me because we were intimate."

"Gross. Don't remind me." Sterling shuddered. "The idea of you with that potato head man makes me physically sick to my stomach."

"What does that even mean?"

"He looks like Mr. Potato Head. With his little clip-on smile and Mr. Businessman suit snapped into place."

She shook her head. "Wow. Thanks. I will probably never get that image out of my head. If you must know, something happened in that house I've never been able to explain. And I think my mom might be trapped there."

"Trapped?" His brow furrowed.

She really didn't have the strength for this conversation. And she knew if she recounted the details of her memories, her concerns, and her hypothesis that he would only scoff and dismiss her beliefs. She took the last few steps to the landing and pivoted for the remainder of the final flight of stairs. "It's a long story. Not sure I'm up to it right now. Let's just say something strange happened."

"What?"

Something reached out, triggering her alarms, as they reached the first floor. "I know why you can't hear the piano," she told Sterling, stopping short.

"Because no one is playing it?" he asked.

She put an arm out to stop him. "No. Because someone is here with us."

"Umm, I can see the piano well enough from here to know there is no one sitting at it. And it's not a player piano. Back to the house. What happened to your mom?"

She ignored the question, anxious to connect with the presence. "I can't see who's playing it either. But I can feel them." She closed her eyes and fisted her hand around the quartz hanging from her necklace.

"Ooooh. I get it. A ghost is playing the piano. You know you're not being recorded right now, right?"

"Shhh." She reached out, trying to determine if the entity in the room posed a threat or simply played a song as it had done in life. She felt a jerk, as if a fish had snapped onto a lure and tugged the line. It drew her closer, beckoning. "I think it wants to tell me something."

Sterling stayed close as she crept forward. The music built in intensity, a frenzied rendition of the classical piece.

Let me help you. Who are you?

The music played louder. She eased to the side of the piano, hands out. Heat radiated from the antique instrument. So much history here, so much emotion soaked up in this old wood.

"The keys aren't moving," Sterling noted. "Not saying you're crazy, but there is no way this piano is playing music if the keys aren't moving."

"You're not listening to the right wavelength," she told him.

She sat on the bench and rested her hands on the keys, opening herself to anything she could absorb.

"I'm listening with my real ears to the real world."

The music stopped.

A woman screamed.

CHAPTER TWENTY-SEVEN

Sterling jumped. "Now that I heard!" He ran for the stairs.

She bounded after him, quick steps behind his taking the stairs two at a time.

"Someone help!" a woman cried from a floor above them.

They swung up the second floor landing and continued on.

"Kimberly! Sterling!"

She glanced up to see Kerry's head hanging over the bannister of the third floor. The woman waved at them to hurry. Doors opened and concerned guests drifted into the halls, rubbing sleep from their worried eyes.

She grasped the stair railing and launched herself onto the third floor.

"Over here!" Kerry cried and tore down the hall.

The woman led them to the psych ward. Suzie leaned against a wall clutching her arm.

Goosebumps rose on Kimberly's arms and, though she didn't feel cold, a shiver ran through her.

Sterling reached Suzie a few steps ahead of her. He dropped to his knees. "What's wrong? Are you hurt?"

Kimberly caught up and knelt on the woman's other side, panting to catch her breath. "What happened?"

Suzie held out her arm, revealing three long scratches. "We saw him! He got me."

Sterling rocked back on his heels. "You screamed for help because you scratched your arm? That's it?"

"No!" Kerry said. "We called for help when the ghost appeared. But then it scratched her. I didn't know if she should move or not."

"She's not suffering from a paralyzing neck injury," Sterling said. "Why wouldn't she move?"

"Well, I didn't know what to do! I've never dealt with a ghost-inflicted injury before. I thought maybe Kimberly should examine her."

"It's a scratch," Sterling said.

"That's not a bad idea," Kimberly said. She rested a hand on Suzie's shoulder and read her spectrum. The woman's red chakra blazed in fear. And her indigo chakra resonated, indicating a possible encounter. "Slow, easy breaths," she directed.

"I'm . . . trying," Suzie panted.

"You can do it. Breathe with me." She demonstrated calming breathing, maintaining eye contact. Normally she would assure the victim that spiritual entities couldn't hurt them. But this one had proven he was fully capable of doing so. "I wish Rosie was here. I need some essential oils and chakra stones."

"I can't believe this." Sterling pressed a hand to his chest and leaned against the wall beside Suzie, breathing heavily. "You really scared me and now we're talking about rocks and oils for a scratch."

"We were scared!" Kerry said. "You didn't see what we saw."

"Did you get pictures?" he asked.

"I think so," Kerry said. "I videoed the entire time."

Kimberly lifted Suzie's arm. The scrapes ran down the center of her forearm, almost the entire length from her elbow to her wrist. Blood oozed in droplets from the wounds. Sterling pulled a handkerchief from a pocket and passed it to her. She applied pressure to staunch the seeping blood.

Kerry stared at her phone screen. "It won't turn on. My battery was almost completely—" Her eyes widened. "I think the apparition drained my phone! Suzie, check yours!"

Suzie lifted her phone from the floor beside her with the unscathed arm. "Oh my gosh! Mine is dead too! We had a paranormal encounter!"

"What level encounter is this?" Kerry asked. "First kind? Second?"

"I think you're confusing this with alien encounters. We don't really classify our experiences that way."

"You should! If nothing exists, create your own. It can be the Wantland Scale. A class one or level one something-or-other. Categorize your own types of entities. It would be like on *Ghostbusters*."

Sterling banged his head against the wall. "That was a movie. Made up."

"I know it was made up!" Kerry snapped. "But Kimberly could invent a real scale."

Wouldn't that be something? Her name in the annals of paranormal history for much longer than even reruns of her show would last. If it caught on, the Wantland Scale would reference her contributions to categorizing hauntings like the Richter Scale measured earthquakes.

"I'll think about that," she told Kerry. She lifted the handkerchief from Suzie's arm. "We've stopped the bleeding at least."

"What happened here?"

Kimberly jumped at the unexpected voice and turned to discover Selma behind her.

"The ghost got Suzie!" Kerry announced.

Selma looked to Kimberly for confirmation.

"This does appear to be paranormal in nature. I detected residual ectoplasmic energy when we first arrived on the scene. My skin tingled on contact with the effected arm. Her indigo chakra is resonating as if tweaked by an encounter with another plane of existence."

"And that's all definitive proof," Sterling said with a roll of his eyes.

"Plus I saw it scratch me," Suzie said.

Selma examined the injury. "This looks exactly like the three scrapes on Clara's arm. Same arm. Same scratches. Runs the entire length of the forearm. Enough to raise my eyebrows."

"Also exactly the same as the female guest who left as a result of being scratched."

"Doesn't one scratch pretty much look like any other?" Sterling asked.

He always had to be disagreeable. Kimberly shot him a look before continuing with Selma. "They recorded the encounter but the phones are dead. I've instructed them to come to footage review tomorrow." She turned to Kerry. "Norman Baker's apartment. Not too early, considering how little we've slept."

"Michael, Stan, and TJ are all sound asleep," Sterling pointed out, pushing himself off the floor.

"They can start whenever they like. But I want to be there when we review Kerry and Suzie's phone footage."

"Whatever." Sterling ran a hand down his face. "Can we go on to my room now?"

Kerry and Suzie's faces lit up.

"He needs me to check for presences. Nothing more," Kimberly said. "I think your room is fine now, Sterling. I don't sense anything nearby at the moment. I want to talk to Selma. See you in the morning."

He stared at her for a moment before he headed down the hall to his room. She hated how forlorn he looked as he walked away, but she couldn't stand the thought of these women reporting they'd seen her go to Sterling's room in her robe.

Kerry helped Suzie from the floor and kept a firm grip on her sister until assured she was fine.

"Not even dizzy," Suzie said.

"Thank you, Kimberly. See you tomorrow," Kerry said, one arm around Suzie's waist while guiding her to the stairs.

Reassured Suzie would be fine, Kimberly turned to Selma. "I wanted to talk to you about something that happened during our investigation tonight. You have quite a few entities who were treated at the hospital operated by Norman Baker."

Selma's face crinkled into a smile. "I've long suspected. And now you have proof?"

"Not the sort of proof Sterling would accept. Several of them reached out to me. They're trapped here and want to be released from their suffering."

"Oh. I thought all of our ghost guests were here because they want to stay. They're welcome, you know. Can we do something to make them feel better?"

"Other than freeing them, I don't think so. They experience their treatments and painful end days without relief. So much suffering." She shuddered at the memory of all those hands grasping her, the onslaught of shared pain overloading her system.

"Do you think this is connected with the current issue? Is one of them the ghost wanting revenge and lashing out?"

"I haven't determined that yet. But perhaps. Suzie was attacked here by the psych ward. Maybe they're connected."

"If one of those ghosts is the one scaring my guests then go ahead. I hope you can simply exorcise the troublesome spirit. I don't like the idea of releasing a large number of our guests. If that's the only way to rid us of the one, so be it. But I hope it doesn't come down to that."

"These ghosts aren't guests. They're prisoners, anxious to move on, desperate for release. You didn't feel their suffering the way I did."

Selma's brow knitted together. "Above all, I want to ensure you don't inadvertently send away a spirit who doesn't want to leave. I suppose if you're absolutely certain . . . Let me think about this, please. We maintain a very delicate balance at the hotel. I hesitate to disrupt it."

"Of course. It's late. Let's sleep and discuss this again tomorrow when we're rested."

She trudged up the stairs to the fourth floor, curious about Selma's reaction. Most people would want her to rid their residence or business of restless, unhappy spirits as quickly as possible, no questions asked. Why would Selma balk? These entities weren't discussed during the ghost tour or referred to by names. Releasing them wouldn't affect the hotel's lore. She needed to identify the vengeful spirit fast and convince Selma to allow her to transition the trapped spirits. She couldn't live with herself if she left the hotel knowing the torment they languished in.

She let herself back into her room, slid into her satin pajamas —indigo, of course and crawled under the sheets. Her eyelids drooped. She prayed the footage from tonight provided some evidence and strong clues.

Maybe she should've gone on to Sterling's room so he could rest worry free. Something did plague him around 3:00 a.m. on a routine basis. She needed to help him determine what it was. She genuinely felt no presences on the third floor. The proverbial "Witching Hour" as Sterling referred to it, had drawn to a close for the night. Of course, she knew the spirits had depleted all the energy sources they could and now needed time to recharge. Even if she had detected a spirit, the presence wouldn't have scared her.

What scared her was the potential between her and Sterling. What might have happened if she'd followed him into the room and allowed him to close the door behind him? He shirtless, she in only a robe. Her heart galloped at the thought. They drove each other crazy on one level—but on another level, too. She detected his attraction to her on a visceral level and couldn't deny her mutual feelings.

Weariness overtook her, exhaustion so extreme she could feel herself falling asleep.

In a half-dream, half-cognitive state, she stood on a balcony,

grappling with someone. Someone extraordinarily angry. She tipped backwards over the railing and fell—
—and jerked herself awake.
The piano played *Für Elise*.

CHAPTER TWENTY-EIGHT

KIMBERLY OPENED her eyes and bolted upright when she noticed how bright the room was. She fumbled for her phone on the nightstand. 9:00 a.m. She rubbed her eyes and sat up, astonished she'd slept so late.

After showering hastily and dressing, she hurried down the stairs, mouth watering in anticipation of coffee. She also wanted to talk with Rosie. So much had happened in the night after they'd halted the investigation.

She hurried through the lobby, nodding in response to Marcus' "Good morning, Ms. Wantland!" and then pausing for picture and autograph requests his greeting prompted.

Escaping out the front door, she crossed the parking lot, bounded up the steps to her trailer, and threw open the door.

Only to discover it empty and dark. And cold, but perhaps her disappointment caused the chilly shiver.

No lavender candles filled the space with their calming fragrance and soothing glow. No freshly brewed coffee waited to treat her pounding headache. No tea steeped in the kettle.

She was a grown up. She could light her own candles and make her own coffee. And if she steeped her own tea, she didn't run the risk of having a steaming cup of Super Perk shoved in her hand. Rosie closely guarded the recipe for her most potent blend and foisted it on Kimberly at every turn. Kimberly's nickname for the detested decoction, however, was Super Puke.

She popped a pod in her new coffee machine, sending a silent *thank you* to Sterling. Moving about the space, she lit candles and breathed deeply, ears strained for the sound of the door.

Where was Rosie?

After two cups of coffee and a bowl of oatmeal—again, courtesy of Sterling—she stared at all of the loose-leaf teas and herbs, conceded she had no idea what to do with them, and grabbed a green tea bag. She poured hot water over it in a to-go cup and applied a touch of foundation and eye makeup while it steeped.

At 10:00 a.m. she gave up on Rosie and reached for the door handle, which turned before she touched it.

The open door revealed Sterling, damp hair askew in a most beguiling manner.

His face brightened. "Found you! This explains why you're not in your room or at footage review."

"You've been looking for me? Is there a problem?"

"Not a problem. Just an excited group of people eager for your presence. TJ found something already and our two new recruits from early this morning can't wait to show you their cell phone videos. You have coffee?" He pointed to her cup and flashed a grin.

"I already downed two cups. This is tea. Thank you again for the breakfast supplies."

He craned his neck to look past her. "You alone? Rosie here? Or anyone else?"

Anyone else? Like who? "I haven't seen Rosie. I hoped she went on to footage review. You want some coffee?"

"I'd love some."

"You haven't seen Rosie either? Where is she?"

"I could guess," he said, arching his eyebrows. "Looks like you had oatmeal. Even without Rosie to fix it for you?"

"Of course. I can fend for myself. I'm actually a pretty good cook. I'm just not in a kitchen much these days. Mostly when we're in Albuquerque and I'm able to be home."

Sterling watched the coffee trickle into his cup. "Albuquerque must be nice. You don't seem to have any desire to leave."

"Nah. It's home. No plans to leave. Are you really thinking about moving there?" She kept her voice as casual as possible.

"I am. If I'm going to be working with you, I'd like to be close to headquarters."

"That's great. I think you'll like it. Might be quieter than what you're used to though. And spoiler, we don't have any beaches."

"That's okay. I can adapt. And I'm ready for a slower pace. Maybe even ready to settle down."

Butterflies danced through her stomach as Sterling leaned against the counter and blew on his coffee, his dark eyes watching her. *Ready to settle down? Sterling Wakefield, the playboy who always had a model on his arm?* She wondered if that would be possible. "Albuquerque isn't exactly the middle of nowhere. It just isn't Los Angeles."

"Tell me about your house."

"Not much to tell. Just a regular house. I don't live in a sprawling mansion if that's what you're wondering. I'm sure you'll find something you like if you really do relocate."

"I mean tell me why you wanted it so badly. Your former fiancé mentioned you bought it back. From whom? Your dad didn't leave it to you when he passed?"

"Didn't you say I have a group of people waiting for me? We should go." She started for the door.

"And I seem to recall you saying that the show doesn't start without us."

"Doesn't mean we should leave them waiting."

"Come on. They have hours and hours of footage to look at. This way they'll have more of it completed when we do join them."

She did prefer to see only the exciting bits and avoid the

hours of nothing in between. She'd spent plenty of her life with eyestrain from staring at hours of nothing on screens. "I don't really share this with many people. Unlike you, I don't vomit details from my personal life all over social media."

"You don't really believe I put anything important out there do you?"

"Aside from constantly posting about where you are, who you're with, what you're eating, things that gross you out, things that make you laugh—"

"Okay! We all know I am far more active online than you. And perhaps more than you'd like me to be now that we move in the same circle. Tell you what. You share this with me, I'll share something personal with you. And I pinkie swear not to tell anyone else."

What was she willing to divulge? How much did she trust him? She detected no underlying malice. She moved closer, searching his eyes. His body shifted in response.

"What?" he asked.

Resting a hand on his arm, she read his spectrum. His heart and throat chakras resonated brightest, though his orange chakra throbbed, presumably in response to her presence. She felt warmth, concern, eagerness . . . and a hint of fear. He was offering to share something that made him feel vulnerable.

She held up her pinkie. "Deal. But you go first."

"That wasn't part of the deal."

"That's the counter offer."

"Yeesh. Fine." He crooked his little finger around hers, shook, and took a deep breath. "It was Halloween. I was ten. My mom walked me all over the neighborhood. My legs hurt and my bag was full, so we decided to call it a night and go straight home. But we passed a house decorated to look exactly like a haunted house. I mean, they pulled out all the stops. It looked like a set for a horror movie. Lights flashing, speakers blaring creepy sound effects, spider webs stretched over every corner. The front yard was covered in gravestones with what looked like freshly dug dirt patches in front of them. And they had a grim reaper animatronic thing on the porch with glowing red eyes. This teenage girl called for me to come tour the haunted house. She said they were about to quit for the night and needed to get rid of the rest of their candy. Plus they had cookies and cupcakes."

He paused, took a deep breath, and shuddered.

She could feel his sadness and disappointment at the memory. She attempted to lighten the mood. "It must have turned out okay. You're here so you clearly survived. And your mom was there. Right?"

"Mom asked if I wanted to go inside. A haunted house to end Halloween on a bang. And the teenager started asking if I was scared, if I needed my mommy to go with me. Typical teen jerk garbage. Well, even back then, I already knew some magic tricks and knew ghosts and mythical creatures don't exist. I wasn't scared. I just wanted to go home. But I let her goading get to me and told Mom I'd be back."

She pictured his ten-year-old self squaring his shoulders and marching off to debunk the neighborhood haunted house. "I'll bet you were adorable. What costume did you wear? Not a ghost, I assume."

"No. I went dressed as a physicist."

She couldn't resist smiling. "Of course."

"Anyway, we went from room to room with me identifying all the creepy 'ghoulish' things they intended to spook trick-or-treaters. The 'eyeballs' were obviously peeled grapes. The 'intestines' were pasta noodles. And on and on. The girl grew more and more disgusted with me because I didn't shriek and get scared. Last stop was the kitchen where we met the girl's mom dressed as a witch and handing out cauldron cupcakes, cups of witch's brew, and black cat cookies. I told her she had a lovely home, admired their devotion to the holiday, and thanked her for the treats."

She stifled a giggle. "You were quite something at the age of ten. Sounds like you matured rather early on."

He shrugged. "Mom always said I was born with the personality of a cranky eighty-year-old man. Didn't ever get along well with my own age group. I found them unbearably silly. Anyway, my refusal to scare apparently infuriated this teenage girl. She showed me to the door and gestured to the huge bowl of candy on the porch bench and told me to take all I wanted since it was getting late."

"Yes. She definitely sounds furious. Offering you candy. Unbelievable."

"As I reached in, the grim reaper sprang to life and grabbed me. Scared the shit out of me. I screamed, dropped my cupcake on the porch, and thought I might have a heart attack. And of course the girl laughed and laughed and said something about that finally scared me and I deserved it. My mom dashed down the driveway, pissed they'd tricked a little kid. The grim reaper took his mask off. It was the girl's brother. He yelled at her about giving him the signal. Their mom came to the door, figured out what had happened, and yelled at them both. In all the yelling I managed to deduce that the boy couldn't see well out of the mask and if his sister said to only take one piece, that was code for 'it's a little kid so don't scare them.' If she said to take all you want, that was his signal to scare an older kid. Anyway, their mom apologized and offered a cupcake to replace the one I dropped but I didn't want anything from them anymore. I only wanted to leave."

"That was mean. What a brat. I'm sorry. I definitely received my share of teasing and harassing as a child too, so I understand."

"Taught me a lesson early on. People find all sorts of ways to trick you. Even when you think you can see through all their deception, they'll spring something on you. I'm always vigilant. And that's why no one can pull a fast one on me anymore. The best illusionists in the country can't fool me. I see through it all."

She giggled a little. His brow furrowed at the sound.

"I'm sorry," she said. "I'm not laughing at the situation. That was awful. But now I have an image of little ten-year-old Sterling 'busting' all the Halloween spooks."

"No one has ever fooled me again."

She briefly considered mentioning Amber, the succubus who fooled him pretty well during their previous investigation, but opted not to antagonize him. He was upset enough. "Sometimes things aren't a trick, you know. Some things simply defy explanation."

"Nothing defies explanation. I haven't encountered a single paranormal activity I couldn't science away. Two seasons of *SpookBusters* and not one instance of anything inexplicable."

"Granted, but I suspect you chose your cases based on the outcome you wanted."

He cocked his head. "What do you mean?"

"Well, when we sift through all the thousands of requests submitted to *Wantland Files*, we look for particularly promising and intriguing cases. Obviously. We don't want anything boring or easily explained. My crew vets the potential cases and does some preliminary research to ensure there isn't a simple explanation that will result in a huge waste of time. I'd bet your team did the same sort of thing but came at it from the opposite approach. You wanted cases you could easily disprove as a hoax. The Internet is full of that nonsense."

Sterling did a double take, his eyes wide. "Hoaxes? Nonsense? Doth mine ears deceive me? Kimberly Wantland thinks paranormal claims are hoaxes and nonsense?"

She gave him the look. "*Some* of them, yes. Of course. I've been doing this long enough to know there are a lot of crazies out there looking for attention any way they can get it."

His eyes smoldered over the rim of his cup as he sipped his coffee. He watched her thoughtfully for a moment. "You are full of surprises. I think we're more alike than either of us wants to admit."

She laughed. "I'm not so sure. Come on. We have a footage review to get to."

"Hold up. I shared. Now it's your turn."

She squirmed. "Maybe we could have dinner later and—"

"Dinner invitation accepted. But share now. No backing out. We pinkie swore. Do not violate the sanctity of the pinkie swear."

She sank into her chair. He offered his coffee cup but she held up a hand. Too much coffee at once made her jittery. "You have to understand, telling people this story never resulted in anything good. I alienated my dad. Was the laughing stock at school. Everyone decided I was crazy. So I learned to keep my mouth shut. I don't like to share."

"You don't really think I liked telling how I almost peed my pants on Halloween when I was ten, do you?"

"That's different. You were targeted by jerks. Being picked on isn't the same as hearing and seeing things no one else hears or sees."

Sterling dragged a chair in front of her and straddled it, leaning against the back. "I'm listening. And I promise not to judge."

"Sterling Wakefield, buster of all things paranormal, instigator of the online challenge, believer of nothing? You are *so* going to judge."

He rested a hand on hers. "I want to know you better. We're going to be working together. We need to trust each other. What happened in the house?"

CHAPTER TWENTY-NINE

So FEW PEOPLE ever asked about her past. Even during appearances, interviewers tended to skim over the basic, known facts and ask about current gossip and investigations. She couldn't help but feel suspicious of Sterling's motives.

She read his spectrum again, this time sensing an almost overwhelming surge of compassion from him. Unexpected. Worried she would probably regret sharing, she took a deep breath.

"It wasn't one instance. Really a lot of things. I figured out at a pretty young age that I saw things and heard things that other people didn't. Whispers, glimpses of shadows, images of people in mirrors. Little things I couldn't really understand and didn't know other people didn't experience. Then I started noticing the funny looks. Kids at school decided I was crazy. My mom thought I had an imaginary friend. My dad thought I had a bad habit of talking to myself. I can remember overhearing their concerned conversations, debating if I needed professional help. I didn't know what they were talking about, but I could tell they were upset about me. I realized they didn't know I was responding to actual things I heard."

"Did they ever take you to someone for evaluation?"

She eyed him. "You think I'm crazy, too?"

"Not crazy. But some conditions result in hearing voices and can be controlled by medication."

She scowled. "I'm not schizophrenic. And no, they didn't take me to see anyone. I could tell it bothered them and learned to be quiet about it. They decided I'd grown out of it. But I'd been labeled crazy at school and never shook that general opinion. Once a crazy, always a crazy. No real friends to speak of. No one to talk to about anything." She took in his exquisite physique. "I doubt you ever experienced that."

He shrugged. "I had friends, sure. But I wasn't the most popular guy either. Contrary to what you may have heard, magic tricks don't impress everyone. Although . . . what's this?" He reached behind her ear and produced a square of dark chocolate. "You're so sweet, you make your own line of candy."

She laughed and accepted the chocolate. "I'll bet that one is always popular with the ladies."

"I won't deny that one usually at least got a first date. But we were talking about you. Don't change the subject."

She unwrapped the chocolate and popped it in her mouth. The rich, deep bittersweet goodness melted over her tongue. She noticed Sterling smile his approval. "Chocolate for breakfast. What a terrible influence you are."

"Ah, live a little. Life is short. You and I both know that. So, back to what happened in the house."

"Slave driver," she teased. If she was honest, sharing the story actually felt good. "Most of the things I saw or heard were shadows or residual phrases. I learned to go about my business and not let them bother me. But we had something in our house. Something dark. He was different. Active. I can't remember a time I wasn't aware of him. I sensed him all along. But then he started messing with me. Teasing and tormenting. He knew. He could sense my abilities like I could sense him. I'm not talking about harmless teasing either. Looking back, I'm convinced it wasn't a poltergeist. I think it was a demon. Back then I didn't know how to control my abilities, and I didn't know enough about spiritual entities to categorize them or even realize that different types exist. I only knew things moved among us that other people are completely unaware of."

She closed her eyes. Thinking about the memories took her back to her childhood. Her heart thumped in response to the helplessness, as though she were right back in the situation. Small, powerless, confused. And scared.

"No wonder you fought so hard to protect those little boys last episode. You saw your own experiences mirrored in theirs. Terrorized at a young age by something you couldn't explain. I'm sure that was rough."

Startled by the lack of teasing, she met his gaze. "I didn't even think about that at the time, but you're probably right. The difference is the Williams had a misguided, confused spirit who needed to move on. I think the presence in our home back then was a true demon. I've thought about this so much. It was real evil. And fixated on me. Playing with me. Who could I turn to? My parents didn't want to hear about it and wouldn't have believed me. Especially my dad. So I kept quiet and dealt with it the best I could. There is nothing worse than being doubted. Especially when you know you're right."

He rested a hand on hers. "I can see that. I'll be honest. When I challenged you to let me come on your show, I was sure you were like every other medium and psychic I've encountered. But you're not. I can tell you truly believe in your so-called abilities. I wish I could catch a glimpse. Something so I could know what it is you think you experience."

"*Think* I experience? I do experience these things, Sterling. I wish you could feel something, too. Being open to experiences is important. But I think you need the innate ability as well. I can't tell you for sure why some people can sense and interact with spiritual beings when most can't. But if you were colorblind, you and I would argue what color things are, both of us convinced we were absolutely right. And we would be. But our brains wouldn't interpret colors the same way. I think this is like that. Something allows me awareness. I'm sensitive to the beings moving among us. Maybe you'll experience it with me sometime."

He cocked his head. "Interesting theory. Huh. So what sorts of things did you experience? Can you remember specific examples?"

"Of course I remember. I wish I could forget. It was little things at first—trinkets on my dresser shifted or every piece of clothing in my closet fell to the floor. I'd make my bed in the morning and come home from school to find all the sheets shoved to the end of the bed. I heard whispers, especially at night."

"What did they say?"

"I never understood the words. I'd wake up and listen, but it would stop."

"Maybe you dreamed it?"

"I thought that the first few times. But it continued and happened regularly. You need to remember how young I was when this started. I can't remember a time things like this didn't happen to me. When I was five and six years old, I kept trying to sleep with my parents but Mom insisted it was all in my imagination—'No monsters. Go back to bed.' I didn't question her. But my things kept moving and then later, when I was older, he started manifesting. I saw him. He stood over my bed watching me, every night. He started as a haze, then became stronger and stronger until he was a full dark shadow." She shivered.

"How would he get stronger?"

"I've thought about this a lot. My best guess is batteries. As I got older, I had more electronics in my room. Batteries would offer an energy source. But also, I was getting older. I became more aware of this gift I have and it grew stronger too. I think he could draw from my energy and I became better able to focus and hone in on him."

He rubbed his temples, probably trying to find a solution to her experiences that didn't involve admitting she had a paranormal entity in her childhood home. "I don't really know what caused these disturbances, but I'm sorry you had to go through such rough times. I understand having a thorny relationship with parents."

"It was my life. I dealt with it. What else can we do?"

Sterling leaned forward, propping his chin on his hands, which rested on the chair back. "But you haven't ever investigated there? That's surprising."

"Dad wouldn't let me investigate the house. Not after everything that happened. He and I had a very challenging relationship after my mom—I couldn't wait to graduate high school and escape to college. Far away from Albuquerque. I wanted to run far away, never look back, and forget everything and everyone. Of course, things don't really work that way. Still, kind of ironic I'm back living there all these years later. Dad left it to his sister when he passed away, with strict instructions in his will to never, ever allow me to 'hold a séance in it.' Not remotely what I do but that was how he referred to my investigations."

His brow furrowed. "That seems harsh."

"Some of my mom's things are still in it. For a while, my aunt wouldn't even let me inside. But she lives on the east coast and had no interest in living in it. She got tired of dealing with it and let me buy it. Though she insisted I honor my father's wishes not to bring further shame on the family and never film for the show in the family home. It's even written into the purchase contract."

She didn't dwell on these things. Mostly she tried not to think about them at all. But now she remembered very clearly longing for comfort and for someone to share with, someone who would understand. The pain of losing her mom, especially in such bizarre circumstances, never fully explained, weighed heavily. Opening up to Sterling brought it all back to the surface. Even now, with Michael and Rosie and her crew, her fans, and a much more open-minded world, she still harbored the sense of being alone and isolated. Of not belonging. All those years of being an outcast left deep scars.

"I'm no psychic, but I get the feeling whatever happened to your mom caused the rift between you and your dad."

She nodded and swiped at the tears that brimmed her eyes.

"Oh, hey." Sterling jumped from his chair, pulling her into a hug. He rubbed her back. "I didn't mean to upset you. Really."

"My mom—" She choked and took a deep breath, wiping escaped tears from her cheeks. "Shoot. Now I've messed up my makeup."

"Don't worry about that right now." He nestled his cheek against the top of her head, his hand drawing her snugger against his chest.

Unaccustomed to such warmth and comfort, she breathed in his masculine scent. He rocked her gently and she gave in completely, relaxing into his embrace. *What might it be like to have someone hold you every day?* Someone who would listen and offer advice. Someone to plan with and goof off with. The accumulated loneliness of so many years yawned widely, plummeting her into its ugly cavern.

He continued to hold her quietly, but rather than calming her, the rush of emotions seemed to only make the problem worse. She wept openly.

The trailer door flew open. Michael stomped into the space, but stopped abruptly at the scene in front of him. His jaw dropped open. "What have you done to Kimmy? I sent you to bring her back, not upset her. What the hell, Sterling?"

"I didn't mean to upset her. We were only talking."

She muttered he was telling the truth, but Sterling's chest garbled her words. She lifted her head and nodded. "We were only talking. Sterling didn't do anything." She rubbed at her cheeks, thinking she could gladly lean against that warm chest and be rocked all day. *What is he doing to me? I've never needed anyone. I was fine on my own until Sterling showed up.*

Michael looked at them both rather dubiously but then shrugged. "Sweetie, fix your face. And hurry. You have to see what we caught last night."

CHAPTER THIRTY

ON THE GRAY-SCALE FOOTAGE, Kimberly watched her image as orb after orb floated closer to her, drawn by her psychic energy. They pressed against her, and she knew they drained her energy. A moment later she collapsed. Sterling raced to her side. At least their cameras caught something. Kerry and Suzie's cell phone recordings had turned out to be horribly shaky and useless. No evidence of the revenge-seeking ghost the sisters had been so certain they'd captured. Stan had downloaded their videos to carefully examine before the sisters happily left for a historical tour.

The green tea Kimberly sipped did nothing to soothe her frayed emotions. She needed something more calming. Something medicinal. She needed Rosie, still annoyingly MIA.

TJ looked up from the computer monitor and beamed at her. "This is good, right? This proves all those spirits are here, asking for help."

"It is interesting," Sterling replied. "We certainly didn't see any lights while filming last night."

She, Michael, and TJ stared at him, mouths agape.

The rest of her crew, headphones clamped on their heads,

stared at screens, searching for more evidence of communication attempts and clues.

Since they'd left her trailer, Sterling had sought eye contact, offered encouraging smiles, and patted her shoulder once. He was even feigning being impressed by the orbs. Clearly, he was willing to do anything to cheer her up. She waved away his concern and repeatedly assured him she was fine, unwilling to let him know how much their discussion unnerved her. Although bursting into tears on his shoulder had probably tipped him off.

"Elise," Michael said, "what else do you have for us?"

Elise shuffled her loose newspaper clippings, downloaded articles, and scattered manila envelopes. "I didn't find much more than I already had on Norman Baker. He didn't die anywhere near here, though, I can tell you that. He passed away in Florida at the age of seventy-five with a diagnosis of cirrhosis."

"So nothing sudden, no reason to think he may have found his way back to Eureka Springs for some unfinished business?" Kimberly said.

"Nothing. He'd served his jail time for practicing medicine without a license and moved on. Nowhere near the hotel. And he was buried in Muscatine, Iowa."

"I didn't think I felt his presence here. Besides, what revenge would he be seeking?"

"I didn't think it was him wanting revenge," Michael said. "I thought perhaps one of his patients. After what you experienced last night, I think they have every reason to want revenge."

"But if he isn't here, revenge isn't possible." Kimberly pressed her fingers to her temples, attempting to massage away the developing headache. "Two nights in and we still don't know what we're trying to exorcise."

"Let's look at the footage again," Michael suggested. "TJ? Can you bring that back up?"

"Sure thing." TJ clicked his mouse and tapped a few keys. "So this is where we saw the girl in the mirror. Here is where Ms. Wantland connected psychically with the spirits. And then my favorite part, where the orbs appear. So awesome."

She again watched the gray footage that had so excited Michael—pale orbs of light materialized from the walls and ceiling and drifted toward her, closer and closer. "This supports what I saw and felt. All the spirits stuck here and suffering reached out to me. They overwhelmed me but I don't think they intended to. I think they only want help."

"You'll help them, right?" TJ asked. "No way we would leave them here like that."

"I spoke briefly with Selma. She doesn't want any of her residents to leave except the one scaring her still-living guests."

"But . . . we can't." TJ's face fell. "We can't leave them."

"I haven't given up," she assured him. "I'll keep working on Selma. She's too good of a person to want to allow spirits to continue suffering. Meanwhile, I think we can rule out Norman Baker as a potential suspect. And probably his patients, which sadly appear to remain in large numbers. That leaves us still completely clueless. Who else has reason to want revenge?"

She glanced at Sterling and discovered him staring at her. The piercing gaze sent her stomach quivering. He tried to cover with a shy smile, but she'd seen the intensity.

Elise rifled through her papers again. "Honestly, a lot of people have died here over the years. You guys all went on the ghost tour. You heard. That only grazed the surface. There were fires where people burned to death. The building has been here a long time and housed a lot of people over the years. I could go on and on."

She pressed her fingers to her temples, losing the battle against the increasing headache. "I warned you, Michael. There's so much activity here. I'm not sure I can ever pinpoint the source. Even Sterling saw a ghost last night."

Michael's jaw dropped. "What?"

Sterling jumped to his feet. "I never said I thought it was a ghost."

His reaction surprised her. "A young woman in a white gown? Remember? Said you thought it was me for a minute? You were convinced when you showed up at my door in the middle of the night. Breathless and shirtless."

His brow furrowed. "I said I didn't know what happened. At least I don't hear things. You claimed to hear a piano playing and crept around the hotel in your robe."

Michael held up his hands. "Whoa, whoa, whoa. What is this about you sneaking around in your pajamas with Sterling?"

"I was in pajamas," Sterling corrected. "She was in a robe. See?" Sterling help up his phone, displaying the picture Kerry and Suzie snapped of the two of them, Sterling's arms curled around her.

She thought Sterling's encounter the night before and their shared stories in the trailer had resulted in bonding. She honestly thought he was beginning to entertain the idea maybe he didn't know everything. The memory of him cradling and rocking her still fresh on her mind, his attitude confounded her. He appeared to be quite irritated. And trying to shift attention away from the experience he now wanted to deny. When would she learn not to let her guard down? No hug was worth this frustration.

Michael cocked an eyebrow at her.

"Hold on. Let me start this story from the beginning, so no one gets the wrong idea." She reached into her quilted Coach bag, indigo, designed exclusively for her, and withdrew her phone. "After last night's disaster of an investigation, I went back to my room disgusted and frustrated. Something started interacting with me, and I think it was Ms. Theodora. Startled me at first, but as it turned out, nothing malicious or threatening about the encounter. In fact, I think she wanted me to take a bath and relax. Watch." She played the snippet of video. A few rattles and thumps emanated from the bathroom.

Sterling pantomimed holding a camera in front of his face,

his eyes wide. He glanced around and breathed rapidly as though terrified. "We are in the bathroom. There are noises in the bathroom. I'm so scared."

TJ snorted, then caught himself, likely because he remembered he didn't like Sterling. But then he offered a fist to Sterling who bumped it. "Good one, dude. *Blair Witch*. I couldn't even watch that. Made me nauseous. Like, learn how to hold a camera, right?"

She glared at him. "I never said I was scared. It was actually rather relaxing once I determined what was happening. I've never had a spirit try to take care of me before. You were the one who was scared last night."

Sterling shook his head. "I wasn't scared. Disconcerted perhaps, until I woke up and got my wits about me. But there isn't anything remotely scary on that recording of yours. I mean, you didn't even record inside the bathroom where the noises were. You could've had someone in there—" His face hardened into a scowl. "Who was in the bathroom? Was it Jason? Sure you were all alone having a bath. That's why you were in a robe. You were screwing around with your ex."

Every face in the room turned to stare at her, even the ones with headphones on who could supposedly barely hear.

She crossed her arms. "No one was in the room with me. I've told you what happened and I recorded it the best I could until my battery went dead. I would have recorded in the bathroom if I could have. End of story."

"Was he still hiding in the bathroom while I was sitting there on your bed?"

"Shirtless, apparently." Michael sounded breathless. "Sweetie, you are making up for lost time. Color me impressed."

She gritted her teeth. "Actually, I think I'm ready to reaffirm my vow of celibacy and swear off men completely. Forever. Can we please focus on footage review? That's what we're here to do."

"I don't think that's nearly as fun as discussing your little ménage à trois last night," Michael teased. She could tell he wanted juicy details, though she had none to give. The look on her face must have convinced him to move on. "But sure, let's just do our work. Sterling mentioned you heard a piano playing? Did I actually sleep through an opportunity to belt out some Broadway tunes?"

"No," Sterling said. The sharp edge in his voice cut through her. "She imagined it. Or, I'm more inclined to think made it up. I can't believe I was actually starting to believe you. This was a trick. You made it up to lure me out of your room, didn't you? So Jason could sneak out while we were gone." The betrayal in his eyes was more than she could handle.

How could he think such a thing about her? He was the one with a new woman on his arm every other day. She might as well have joined a convent when she turned eighteen. "Jason wasn't there, Sterling. Not ever. He hasn't been in my room. Period. You were the only man in my room last night."

"Personally, I don't really want to hear any of this," TJ said. "Can we get back to the piano? Ya know, the actual investigation?"

Casting her thanks at TJ, she continued. "I didn't imagine it. And you didn't miss out on show tunes, Michael. He played *Für Elise*."

"Who did?" Michael asked.

"I'm not sure. I mean, I could sense the entity but I have no idea who he was. Didn't Selma say she recently found that piano and returned it to the hotel? Elise, can you try to find out any known history on it?"

"Definitely." Elise scribbled on her pad, apparently pleased to tackle a new project.

"Suzie was attacked right after I heard the piano. Could there be a connection there?"

"Kimberly," Stan said. "Come look at this."

"Please tell me you found something good. We need a break

in this case," she said, crossing to stand behind Stan. *And I need a distraction from my non-existent sex life.*

"I finished looking over the footage from my hand held and started looking at what the sta-cam we left on the hotel grounds captured. We caught the jumper."

CHAPTER THIRTY-ONE

MICHAEL HURRIED to Kimberly's side. "You mean the ghost that jumps from the balcony?"

"I think so," Stan answered. "Watch."

He clicked the mouse, advancing the recording, and an elongated blue orb streaked from a third-floor balcony to the ground.

"Impressive," she said. "That does seem to match the description of her."

Sterling had joined them and watched, arms folded across his chest. "Except we were told it looks exactly like a young woman. In fact, the supposed apparition prompted frantic 911 calls. That looks like a blurry streak of light to me. Not a human at all. Maybe a bug flew in front of the camera."

"I'm going to isolate and further analyze," Stan assured Sterling. "I agree what we caught isn't exactly a spot-on image of a woman, but it may have appeared that way to a human eye. Remember, we're hindered by what the camera records. But we did at least capture someone jumping."

"I strongly disagree," Sterling said. "That is a streak of light. A blip. I see nothing to indicate a human form. That's not a person."

"Duh. It's a ghost. Not a person," TJ said.

Sterling sighed heavily. "It is even less likely to be a ghost than an actual person. But the point I am making is that this image is a shapeless blur, which does not in any way look like a person."

"Give me time," Stan said.

"Time to manipulate the image to look like whatever you want it to resemble?"

"Isolation and analysis isn't manipulation."

"Again, I strongly disagree."

"I'm simply giving us a better look at the image. I'm not changing anything."

"Stan," Kimberly said. "Can you run that back, please? Let me see it again?"

Her camera operator did as she requested, replaying the recording.

"Can you zoom in on the balcony, right before she falls?"

Again, Stan complied.

"There," Kimberly said, pointing to the screen. "Look on the balcony before she falls. See that?"

Michael leaned forward, squinting at the screen. "What is that?"

"Someone else is with her. I'm sure of it. What if she didn't jump? I think she was pushed."

Stan zoomed in again, clicking his mouse, amplifying the image until the balcony filled the screen. Grainy and pixelated, a second image emerged, the hint of a scowling face atop a roughly human form.

"I'll be damned," TJ said. "I never would have noticed that. You're amazing, Ms. Wantland."

Flushing slightly at the praise, she shook her head. "Nah. I have an advantage. I experienced this yesterday on the ghost tour. Psychically. Remember? I connected with a young woman who was pushed by an angry man. She lost her balance and fell from the balcony."

"I'd forgotten that," Michael said. "Though in my defense,

women falling from balconies pales in comparison to Kimmy falling in bed with two guys in the same night."

"Michael!"

"Allegedly falling," he corrected.

"Nope. Not even allegedly. Wasn't in bed with anyone last night."

"Well, we can discuss this later," Michael said. "So, she was pushed by an angry man? Any thoughts on why he was angry? Was he perhaps angry enough to want revenge for something?"

"I'm not sure but I've been experiencing a falling sensation quite a bit during this investigation—"

"I'd say you just keep falling a lot," Sterling said.

"Right into bed, apparently." Michael raised hopeful eyebrows at her.

"If the peanut gallery could close its yaps for a moment, some of us are attempting to sort out a mystery here." She glared at them both until they gestured for her to continue. "What if the falling is important? Could the spirit of this young woman be reaching out to me? Perhaps she wants my help. Elise, do you have anything more on the girl who fell from the balcony? Who evidently was pushed?"

"Evidently implies evidence, my dear," Sterling said. "Of which you have none."

She held up a hand in Sterling's face and waved at Elise to continue.

"Not much more than what I already shared," Elise began. "The girl was a student here during the time it was a conservatory—a boarding school for girls. Her death shocked the community, particularly when the autopsy revealed she was pregnant. I believe I saw that some people in town cast suspicion on the dean at the time, but he vehemently denied involvement or knowledge."

"You mean he was suspected of fathering the child? Or of causing her death?"

Elise wrinkled her nose. "Both."

"Ick."

"Young men at the time often used the laundry baskets to smuggle themselves into the rooms of young ladies who had caught their attention. And the dean reportedly sometimes nabbed the interlopers and rode up in their stead, startling the ladies expecting gentleman callers. But perhaps in this case he—"

"Wait," Kimberly said. "Laundry baskets?"

"Yes. The girls had baskets outside their windows they used to lower their dirty laundry down to be washed. Sometimes these young ladies also used the baskets to hoist suitors into their rooms."

"And the laundry room is the first place this spirit manifested. Something tells me this is worth digging into," Kimberly said.

Elise opened a laptop. Her fingers flew over the keys. "Right. Here it is. The dean was exonerated of any involvement. The accepted story is that the girl's boyfriend and presumed father of the baby belonged to a wealthy family in Eureka Springs. They managed to keep his name out of the scandal. To this day, little is known about either the victim or the father."

"What do you think, Kimmy? Could the angry spirit be her baby's father?"

"I'm not sure. I didn't get any reading on the man at all. You know my visions tend to be hazy. I have a better feeling for the spirit I connect with."

"We need a motive for revenge. That would be the best starting point," Michael mused.

"Obviously true," she admitted. "Until we have that break, we're groping in the dark."

"I'm not sure we'll get lucky two nights in a row, but I'm definitely leaving a sta-cam out there again," Stan said.

"Sure. Of course," Michael agreed. "Where do we want to focus the investigation tonight, Kimmy? More psych ward? Hang out back and hope for another appearance there? Someplace new?"

She closed her eyes and grabbed her quartz. She tuned everyone out, pushed aside thoughts of Jason and Sterling, tried to stop wondering where the heck Rosie was, and summoned all her energy. She opened herself to input, reaching out, hoping for direction. Anything. *Where do we need to go?* She saw washers and driers, Clara, the morgue and the spa. She remembered hearing something utter, "Revenge," during her massage.

"The laundry room. Let's go where it all began. I can't imagine how the laundry room plays into all this, but we don't have anything else right now and the laundry room is pulling me."

Michael nodded. "Okay. Laundry room it is. Let's hope we stir something up."

CHAPTER THIRTY-TWO

KIMBERLY SIPPED HER TEA, nodding at the story Jason told. "Of course I remember. How could I forget?"

Jason leaned on his elbows, the menu in front of him ignored. "The look on that cow's face!" He burst into laughter, clapping his hands.

"Oh, no! I'd forgotten about the cow." She threw her head back and laughed. "What were we thinking?"

"We were young. Though you haven't changed a bit. Haven't aged a day."

"Stop. I'm a mess. My stylist didn't show up this morning and I'm only wearing a bit of makeup. Didn't sleep last night, either, so I know I look dreadful."

"You've never looked better. You don't need makeup. Your complexion is flawless."

She lifted her teacup, unsure where to look or what to say, and hoped it hid her blush. "Thank you. You're too kind. I try not to appear in public without at least a little makeup. "

The waiter sidled to their table, hands clasped in front of him. "Have you decided? Or do you need a few more minutes?"

"I haven't even looked," Jason said, fumbling with his menu.

"But you're known for your pizza. Kimberly, you still like veggie best?"

"Veggie is good."

Jason folded his menu and offered it to the waiter. "Bring us a veggie to share."

They sat outside on the balcony of the Sky Bar overlooking the hotel grounds. Though she'd been here night before last, it was close and fast and Jason seemed so keen to try it, she didn't have the heart to say no.

"You remember my favorite pizza. Thank you for that."

"My pleasure. I'm so glad you agreed to meet me. And hey, eating veggie seems to be working for you. I might as well take a leaf from your book."

She didn't know quite how to react to all his compliments. "So how is work?"

"It's great. I mean, I haven't achieved anything like you have obviously. But I was promoted to manager a couple years ago. I travel some. It's good."

"That's good. I'm glad you're doing well. Your parents are okay?"

"They're fine. Loving retirement. Traveling. Volunteering. Mom says she's finally doing all the things she's waited her entire life to get to do. She, uh, reminds me from time to time she expected to be spoiling grandchildren by now." He cleared his throat.

She laughed again. "That doesn't surprise me. She used to tell me she hoped we wouldn't wait too long. I really liked her. She was good to me."

Though she wanted to appear calm, her stomach quivered. She marveled at how easily they picked back up basically where they left off. Talking with him was easy, like those six years hadn't happened at all. Except of course, they were ignoring the final unbearable months at the end, leading to the breakup. Still, there was a comfort level she hadn't anticipated. They had history. They knew each other. He liked her before she was famous, before she had anything.

"This is nice," Jason said.

"It really is."

"You sound surprised."

"Aren't you? I don't think most exes have lunch together and reminisce about the good old days."

He nodded. "That's the way I think about us too. The good old days."

"Your mom deserves those grandkids. I'm not sure I was ever the right woman to provide them. Have you found another candidate? Maybe someone your mom likes even better?"

He took her hand between his. "Not even close. I haven't found anyone I enjoy being around like I enjoyed being with you. Anytime I go out with someone, the date fizzles because I can't stop comparing her to you. No one compares to you. We laughed. We had fun. We understood each other. You're intelligent and we had wonderful, in-depth conversations. Mom and Dad bring you up from time to time. They say it's a shame we couldn't make it work."

"Really? That's rather surprising." Her heart thumped but she didn't retract her hand.

"They watch your show religiously, too. Mom has a *Wantland Files* T-shirt and coffee mug. She tells all her friends we used to date. That you were nearly her daughter-in-law."

Her heart melted a little bit. "I wouldn't have expected that. That's sweet."

"What about you? Are you seeing anyone? Sterling Wakefield, huh? Right here on set."

"No, not Sterling. He doubts my abilities as much as you always did. I don't really date. I'm too busy." She withdrew her hand. "I do remember the good times. And I also remember the demands of the paranormal investigations on my time was part of what pushed you away. It's only worse now, Jason. I have no personal life."

"I wasn't there for you. I was selfish. I truly regret that now. I don't have any excuse except maybe that we were still young. And I was stupid. Could you forgive me?"

"There's nothing to forgive. I'm not angry. Really. I got over it long ago. But nothing has changed for me. If anything, it's only gotten worse. My career still relies on my psychic abilities that you considered hogwash."

"I regret that too. I've grown a lot in six years, Kimberly. I promise. I thought I knew everything then. Now I realize what a closed-minded fool I was. Lately I've been thinking about you a lot. I screwed up. I think I could be far stronger and more supportive now. Do you think you could ever give me a second chance?"

She would have given anything to hear him say that six years ago. "Wow. I didn't expect that."

"We've wasted a lot of time already. I don't see any reason to waste more if there is any way you'd give me another shot. I want you to know exactly how I feel."

The waiter approached with their pizza and served a slice to each of them. "Careful. It's very hot," he cautioned before leaving them to enjoy.

Finding the pizza too hot to touch, she lifted her fork and cut a bite from her slice. She blew on it, careful not to look at Jason. Rather like the first time they'd met. She'd tried not to look at him then, too. They had both enrolled in the same block course to satisfy a requirement. He'd slid into the seat beside her and did a double take. She'd spent the entire lecture pretending she hadn't noticed, keeping her eyes on her spiral or the professor as though she wore blinders. At the end of class, she gathered her things quickly. But not quickly enough. He'd jumped from his seat, stepped to her side, and extended a hand in greeting. "Jason Caraway. Yes, like the seed. And yes, I can take your cares away." She'd sat there speechless, much like she was now. His ability to startle her hadn't changed.

They were about as unalike as two people could be, and yet

mutually attracted. And frankly, the theatre department, though teeming with excellent male best friends, did not offer a slew of datable guys. Those who were interested in girls paired up with the most attractive and talented amongst their fellow thespians. She did not qualify as either. At least not her freshman or sophomore years.

Words from her childhood had echoed during college. "Late bloomer," Dad often called her when she was growing up. "She's the tortoise, not the hare," he'd said to Mom many times, despite straight A's and teachers' praise. Dad noticed only her social awkwardness and couldn't see her strengths—and didn't want to acknowledge her gifts.

She'd met Michael her freshman year. Flamboyant and outspoken, friends with everyone, he didn't waste a moment of his life caring what anyone else thought of him. She'd been bent over a water fountain in the hallway, slurping water while awaiting her first audition fall semester (a terrible idea since her nervous bladder kept her running to the bathroom every few minutes) when she'd felt a tap on her shoulder. She'd turned, wiping dripping water from her mouth, to face the tall, lanky, beaming boy. "Hi, I'm Michael. We haven't met yet." *Way too happy*, she'd thought at the time.

But she'd come to rely on that cheerfulness, as well as his fearless openness, his willingness to risk looking like a fool to make a scene great. They wound up in several of the same classes each semester, partnered often on classroom exercises and scene studies. Gradually, she'd learned to let her guard down and take chances, too. The first time her class burst into laughter during one of her scenes, at something she'd done, she thought she might burst with happiness. The semesters passed quickly, with no time to even think about boys or dating.

And then Jason held out his hand that first day of class second semester junior year. Probably his next comment, "Didn't I see you on stage last month? I only went for extra credit but then I was blown away. And you were incredible," led to her stunned nod when he asked her out. What girl could say no to a date request on the heels of that compliment? And then he'd swept her off her feet.

"Your silence is saying a lot," Jason said, his pizza still untouched. A breeze blew across the balcony. "Loud and clear."

"I'm sorry. I kind of zoned out. I was thinking about our first date."

His creased brow relaxed. "Oh! The official or unofficial first date?"

She laughed. "The very first. Retroactively official in my mind."

"I'm glad to hear that. It was only unofficial initially because you insisted we 'just hang out' that first time." He reached across the table and took her hand. "Can you at least think about it? Can you give me that much? I'm sure it's a lot to process after six years apart, but we were good together. And I think we'd be even better now."

"I . . . I'll think about it, but I don't want to give you false hope. Life is complicated. We went down different paths. I don't know how we would make it work now."

"I moved to Albuquerque for you once. I can do it again."

"Oh, Jason. You were miserable there. Don't you remember?" Curiosity got the better of her. "Where are you living now?"

"Back in Tulsa. Near my family."

"Of course. That makes sense."

"If you can, stop by on your way back home. Mom would love to see you."

See his mom? That could be the start down a path she shouldn't even consider. Yet her heart thumped as images of his smiling mother played through her mind like a nostalgic old family movie. His mother, Pam, always included her in their holidays and celebrations. She remembered the beautifully wrapped Christmas gifts under his family's tree, the thoughtfulness of the gifts always a moving surprise. Pam baked birthday cakes for her during college and the subsequent years they'd lived in Tulsa. Far from her own home in Albuquerque, she'd come to confide in Pam as she would have her own mother, had life gone a different direction. Until Albuquerque pulled her back.

"I'll see if I can squeeze in a visit," she said.

Kerry and Suzie followed a waiter to a table. Kerry spotted her, then honed in on Jason like a hawk and nudged Suzie with an elbow. Their cell phones were in their hands before Kimberly even realized what the women scowled about.

Kerry stormed to their table, Suzie trailing in her wake. "I can't believe you're stepping out on Sterling. Really? Less than twelve hours after we discovered you naked with Sterling—"

"Not naked!" she corrected.

"We find you holding hands with a stranger?"

Jason dropped her hand and retracted his arm as if informed he was handling a viper. "Naked? You said you're not dating him. What, is it just sex? That's not the Kimmy I knew."

Kerry's and Suzie's jaws dropped.

Kerry held out her phone. "Say that again."

Kimberly held up a hand. "Don't repeat—"

Jason frowned. "I said that's not the Kimmy I knew."

Kerry glanced askance. "Suzie Q? Do you know what we did?"

"I think we solved the mystery of the hated nickname."

"Hated?" Jason studied her. "You hate being called Kimmy? Since when?"

"Isn't it obvious?" she whispered. "Can we please not—"

"You said you were over our break up. You said you weren't mad anymore."

"Breakup? He's not a stranger," Kerry said, licking her lips. "They have history."

"You're her old boyfriend?" Suzie's eyes shone.

The waiter attempting to seat the distracted women plucked at Kerry's sleeve. "Ladies, your table—"

"Shh! Just a minute," Kerry said.

Kimberly hung her head in her hands while everyone spoke

at once. The two women peppered them with questions as to the nature of their relationship, past and current. Jason demanded to know the nature of her relationship with Sterling. And the waiter attempted to cajole the women to their waiting table.

Her head throbbed. She clutched at her quartz.

Kerry noticed the movement. "Sterling gave her that necklace, you know."

She took a deep breath and stood. "I give up. Jason, thank you for the lovely lunch. I'm sorry we were interrupted. Welcome to my world. Ladies . . . " Nothing she wanted to say should be uttered in public, particularly with the number of cell phones trained on her. "If you'll excuse me." She picked up her indigo Coach bag and exited the balcony, head held high.

She felt dozens of eyes following her as she left.

CHAPTER THIRTY-THREE

THE SCENT OF LAVENDER, sandalwood, and sage greeted Kimberly when she opened her trailer door. The electric teakettle whistled. And Rosie measured tealeaves into a cup.

She crossed the trailer and grabbed Rosie in a hug.

"Hey!" her stylist protested when tea leaves spilled to the floor.

The trailer was warmer and more comforting with Rosie in it. Her worry and annoyance with the missing woman resurfaced above the relief. "Sorry. But where have you been?"

"With Lorenzo. He took me to brunch. After an incredible night."

Rosie appeared to be blushing. Rosie never blushed. She contemplated what the guy did to cause this reaction, then shook her head, realizing she had no desire to have those images in her mind.

"But after a lengthy brunch I realized I hadn't checked in and saw your texts. Plus the Sky Bar Pizza Scandal. So I hurried over. Knew you'd need relaxing tea to help you cope with being harassed in public."

"What scandal? There is no scandal. I had lunch with an old friend."

"An old *boy*friend. And girl, your fans are not digging this. The shippers are pissed. Wait until they figure out he was your fiancé."

"I'm not going to let total strangers dictate who I have lunch with. That is ridiculous."

"Look at this." Rosie turned her phone so she could see the screen. A picture of her beaming at Jason as he held her hand at lunch had thousands of comments, all of them along the lines of

Who is this asshole?

Where was Sterling?

Why is Kimberly stepping out on Sterling??

and all tagged *#cheater*.

"This is why I never look at Twitter. Who are these people and why do they think they have any say in my personal life?"

"They're your fans and they keep your show on the air by watching it every week."

"Great. But that doesn't mean they can butt into my personal life. And come interrupt my meals with friends."

Rosie gave her the look and shoved a mug of tea into her hands. "So how was lunch? Must have been awkward, right?"

"It really wasn't. Surprisingly. We chatted and caught up. He's a manager now, so that's good."

"But he's not dating anyone."

"You sound so sure."

"Sweetie, he wouldn't be here having lunch with you if he had a girl back home."

She didn't reply.

"So? What does he want?"

"I think he just wanted to say that he's sorry and put some closure on things. We ended on a pretty sour note. Now we can put that behind us and move on."

"Girl, it wouldn't have ended if it hadn't gone sour. That's why we break up. If I told you I was meeting Donovan for lunch, don't you think you'd be a little concerned?"

"I'd be very concerned considering he stole your car and cheated on you with your best friend. I think I'd be even more concerned if you reconnected with Stuart. The guy who claimed his mother was in the hospital and asked you to help pay the medical bills."

Rosie shuddered. "Stuart. I'd forgotten that loser. Why'd you bring him back up?"

"Or Conrad. The freeloader who moved in with you, ate all your food, didn't help pay rent or bills. And was always on the verge of his big break. Remember how you called him Studly?"

Rosie covered her eyes. "Kimberly, stop! I don't want to think about any past boyfriends. I have no idea how you sat through an entire lunch with one."

"This is different. You weren't engaged to Donovan or Stuart or Conrad. And you didn't invest years in a relationship with any of them."

"Or any guy. Yet. I'm just saying. You need to remember why you two went your separate ways, that's all. I'm not buying the closure thing. You're acting funny. Something happened at lunch." Rosie always read her like a book.

"He asked if I would take him back," she admitted. "Or at least consider it."

"Wow. That's quite a lunch."

"I know. I didn't see it coming at all."

"Really? The guy comes all the way to Eureka Springs to see you—"

"He's living in Tulsa again. It's not *that* far."

"—begs for a date, and you don't think he wants to get together with you? Sometimes you're a bit of a nitwit for someone who has a sixth sense and second sight."

"Thanks."

"I, uh, actually wanted to talk to you about something. Speaking of unexpected lunches." Rosie's tone changed from teasing to serious. Rosie rarely did serious.

She sat forward in her chair. "What is it?"

The door opened. Sterling stomped into the trailer and flopped into a chair. "Hey, Rosie. Have you set her straight yet?"

Rosie shrugged. "You know I've been trying for years. She doesn't really listen to me."

She paused blowing on her tea. "Hey. I listen to you."

Rosie gave her the look and moved to the makeup station. "When?" Whatever she'd been about to share would have to wait apparently.

Sterling rested his forearms on his thighs. "I mean today's issue. Have you seen Twitter?"

She shrugged. "Yes. Rosie showed me. It's nothing."

"Nothing? We're trending, which would be great. Except it's angry trending. People watch you. You need to be more careful. As your media specialist—"

"You think I don't know I'm scrutinized? I've lived this way for years." She held out her hand to allow Rosie to massage essential oils into it.

Sterling lifted an eyebrow. "Then you should have known better than to invite this current outrage."

"Outrage? I had lunch with an old friend. Why should that outrage anyone? I think it's ludicrous this is even being discussed. You guys need to mind your own business."

"As the media specialist for the show, it *is* my business. Twitter is blowing up with pictures of you with some guy when we've been trying to spin a potential romance between the two of us. Now the fans are disgruntled and that isn't good for the show. We need everyone to love Kimberly Wantland and watch our show religiously. Not slut shame you."

"*Slut* shame? How dare you! I haven't been on a date in years. No one cares more about my show than I do. I don't need you spinning anything. And you call me a liar? We all know there's nothing going on between us. Be honest, oh media specialist guru." She leaned back, heart racing and breathing rapid. So "spinning" false feelings explained his recent kindnesses and invitations for dinner? How gullible she was to think he might actually be developing affection for her.

"Relax," Rosie admonished her. "Getting riled up won't help anything."

Sterling ran his fingers through his hair. Somehow it looked even better mussed. "Look, I don't want to butt into your business, but this is a bad idea all around. Tell her the rule, Rosie."

Rosie, rubbing lavender oil into Kimberly's hand, frowned. "What rule?"

"The never go back rule. You absolutely cannot get back together with an ex."

Rosie hesitated.

Kimberly laughed. "You're asking the wrong person. Rosie has been known to go back a time or two. Or three."

"What? I get lonely, okay?"

"And I'm not getting back together with Jason. So calm down." She sipped her tea. "Are we going to talk about the ghost in your room last night?"

Rosie did a double take. "Sterling saw a ghost last night?"

"If you'd been at footage review, you would have heard all about it. A girl in a white gown."

"Sterling saw a ghost last night?" Rosie repeated, looking at him for confirmation.

Sterling squirmed. "I don't know what I saw. Let's not call it a ghost."

"Spectral manifestation?" she suggested.

"Unknown vision. Perhaps an illusion my mind conjured before I was fully awake."

"You told me you were fully awake. Even thought it was me and followed her into the bathroom. You were pretty shaken."

"I'm less convinced now. Although I might feel better if you stayed with me tonight. Just in case."

Rosie laughed. "I agree. That's the safest option. Definitely." She pushed his arm. "You nut. You're so ornery."

"I made dinner reservations. No backing out. You promised me dinner."

He burst into her trailer, chewed her out for having lunch with a friend, and criticized her for damaging the show's popularity. Now he jokingly invited her to spend the night with him and expected to have dinner together. And guys thought women were confounding. "I guess I did promise."

"Where are you going?" Rosie asked.

Sterling shook his head. "That's a secret. I don't want anyone showing up unexpectedly. Kimberly and I have some things to discuss."

Rosie's eyebrows arched. "I'll be waiting to hear about that when we prep for the shoot tonight."

CHAPTER THIRTY-FOUR

Kimberly didn't know how Sterling managed to secure a reservation at The Grotto, much less a secluded table adjacent to the natural spring babbling beside them at short notice. But she approved. The low light, the candle on the table, the natural stone wall of the historic building all combined for a superb ambience. She felt more relaxed than she had all day.

She finished her salad and folded her arms on the table, meeting Sterling's gaze. "Have you ever even entertained the idea that perhaps you're sensitive?"

Sterling shrugged in an "aw, shucks" gesture. "What can I say? I admit to being a sensitive guy."

"Not what I meant. Sensitive as in sensitive to paranormal activity. You've told me about repeated experiences at three in the morning. And you're the first person in the crew to actually see a ghost on this investigation. Not see evidence on a recording. To actually see a ghost."

He rubbed the back of his neck. "This isn't really the conversation I wanted to have tonight. How was your salad?"

"I almost licked the plate." She took in the natural rock walls and the running stream. "This really is fabulous. What a great place."

"Agreed. Coming early helped get a good table. And I made sure no one else would be here."

"Really? How?"

"I asked around the crew to see what everyone else was doing for dinner. Then I bumped into Jason in the lobby. He asked me if I knew where you were going for dinner and I told him I was taking you to Caribe, this great little Caribbean cantina that uses locally grown food. I suspect he's at a table there right now, waiting for us to walk in. If he could get a table. I tried for reservations there but they were booked." He watched her carefully as he sipped from his water glass.

"Mean, but ingenious."

"You're not mad I tricked him?"

She shrugged. "I'm enjoying this. And the solitude is refreshing. I don't think anyone has noticed us. Or if they did, they're being really chill about it." Her cell phone lit up with a text. She knew the number. "That's the woman who stays in my house while I'm away."

More drama last night.

"Damn," she said, returning the phone and wishing for a drink.

"What's up?"

"She knows to watch for anything unusual around the house. Apparently something happened last night."

"I think you ought to investigate your house. Seems like the perfect *Wantland* episode. Where it all began."

"Like I said, my dad forbid it in his will. He says I brought enough shame on the family without dragging cameras into the home where my mother died and making a circus out of our family tragedy. He knew I wanted to investigate. Even though my aunt let me buy it back, she insisted I at least honor his last wishes and never record a show there."

"Because of your mom? You never told me what happened," he murmured.

"Yes I did. She died."

"You know what I mean. Sounds like the circumstances were questionable."

She tapped her foot. "They were . . . unresolved. And thanks to my dad and now my aunt, they'll probably stay that way."

"I'll bet Jason knows the story."

Lunch still fresh on her mind, she bristled. "Of course he does. He's the only one." She considered flagging down the waiter and ordering a glass of red wine but knew Sterling would revel in her rule breaking.

"You didn't tell Michael?"

"Oh, right. Michael. Yes, he knows."

"So what's one more?"

"This is how super villains learn secret identities. One person finds out, then one more, then one more. Pretty soon the entire town knows."

He sat back and crossed his arms, eyeing her closely. "Now I have to reshuffle my preconceived notions of you yet again. Never pegged you as the comic book type. Figured you were more cerebral than that."

"I believe I mentioned my lonely, friendless childhood. I filled it with all sorts of reading materials. Besides, I kind of related to—" She turned away, reached for the wine glass that wasn't there, and drank deeply from her green tea instead. "You know, I'd say Cerebro would be a terrific nickname except it's already taken."

"Seriously? Who is he?"

"Seriously? How can you not know about the X-Men? The mutants? At least Hugh Jackman." She could almost hear the hearts around his name as she said it.

"Ohhh. Wolverine. That one I know. Never paid much attention to those stories. Of course, I don't relate. I'm not concealing a secret ability." He leaned forward and sought eye contact. "I've been told I look a little like Hugh Jackman."

She drained her teacup. Apparently he'd heard the little

hearts, too. "Really?" She searched for the waiter. *Where did he disappear to?*

Sterling flexed a bicep. "Maybe not as ripped. Okay, not ripped at all." He grinned sheepishly.

Having seen him shirtless, she knew that wasn't true. "Oh, please. You look good and you know it. Women fall all over you."

"I didn't have two women in my bed last night."

"And I didn't have two men. That's all in your mind. Pinkie promise." She held out her hand, little finger extended.

He didn't offer his. "I kind of doubt the veracity of your pinkie promises. We pinkie swore earlier and you haven't fulfilled your end of the deal. What happened to your mom?"

She puffed her cheeks and blew out a long sigh. A quick glance assured her the other diners continued to pay more attention to their food than to her. Their isolated table made eavesdropping all but impossible.

"My dad wasn't home from work yet. Mom's hours ended earlier in the day so she could be home shortly after I got home from school. That day, I ran down to see her when I heard the door. We met in the kitchen, like always. She made a snack for me, like always. Cheese and crackers that afternoon. I remember her saying, 'Cheers,' and toasting with one before popping it in her mouth. She said she was going to make spaghetti and meatballs for dinner." She paused to dab her eyes.

Sterling reached for her hand as the waiter appeared with their meals.

"Can I bring anything else?" he asked as he gathered their salad plates. "More tea, perhaps?"

"Yes, bring her more green tea." Sterling lifted an eyebrow. "And maybe some wine?"

She blew her nose and shook her head. "I can't. Really. But you go ahead. A glass shouldn't bother you."

"What's your favorite? What would you order if you intended to drink?"

"Merlot."

"Excellent taste. Bring us your best merlot," he instructed the waiter. "A single glass."

Sterling sliced into his steak, eyes on the plate as he cut the slice into bite-sized pieces. "So, cheese and crackers," he prompted, as casually as if commenting on her blouse.

Which he hadn't done yet, and she picked this because she thought he'd like it. She reached across the table and forked a bite of steak from his plate. "Cheers."

He feigned a scowl. "Alright, you. Next time we go out, I'm ordering steak for you. Enough of this fish preference ruse."

She nudged her plate toward him. "Have some of my salmon. Sharing is better. This way we can order two favorites and get to enjoy both."

His eyes practically glowed in the candlelight. He took a bite of the proffered fish. "You're right. Two is better than one."

She ducked her head to hide the flush she felt certain pinked her cheeks. Why did she encourage this? She didn't need the complication of a romantic entanglement at work. If Sterling even had any feelings for her. This afternoon he seemed focused only on increasing their fan base. Tonight he seemed far friendlier.

The waiter returned with the wine. Uncertain where to place it, he held it over the table waiting for instruction.

"Here," Sterling directed. "She doesn't drink."

"Yes, sir. Enjoy your meals." He clasped his hands together and backed away.

Sterling sipped and encouraged her to continue. "So, cheese and crackers?"

"Right. After the snack, I went to my room. Mom started cooking. Maybe thirty minutes later, I heard something in the kitchen."

"Heard what?"

"It sounded like a scuffle. Then I heard a pot clang and a loud thump. It scared me so I started downstairs to see what happened. Halfway down, I heard my mom call me. From upstairs. Which made no sense. Their master bedroom was downstairs. Besides I would have heard her footsteps if she came up."

"Maybe an echo from downstairs?"

"I thought the same sort of thing, though it didn't sound like it. Confused, I turned and went back up, calling for her. I went toward the loft, but then she called again. From my bedroom. It was no echo. I knew she hadn't been in my room and couldn't have passed me on the stairs. I crept to my room, pushed the door wide . . ."

She closed her eyes at the memory and shook her head.

"And?"

"You won't believe me. I know you won't. But I saw her sitting on my bed. Except it wasn't her. She looked wrong. Translucent, like a mist. She reminded me of the projection of Princess Leia in *Star Wars*. I could see her, but I could see through her. I think I said, 'Mom?' She held her arms out to me. I was so scared I backed away. I turned and ran downstairs to the kitchen. And there she was sprawled on the floor."

Sterling grabbed her hand and squeezed as tears spilled down her cheeks. "I am so sorry. I didn't realize you were there when she . . . I don't know what to say."

She took a deep breath. "I ran back upstairs to my room but she was gone. My bed was empty. I realized I should call 911. My dad walked in the door as I was fumbling with the phone. I was shaking so hard I couldn't dial. He called and then he stood over her, rubbing his face and crying. He scooped me up and collapsed into a chair. Asked if I knew what happened. Of course, I had no idea. But then I told him she was still in the house, that I'd seen her and I needed to find where she went. I tried to get out of his lap, but he held me close. The paramedics arrived. While they tried to resuscitate her, I searched every room in the house. I didn't see her anywhere. Maybe if I'd called for help faster, she could have been saved. She was pronounced on the scene."

She raised her face and found Sterling's eyes full of sorrow and sympathy.

"I'm so sorry. How old were you?"

"Ten."

"What a nightmare. What . . . took her? What caused it?"

"We don't know. That's the strangest part. The autopsy revealed nothing. She was determined to be in the peak of health. And yet she fell down dead."

"Wait, what? That's not possible."

"And yet, that's what happened."

"But that doesn't make any sense. Something had to cause her death."

"I'm sure something did. But medically speaking, she was perfect. Tore my dad up. And I only made it worse, insisting she was still in the house. He grew angry with me. So I stopped talking about it. But I watched for her. I wanted so badly to see her again. I think she wanted to hug me, to say goodbye, when she reached for me. And I was so scared, I ran away. I didn't say goodbye. That was the first time I truly realized I see ghosts."

"Did you ever think you saw her again?"

"Sometimes. Maybe. Not like that first time, when I saw her clearly and she smiled and reached for me. But once in a while as I fell asleep or woke up, I detected a presence and thought I caught a glimpse of her. And occasionally I smelled her lavender and freesia perfume. And I didn't feel as threatened by the other presence. The one I think may have been a demon. I think she protected me from him. In fact, I wonder if that's what killed her." She spoke the last bit to her plate, afraid of his reaction.

"You think a demon killed your mom?"

"I heard some sort of scuffle before I found her dead. Something caused it. But there were no marks on her. Why not the demon? The doctors couldn't explain it."

"But maybe they overlooked something or . . . I don't know. Something other than a demon."

"And why are you so sure?"

"Because demons don't exist."

"You haven't seen one yourself, perhaps. Or maybe you have but won't admit it. That doesn't mean they don't exist. I don't know for sure this presence was a demon. But I know there was something in that house. And I think it killed my mom. I worry about her being stuck there with some horrible thing that killed her. Alone for so many years. I left. Then Dad passed away. Aunt Dolly couldn't keep renters in it, and it sat empty. She sold it to me but insists on no ghost hunting. Mom might still be there. And I could help her transition. At least I have someone staying in the house now. But I can't investigate."

Sterling eyed her. "It's your house. How can they possibly enforce that?"

"I don't want to cause a rift. Unless Aunt Dolly eases up and gives permission on his behalf, I can't do any paranormal investigating there."

He finished his food. "I'll call a friend of mine. An attorney. I'll see what he says." He downed the remainder of the wine. "Let's go bust some ghosts."

CHAPTER THIRTY-FIVE

KIMBERLY SHOOK out her arms and legs, hoping to dissipate the nervous energy. All Rosie's massage and aroma therapy, all her pre-investigation relaxation exercises, and all Michael's assurances tonight would be the night were lost in a sea of anxiety, waves tossing her like a bit of driftwood.

She shivered, her thin blouse no barrier against the clammy air. Still fully illuminated, the laundry room nonetheless seeped gloom and despair. Without the usual warmth from tumbling driers and the cheery chatter of employees, the room sulked, dank and dreary.

Another guest attacked. When Selma reached out to her, requesting investigation and assistance, she'd reported Clara's experience only. The attacks had continued, but they were sporadic.

Though she was here to solve the problem, she couldn't help but think she was escalating it instead. An attack a day since she'd arrived. Two nights raised only more questions. Sure, they'd ruled out a couple of leads but they'd discovered many more.

Sterling leaned against the wall, picking at his fingernails. He glanced at her and gestured her over.

No desire to revisit their dinner conversation, she shook her head. Clutching her quartz, she breathed deeply, willing herself to relax.

Sterling came to her. "Hey, ummm . . ."

"Really, Sterling, not right now. I need to relax and don't want to talk about anything personal. Please."

"Yeah, I get that. But when we got back from dinner, and I went to my room, all the lights were on. I know I turned them off."

Breathe in. Gather the stress. Breathe out. Relax. "Maybe you forgot. It happens."

"I know I turned them off. Plus, the lamp was on and I haven't used it even once. I couldn't find the switch."

"Oh. Well—"

"And the water was running in the sink. And the bathtub."

"Okay, I can't even see the absent-minded professor doing that."

"So how'd you get into my room?"

"Get into your . . . I went straight to my trailer for pre-show prep and makeup. Rosie will tell you."

At the sound of her name, Rosie joined them. "Tell him what, girl? That your lipstick shade is Cute and Kissable?"

Not in the mood. She loved her Rosie, but didn't feel flirty or playful at the moment. She pressed her fingers to her temples. "That I didn't sneak off to his room. I was in the trailer with you until we came here together."

"As much as I'd like to imagine her sneaking off for a quickie before the show, alas, she did not leave my side."

"Rosie!" Even Sterling blushed a bit at her suggestion.

"I think Jack has been messing with him."

Sterling sighed. "Look, I know someone was in my room. I called housekeeping and they assured me no one has been in my room since this morning. And they would never leave lights on and water running. Was it TJ? Who's messing with me?"

Selma appeared at her side, laughing softly. "I told you Jack would have fun with you, Sterling. Relax and enjoy. There's no stopping him." The older woman pulled her aside. "Kimberly, I've given a lot of thought to our previous conversation. I don't feel good about releasing additional spirits. Let's focus on the one scratching the guests and him alone."

Why would she feel so strongly about keeping ghosts who were miserable in the hotel? "If you'd look at the footage we recorded, I think you might change your mind. I know what I saw and felt."

Selma patted her arm. "Just the one ghost. Leave the rest."

Elise joined the cluster. "Kimberly, I spent the afternoon trying to track down more information on the student who jumped to her death."

Finally, some information. "And?"

"I didn't find anything."

She couldn't hide the disappointment. "I was really hoping for something more to go on tonight."

"Sorry," Elise said. "This happened back in the early nineteen hundreds. No Internet to look up news articles. And not much in the local paper. Like I said, the death was covered up and kept quiet. They intentionally hushed it up."

"Okay. I appreciate your work. Keep digging I guess."

Everyone looked to her to solve this. Without a starting point, she didn't know who to reach out to. She needed to make progress. No one else would be scratched by the angry ghost on her watch. She knew if she could find him and connect, she could resolve whatever revenge motivated his lashing out.

Michael clapped his hands once. "Let's flip the lights and go dark."

Standing in the dark space, she clutched her quartz and breathed deeply. The room seemed to breathe too, a desolate sigh as if resigning itself to this intrusion. She sent positive energy into the space, reassurance she meant no harm. She wanted only to help.

Michael spoke softly, "And five, four, three . . . "

She knew he silently finished counting down on his fingers.

They'd done this for years. Time to begin. "Whoever haunts this hotel seeking revenge, can you tell me what's wrong? I know you are restless. Revenge rarely ends well, though. And right now, you're only hurting innocent people. Let me help you resolve this."

Something ruffled her hair. A slight chill played across the back of her neck. The basement room had no windows and no exterior doors—no source for a breeze. She concentrated, hoping to detect a presence. She shivered as something passed behind her again, a quiet, whispered kiss against her ear. She couldn't make out the words, only the soft cadence of a voice.

She turned her head toward the sound, ears straining. *Come on. Talk to me.* "Who is with us?"

"Kimmy, talk to me," Michael said. "What's happening?"

"Not sure. I thought I heard something. Maybe someone trying to connect."

"Guys?" Michael asked. "What do you see? Anything around Kimmy?"

"Sweeping the room," Stan said. "So far nothing. You get anything on the mike?"

"I didn't. Thermoscan indicating minor temperature fluctuations. Nothing exciting yet. Elise, how's the KII?"

"Higher EMF than the ambient control reading from earlier, but not spiking. Nothing crazy."

"I thought I might have seen a shadow on the FLIR," TJ said, "but just a blip. Might've been nothing."

Another whisper hissed behind her, trailing another cold kiss of breath against her ear. "I hear you, but I don't understand. Can you tell me who you are?" Silence. "Something is trying to manifest but either isn't strong enough or isn't completely convinced it wants to. Do we want to bring in a few batteries?"

"Not if there's another way," Michael said. "I don't want to risk unintentionally charging up something we don't want to deal with."

Another whisper, frustratingly close and yet maddeningly unintelligible.

Draining her psychic energy this early in the investigation would simply result in another early night with no results. But she reached out, pushing as much as she dared. The whispers had been real. Someone wanted to communicate.

She visualized casting a fishing line over and over. When nothing bit, she changed to a lighthouse shining her beacon as far as she could. *Come back. Talk to me.* Her hand fisted so tightly around the quartz, it ached and throbbed. Her temples pulsed from the strain.

The voice in her ear, clear and strong, said only two words.

She gasped and whirled. Something had stood behind her. She knew without a doubt. But though her sixth sense tingled from the apparition's residue, nothing remained. It had ghosted, so to speak.

"Kimmy, what is it?"

"Did anyone catch anything behind me?"

"I had my camera on you," Stan said, "but didn't happen to see anything. Might show up during review."

"Nothing visible on the FLIR," TJ said.

"I saw a brief spike in EMF but nothing alarming," Elise said.

She held her hands out as if she could ward off the spirit toying with her. "Brief audible directly behind me. Female in nature. Possible physical manifestation. I felt something but cannot confirm by visual."

"What did it say?" Michael asked.

"He's coming."

CHAPTER THIRTY-SIX

THE ROOM BRISTLED with hushed anticipation. Her crew shuffled. Her eyes widened and her ears strained, anxious for something further.

"Who is?" Selma asked, anxiety in her normally unflappable voice. "Who's coming?"

"Ms. Reddick, are you okay?" Michael asked. "If this is too stressful for you, maybe you should go on to bed. We can update you tomorrow."

"No. No, I'm sorry," Selma replied. "I'll be quiet."

"Okay, guys. Cute. Very funny." Sterling spoke from the position he'd taken up at the back of the room. "Seriously. Stop it. Who the hell is poking me in the back?"

She heard scuffling sounds and assumed Sterling turned circles, trying to catch his antagonist.

"TJ? Is that you?"

"Dude. I'm over here by Ms. Wantland. Get a grip, Noob."

"What the hell did you call me? Okay, seriously. Stop messing with me. I get it. Haze the new guy. Ha ha. You've had your joke."

"No one is near you, Sterling," Michael said. "Stan is by me. I see you on his camera. You're alone."

"Holy shit," TJ said. "Not according to the FLIR he isn't. I'm seeing a heat signature directly behind him."

"What?" Sterling demanded. "What's behind me?"

"Let me see." Kimberly moved to stand beside TJ. His display indeed indicated a possible presence.

"EMF spiking," Elise announced.

"Temperature around Sterling dropping," Michael said. "I'm moving closer."

"Someone pulled my hair," Sterling said. "So not cool."

"Sterling, be still," she instructed. "We're detecting a manifestation near you."

"Oh, stop trying to sound science-y. You know I don't believe a ghost is harassing me."

She felt a presence, cold and hostile, drifting like a fog through the room. This was not the same spirit who had whispered in her ear, who seemed to have fled after its warning. This one was different. Angry. Maybe they were finally getting somewhere. She needed to connect and determine what motivated it.

Closing her eyes, she reached out with her psychic energy, inviting the presence to come to her. If she connected, she could get an idea what it wanted, why it was angry. She focused, trying to determine precisely where the entity was in the room.

"Holy shit!" TJ's outburst in the silence sent a jolt through her nervous system. "Something is all over Sterling. I can see it. Like a cloud around him."

"This is not funny," Sterling said, brushing his hands over his arms. "I feel like I have spider webs all over me. How are you doing this? And what is it?"

She peered at the FLIR images. A roughly human form hovered behind Sterling, while a dark cloud surrounded him, tendrils passing over his arms. "This is it! We have a confirmed manifestation. Immediately behind Sterling. Human form. Or human-ish at least. Appears to be extending its energy field around Sterling, possibly with the intent to antagonize. This is not a repeater. We have an intelligent specter."

"EMF approaching one hundred thirty," Elise said.

"Kimmy, get over there. See if you can make contact or something."

"Already on it."

Sterling yelped. "I call uncle. That's all I can take. Kimberly, please. Make them stop."

"Be still, Sterling. I'm coming to you. I think this ghost feeds off fear so try to stay calm." The panic in his voice sent anxiety pulsing through her. She took several deep breaths and focused on calming her racing heart. Whatever this thing was, it delighted in tormenting and frightening people. She felt grotesque glee alongside the raging anger throbbing through the room, the energy radiating, pulsating as it grew in strength.

Sterling latched onto her the moment she reached his side.

"Shhh. It's okay," she soothed him. "Deep breaths. It can't hurt you." Though that last bit might not be true, she had to calm him down.

"How are you doing this? And why?" The betrayal in his voice cut her to the quick.

She threw her arms around him, tightening him against her, and enveloped him in her psychic energy. Thinking only positive thoughts, she envisioned her heart chakra spinning green and bright and willed friendship and compassion down her arms and through her fingertips. The specter attempted to further poke and prod Sterling but her barrier shielded him from the nasty little presence. Holding tight to Sterling, she absorbed the impact from the would-be antagonist. Putting herself between them offered a brief connection and some insight.

Anger, fury, hate. Images of scratching. Revenge.

Sterling gasped. "What did you do?"

"You wouldn't believe me if I told you."

"It's gone. How—"

She shivered and shook off the aftertaste of negative energy the specter coated her with. "The power of a hug. But it isn't gone. It only moved away from you. I still feel him."

"Feel what?" Sterling asked.

"Our culprit. Jasper the Angry Ghost. Mr. Revenge. Whatever you want to call him."

"Kimmy," Michael said. "Can you speak up? Did you say this is the one?"

She turned to face Stan's camera. "This is him. He doesn't want to connect but I got through for a moment. He's vicious. I saw scratched arms. Felt his anger and lust for revenge.'"

"I felt sick with dread," Sterling said. "But when you hugged me, it went away. I felt warmth and encouragement. What did you do?"

She rested a hand on his arm. "I used my chakras that you don't believe in—"

Something shoved her from behind, sending her sprawling forward. She landed hard on her palms and knees.

Sterling knelt beside her. "Are you okay?"

The lights flickered on and off. The washers and driers spun to life, then fell silent. The crew twisted left and right attempting to capture the sporadic activity. The lights went out, plunging the room into darkness. All the lights on the washing machines lit up at once.

She scrambled off the floor, alarmed by her crew crying out.

"I felt a cold gust," Michael said.

"Something brushed my arm," Elise called. "EMF over one fifty. Unreal."

"This thing is all over the place," TJ said. "I can't keep a bead on him."

Stan cried out, then apologized for the outburst. "Sorry. I saw a face swoop at my camera. Startled me."

Everything went quiet.

Rosie screamed. "My arm! Something cut my arm!"

CHAPTER THIRTY-SEVEN

THE SOUND of Rosie crying out in pain chilled Kimberly to the bone. She hurried to her stylist. Selma already stood beside Rosie, inspecting the injury.

"Looks exactly like Clara's cuts," Selma commented.

"And Suzie's." She took Rosie's arm in her hands, accepting the tissue Michael handed her to blot the seeping wound. "You okay?"

Rosie sniffed but nodded. "I'm not usually directly involved like this. It scared me."

"Understandable." Her stylist shook. "I'm sorry. Breathe and try to relax."

Rosie laughed softly. "This is a switch. I'm supposed to help you recover after an experience."

"I know. You're not supposed to be in harm's way." She gritted her teeth. "This has gone too far. Selma, can you bandage Rosie's arm?"

"Of course, dear."

"Really, Kimberly, I'm fine," Rosie protested. Her shaky voice belied the truth.

Kimberly squared her shoulders and wrapped her hand

around her quartz. Taking a deep breath, she concentrated all her energy toward her indigo chakra.

"Come to me!" she commanded. "I won't let you hurt or scare anyone any longer." She held out her arm. "Want to scratch someone? Scratch me."

"Kimmy, maybe you shouldn't antagonize—"

"I don't care. I'm the one he should deal with instead of skulking around tormenting and terrifying people."

The room didn't so much as whisper to her. The tomb-like silence pounded her eardrums. Or perhaps that was only her blood whooshing through her ears.

The washing machine lights continued to blink, appearing to race around the room like the fairway of an amusement park.

"I don't see anything," TJ whispered. "Is it gone?"

"Can't be," Michael said. "The lights are still freaking out."

"And EMF nearing one sixty," Elise added.

"Where is it?" TJ asked. "I got nothing."

"I'm trying to pinpoint. Everyone quiet." Kimberly cast a wider net. "Where are you? You coward. Come deal with someone who can handle you."

No one moved.

No one breathed.

She shivered.

A slight breeze lifted tendrils of her hair. Her skin crackled with energy. The air around her turned frigid.

A rush of air gusted against her, knocking the wind out of her. Gasping, she watched the image of a rotting corpse materialize on the far side of the room. It rose toward the ceiling and flew across the room directly at her. Instinctively, she threw her hands up to block the specter.

It passed through her. She tasted decay and earth, cobwebs and dust. The stench of death filled her nostrils. She held her breath.

This is what I have become, a voice hissed in her ear. *Revenge.*

She turned around in time to see the specter blast out the door and turn down the hall.

The door slammed shut.

She ran after him. "Don't let him get away. That's our ghost."

She slammed into the door, throwing it open, and raced down the hall.

Only dimly aware of the shuffling sounds indicating her crew hustled behind her, she channeled everything into keeping a bead on the ghost. The crew knew how to do their job and depended on her to lead the way.

She ran past the spa. Realizing she'd lost the thread, she turned to retrace her steps. The trail went cold in the middle of the hall.

She spun in a circle, feeling, casting about, until the ceiling drew her attention. Of course. Ghosts weren't limited to floors and hallways. He'd taken a shortcut upstairs.

She tore down the hall, took the stairs two at a time, and burst into the lobby, startling the young man at the desk. He smoothed his hair and waved. She doubled over to catch her breath.

Her crew caught up with her. Rosie rested a hand on her back. "You okay? Need to recharge?"

"I think I'm okay. He definitely used me as a springboard and took some energy, but he was already hot. He didn't need me. He was only making a point."

"I'm not surprised," Michael said between gulps of air. "The way he messed with the lights and machinery."

TJ swept the room with the FLIR. "Seriously. He owned that laundry room."

Sterling scowled. "Who did what to the laundry room?"

TJ gave him an eye roll from hell. "The ghost. He owned the laundry room. Jeez. How old are you, old man?"

"Old enough to be annoyed by your slang. Speak English."

"Chill, old dude."

Kimberly held up her hands. "Everyone chill. TJ, are you getting anything? Stan?"

"I've got something!" TJ said. "Two figures coming this way from the conservatory!"

"Yeah, we all see those." Sterling pushed the FLIR down.

"Hey!"

"Look with your eyes. They're human."

Two twenty-something girls teetered toward them on heels, champagne sloshing from plastic flutes with each step. They leaned on each other and giggled.

"Oh, honey. Why do brides do that to their bridesmaids?" Michael asked, clucking his tongue. "Those dresses are hideous."

"And those girls are a train wreck," Kimberly said, noting they'd spotted Sterling.

"Meh." Rosie shrugged. "I know train wreck. They're a big hot mess. I wouldn't go train wreck yet."

"Oh. Em. Gee." One of the girls staggered over to Sterling and leaned on his arm, blinking her matted eyelashes at him. "Are you guys chasing a ghost?"

The other girl stumbled with a giggled, "Woops!" and fell against his other arm. "Ohmygosh I'd be so scared."

Kimberly took a step toward Sterling, fists balled.

Rosie grabbed her arm. "Save your strength, sweetie. Let a pro handle this. I've got your back."

Rolling up her sleeves, Rosie moved to intervene. But Sterling extricated himself.

"Sorry, girls," he said, sliding deftly out of range. "I'm only along for the ride. See that guy? With the camera? His name is TJ. You should've seen him a few minutes ago. He stood up to the ghost while I hid in the corner."

Two heads swiveled toward TJ. Four thickly-lashed eyelids batted at him.

TJ shuffled his feet, cleared his throat, and shrugged. "I did. Yeah. Totally. Ghosts . . . no big thang."

The girls shifted their attentions, wobbling to flank TJ. "Aren't you ever scared?"

"Nah. Ghosts can't hurt us. They're just residual energy," TJ said. "Well, most of the time."

Michael cleared his throat. "We were trailing a ghost. And our time is extremely limited, so if you ladies will excuse us."

TJ juggled his camera in one hand and extended the other. "Nice to meet you both. Maybe I'll bump into you sometime tomorrow."

One of the girls thrust a hand inside her clutch and fished out a room key, which she pressed into TJ's hand. "Come see us later tonight. The number is on the key."

The girls giggled and tottered toward the elevator, turning over their shoulders to wave at TJ while they waited for the lift.

TJ stared at the key in his hand, stunned expression on his face.

Sterling clapped him on the shoulder. "Well played."

"Um, thanks, I guess." He held up the key. "What do you think I should do with this?"

Kimberly wanted to give her opinion of what he should do with it, but held her tongue, preferring to hear Sterling's advice.

"You do what you think is appropriate."

"What would you do?" TJ asked.

"I demonstrated what I would do. I had no interest in that key. Those girls had a good time at a friend's wedding tonight, but they're not thinking clearly. Why else would they have approached someone so much older?" He gestured to himself.

"Because he's famous," Kimberly muttered to Rosie. "And still on TV thanks to my show, of course."

Rosie nodded. "Mmm-hmm. You got that right. Well, and he's hot. Who wouldn't want to hit that?"

She raised her eyebrows. "Seriously?"

"Objectively speaking, of course. I'm not saying I have any intentions of making a play for him. But I can appreciate a fine man."

TJ stuffed the key into the pocket of his jeans, blushing bright pink when she caught his eye.

Michael cleared his throat. "Shall we?"

She closed her eyes and attempted to find the ghost's residual plasma burning behind him. After wandering the lobby several minutes, hand clasped about her crystal, she gritted her teeth. "Thanks to that interruption, the trail has gone cold."

"Don't look at me," Sterling said. "I helped get rid of them."

True. And her estimation of him ratcheted up a few notches as a result. He had deflected their advances so skillfully he seemed to have practice. Maybe not quite the player she imagined him to be. Or had been Twitter'ed into believing. Plus, he'd managed to interact with TJ without either of them snapping at each other.

"What next, sweetie?" Michael asked.

"Let's try the usual approach. Fan out and see what we stumble onto. I'm ready to find this guy and end this tonight."

Sterling approached and rested a hand on her lower back, sending a warm thrill up her spine. "Do you mind if I stay by you?"

"Going to keep an eye on me? Watch for sleight of hand?"

He cocked his head. "How did you do it? I confess you've confounded me. You probably don't want to share your secret but I'd like to know. Something really made my skin crawl. It wasn't my imagination."

She crossed her arms. "Did you ever consider other people don't invent or imagine their alarming experiences? That's why they call me for help. Just like you did." She nudged him with an elbow.

He smirked. "That hug was worth it. If you hug everyone like that, no wonder you get thousands of requests every day."

A warm flush crept up her cheeks. "No way. I save those for special occasions." She didn't mention it drained her chakras.

"Well, I'm going to stick by your side in case one of us needs help."

Rosie leaned against her. "I was going to ask if you needed to recharge but I can see you're pretty fired up already."

She narrowed her eyes at Rosie's insinuation. "Don't try to get out of work like that. How's the arm, though?"

"It's just a scratch. Shook me up more than anything."

She didn't like the brooding look in her stylist's eyes. A brooding Rosie was never a good thing. She raised an eyebrow but Rosie shook her head.

"We'll talk later."

Rosie wanted to talk? Something was bothering her.

"Ms. Wantland." TJ's hushed voice grabbed her attention. "Something by the stairs."

"Are those girls back?"

"No, ma'am. Single entity. Hovering near the staircase."

"Hovering?"

"Appears to be. Trailing, diffuse edge several inches off the floor."

"I'm not as fully charged as I thought," she told Rosie. "TJ spotted a presence before I felt it."

Awareness coupled with the spirit's willingness to bond resulted in a strong connection. She breathed deeply and allowed the full connection the ghost appeared to be inviting. Their two cognitions clicked together.

"It's Ms. Theodora," she said as images of bedpans, syringes, vials of medication (or the mixture she injected into her patients believing it was mediation), blankets, and weeping patients played through her mind. "I'll follow her. The rest of you spread out wherever we aren't."

Ms. Theodora lifted a translucent hand, beckoned, then turned and floated up the staircase.

Kimberly allowed energy to flow along her connection to Ms. Theodora. The nurse's apron and cap appeared. Sharing energy with a ghost willing to communicate could mean the difference between gleaning new information and walking away with nothing. She'd learned early on how to balance the ebb and flow, like someone learning their tolerance for alcohol. She could still be caught off guard but in general knew her limits.

"Michael, sta-cam on the piano tonight?" she called over her shoulder.

"Already set it up," Stan replied, trailing behind her, camera recording her interactions.

"I'm staying with Kimberly," Sterling announced, long legs vaulting him up the stairs to her side.

"We remaining girls should stick together," Rosie said, presumably pairing off with Elise.

"What exactly do you 'see' that you're following?" Sterling asked as they neared the second floor landing.

"A ghost. I thought we'd established that."

"But what does it look like? Like the librarian in *Ghostbusters*?"

"Actually, yes, though not as clearly defined."

High-pitched giggling preceded a little girl skipping down the hall. She jumped to avoid a collision. "Whoa! Slow down, sweetie. Shouldn't you be in bed?"

The girl continued without so much as a glance.

Sterling grabbed her arm. "Who are you talking to?"

"That little girl. Right there." His furrowed brow told her he wasn't teasing. "You didn't see her?"

He looked up and down the hall. "We're completely alone."

"Well, *that* ghost looked like a little girl."

Ms. Theodora beckoned again.

"Interesting. She wants us here on the second floor. I was sure she'd take us up to three. To the psych ward."

"I wish I could see what you see," Sterling said.

"Me too. Although you felt a ghost in the laundry room. Similar to when I passed out near the psych ward during the tour. Imagine not only one but dozens of ghosts pulling at you. That was a tactile experience if not visual."

"But I want to see something. I want . . . " He gestured as if he couldn't find the right word.

"Yes?"

"I want proof you're not scamming me like all the others. I don't think you are, but I want something tangible."

"I can't let you see through my eyes any more than I can see through yours. And trust me, some days I'd gladly swap."

"It's possible, though, that you set something up in the laundry room to make me feel weird. Or you could have hallucinations and truly believe you see something. That at least would be honest. You wouldn't intentionally be tricking me."

She stopped, leaving Ms. Theodora tapping her foot, and swept a lock of hair behind her ear. Stan remained inconspicuous, but she felt the ever-present lens on her. She met Sterling's gaze directly. "Has anyone ever told you they loved you?"

He raised an eyebrow and huffed. "Of course."

"Did you believe them?"

"Well, yeah."

"Why? How did you know? What convinced you?"

"I don't—people show you they love you. Do nice things. Gaze at you adoringly."

"But people confuse a lot of things with love. Infatuation, desire, celebrity crushes. To name only a few. And people will do just about anything to get what they want."

He scrubbed the back of his neck. "I suppose there is truth to that."

"Sometimes people truly believe they're in love but when push comes to shove realize they were mistaken."

"These two things really aren't comparable. You're comparing human emotion with imaginary ghost visions."

She grasped both sides of his face. "Do I look confused? Out of my mind? Because right now I'm more certain I see a ghost impatiently waving to us than I'm certain anyone ever truly loved me."

He brought his hand to rest on hers. "You definitely appear completely lucid."

He leaned closer and she forgot all about Ms. Theodora. She

heard the whir of Stan's camera zooming in for a close shot. *The Internet will go rabid, salivating all over this clip.*

Was he only playing for the camera? Hoping to send the fans into a wild frenzy? Though she could easily allow herself to keep going, she didn't want their first kiss on camera. She needed to know for sure it wasn't a publicity stunt, that he truly felt something for her. If she ever kissed him, she wanted it to be real. She broke away, sure—and hoping—he could see the disappointment in her eyes.

He took a deep breath and shuffled his feet. "Right. Sorry."

"I'm sorry, too. But I—"

"I know. Not in front of the camera."

"Hey, Wakefield," Stan said. "Which room are you in?"

"Two eighteen. Why?"

"I thought I saw a shadow in front of that room."

"My room?" Sterling twisted to peer down the hall.

"Ms. Theodora is down there. Which room is yours?"

Sterling led her toward his room until she grabbed his arm and tugged.

"You almost walked into her. Don't you feel how cold it is here?"

He looked at her like she had eight eyes. "Yes, but vents blow cold air."

"Not if the building doesn't have heat and air. She's right here in front of your room. And she seems to want us to go inside."

CHAPTER THIRTY-EIGHT

STERLING UNLOCKED his door and held it open for Kimberly.

She gestured Ms. Theodora inside ahead of them. "This is Jack's room. The teenage boy who teases and pranks guests. Why did she bring us here?"

"You're the Ghost Whisperer. Not me." Sterling flopped on his bed.

"You saw a ghost though. Last night."

He squirmed. "I probably dreamed it."

"Don't dismiss your experience. You said a girl in a white gown. Right?"

He nodded.

"How young?" She held her hand near her knee. "Little?"

"No. Not a child. A young woman. About your height."

"Right. You thought it was me at first for some inexplicable reason. I remember." The young woman in the mirror wore a gown. Was she his visitor? "White gown as in a hospital gown?"

"No. A nightgown. Lacy, I think. Ruffles maybe at the hem and cuffs."

"So not a patient. Probably not one of Norman Baker's victims. Could she be one of the girls from the Conservatory?"

Sterling blinked. "Are you asking me? Or the ghost?"

"Oh, sorry. Ms. Theodora dissipated. She must have used up all her energy bringing us to the room. Shame. I was hoping she'd show me something important."

"Such as?"

"I'm not sure." She looked around the room, then back at Sterling. "I'm sorry I didn't come back with you last night when you asked for help. I shouldn't have dismissed your fear like I did."

Sterling waved away her concern. "I wouldn't say fear. It was nothing. Just a nightmare. I overreacted."

"Well, no more. Stan, can we set up a camera in here? We discussed leaving one to try to catch Jack, but opted to focus more on our vengeful intruder."

"Wait," Sterling said. "Leave one in my room all the time?"

"We're pretty stretched on cameras, " Stan said. "But I can pull one from the grounds or the third floor. Rearrange a little bit to make sure we keep as much in the shot as possible."

"Hold up. I don't want a camera in my room while I'm asleep. That's creepy."

"Says The Almighty Social Media Guru who posts anything and everything online?"

"I told you I don't post anything that's truly personal."

"The intimate photo of us after a couple's massage wasn't personal?" Apparently that meant more to her than it did to him. "We don't use footage unless it captures something intriguing. Even though you posted the massage photo." She narrowed her eyes at him.

"So you're out for revenge now?"

"No. Just reminding you of the obvious. You're happy to post things others consider personal. Anyway, you'll get used to the camera. It'll be like it isn't even there."

"I doubt that. I don't think I'll be able to sleep at all with a camera on me."

That sounded final. His chakras lit up in a display so bright, she felt out of sorts. Kind of like a solar flare disrupting Earth's electronic field. His energies were blocked and he didn't know what to do about it.

She rested a hand on his sternum, closed her eyes, and sent her own energy to calm and soothe him.

His torso caved around her touch, hips rocking away from her. "Whoa there, Miss Not In Front of the Cameras. I won't be held liable for the consequences of your actions."

He did not, however, break away from her touch.

"Relax. You've let yourself get worked up."

He tugged at his pant leg. "Do I really have to explain you're working things up, too?"

Stan attempted and failed to stifle a laugh.

"I was trying for the opposite effect." She gave up, dropping her hand. "Stan, can you angle a camera in here to capture most of the room in the frame?"

The camera operator eyed the room and nodded. "Most of it. I think so."

Sterling adjusted his black jeans and tugged the hem of his T-shirt. "You're putting a camera in here against my wishes?"

"I feel strongly this room factors into the mystery. I don't know how. We need a camera in here if we hope to glean any clues that might help us understand what's going on." She would never admit it, but deep down she enjoyed making him squirm.

"Fine. But I'm not sleeping in here with a camera. I'll crash in your room tonight."

"Uh, no you won't. We're not doing that again."

His eyebrows shot up and his lips twitched into a smirk. "Why not? We had such a good time last time."

"Stop that!"

"We might as well start booking us into the same room. Why bother with separate when we wind up together anyway?"

Her face hardened into a scowl. "You know nothing happened between us."

He stepped closer, leaning over her. "Rooming together. Couples massage. Come on. Why deny it?"

Her heart raced at his nearness. *Damn it.* How did he do this to her? He spun the situation to his benefit yet again.

A ruckus in the hallway spared her from answering his question.

"Did anyone see where Kimmy went?"

She opened the door, breathing more easily with distance between her and Sterling, and stuck her head out. "We're here in Sterling's room."

Michael muttered something that sounded suspiciously snarky, then raised his voice. "We have activity on three."

She gestured to Stan to follow. "I knew three would be hot. Camera in here later." She shot a look at Sterling.

"Okay, but if the camera is in here, I'll be in your room."

Pushing past a ghost tour, registering but ignoring the murmurs and camera flashes, she hurried up the flight of stairs to the third floor. She found Rosie leaning against a wall, pale and quiet.

Elise stood nearby, dictating into a digital recorder. "Witness reports visual sighting and physical contact."

Rosie perked up a bit at the sight of her friend. "I saw a freakin' ghost, Kimberly. I swear I saw a ghost. And it, like, flew through me."

Kimberly pulled Rosie into a hug. Her stylist's skin crackled with residual energy. "It's okay. You're okay. Did you hear anything?"

"No. He appeared and then . . . " Rosie shuddered. "I don't know how else to describe it. He came toward me very quickly and then passed through me."

"Deep breaths. You're okay. I feel the energy on you from contact with a spirit. I know it's disconcerting, but it will wear off." She looked at her crew. "Anyone catch anything?"

Elise lifted the digital recorder. "I was right by her with this, trying to draw someone out with an EVP session. I've made note on the recording. If he responded, we may be able to hear it."

"That's something at least. Any chance we caught a visual?"

"The sta-cams are aimed the other way. Toward the psych ward," TJ said. "And I was checking the first floor with Michael."

"Not important." She rubbed Rosie's arms. "I'm afraid he targeted you to antagonize me. I'm so sorry."

Sterling leaned against the wall and crossed his arms but said nothing.

Michael cleared his throat. "More evidence this spirit is hostile. Rosie, you're done for the night. If there's any chance Kimmy is correct and this guy is targeting you, we have to keep you out of harm's way."

Rosie turned to Kimberly. "Is that okay?"

"Okay? I'm with Michael. I insist. Go ahead while he's drained from manifesting."

Rosie hugged her and headed down the stairs.

Michael turned to her. "Kimmy, anything?"

"I'm so worked up right now. Give me a few minutes to calm down."

TJ approached Sterling, digging in his pocket. "You remember those girls?"

"The two bridesmaids blown away by your paranormal bravery? Those girls? I remember."

TJ held out the room key. "Look. That's their room. Right there."

"So it is."

"What should I do?"

"What do you want to do?"

TJ turned the key over and over. He bent down and pushed the key under the door, then looked at Sterling.

"How do you feel?" Sterling asked.

TJ contemplated the question. "I feel good."

"You made the right decision." Sterling clapped him on the back. "I'm proud of you, son."

TJ wrinkled his nose. "Son?"

"Well, if you're going to call me old man, I think it's only appropriate I call you son."

"Old, yes. But not old enough to be my actual dad."

She smiled at Sterling. He never ceased to surprise her.

He noticed. "What?"

"You handled that well."

He shrugged. "Now that I'm a dad, I need to set a good example."

TJ shook his head. "Dude, you are so not my dad."

Sterling draped his arm around her shoulders. "Your mom and I want you to know how important it is to save yourself for just the right—"

She threw her hands in the air. "You two drive me crazy."

CHAPTER THIRTY-NINE

KIMBERLY CLOSED and bolted the door behind her. She trudged to the bathroom and shrugged out of her clothes. Stepping into a hot shower, she scrubbed her face clean of makeup. Her head throbbed. A dull pain behind her eyes stabbed at her. After toweling off, she pulled on her pajamas and fell gratefully into bed.

Nothing further had revealed itself that night. The encounter with the ghost bent on revenge left her drained. Every muscle ached. Perhaps it was for the best the ghost had not revealed itself again. Hopefully footage review would uncover something in the morning. For the moment, she wanted nothing more than a few hours of sleep.

Sterling and TJ though. How funny was that? She never would've seen that coming. Though TJ balked at Sterling referring to him as "son," he didn't seem truly upset by it. She would love to see them continue to get along better. TJ's point was valid. Sterling wasn't old enough to be his father. Maybe an older brother of sorts.

Her drained brain screamed for rest, but sleep eluded her. Mentally, spiritually, and physically exhausted, she was also overly stimulated. She glanced at the clock. 4:10 a.m. In precious few hours, light would filter into her room and the hotel would wake with the bustle of activity. She had to sleep. She rolled onto her back and rested her hands on her stomach, breathing slowly in and out, attempting to push all thoughts from her mind.

Concern for Rosie reared up to fill her emptied thoughts. Nothing like this had ever happened before. This was an intelligent ghost, she was sure. That spirit knew Rosie was important to her, probably due to her reaction when it scratched Rosie. Why? What could be prompting this? What happened to the ghost that so inflamed it with the desire for revenge?

She woke to frantic rapping. Her eyes flew open.

A dark figure stood above her.

She sat up, suddenly wide awake once more.

The shadow disappeared but the rapid knocking continued. She gritted her teeth. If that was Sterling again . . .

She stood and started for the bathroom to grab her robe but realized he'd seen her in pajamas more than once. What did it matter?

She cracked the door. Rosie and Elise stood in the hallway, fists still raised from rapping on the door. Their wide eyes put her on alert.

"What is it?" she asked.

"We heard it," Rosie said, voice quavering.

"Heard what?"

"The gurney," Elise said. "The wheels rolling down the hallway. Started about fifteen minutes ago as we turned out lights and tried to sleep. Sounds like the guy described it on the ghost tour."

Rosie shivered. "Can you please come see what it is? I can't sleep not knowing what's walking up and down the hall."

Mindful of the last time she declined to check into a disturbance, she nodded, grabbed her key, and followed them downstairs.

The two women stopped as they neared the third floor landing. Rosie held out an arm to stop Kimberly.

Elise cocked her head and whispered, "I don't hear anything."

They tiptoed the remaining steps. All three heads swiveled to peer down the hall, toward the elevator to the morgue.

Dim lights.

Silence.

No one.

She'd never seen it so dead. So to speak.

She sighed, tense muscles relaxing. "I guess I missed it."

"Sorry to disturb you," Rosie said. "We probably woke you."

"Don't worry about it. We have to look into every possible lead."

She walked with them back to their room.

Until Elise stopped. "Listen. Hear that?"

A faint creaking sound, like wheels rolling along a hardwood floor.

Rosie's eyes widened. She clutched Kimberly's arm with both hands. Hard. "That's it, girl. That's what we heard."

Kimberly turned slowly to face the psych ward.

The faint imprint of a nurse had materialized at the end of the hall. Wispy and diffuse, she pushed a gurney before her, demeanor solemn.

"Do you two see that?"

"See what?" Rosie asked.

"I don't see anything," Elise said, "but I have the digital recorder going and a hand-cam."

Of course Elise carried equipment. The woman was always on the ball. A momentary burst of gratitude for the crew surged.

She held completely still, hoping not to disturb the ghost, which continued its slow progress down the hall.

"Kimberly, can you describe what you see?" Elise asked.

Right. Of course. "Semi-transparent manifestation. Diffuse trailing edges. Fog-like. I see the image of a woman in old-fashioned nurse's attire, not scrubs, pushing a gurney down the hall. The gurney is draped with a sheet, covering presumably a corpse."

Elise panned the camera to the other end of the hallway. "Down there is where the elevator was that once led to the morgue. Norman Baker gave his nurses strict instructions to remove deceased patients' bodies to the morgue in the middle of the night while the other patients slept."

Rosie looked down the hall toward the morgue, then swiveled her head and stared in the other direction. "Hold up. Is she going to walk straight past us?"

"Yes. She's nearly here."

"No more ghosts for me tonight." Rosie pressed her back against the door and jiggled the handle. "Shoot. The key."

"I'm confident this is a loop, Rosie. A recording stuck in motion, repeating actions from life. You know that. The nurse will simply drift past us. She won't interact."

"No offense, but I'm not taking chances. I want in my room."

The creaking grew louder as Rosie struggled to cram the clunky key into the lock. "Come on."

Elise remained beside Kimberly. "I'm doing my best to follow the manifestation based on the squeaking wheels and your visual path."

"Thanks, Elise. No one could do better."

The door opened behind them and Rosie tumbled into the room, clicking the door firmly shut.

"Rosie, doors don't stop ghosts, sweetie."

The door opened slightly, and Rosie peeped through the gap. "I'm hoping it will at least discourage her. But I'll leave it cracked in case you need to duck in too."

Kimberly sucked in a breath as the manifestation floated even with them. The clarity of this apparition was remarkable. This wasn't simply a blob or a smudge of light on a recording.

The energy level at Crescent was staggering. And exciting. She gripped Elise's arm and stifled a squeal.

"Hey," Elise whispered. "Don't shake my camera."

The nurse stopped. Her head turned to face them. One misty finger drifted in front of her pursed mouth. "Shhh."

Kimberly froze, heart hammering. Was that part of a loop? Did the ghost nurse shush someone every night? Or was she responding to Elise's comment? No one but her had seen that. No way would she further frighten Rosie by sharing what she'd witnessed.

The nurse returned her hand to the gurney and resumed her mission to, presumably, the morgue.

Kimberly stepped away from the wall and followed the apparition.

"What are you doing?" Rosie asked behind her.

She held out a hand and waved her off, focused on the nurse.

When the nurse halted the gurney in front of what used to be the elevator, Kimberly chanced moving closer until she stood directly beside the draped figure.

She stared at the lumpy sheet, the outline of a body. Who lay beneath it?

The sheet shifted, jarring her so abruptly she jumped.

When nothing further happened, she couldn't stop herself. She needed to know. Something compelled her to reach out, grasp the edge of the sheet, and lift.

The young woman from the mirror. The one she'd connected with. The one who'd died an agonizing death from an abdominal tumor. Locked away from family, injected with painful shots several times a day. Alone.

The young woman's eyes flew open.

Kimberly dropped the sheet with a jolt and jumped backwards. She may have screamed a little too, since Rosie and Elise asked if she was okay and what happened.

The sheet shifted again as the young woman rose slowly off

the table into a sitting position. The sheet dropped into her lap. Her mouth moved. "Help me."

The nurse rested a hand against the young woman's sternum and pushed the corpse back into a prone position, then readjusted the sheet.

The nurse stared directly at her.

"I . . . I'm sorry for—"

"Shhh!"

CHAPTER FORTY

THE COFFEE MACHINE hissed and dispensed a cup of hot elixir. Kimberly lifted the cup and sat in her makeup chair.

Rosie was late. Again. She longed for her stylist's presence. She needed to see that Rosie was okay. How could she have let that vicious ghost hurt and terrorize her best friend?

Placing the scalding coffee on the counter, she rested her head in her hands and pressed against her temples.

She thought she might've slept three hours but wasn't certain when she'd actually fallen asleep. Once the nurse and the gurney dissipated, she'd remained with Rosie and Elise in their room for about half an hour, verifying for Rosie that the loop wouldn't repeat again.

Loop? Could she call it a loop without doubt? The nurse might have been responding to their presence and the sounds they made. If she saw the manifestation repeat in precisely the same manner, including the nurse's shushing, she would feel inclined to believe it was a loop. If it wasn't?

She certainly couldn't attribute the rising corpse to a loop. No way that ever happened in life. For the third time in this investigation, the same ghost reached out to her for help.

She had to help that young woman.

The trailer door opened.

Rosie.

"Morning, girl. Are you as miserably exhausted as I am?"

"Throbbing head. Aching eyes. My face feels swollen and stiff. Sinuses stuffy." She scrutinized herself in the mirror. "Bags under my eyes. Great. Making you work for your paycheck today."

Rosie nodded. "Ditto to all those symptoms. I see you already made yourself coffee."

Kimberly jumped to her feet. "I'll make you some, too."

"Sit," Rosie instructed. "This investigation is topsy-turvy enough without you serving me coffee."

"Least I can do," she said, popping a fresh pod into the machine. "How's your arm?"

Rosie plugged in the wand and fussed with brushes. "Doesn't even hurt. It's nothing. Really."

"Look me in the eye and tell me that." She held out the cup.

Rosie accepted the coffee. They both sipped.

"Okay, it shook me," Rosie said. "I'm a bundle of nerves. And I think I'm getting old."

"Old? You're younger than I am. And I think you're contractually obligated to refrain from using the 'o' word in my presence."

"Not younger by much. And not at all if we measure in boyfriend years. Guys like the jerks I've had add extra years. It's a complicated algorithm, but I'm beyond middle aged in boyfriend years."

Kimberly laughed and sipped her coffee. It had cooled enough she gulped and relished the warmth radiating through her stomach. "What would I do without you?"

Rosie took a deep breath, her demeanor all business. "Let's talk about that."

Kimberly froze mid-drink, the warmth of the coffee no

match for the chill her stylist's words sent through her. "About what?"

"Lorenzo asked me to stay with him here in Eureka Springs."

A hard knot formed in her stomach. "What? For a week or two? Like a little vacation?"

Rosie wouldn't meet her eyes. "No. He means permanently."

She tried to force a laugh. "But that's silly. That would never work. What about the show?"

Rosie fiddled with makeup brushes, staring so intently she seemed to have forgotten the function of each.

"Rosie? You told him no, right?"

Rosie leaned against the counter. "I told him I would think about it. And I am thinking about it. Eureka Springs is beautiful. It's quiet with a great artistic community. I could see living here."

Kimberly's heart skipped a beat. Rosie couldn't be serious. She couldn't. "Maybe eventually. You could retire here. But—"

"What if Lorenzo doesn't wait for eventually? I've never dated anyone like him, Kimberly. I don't know if I can walk away from this. How many chances will I have in the future? I'm not like you, dating two guys at once."

"Oh, stop. You know I'm not dating even one guy, let alone two. You're the one who always has a guy."

"Not good guys. Jerks just looking to use me. Looking for some gullible fool who will pay their bills and give them money. I'm such an idiot. And I never realized it until someone started treating me better." Rosie's voice cracked and a tear rolled down her cheek.

Kimberly jumped to her feet and enveloped Rosie in a hug, clutching tightly as if holding on would keep her firmly planted in her life. "But the show. We need you. I need you."

"You have Sterling now. You can get another stylist. I'm replaceable."

Tears threatened. "You are not replaceable. How can you

even think that? I told you this show doesn't go on without you. I'm so sorry I didn't protect you from this ghost. I promise I will stop it from hurting anyone else. Or you again."

Rosie pulled away. "That's not . . . it's a scratch. I'll be fine. But I'm thinking about my future. Even the best shows don't last forever, and what will I have when it ends? I don't mean money. That's not what this is about. I mean, what life will I have? I've bounced from one loser to another. Now I've found someone who treats me like a queen. I don't want to lose him."

"I'm glad you have someone treating you better now. Really. You deserve it. But to throw everything away for him? If Lorenzo really cares for you, he will make allowances for your job. Because he will want you to be happy and have something independent of him. If you quit to stay here with him, you will be totally dependent on a guy. Has that ever worked out for you? Please don't put yourself in that situation. Even if he's the greatest guy on the planet, and the relationship is strong and healthy, you don't want to be dependent. That's not you. And frankly, it's not healthy for anyone."

Rosie seemed to consider the argument. "Well, I'm here today and we need to get you ready for footage review. No more blubbering. Here, dry your eyes."

She accepted the tissue and blotted her leaking tear ducts.

Rosie selected eye shadow to match her blouse and prepped essential oils to apply.

Kimberly sipped her coffee, knowing no amount of relaxation techniques would bring balance. Not after the gaping rift Rosie had rent between them. She had basically dropped a nuclear bomb on their friendship.

How could Rosie even consider leaving? They'd commiserated about and celebrated their single status for years. Another stylist? How could she even suggest such a thing?

Rosie massaged lavender oil into her hands, then shifted to her temples. "Soothing breaths. In and out."

She did as instructed but all she could think about was Rosie leaving. She should be thinking about footage review and reveling in the incredible encounter with the nurse.

The door opened and Sterling's long legs carried him into the trailer. He yawned. "Morning, ladies. Anyone get any sleep?" Rubbing his eyes, he grabbed a cup and a pod.

"Nope," Rosie said. "Not after the encounter we had."

"Uh-oh," Sterling said as the coffee machine hissed a third time. "Pesky ghosts last night?"

"I ran for Kimberly. Scared the bejeezus out of me." Rosie shuddered. "And I could only hear the wheels. I couldn't even see her."

"One of the most remarkable apparitions I've witnessed," Kimberly said. "Full body, well defined. The nurse with the gurney."

Sterling carried his coffee and leaned against the makeup counter. Kimberly tried not to notice his butt reflected in the mirror. But she did. And felt her face flush. Then she remembered him dropping his towel at their massage and flushed again. Rosie noticed, followed her eyes, and smiled knowingly. Between memories of Sterling shirtless and Rosie's bombshell announcement, she was a mess.

"So that's where you were last night."

Kimberly furrowed her brow. "What do you mean?"

"I went by your room and you weren't there."

"Why were you at my room in the middle of the night this time?"

"I told you if you had them leave a camera in my room I would crash at your place. Kinda wondered where you were. Glad you were with Rosie."

"I told you there is no way you're sleeping in my room again. Presumably you went back and slept fine, as I predicted you would?"

"Nope. I went to Michael's apartment suite and he let me in." Sterling yawned and stretched, his biceps straining against his black T-shirt. "I think I'll run to Mud Street Café for cinnamon rolls again. What can I bring my favorite ghost enthusiast?"

"Favorite, huh? I don't think the competition is very stiff."

He gave her a teasing look. "No, the competition isn't."

Another double entendre. Heat crept up her face and spread through her cheeks. "It's like being the best of your least favorite thing. Nothing for me, thanks. I can't eat right now. Maybe later if this headache wears off."

"Rosie? Anything?"

"Lorenzo and I are having lunch later. I'll pass, thanks."

"What about you, Kimberly? Any lunch plans?"

Though he kept his voice casual, she noticed he tensed and his red chakra lit up with jealousy. She suspected he really wanted to know if she had plans with Jason.

"No plans right now."

His red chakra eased back to normal, orange and green spinning more vibrantly. "You know, I saw Jason at the bar last night."

She waited but he said nothing more. "Is there more to that story or . . ."

He shrugged. "Just saying. Looked like he was hoping to pick someone up."

She bristled. "Or maybe he simply wanted a drink."

"Whoa. Didn't mean to offend. I'll let you two do your thing. See you at review."

"He so clearly wanted to offend," she said after the door closed behind him. "Why else would he even mention Jason?"

"He's checking your interest level. Poking the bear to see how much you growl. And you growled a bit. What's the story?" Rosie picked up a sponge and dabbed on foundation.

"Can we not discuss this? Remember the good ol' days when we didn't talk about guys unless we were laughing at your most recent escapade?"

"And now you think I'll pass on the opportunity to be entertained by your escapades? Yeah, right." Rosie opened Twitter on her phone. "Look at these pictures of you and Sterling at The Grotto. Your fans are into him. Big time. I don't know why you're fighting this."

She took the phone. "Are you kidding me? I actually thought we went unnoticed. Who took these?" She scrolled through some of the comments. *So many hearts. Ugh. Gross.* And the sappy comments made her cringe.

#Kimberlingisathing
Ship this so hard.
These 2 together makes me so happy I cried.
Jason – get out and stay away

"I don't believe this. I seriously cannot believe the nerve."

Rosie blanched. "I was hoping you wouldn't see the Wantland baby hashtag."

"Wait. What? Wantland *baby?*"

"Oh. I assumed that's what set you off. Yep. Quite a few of the shippers are hoping for a Kimberling baby."

"Can people please stay out of my business? Why would anyone care if I have a baby or don't?"

"At least they love you and Sterling together. Gotta enjoy that."

"As two professionals working together, sure. Suggesting we go make a baby just for kicks and grins, not so much. And they are absolutely unfair to Jason. Listen to this. 'Stay away from Kimberly or else.' 'Don't come between Kimberling or I will find you.' 'You can't compare to Sterling, loser, get out.' They've all tweeted at Jason, which means he's seeing all this hatefulness. How did anyone even know who he was?"

"He posted pics of himself with you and tagged you in them, of course."

"It's not fair to him. This is crossing the line. Poor Jason."

"Poor Jason? He knew what he was flirting with when he came sniffing around after you. Or he should have unless he's suffering from amnesia. Isn't this why he dumped you?"

She winced at the reminder of being dumped. "No. I wasn't getting attention like this back then. He couldn't handle the time commitment. Said I was putting paranormal investigations before him. And he thought I was wasting time on 'frivolous pursuits' instead of building a future."

"And you didn't dump his ass for that?"

"I had no idea I would eventually have a successful show like this. And I'd heard my dad running down my 'obsession with ghosts' all my life. For that matter, Sterling thinks it's nonsense, too."

"But now that you're famous, Jason comes crawling back? At least Sterling understands being in the public eye. He doesn't like you just because you're a celebrity."

"Jason liked me before I was a celebrity. For a while, anyway. And Sterling has gained a lot of new fans and attention piggybacking off my success. Not so sure he's that much different. What I need is a man who really gets me. Maybe another sensitive who also experiences paranormal energy."

"Well, I agree with Sterling that you're too good for Jason. I also agree with the shippers. I think you and Sterling are good together."

Kimberly's phone rang, the specific ringtone diverting her attention from her fantasy about an Agent Mulder-style sensitive, with dark brooding eyes and empathic abilities, who completely understood and supported her. She shook off the image, reserving the right to dream later, and accepted the call. "Hey, Angela. Everything okay?"

Rosie paused the makeup application while she listened.

"No, you're not bothering me at all. I'm glad you called. I agree. I think that's significant. Thank you."

"What was that?" Rosie asked after she hung up.

"My house sitter, Angela. I asked her to keep me apprised of any unusual occurrences in the house. She says she woke up in the middle of the night to a woman's voice. Truly thought someone else was in the house. But she searched and no one was there."

"Is that a big surprise, really? You already consider it active, right? You grew up with spirits there."

"Yes. But she swears the voice said, 'Kimberly.'"

CHAPTER FORTY-ONE

FOOTAGE REVIEW HAD NEVER BEEN SO HOPPING. Though the back of her mind churned with potential explanations for the female voice in her childhood home, the majority of her attention was occupied with more findings than anyone expected. She acted as ringmaster to a circus, circling from one monitor to the next as her crew discovered clues.

"Unreal," Michael said. "Look at this footage. Your face. Your clothes! Look at your blouse billow."

She leaned over his shoulder, peering at his monitor. Someone had caught the specter as it flew over her. Her face contorted like someone bracing for impact while her hair blew behind her.

"I told you this one is powerful," she said. "Any entity that can corporealize solidly enough to inflict injury on a living being is a serious force."

"How do we deal with that?" TJ asked. "I mean if it's that strong. What if it doesn't want to go?"

She tossed back a cup of coffee and crushed the cup, masking that the same fear concerned her. "They always have a weakness. We have to find his. Unfortunately, we have no idea who he was, why he's so bent on revenge, or why he only began manifesting six months ago."

"Normally a presence tied to a location repeats regularly. Right, Ms. Wantland?"

She nodded and beamed at her protégé. "That's right. But this one hasn't. What set him off? When he flew past me, I heard him say, 'This is what I have become. Revenge.' Did we capture any audio?"

"Not yet," Stan said. "Still reviewing."

"Ms. Wantland? I'm worried about Sterling," TJ said. "Look at this recording. The thing really went after him."

She crossed to TJ's station and watched the footage of Sterling as the ghost tormented him. "I truly believe this ghost feeds off fear. We all believe in ghosts and cope with them regularly. Sterling on the other hand doesn't believe and couldn't explain away what was happening, which left him feeling vulnerable."

"He probably didn't learn his lesson. Maybe we should keep an eye on him tonight. You might need to protect him again."

She rested a hand on his shoulder. What a relief that the hard feelings between them seemed to be lessening. "I agree. Doubt he transformed into a believer in one night. Good idea."

Sterling entered the room, white paper bags clutched in his hands. "Cinnamon rolls!"

The crew broke away from their stations and descended on him. Michael held out his headphones.

"Kimmy, we both know you aren't eating a cinnamon roll. So watch this while I grab one. It's paused where you should start."

"Good night last night?" she whispered as she accepted the headphones.

"Honey, not as good as it could have been if he wasn't straight and completely fixated on you."

She shook her head to object, but also blushed. She slid into the seat. When she depressed "Play," she saw a hallway but couldn't tell exactly which one she was viewing. Maybe second floor?

A white shape materialized and drifted down the hallway, stopping in front of a door. The image resolved into a young woman in a white nightgown.

She squinted at the screen. "Which room did she stop at?"

"That's Sterling's room," Stan said. "Same room we followed Ms. Theodora to last night. I'm reviewing the footage from the sta-cam I left in there afterwards."

"I thought so. Sterling told me he saw a young woman in his room." Guilt for dismissing him gnawed at her stomach. Plus the sweet cinnamon roll aroma had reached her. Her stomach chewed her out for not nabbing one.

Michael's brow knitted together as he swallowed. "Is that your stomach? Good grief, did you eat yet, sweetie?"

"I'm fine. No empty carbs, thank you."

He shrugged. "Pretty good image, right?"

"It's so clear. And I told Stan—"

Stan jumped out of his seat. "Whoa! You were right to leave a sta-cam in Sterling's room. She came back. And you've got to hear this!"

She joined Stan and clamped the headphones over her ears. Sure enough, a hazy image moved into view, drifting through the room and toward the bathroom. As the filmy, lacy nightgown drifted past the lens, the microphone caught a soft voice. *Must tell.*

She jumped, pulling the headphones off. "What did she say?"

"What is it?" Michael asked.

"Here." She offered the headphones to him. "What do you think she said?"

Michael bit into a roll as he joined her, closing his eyes and chewing as he listened. His eyes widened. He swallowed and listened a second time before removing the headphones. "Sounded like 'must tell' to me but what the heck does that mean?"

"I don't know yet what it means but when I connected with a young woman on the ghost tour, she was thinking, 'Must tell.'

And when she fell, her last thought was that she didn't get to tell."

"Tell what? This must be significant."

"I agree. I'm convinced this young woman in the white nightgown is important. What if our young woman in the white nightgown is the same young woman reported to leap from the balcony? We know the student was pregnant. We've learned she was pushed. Did someone push her because of something she knew? Something they didn't want her to be able to tell anyone?"

Elise licked sugar from her coated fingers. "The girls who attended the school were all from wealthy families. They were so secluded and chaperoned, what could one of them have possibly known that would be serious enough to kill for? Even their outside correspondence was limited to the list of people supplied to the school by their parents. What could she have known?"

Kimberly shook her head. "We've learned a few things but not enough to tie it all together."

Kimberly closed her eyes, trying to remember everything she could from when she connected during the ghost tour. "So this ghost wanders the halls. She falls from a balcony on three. And she desperately wanted to tell someone about something. If we assume this is Sarah Hawthorne, we have to figure out what troubled her so badly she's still here trying to resolve the issue."

Michael propped his chin on a fist. "But the ghost scaring and hurting guests is a guy. We're not looking for a female. And Selma made it clear we're only to focus on him."

"But Michael—"

"Focus on the job, Kimmy. Selma insisted."

"Some of the other ghosts are reaching out though. I can't ignore that. And this girl keeps appearing. Something huge must be bothering her."

He raised his eyebrows. "Only if it's tied to Mr. Revenge. Got it?"

Stan spoke up. "Hey, guys? I managed to isolate and enhance the face from the girl."

They clustered around his screen.

She stared at the figure, white lacy gown, dark hair, and sad eyes.

Elise flipped through a manila folder, pages rustling. "I have a picture from a newspaper article about Sarah Hawthorne. The only article and the only picture I could find. I should have that. Here it is!"

Kimberly accepted the image and passed it along.

Stan held it beside his isolated image. "It's her, isn't it?"

No snarky reply from Sterling. She turned to see why he wasn't jumping all over the opportunity to utter disparaging remarks. He took the photo of the young woman. He looked back and forth from the picture in his hand to the wandering spirit on Stan's screen.

"Sterling?" she prompted.

"This . . . " He shook his head. "This can't be."

"What is it?" she asked, moving to stand beside him.

"That looks like the girl I saw in my room. That's the girl in the nightgown." Sterling leaned closer. "How did you do that?"

Stan shrugged. "Tweaked it a bit to make it a little clearer."

"No, but . . . that's exactly the girl I saw . . . well, imagined in my room the other night. How did you recreate something from my imagination?"

Kimberly patted his arm. "I told you not to discount that experience."

"This is nuts. This is not possible. You must have had Stan recreate the picture from the newspaper."

"And somehow we all knew what the ghost in your room looked like? That makes no sense."

He shook his head. "No. No, I must be seeing something there that isn't. The suggestion is making my mind bend it's memory to match the image you created."

TJ wrinkled his nose. "That actually sounds crazier than ghosts."

Kimberly beamed at him. "You saw a ghost. Accept it, my fellow experiencer."

"Great. I'm going crazy, and you're thrilled about it."

"No. We have more in common now. You said you wanted to see."

"I also said I didn't want a camera in my room. And this is why. I could have been sleeping in there. With . . . something."

She laughed. "You *would* have been sleeping in there if not for the camera. This is no different than jumping in a lake and acting surprised you have fish swimming all around you. We have residual spiritual energy around us all the time."

Sterling glanced sideways at TJ. "Did she just suggest I swim with the fishes?"

"Dude! Was that supposed to be Brando?" TJ laughed and shook his head. "I have more activity on three, Ms. Wantland. And Sterling." He scooted over and allowed them to see his screen.

Sterling seemed to decide to let his concern about a nervous breakdown go for now. She watched him accept TJ's invitation to view footage and joined him.

Orbs danced around the end of the hallway near the psych ward. "Did this camera get anything around four thirty in the morning? That would have been when Elise and Rosie first heard the nurse rolling the gurney."

"I didn't see anything that defined," TJ said. "The orbs quit flying around then, though. And I've noted some shadows I'm going to zoom in on later."

"I'm looking at my hand-cam right now," Elise said. "I already listened to the digital recorder I had. I didn't hear much."

"What about the shushing?" Kimberly asked.

"The what?"

"Oh, right. I didn't say anything. The nurse shushed us when you told me not to shake your hand."

Elise's eyes widened. "She did? I thought you said—"

"I know. I said it was a loop repeater. And maybe she shushed someone in her life. We don't know. But I wondered if you captured it."

"Not that jumped out at me. But I will go back now and listen more carefully. Maybe attempt to filter some of the ambient noise."

Stan waved at her. "Speaking of sounds. I think I have something. Not the clearest EVP I've ever heard. But distinct and potentially left by our ghost."

"What is it?" she asked, hurrying to his side and reaching for the headphones.

"I won't bias your experience by telling you what it sounds like to me. As Sterling would say, let's be objective here."

Sterling's eyes crinkled around the edges and his gaze didn't glow with his usual playfulness. He seemed to try to mask how shaken he was with brevity. "I haven't seen anything objective or unbiased yet today, but I appreciate the shout-out, Stan the Man."

Stan rolled his eyes but his shoulders shook with a laugh. "You work on that one all summer?"

Michael left his own station to see what Stan found. "I want to hear."

She pressed the headphones over her ears and Stan played the audio for her.

A faint crackling preceded a deep voice. *Sarah.*

She passed the headphones on to Michael. After he listened, Sterling took a turn as well.

"Honestly," Sterling said, "that sounded like a record player needle skipping on an old LP to me."

"Your ear isn't trained yet," Michael said. "Give it time. Kimmy?"

"I heard Sarah pretty plainly."

Michael nodded. "Yep. Sarah."

Stan grinned. "I thought Sarah as well."

Sterling's face twisted into a skeptical smirk. "Seriously? You all heard a name? Let me hear that again."

He listened but shook his head. "Sorry. Sounds like footsteps or something. I hear two beats, but it in no way resembles a word to me. You're really reaching on this one."

"Hold on," Elise said. "Sarah as in Sarah Hawthorne? Is he calling her?"

A shiver of excitement buzzed through Kimberly. "Could there be a connection between our ghost and Sarah?"

"We're making it up as we go, so I think you can write in any plot twist you want," Sterling said.

TJ shook his head. "Just wait, old man. You'll learn this stuff is for realz. We will make a believer out of you."

Sterling clapped him on the shoulder. "Son, some day when you're as old as I am, you'll look back on this moment and wonder why the hell you believed in things like ghosts and saying things like 'realz.'"

The door squeaked open and Selma joined them. "Morning. How's it coming? Any closer? The entire staff is on edge and my laundry crew is afraid to go in the laundry room."

Kimberly noticed Selma leaned on a cane today and drew back a chair, gesturing for the woman to sit. "I think we're finally making some progress."

"Excellent. Thank you, dear. My hip is flaring up on me today," Selma said, easing into the chair. "I had a message Elise was looking for me."

"Yes. We wanted to ask you about the piano in the lobby."

Selma rested the cane against the table. "Our new piano? Well, not new at all. Our recently reacquired old piano? It came to Crescent back during the Conservatory years. Why the interest?"

"I've heard it playing," Kimberly said.

"Really? I thought I heard it playing myself but figured my mind was tricking me. Heard a song my late husband used to play for me."

Kimberly's pulse quickened. "Was it *Für Elise?*"

"No," Selma said. "*Blue Danube*. Why do you ask?"

"I thought I figured out the mystery for a moment there." Though that explanation would have been less exciting than a clue to their mystery ghost. "I've heard the piano playing *Für Elise* a number of times. And I saw a young man playing it."

"The piano has a rather infamous history," Elise said. "Did you know that, Ms. Reddick?"

"Our piano? Girls learned lessons on it. Nothing scandalous about that. I was so glad I tracked it down and it was for sale that I snatched it up."

"Not scandal. And not here at the hotel." Elise opened a spiral notebook, licked a finger, and flipped through several pages. Adjusting her glasses, she continued. "There are many holes in the history I've pieced together of course, but nearly every owner I found since the piano left the Crescent experienced tragedy in their life after acquiring it."

"Such as?" Selma asked.

"A Hollywood starlet who got her start in Ziegfeld's Follies and then moved to Los Angeles died mysteriously after playing the piano at a party hosted by the producer who owned it at the time. I haven't determined yet exactly how it made it's way to California. The producer's toddler daughter became violently ill after she was allowed to bang on the keys. After that, he got rid of it. A wealthy business owner bought it for his wife, who soon after died in a boating accident."

"So everyone who plays this piano dies?" Kimberly asked.

"Dies. Becomes gravely sick. Disappears. Loses something or someone close to them. It goes on and on."

Sterling cleared his throat. "I hate to break it to you, but tragedy strikes people every day. You're forming causation where none exists. This is merely coincidence. Sad, to be sure. But you can't blame the piano for accidents and illness that would have happened anyway."

"It's not the piano," Kimberly said.

Sterling's eyebrows shot up. "Sorry. I guess I misunderstood. I thought that was where this discussion was going."

"That's silly. The piano is merely a musical instrument."

"Yes. Right. Simply an inanimate object incapable of causing death and destruction. I thought you were about to say it's cursed or something."

"Cursed? No. But it sounds like it's haunted."

Sterling hung his head, his shoulders slumped. "For juuust a moment there I actually thought we agreed on something. I'm sorry. The piano is what now?"

"Haunted. Maybe. I can't say for sure without more investigation. But a haunted object often causes a path of destruction wherever it goes. Sounds like that could be the case with the piano. The piano isn't causing these tragedies. A ghost is."

"And how could a piano be haunted?"

"The same way a house can be haunted. A ghost has attached itself to it. The ghost's energy is affecting the environment around it. If the ghost is angry or vengeful, the negative energy can suffuse the area around it and potentially impact the people in the vicinity."

Sterling nodded, his mouth pressed into a tight line. He shrugged. "Sure."

"Selma," she said, opting to ignore Sterling's skepticism for the moment, "when did you bring the piano back to Crescent?"

"Well, let me think. It was after our Paranormal Weekend in February, I know that. I'd need to check but probably around six months ago."

She blinked. "And when did you say Clara's experience in the laundry room occurred?"

Selma sat up straight. "Within six months ago. And now you mention it, I know that was shortly after the piano arrived. I remember walking past it in the lobby and thinking how nice it looked back home while I was headed to the laundry room to hear what all the fuss was about."

"This cannot be a coincidence."

Sterling raised a finger. "It absolutely can be a coincidence."

Stan turned a camera on her. She spoke directly into it.

"When Selma brought the piano back home to Crescent Hotel, she may also have unintentionally brought a new ghost. Which would explain why this manifestation is new. We have to figure out who he is and what he wants."

CHAPTER FORTY-TWO

When Stan lowered the camera, Kimberly turned to Michael, who rewarded her with two thumbs up. "Good job, Kim—Kimberly. I assume tonight's focus will be the piano?"

"Definitely. I will attempt to connect with the ghost attached to it. We're finally making progress."

"Agreed." Michael high-fived her and moved around the room patting his crew on the back.

She glanced at Sterling, surprised by his silence. He shook his head and rolled his eyes before he noticed her watching.

"Ready, Sterling?" Stan called. The two men moved to a corner.

Disappointment settled in her stomach. "Michael, is Sterling still filming Confidential Corners?"

Michael's brow furrowed. "Well, yes. That's the format of the show now, sweetie."

"Oh." Despite her attempts to cover her displeasure, her shoulders slumped under the weight of the news.

"Aw, hey, now." Michael curled an arm around her. "You didn't think his silence this investigation meant he agreed with you, did you?"

She shrugged. "He did see a ghost. And freaked out in the laundry room when he felt a ghost."

"True. But he doesn't accept our explanations. And that's okay. He's bringing a whole new demographic to the show. Rand-Meier is over the moon."

"Has he called you once so far this week?"

"Nope. And that's the best possible scenario we could hope for. So don't pout."

Sure. Don't pout. He always called to check in when I was the sole host.

In his corner, Sterling yammered away about sleight of hand and trick photography.

"Look at it this way, Ms. Wantland," TJ piped up, clearly having been cavesdropping. "All the people who watch to see Sterling's Confidential Corners wouldn't have watched to see you tracking down ghosts. So he's helping you, even if he makes you crazy."

She crossed her arms. "He does make me crazy. I'm not sure it's worth it."

TJ continued. "Plus all the hardcore shippers. They probably already loved you, but now they'll never miss a single episode."

She narrowed her eyes. "That's not helping one bit."

"It should," Michael said. "At least TJ has seen the light. If ratings trend down at all, suddenly we're sweating renewal. Ratings tick up like they did for your season finale, we're guaranteed another year. At least. We may be able to negotiate a multi-year contract if this year explodes like I think it will."

"I know he's kind of a pain in the butt," TJ said, "but he's not as bad as I thought. Once you get used to him."

"*Et tu,* TJ?"

TJ pushed his glasses up his nose and blinked at her, brows wrinkled. "What? I like my job."

"Fine. Everyone loves Sterling. Sterling is the bomb. Who cares about Kimberly anymore?"

Michael gave her an eye roll from hell. "Puh-leeze. No pity

parties. You go get some lunch and take a nap. This nonsense is exhaustion talking."

"Fine." She headed for the door.

"I speak your language, sweetie," Michael called after her. "I know that means you're not fine. I mean it. Get some rest."

After briefly contemplating the Sky Bar, she stomped her way downstairs. Too much pizza lately. She needed an infusion of phytochemicals and antioxidants.

The elevator door opened as she crossed the lobby. Jason stepped out directly in front of her.

He beamed. "Kimmy! I was hoping to bump into you. Can we grab lunch?"

The rush of familiarity at the sight and sound of him surprised her. "I do need food. Do you know someplace nearby?"

"Lots of places. But one I've really wanted to try. Shall we?" He held out his arm for her.

She looped her arm through his, grateful lunch plans were solved. And grateful for the comfortable company. Odd that they could slide right back into their easy friendship, as though the terrible breakup had never occurred.

He led her to a Toyota Prius and opened the passenger door. "Okay if I drive?"

"Of course. Is this an electric car?"

"Hybrid." He closed the door and climbed into the driver's seat.

She ran a hand over the console. "This is really nice."

He shrugged. "It's no i8. But it's a nice ride and gets good mileage. And I feel better reducing my carbon footprint."

"That's awesome. You always were concerned about the environment."

"If we all do a little bit, it adds up. Besides, I figure, no wife, no kids, I can spend a bit on a car that makes me happy. What about you?"

She almost lied, embarrassed she didn't own an impressive or exciting vehicle. But what if he asked to see it? Better to tell the truth. "Nothing impressive, I'm afraid."

"Seriously? You could be driving anything."

You're Kimberly freakin' Wantland. "I suppose. Cars never excited me. Plus, the show could end and I'd be jobless and it would all be gone like that. Then what?"

He nodded. "Well, a good financial advisor might help you sleep better at night."

"I mean I have one. It's just . . . it's silly."

"Sounds like maybe you need something else in your life besides the show."

His tone caught her by surprise. She looked up to find his eyes burned with meaning. She flushed. "Where exactly did you want to eat?"

He shifted gears and backed out of his parking space. "Actually, I have an even better idea. How much time do you have?"

"I'm supposed to eat and nap. Rest up for tonight." She thought of Sterling delivering his "intelligent counter argument" in his Confidential Corner and Michael's lack of sympathy. "But what did you have in mind?"

CHAPTER FORTY-THREE

THE CLERK at the Onyx Cave cash register counted back Jason's change while staring at Kimberly. "Seventeen, eighteen, nineteen, and one makes twenty."

She offered a smile, shifting back and forth. *Why won't he stop staring?* "Are you sure you don't want me to pay for my ticket, Jason?"

"Don't be silly, Kimmy. This is my treat."

The clerk choked and coughed. "You're . . . you're . . . "

She glanced back, disconcerted to find him still gazing at her, eyes bulging.

"Yep. This is Kimberly Wantland," Jason said, tucking his wallet back into his pocket.

"And you're the . . . you nicknamed her Kimmy. You're the new guy coming between her and Sterling." He grabbed her wrist. "Hang on! I gotta call my wife!"

"New guy?" Jason said. "I'm the old flame, not a new guy. We were engaged for crying out loud. Sterling is the new guy. Sheesh."

The clerk gave no indication he'd heard a word Jason said. He listened intently to the phone in his hand. "Honey? You gotta get down here. You'll never believe who's here. And you'll never forgive me if you don't get to take a picture with her."

Kimberly massaged her wrist, which he'd only let go of in order to dial the phone. "I'm flattered, really. But we're on a bit of a time restriction—"

He hung up the phone. "She'll be right over."

"How long is this tour?" Jason asked. "We need to grab lunch before she goes back to work."

"My wife will make you lunch!"

Everywhere she went. To think only a few years ago she could walk down the street without being recognized and offered gifts and asked for selfies. What was it about being on television that made people go gaga over you? *I'm just a normal person. Who can communicate with spirits.* "Oh, no. Thank you. No need to impose."

"It's not an imposition! She'd be thrilled to make lunch for Kimberly Wantland!"

The door opened and an older woman blustered into the combination lobby and gift shop. "Earl, this better be—Oh my God! It's Kimberly Wantland."

Earl beamed. "I told you you'd never believe it."

The woman clutched her chest. "This is the best birthday gift ever, Earl. I can't believe I thought you really didn't get me anything this year. When you had this surprise planned all along."

Earl blinked a few times before recovering with a big smile. "Only the best for my Edith."

Jason rolled his eyes. "We really need to be—"

Kimberly sensed a deep sadness in the woman and extended her hand. "Nice to meet you, Edith. And happy birthday."

Edith clasped her hand in both of her own, shaking vigorously. "I can't believe this. I really can't. I've watched every one of your shows and probably all the repeats, too. And now here you are to talk to my mama for me." Tears filled her eyes.

Earl rubbed the back of his neck. "Now, Edith. This is just a meet and say hello."

"Oh. Of course." Edith wiped her eyes and sniffed. "We probably can't afford anything more than that. Excuse my presumption."

"And we need to move on with the tour," Jason said, placing a hand on her lower back and steering her toward the cave entrance.

Kimberly dug in her heels, aware she would probably regret this decision. "What's your mother's name?"

Hope lit Edith's eyes. "Opal."

She felt nothing in the room around them. "And where is she?"

"She never left the house when she died. I know she didn't. It's right there." Edith pointed over her shoulder.

Earl rested a hand on his wife's shoulder. "Edith, I didn't—"

"What better time to reach out to her than on your birthday?" Kimberly said. "Your mother will probably be eager to connect on such a special day. Let's go see."

CHAPTER FORTY-FOUR

EDITH LED the way from the cave entrance to a small house nearby. "Mama lived here with us until she passed away. Lived to be ninety-eight and claimed her health was due to the spring water. She believed in the healing properties."

Jason leaned close, whispering in her ear. "Sure. Let's hope she only bathed in it. Drinking untreated water never added years onto anyone's life."

"She's having a hard time today. She misses her mother. I can feel it. And her spectrum is out of adjustment."

"Right. Spectrum and chakras. I'd kind of forgotten about that."

"Really? You used to love when I read your spectrum and adjusted your chakras."

"Of course I did. That was your version of foreplay. I knew what would happen afterwards."

Her face grew hot. Was this something she wanted to discuss with him? Particularly right now? "That's not true."

He eyed her. "Really? I seem to remember—"

"Okay, so maybe I enjoyed it," she admitted, sure her cheeks were bright pink.

"Maybe later you can evaluate my chakras. See if I need an adjustment."

"Stop that!" She half-heartedly punched his shoulder.

Earl and Edith stood before their home, watching her banter with Jason. Edith's brow furrowed as she glanced back and forth between the two of them. Guilt ran through her, followed quickly by irritation. Why should she feel guilty?

Though Earl and Edith's home lacked the extravagant latticework, wrap-around porches, and elegant shapes of the Victorian-era homes on Spring Street in town, Kimberly sensed the age of the building as Earl opened the door and Edith gestured them inside.

Assaulted by floral designs in bright colors vying for her attention, Kimberly cringed but looked past the brightly patterned couch that clashed with the golden striped wallpaper and the daisy drapes, as well as the figurines and trinkets and commemorative plates covering every surface of the room. She inhaled deeply. "You've been baking. Chocolate chip cookies?"

"Yes! Let me get the plate!" Edith turned, presumably for the kitchen.

"I'm not hungry," she lied. She moved further into the home, drawn down a hallway. "Tell me about your mother. Why do you think she's still here?"

"I hear her at night sometimes. Plus she moves things around."

Kimberly continued to move along the hallway, walls lined with black and white photographs of stoic people and shelves crammed with angel figurines in various poses of prayer. Allowing herself to be drawn by whatever force pulled at her, she stopped in front of a closed door. She placed a hand against the wood and breathed deeply.

"That was Mom's room," Edith whispered. "Incredible. I knew you were real. Knew you aren't a fake, no matter what Sterling says."

The edges of her mouth twitched, but Kimberly fought the

urge to pump a fist in the air. *Take that, Sterling.* "May I go inside her room?"

"Yes, of course. Please." Edith turned the knob and pushed the door open.

Nothing dreadful assaulted her. She sensed no anger or betrayal. No shock or fear. None of the typical residual emotions that accompanied an entity confused by the loss of its body though it lingered in this world. The room smelled vaguely of baby powder and lemon.

"You said you hear her at night? What does she say to you?"

"It's not always words," Edith said. "Sometimes I hear her shuffling down the hall toward the bathroom. When you care for someone for years like Earl and I cared for Mom, you know them, you know? You just . . . know."

She nodded, though she didn't share the experience of caring for her mother into old age. Despite the short time they shared, she remembered her mother's scent, her walk, her voice, her warm embrace. She swallowed hard and squeezed her eyes closed. *Not now. This is about Edith's mother.*

Jason left Edith and Earl hovering in the doorway and joined her in the room. He leaned close, whispering in her ear. "Could you speed this along? I thought this afternoon would be just the two of us." He glanced at his watch.

Her forehead furrowed. "Quiet would help. You're distracting my focus. I'm attempting to connect."

"They're not even paying you and they're cutting into our time. And no one will even see this. Your crew isn't here to film."

Earl's phone mimicked the sound of a camera as he snapped a shot of her.

She raised an eyebrow at Jason. "Everyone sees everything I do. Doesn't matter if the crew is with me or not."

"So make up something and let's get out of here."

She felt her jaw tighten. *Make up something?* Aware he was disturbing her chakra alignment and upsetting her balance, she clasped her quartz, closed her eyes, and breathed deeply.

"That's the necklace Sterling gave her," Edith whispered. "Those two are adorable together. Wish he was here. Who's this guy?"

"He's the new guy that showed up at their investigation at the Crescent. I told you about it."

"How'd you know?"

"Cuz I'm on that Twitter. You should get on it too so you can see the latest news."

"That Twitter," Edith said. "I can't make head nor tail out of that mess. No thanks."

"You're missing out. Think this boy's name is Jarrod or something like that."

"It's Jason." The hard, biting tone in Jason's voice, as though his teeth ground together, brought back memories of their arguments over her gift. "And I'm not the new—"

"Okay. Everybody out but Edith. I need to focus and I need quiet."

Jason slanted his eyes at her but followed Earl down the hall.

"Girls only, I guess," Earl said. "Why don't we go find those cookies Edith baked?"

She sat on the bed, breathing deeply and reaching out with her sixth sense, inviting connection.

"This is where she passed," Edith murmured.

"Talk about her," she encouraged. "What was she like? What do you think she's trying to say? What moves around?"

"She worked hard," Edith said. "Her whole life. She remembered the Great Depression and never took a thing for granted. And she was so independent. She didn't want to 'burden' Earl and me. Her word, not mine. She was no burden."

Edith's voice caught in her throat. Kimberly rested a hand on her arm. "I know. I lost my mom, too."

"I'm so worried that she's trapped here. That she's trying to tell me something. I'm scared she's hurting or suffering and doesn't know how to move on. She had such a hard life. Sacrificed so much for my brothers and me. I want her to be able to move on and finally rest. Does that make sense?"

"Of course. Do you have something of hers? Maybe something very special?"

Edith seemed to ponder the question before she rose from the bed and went to the closet. She returned with a threadbare, faded yellow blanket, frayed on the edges. "This was my baby blanket. The first one, before she knew I was a girl. No ultrasounds back in those days. After four boys, she was so delighted to have a baby girl, everything she dressed me in from then on was pink."

She accepted the blanket, clasping it gently in her hands. A shiver ran through her. She strained her ears for any whispers, any rustling, any indication someone else was in the room with them. "Go ahead and talk to her."

"What do I say?"

"Whatever you want to tell her."

Edith cleared her throat. "Mama. I miss you. I really do."

A doll fell from a shelf.

Edith gasped. "That's what moves. The doll. I find it in different places in the room. At first I thought Earl was messing with me. But it moves while he's over at the cave. So I know it isn't him."

"Is the doll special to her?"

"Yes. The only doll she had growing up. She kept it all these years."

"Opal, we're listening. Your daughter Edith would love to talk to you today. It's her birthday. Do you remember?"

Movement caught her attention. The drapes fluttered.

"Do you hear anything?" Edith asked.

She held up a hand. Clasping her quartz, she reached out to the spiritual plane, coaxing anyone nearby to visit. Without much to go on, all she could do was hope Opal, if she did indeed remain, was as eager to communicate as Edith.

In her mind, she saw an image of a baby swaddled in a yellow blanket. Though the blanket in the image was brand new, not in its current tattered state, she recognized it as the blanket she currently held on her lap. "I see something. I think your mother is reaching out."

Random images of balloons, birthday cakes, wrapped packages, and wiggly groups of children raced through her mind. She smiled. "Your mother says happy birthday."

"She's here?" Edith gasped. "You know it's her?"

"She's sharing memories with me. I see you as a little girl opening presents. Wait. Now you're older. Having dinner together."

"Is she okay? Is she hurting?"

"I don't feel anything negative at all. She seems . . . content."

"You've said on your show that spirits normally remain when they suffer a sudden loss of their body. Usually due to a traumatic event. But she didn't."

"I'm sensing she stayed intentionally. I think she wants to wait for you before she crosses over."

"But why doesn't she want to go be with Dad?"

The images changed. She saw a clinic. A hospital, perhaps. Nurses. A doctor. These images were new, the clinic modern and the staff in scrubs. Worry and concern consumed her, accompanied by an image of Edith in a hospital gown. Was Opal trying to tell her Edith was ill? Did Edith know? "When did you last see your doctor, Edith?"

"I guess I'm due for a check up. Why?"

Earl's deep voice startled her from the doorway. "She's overdue. Edith is one of those who takes care of everyone and everything but herself."

"I think your mother is still trying to take care of her little girl from beyond the grave. I believe she wants me to tell you to go see your doctor."

"I told you not to ignore those fainting spells, Edith. You wouldn't listen to me. I hope you'll listen to your mother."

"But she's okay?" Edith repeated.

"She seems fine. Worried about you. But not hurting or unhappy."

"I'll call the office and make an appointment. What do I do about Mama?"

"Well, that depends. I can attempt to help her move on, if you'd like. But I cannot force a spirit to leave a location. And your mother doesn't seem inclined to leave. Does her presence disturb you?"

"No! She doesn't upset me. I was only concerned she was trapped and miserable. You're sure she's okay?"

"I am."

"So we leave her be? Forever?"

"Leaving things as they are would be my recommendation. She wants to stay with you and as long as she isn't upsetting anyone, why try to force her out? She may settle down once you've seen a doctor. I have the feeling she wants to cross with you when that time comes. But take care of yourself so that time is far off in the future."

"Amen," Earl whispered. "I need you around a while yet Edith. This old man can't function without you anymore."

"Oh, stop, Earl." Edith swiped at her cheek. "I'm not going anywhere."

Earl sat on the bed beside her and brought her head to his shoulder. "I've been lucky to have you all this time and can't imagine living without you. You know I've been worried. Let's get you to the doctor and make sure you're okay."

"I will, I will. Now stop making a scene in front of company, you great big goofball. I'm not going anywhere. You ever know me to give up on anything?"

"Never. You're my scrappy little fighter. One of the many reasons I love you."

Edith wiped her eyes again. "I feel so much better knowing Mom isn't unhappy. I've been so worried."

Earl hugged her. "Happy birthday. And stick around for more."

Jason rolled up and down on the balls of his feet. "Kimmy, maybe we should . . . " He jabbed a thumb over his shoulder toward the door.

"Yes, we will leave you two alone and go ahead through the cave if that's okay."

Earl hopped to his feet. "I'll walk you back and get you started."

"Pleasure to meet you, Edith. And happy birthday." She extended her hand.

Edith pressed past her hand and dove in for a hug. "Thank you so much for this."

CHAPTER FORTY-FIVE

EARL LED THE WAY BACK, reached under the counter, and handed them what looked like a walkie-talkie. "There are places along the walk where you can listen to facts and information about the cave. I'm so glad you stopped by today. I really can't thank you enough."

Kimberly waved away his continued thanks. "It's what I do. Glad to help."

She ducked her head as she entered the cave and walked in silence until she spotted the first marker indicating a tour stop and clicked the button on the device.

Jason placed his hands on her waist and spun her to face him. "I think we should talk. What was that?"

"What was what?"

"This was supposed to be our time. Time for us to catch up and talk about us."

"And here we are spelunking, just the two of us, like you planned."

"After a side trip for you to talk to a ghost."

She didn't miss the sarcastic note layered over the word ghost. Her Duchovny-like ghost hunting fantasy partner made another appearance in her psyche. Was it too much to ask for a little understanding? "Are you honestly begrudging the few minutes I spent helping that woman?"

"Helping? You made up a story about her mother watching over her from the grave."

She balled her fists and willed herself to relax. This was supposed to be her break. Time away to relax and get her mind off things. *Breathe in. You are not crazy. Breathe out. Don't allow him to take this away from you.* "I didn't invent anything. But let's suppose I did, in fact, make it up. She is now at peace knowing her mother isn't suffering. That helps. She needs to go to the doctor and now intends to. You heard the bit where her husband mentioned fainting spells, right?"

"I don't know how you did that. Could you tell something was off or did you just get lucky? Or did the husband reach out to you before we showed up? Was this planned all along?"

Her jaw dropped. "Do you hear yourself? Coming here was your idea. Spur of the moment. I was walking out the door to find food. You sound exactly like Sterling right now and frankly I needed a break from his caustic skepticism. I thought you were more understanding and open-minded now."

Jason's scowl relaxed. "I did say that. You're right. I did."

His phone pinged. He stared at the screen and then scowled.

"How are you getting reception in a cave?" she asked.

"Not sure. But I am sure I'm tired of being described as interfering and butting in. Your fans are eating me alive. Look at this. Earl apparently tweeted a picture of us here at the cave and I'm being called all sorts of nasty names as a result."

"I'm sorry. I did warn you. It's only worse since we went our separate ways."

"How do you stand it?"

"I turn off notifications and don't open apps."

"No, I mean, how do you stand people commenting on everything you do? Thinking they have some say in your life?"

"I don't like it. But it comes with the territory. I'm able to reach so many people with my show now. And I love that. This is the downside of it. Can't have one without the other."

He took her hand. "You won't always have the show. What will you do when it ends? What will you have then?"

She pulled her hand away. "Why is everyone talking about the show ending? I'm more popular now than ever. As much as I hate to admit it, Sterling helped increase viewership and has stirred things up. Another instance of taking the good with the bad."

"But after it ends?"

"I'm not thinking about that now. I'm focused on making the show great while I have the opportunity and helping as many people as I can. No job lasts forever. You'll eventually retire too."

"I know. And I am thinking about my future. What I want it to look like. And who I want in it." He curled an arm around her waist and leaned close. "I made a mistake six years ago. I want you back in my life."

He leaned closer still. Fearful he was going for a kiss, she ducked out of his embrace. "Jason. You're moving far too fast. It has been six years, after all."

"It doesn't feel like it. You said so yourself, how easy it is to slide right back into conversation." He curled his arm around her waist again.

She slid away. "Conversation is one thing. Being physically intimate is another. I think I want to go back to the hotel."

His phone sounded again. A glance at it renewed his scowl. "Nice. Here's someone calling me . . . I'm not even going to say it out loud. It's that offensive. How can people sit behind their screens and feel justified calling people nasty names? Why do they care if I spend time with you?"

"They're trolls, Jason. Stop looking at every comment. You'll drive yourself crazy."

"Here someone says, 'She looks happiest with him' and added a—Is this a picture of you with Sterling . . . undressed?"

She glanced at his phone. "He snapped that during a massage and then tweeted it after I asked him not to."

"You two got a massage together?"

"It wasn't like that." She reconsidered. "Okay, it was like that, but it's a long story. Can we not do this?"

"I had high hopes when I came to see you, Kimmy. I thought we could recapture the spark. Come on. Let's finish the tour and take you back to what's important to you."

CHAPTER FORTY-SIX

"He had high hopes?" Rosie exclaimed. "When he showed up unannounced and waylaid you? 'I'll take you back to what's important to you?' I cannot stand passive-aggressive comments like that. He's trying to guilt you into doing what he wants. Don't fall for it."

Rosie resumed twirling locks of hair into luscious waves.

Kimberly pursed her lips and gave her the look in the mirror.

Rosie shook her head. "Don't say it. Don't you dare say it."

Kimberly bit down on her lip and squeezed her eyes shut, shoulders shaking with suppressed laughter.

"Look, this is a case of learning from my mistakes and saving yourself a lot of heartache. So stop already."

Shoulders quaking, she managed to keep her voice even. "I didn't say a word."

"Fine. Eduardo Ignacio Esposito the Third. Otherwise known as 'Iggy.'"

The both burst into laughter as the trailer door opened and Sterling entered.

"What's so funny?" he asked.

"Rosie giving relationship advice with the disastrous 'Epic Saga of Iggy' lurking in her past."

Rosie clicked her tongue. "No. That's tragic. What's funny is that Jason showed up after six years and expected Kimberly to leap into his open arms and take him back."

Sterling's narrowed eyes ended her laughter. "Really? Was that the point to sneaking off to the caves?"

"How did you—?"

He held up his phone, displaying the photo on Twitter.

"Of course. Earl tweeted. Well, I thought Jason and I were going to get lunch. But, yeah, I think he had other ideas."

"I'll be damned. So you didn't even get food?"

"I'm fine."

"That jerk. I ought to wring his neck. So what happened? What did he do?"

Rosie brushed blush on her cheeks as she continued. "He told me how he feels. That he wants me back in his life. Suggested I consider what will happen when the show ends. Hinted I'd be all alone and miserable."

Sterling snorted, a sound she hadn't yet heard him produce. "Like hell. *He* might be alone and miserable—and probably is—but that will never be you."

"Mmm-hmm. That's right," Rosie agreed. "We may wind up old maids rattling around in your haunted house, but you'll never be alone."

Her eyes actually threatened to tear. "That's sweet but won't happen if a certain someone gets his way."

"With my history? Seems highly unlikely."

"But back to Jason," Sterling said. "Please tell me—"

"I said no."

"So he left?"

"I don't know what he's doing. We had an awkwardly silent drive back to the hotel. I mean, he did at least come find me and make the effort to admit he was wrong. And he said he made a mistake. That's more than any other guy has ever done. I was actually thinking maybe I should try making a relationship work. But then this afternoon he got frustrated with people paying attention to me and scoffed at my abilities. I got upset."

Sterling nodded. "With good reason. Don't second-guess yourself. You want to try making a relationship work, fine. But not with Mr. Potato Head. Is he impressed with your success or jealous and threatened by it? He doesn't even seem to know. What you need is someone who can relate and understand. Someone at your level."

"Close your eyes." Rosie dusted her face with powder. "If only we knew the perfect guy who could totally understand the demands of a television show."

"What I need," she said, glaring at Rosie, "is someone who doesn't consider my interactions with spirits a joke. Or a hoax." Once again, her buff fantasy boyfriend appeared in her mind, this time shirtless. His chest and biceps vaguely resembled Sterling's, so she quickly shooed him back into the deep recesses of her psyche.

The trailer door opened and in walked Michael, phone pressed to his ear. He scowled at her. She tossed her hands in the air and mouthed, "What?"

"Yes, sir. I understand, sir. I'll talk to her." Michael hung up. "You went off with Jason for some side investigation? And didn't bother to tell me?"

"That's not what happened at all."

"That pretty much is exactly what happened," Sterling said.

"Well, however it happened, RandMeier gave me an earful about you conducting unapproved investigations. Your contract contains a clause limiting investigations outside the parameters of the show and conflicts of interest, blah, blah, blah."

"This was in no way a conflict of interest. I wasn't paid. The couple didn't approach the show and get turned down. It was a spur-of-the-moment thing to help out. Jeez."

"You need to focus, Kimmy. I feel like you're all over the place this week. Why run off with Jason? Why waste valuable time like that?"

"Valuable? It was break time. You sent me away."

"To rest and eat. You did neither. Now you're hungry and probably completely depleted."

"I'm not depleted. This was nothing. A throw away. The woman's mom was right there, eager to give her daughter a message. It cost nothing."

"You didn't know that going in. Why risk it?"

"Because I'd give anything for the chance to talk to my mom one more time. I will never have that opportunity thanks to my dad and my aunt. But I was able to give that to Edith. It ticked off Jason, Sterling, you, RandMeier, and probably everyone else. But I would do it again. She got to know her mom is proud of her and watching over her—" She choked on the words and scrubbed at the unwanted tears streaking her cheeks.

Michael draped an arm around her shoulders, patting her arm. "Okay. It's okay. I get it. I'll take care of RandMeier."

Sterling shifted. "Well, if it ticked off Jason, then it wasn't a total waste of time."

Rosie stuffed a tissue into her hand.

"Sorry, girl. Ruined my makeup."

"Eh. It can be fixed. Two minutes tops."

The door opened and TJ stumbled inside, gasping for breath.

"Kid," Sterling said. "Less computer screen, more exercise."

TJ held up a hand and bent forward, fighting to draw air. He wriggled an inhaler from his pocket and sucked a puff into his laboring lungs. "Another . . . scratching," he rasped.

She shot from her seat.

Michael bent over TJ, a hand on his back. "You okay?"

"No one told me the little guy has asthma," Sterling commented.

"It's well controlled," Michael said. "First attack he's had on set."

"Here," Sterling said. "I'll give you my cell number. From now on text me with anything important. You don't need to be running around. You're not an errand boy."

Michael stared off in space. "An errand boy. Is that like a pool boy? Why don't we have an errand boy? Do we need to hire one?"

Sterling clapped him on the back. "Not now. I'm here!"

"Thanks. You're so helpful." The sarcasm dripping from his words left no doubt in her mind he was envisioning a hot guy dashing about, fulfilling his every command, clad in tight shorts.

He could have his errand boy when she got her ripped sensitive partner.

CHAPTER FORTY-SEVEN

Selma waited for them in the lobby hovering over a young woman cradling an arm. Kimberly pegged the woman in her mid-twenties.

Selma waved them over and lifted a tissue from the woman's arm. "Look."

Stan swooped in with his camera, catching wide shots of the faces, then zooming on the arm.

A group of onlookers clustered nearby, whispering, brows furrowed.

Kimberly made eye contact and gauged the woman. She extended a hand. "Kimberly Wantland."

The woman shook with her good arm. "Elizabeth."

She closed her eyes. The hairs on her arm stood on end, electrified by ectoplasmic residue.

"Identical to the others," Selma said.

Sterling sighed. "All the scrapes look alike because they're all scrapes. A scrape is a scrape is a scrape."

"Identically placed. Identical in length," Selma pointed out.

"Oh? Is someone taking notes? Sketching diagrams? Measuring with calibrated calipers? Or is everyone relying on faulty memory?"

"It's the right arm, every time," Selma said. "And we did take pictures."

"For that matter, subsequent scrapes could be copycats."

Elizabeth glared at him. "Are you suggesting I cut my own arm? For attention?"

TJ, apparently recovered, moved next to her. "No one would do that, Sterling. Don't insult her."

Kimberly released Elizabeth's arm. "I can sense that you're telling the truth and feel evidence of contact with a spiritual entity."

Elizabeth jerked her chin at Sterling. "Is he always like that?"

"He is," TJ said. "Don't worry. It's for the cameras. Nothing personal."

Kimberly offered an apology. "I feel responsible for your injury. If I'd stopped this entity, you wouldn't have been hurt."

"You'll get him, Kimmy," Michael said. "You warned me the sheer number of spirits would complicate this investigation."

Selma nodded. "No one blames you, Kimberly. Don't get discouraged. He's a tricky one, but you'll get him."

What if I don't get him? "I appreciate the support but we've barely gotten near him. Something needs to give on this case."

Elizabeth smiled at TJ. "Thanks for sticking up for me. That was cool."

TJ blushed. "Sure. It's all good. Seriously, Sterling didn't mean anything by it. It's for the cameras."

"He looked pretty serious to me."

"I know, right? I mean, he doesn't believe in ghosts. But he's cool. We're friends."

"Cool. Hey, I was about to go check out the gardens. You wanna come with?"

"I . . . yeah! Ms. Wantland?"

"Go ahead. We have a couple of hours before we'll be filming again."

"Cool! Thanks!"

Sterling watched them leave through the back door. "I'll be darned. He said we're friends."

She rested a hand on his arm. "See? Who would have believed this could happen? Makes ghosts seem easy to believe in, in comparison."

Sterling threw his head back and laughed. "No. No, it doesn't. Much easier to believe I can win someone over than to believe ghosts are real. Good play though."

Elise burst into the lobby, appearing to have dashed up the front steps, possibly two at a time judging by the way she gulped for breath. "Ms. Wantland! I've been at the library this afternoon. They have a collection of very old books from the area tucked away. You won't believe what I found."

Kimberly stepped toward her researcher, the woman's excited state affecting her own mood. Could this be the break she needed? "Regarding the investigation? What is it? Let me see."

Elise grasped her glasses and pushed them back in place. "I couldn't take the book off the premises. The risk of damage, even exercising utmost care, would be too great to—"

She waved her hand as though to drag the information out. "To the point, Elise. What did you find?"

"The diary of one of the girls who attended the conservatory. And who was close friends with a girl named Sarah."

Kimberly held back a small squeal of delight. "Maybe Sarah Hawthorne?"

A huge grin split Elise's face as she nodded. "After skimming through it, I think so. I jotted down a few notes." She flipped through her spiral and read. "'Sarah has caught the fancy of one of the laundry boys. I daresay he has turned her head in return, as she brings the conversation back to him rather frequently and speaks of him fondly.'"

"The *laundry* boy?" She grabbed Elise's arm in excitement.

"Exactly."

"This has to be the connection."

"There's nothing to signify a connection," Sterling said. "Do any of the diary entries describe the laundry boy as a raving lunatic who got his rocks off by inflicting injury on women?"

Elise scanned her notes and flipped a few pages, engrossed in thought. "Nothing I've found yet."

Sterling shook his head slightly. "That was sarcasm. My point is that you're seeing a connection you want to see when none exists."

Selma spoke up. "Now hold on, Negative Nelly. Let her finish. She may have more to tell us."

"Well, I . . . I didn't get through the entire diary. I wanted to make sure Ms. Wantland agreed it was worth spending more time on it."

"It's the most promising lead yet. Good job, Elise. Do you have more?"

Elise flipped back to the page where she'd left off. "'Sarah came to my room after curfew this night. How she managed it, I do not know. Nathan took her for a stroll through the gardens today. Miss Frakes followed them, reported Sarah, scowling the entire time. Nathan is a gentleman by birth, but alas his family, like so many, lost all in our Great Depression. He was turned out to find his own way. Sarah says she saw Miss Frakes furiously writing a letter, face pinched, and fears the woman is reporting Nathan's interest to her parents. And she doubts they will approve of someone who has fallen so low.'"

Kimberly considered dancing or turning a cartwheel but opted to maintain decorum. "Michael, this sounds promising. I suggest we send her back to glean as much as she can about Sarah."

Michael rubbed his chin. "I'm not saying I agree with Sterling, but I kinda agree with Sterling. Even if this is a student from the Conservatory, how does this tie in to the ghost we're here to expel?"

Sterling threw an arm around Michael's shoulders. "Yes. Good, my apprentice. Come to the dark side."

Michael brushed him off. "I said I don't agree. I'm just hesitant to pounce on this."

"You're learning, my padawan."

"Dude, please," TJ said. "Padawans are Jedi apprentices. Not a correct dark side reference."

Kimberly rubbed her temples. "All of you stop! That spirit said the name Sarah. It must tie together."

"I'll trust your instinct on this, Kimmy. Elise, go ahead and see if you can find something more. How late is the library open?"

"Nine, I think."

"That should give you ample time. We will start at nightfall, like always. Maybe you can find something to definitely connect them."

"I'm on it!" Elise turned for the door.

"Hurry," Kimberly called after her. "Anything referencing Sarah."

"You really think this could be it?" Selma asked.

"Something tells me yes. We need to unravel exactly what happened to Sarah and Nathan."

"I'm not completely convinced," Michael said.

"But how often is Kimberly wrong?" Selma asked.

Michael frowned. "I'm adhering to your rules, Ms. Reddick. You insisted we refrain from disturbing any other occupants. If you want to grant us a little more wiggle room, I'll ease up."

"What if I can get the ghost to respond to the name Nathan?" Kimberly asked.

"That would definitely be a step in the right direction," Michael said.

"Do what you need to do, Kimberly," Selma said, laying a hand on her arm. "I didn't mean to inhibit you. I'm worried . . . about something I shouldn't be worried about. If my husband is still here, I don't want him accidentally sent away. Foolish, I know. I don't even know for sure he's here with me."

Kimberly rested a hand over Selma's. "I understand. And I'll be careful. I promise."

"I know you will, dear. Now, get that ghost."

"Rosie, I need your help. I need to be fully charged and focused in a few hours. When the sun sets tonight, Nathan and I have a date, whether he likes it or not."

CHAPTER FORTY-EIGHT

KIMBERLY FORCED down a swallow of the hated brew, pushed the teacup away, and gagged, willing herself not to vomit in the hotel lobby. "No more. I can't, Rosie."

"You have to. We've massaged and relaxed you. Played soothing nature sounds to root you in Mother Earth. I've aligned and charged your chakras. Burned incense and candles. You're wearing all your crystals. I have bundles of sage to burn plus the chakra stones for emergency energy restoration and an assortment of teas on hand. The only thing left in my personal arsenal is the Super Perk."

"I got about half of it down. That's a new record."

"These are desperate times. Drink."

"Not nearly that desperate. I can't focus on spirits if I'm hunched over a toilet hurling Super Perk."

"Ick," Sterling said behind her. "I'm guessing if you think you might hurl you won't want this." He held out a paper bag.

"I'll be fine if I don't drink any more tea. What's in the bag?"

Rosie cocked an eyebrow. "You've never once puked that up. Stop being a baby."

"I haven't puked because I know my limit. And thank you,

Sterling. I will enjoy whatever you brought me after the investigation tonight."

"It's some quinoa and mixed veggies."

"Quinoa and veggies? Really?" She pulled the to-go box from the bag. It smelled heavenly. "This ought to be light enough to eat before investigation."

She only meant to eat a few bites, but it tasted so good and was loaded with so many antioxidants, she devoured forkful after forkful until the plastic tines chased the last few grains. She sighed contentedly and only then noticed the silence—her crew watched her, stunned.

Michael pressed one hand to his cheek, slowly shaking his head. "I can't believe you got her to eat right before an investigation."

"Oh, stop," she chided them. "You've all seen me eat before."

Sterling held up his hands as if to stop applause. "Really. It's not that much of a challenge. She eats seeds and nuts and leafy things. And then there's a thing called the Internet to find a restaurant. Not rocket science. Or magic. Just have to know what she can't resist."

"Don't break your arm patting yourself on the back there, Sterling. But seriously, thank you. It was perfect. And got rid of the Super Perk aftertaste." She beamed at him despite his self-satisfied smirk.

He broke eye contact and rubbed the back of his neck. "Anytime." He wandered to Michael's side, watched Stan's computer monitor for a moment, then glanced back at her.

Rosie dug a sharp elbow into her ribs. "Guys don't blush like that at girls they don't like."

So she hadn't imagined that flush. "Oh, stop." She peered for the hundredth time at the door. Still no Elise.

"Kimmy. Er, Kimberly. Whatever. We're wasting time. The sun set thirty minutes ago. I think we need to start. If Elise finds something, she can fill you in later."

She wrung her hands. "Yes. Okay. Let's start here at the piano."

Ambient light shown through the rounded windows that stretched floor to ceiling in the lobby. The front desk remained manned by two fresh-faced and wide-eyed receptionists. Ghost tours milled in the lobby, traipsed up the stairs, and flashed untold numbers of pictures.

Ideally, she'd work the piano at 3 a.m. Too much living activity buzzed in the space for a perfect investigation. The noise and distractions would interfere, complicating the process of reading all the frequencies and tuning into the right one. Even if Nathan and Sarah drifted somewhere in the hotel, lost and confused, she might not be able to detect them, much less call them to her. And the amount of energy required would be increased to combat the distractions.

"Kimmy? You sure about this?"

Her friend and director knew her too well. He saw and understood her hesitation.

What choice did she have? The piano drew her to it, tugging at her sleeve like an impatient toddler. Laundry room again? Third floor? They had sta-cams there. Any activity would be caught on camera. Outside? Perhaps hope to catch the plummeting girl falling from the third floor balcony? Ditto. Sta-cams could record that. If only Elise would come back and bring her something that would tie it all together.

"Yes." Then more firmly. "Yes. I'm sure the piano is important. I wish the lobby was darker and quieter, but I think anything else would be a waste of time. We can always come back later if I'm unable to draw anyone out and connect."

"Would that then make starting here a waste of time?" Sterling asked. "I'm just along for the ride, so makes no difference to me. But if you need it dark and quiet in the lobby, this isn't the time to be here."

"You need it dark and quiet? You got it, Ms. Wantland!"

The voice was somehow familiar and yet she couldn't put a

face to it. She turned over her shoulder to find Kerry and Suzie front and center in the throng of hotel guests amassing to watch.

"Hello, ladies. I think I'll be okay—"

Kerry turned to face the wiggling crowd behind her. "Listen! Suzie and I are about to get to see an actual *Wantland Files* investigation. Do you realize what kind of opportunity this is? Do you understand the likelihood any of us will ever have the chance to experience this again?"

"It's none!" Suzie chimed in.

"That's right. None! So everyone needs to be still, be quiet, and be considerate of the professionals working here tonight."

A hush fell over the room. Even the murmuring ghost tour participants zipped it.

Kerry turned back around, smile wide as she gave a thumbs-up to the crew. Suzie held her clutched fists against her chest, appearing as though she might burst into a tiny explosion of excitement at any moment.

Michael clapped once, decision made. "Thank you all for your cooperation," he called to those milling about. He addressed the crew more quietly. "Let's roll in five. Set up a perimeter to hold back anyone who wanders through after we get started and doesn't know what's happening. Keep an eye out for camera clowns. We have some live wires in this audience. Stan, sta-cams set and rolling?"

Sterling pressed closer to her. "Camera clowns?"

"People desperate to pop up in front of a lens and make fools of themselves. Make faces. Pick noses. Flip the double bird. Sometimes they yell gibberish or obscenities. Ruins any chance of EVP."

"With so many people on set, surely no one could get that close?"

"Your naiveté is almost adorable. Would you notice someone who crawled up behind you and then sprang in front of your face? You wouldn't. Not until the shock nearly gave you a heart attack."

He lifted an eyebrow, seemed to consider, then nodded, the closest he'd come to saying she was right about something.

"Don't worry, Ms. Wantland! We won't let anyone ruin things!" Kerry called above the growing hum of the crowd.

"The quiet didn't last long. Maybe we should wait until later." She grasped her quartz and breathed deeply.

"You okay?" Sterling asked.

"Anxious. Frustrated. Worried I won't make any progress tonight."

"So basically, your normal self."

"Listen to the general hubbub in this room. All the breathing and shuffling. Add whispering and how can anyone think, much less accomplish something as delicate as connecting with a ghost?"

He placed his hands on her shoulders and rubbed, slowly. "Relax," he whispered in her ear. "You're working yourself up. This group of people is on your side. Their energy is positive. They want to see a ghost. And I remember you distinctly telling me ghosts don't only come out at night or at midnight. That they're all around us, all the time. Like fish in a pond, right?"

"But if I can't focus—"

"You can. You're Kimberly freakin' Wantland. And nobody is going to stop you from doing your job. You got this."

She closed her eyes and relaxed into the rhythmic kneading of his hands, soothing and effective. Somehow his deft fingers found the knots and tense muscles and eased them, coaxing them to let go a little. He was almost as good as Rosie. And on one level, much, much better. "That's . . . really nice."

"Good."

Phone cameras clicked and the whispering crescendoed to a full on ruckus.

She opened her eyes and discovered him posing for the cameras. "Well, there you go. Publicity achieved," she said, shrugging his hands off her shoulders. Why did she keep letting herself think he did anything for any reason other than attention?

"Kimberly, wait. I wasn't—" He reached for her but she leaned away.

"Ready, Michael?"

"Ready when you are, Kimmy! I'll count down, then you talk us in."

Rosie dashed to in to powder their noses and run her fingers through their hair, smoothing Kimberly's flyaway wisps but tousling Sterling's loose ends. "There's our rakish ne'er-do-well," she said with a wink before dashing out of frame.

"Ne'er-do-well? What decade is this? And did I miss a meeting? I've been designated a scamp?"

"It's Rosie. Let her do her thing. It looks good that way. I like it."

"Really?" He patted his head as if trying to detect what exactly Rosie had done.

"Let's get this ghost. Tonight."

CHAPTER FORTY-NINE

Michael held up all five fingers, counting down as he spoke. "In five, four, three . . . " He held up two fingers, then pointed to her.

She faced Stan's camera. "We've explored Crescent Hotel thoroughly. And we've seen a lot of activity. Miss Theodora asked us to leave. We discovered spirits trapped on the third floor in the old psych wing, suffering their last agonizing days over and over again. We've seen a young woman in a white nightgown drifting through the halls and captured footage of the infamous jumping girl. We shook things up in the laundry room, encountering a ghost who claims he wants revenge. But revenge for what? And we're still unclear who exactly is terrorizing the hotel guests."

"I wasn't terrorized," a voice in the crowd whispered.

"Shhhhh!" Someone, likely Kerry, shushed the speaker.

Kimberly took a deep breath, gritted her teeth, and continued. "Tonight I'm focusing on the piano here in the lobby. I heard it playing during our stay here, while no living person sat on this bench. I have a theory as to the identity of our revenge-seeking ghost, but so far, no proof."

Sterling cleared his throat but said nothing.

A voice from the crowd called out. "Come on, Sterling. Nothing? What do you think about her looking for proof to support her theory?"

Kimberly's head snapped to face the heckler before she could remind herself to ignore him and remain in control. She shook her head and faced the camera, train of thought lost. Rattled, she tried to remember what she'd just said.

"Hey! Shut it!" Kerry said.

The heckler didn't shut it. "Sterling is supposed to give his take. Let's hear it. Isn't that why you're here? Or are you going soft?"

Sterling cleared his throat again. "I will make my case separately, in the Confidential Corner segments of the show. Now, if you please, we're trying to work here."

The man made the sound of a whip cracking. Several times. "Pussy whipped. You got a thing for Wantland and now you're going ghost on us."

"How dare you—" Kerry attempted again to intervene.

The man booed. "Bring back *SpookBusters*. That show was way better!"

Kimberly felt tears beginning to pool and cursed herself for letting this buffoon under her skin. She willed herself not to let him see how badly he upset her. "Sir, if you don't care for my show, you're welcome to—"

Sterling stepped in front of her. "You're welcome to get the hell out of here. How dare you? I don't give two cents for your opinion of me but I'll be damned if you run down my new show or Kimberly. I like it here. I don't want to go back. Pussy whipped? You are a sad, lonely man, clearly eaten up with jealousy that I get to spend every day with this gorgeous, successful, strong woman. If you can't keep your mouth shut, I will personally come over there and throw you out the front door."

A moment of silence engulfed the room, as if everyone waited to see how the man would respond. When he said no more, applause erupted to fill the space.

Michael called to her. "Don't worry, Kimmy. We will edit that garbage right out. You keep going, sweetie."

Sterling returned to his place beside her. "Like hell, he'll cut that," he whispered. "I'll give up my Confidential Corner before we cut that little tidbit. That was gold."

She tucked her hair behind her ear and collected her thoughts. She would never, ever agree to investigate an occupied building again. This was exactly what she feared would happen. And still she couldn't remember what she had last said.

Sterling spoke up. "Kimberly, you were explaining you opted to start tonight here at the piano. You're attempting to prove a theory you have about the identity of the angry ghost."

She smiled as relief and gratitude surged through her. "Thank you, Sterling. Yes. I think the spirit is attached to the piano in some way. I hope it can give us some clues."

She faced the piano, breathing in deeply. Holding her hands over the instrument, she waited for something to tap into her spiritual energy, maybe even allow a connection.

Her thoughts were difficult to focus, however. She couldn't believe how handily Sterling had shut down the heckler. And with such conviction. He'd stepped in front of her protectively, one arm out to block her from the man. Jason never stood up for her like that. Sterling had even said he would rather be on her show than have *SpookBusters* back. And he didn't deny the man's accusation he had a thing for her. She flushed.

"Kimmy? Anything?" Michael's voice jarred her from her thoughts.

"Not yet," she said, but didn't admit she hadn't focused due to fantasizing about Sterling.

She closed her eyes, pushed aside all thoughts of the crowd, the heckler, Jason, Rosie contemplating leaving the show, and Sterling. She rested her fingertips on the edge of the piano and reached out, opening herself to any information the piano could give her.

She envisioned her indigo chakra and put all her energy into it, allowing it to grow and resonate fully to help her connect to the spiritual plane. Her surroundings faded.

The wood seemed warm to her touch. Snatches of conversation, whispered whimpers, impassioned pleas raced around her, swirling, building in intensity. All the shock, anguish, horror, and pain the piano had soaked up during its history disgorged itself into her. Rage and revenge eased into loneliness and desperation. She intuited the piano had sat in storage many years. Sudden illness and death were both punctuated with brief flares of delight. The piano was sharing its bitter, ill-fated history with her.

She fought to maintain control over the deep abyss the dark energy threatened to drag her into.

What started all of this? What initial tragedy sent the piano down this terrible path?

And then she saw them. The young man who'd appeared to her the night she'd heard the piano play, and beside him this time, the young woman—the one in the infamous bar photo cradling an infant, the one she'd seen drifting the halls and Sterling's room, the one she'd connected with, desperate to tell someone something before she was pushed from the balcony.

They smiled, the young man's fingers dancing over the keys, his face aglow with delight as she clapped and praised him.

This moment in time jolted her emotionally and physically. She gasped at the shock of being yanked from sinking into utter desolation to rising on pure, carefree passion.

Who? Who is the angry spirit? Who joined you here and terrorizes the guests?

Nothing.

Sarah? Nathan? Please. I want to help.

Even as she begged, she knew nothing would come of it. Might as well yell at a television or movie screen. History unfurled in front of her. A recording, nothing more. And the piano could only share moments it had been directly involved in.

Whatever catastrophic event had sparked the piano's journey wasn't in these memories.

But how could that be? Shouldn't the piano be involved in the incident that so thoroughly devastated it?

She needed a spirit. One willing to connect and communicate with her. Sarah or Nathan. Something told her one or both of them was involved. But how could she lure them to her and convince them to help?

She lifted her hands from the piano and severed the connection. It had told her everything it could. No sense wasting more energy. She had already drained more than she wanted to admit.

She staggered backward and bumped against Sterling.

"I've got you," he murmured. "I won't let you fall."

She raised her hands to her temples and willed the ground to stop spinning. "A bit woozy. I'm okay."

"Woozy is not okay." He grabbed her elbow and held firmly. "Michael? Rosie?"

"Kimmy knows her limits."

"And pushes herself past them every time. I've seen her pass out more times than I can count. Not anymore. Not while I'm here."

She allowed him to ease her onto the piano bench. The crew closed in, watching and recording as Sterling fussed over her.

"Rosie," he instructed. "Get her some of that nasty tea she hates."

Her assistant remained motionless, watching, waiting perhaps for some sign her services were not wanted. Kimberly didn't tell her no. She had never once asked for help or even admitted she needed it. And she never would. But Sterling insisting on caring for her was different. Something deep inside found comfort in his concern.

"Okaaay . . ." Rosie finally said, backing away slowly as if still waiting for an objection from her boss.

Sterling gathered her hair away from her neck and fanned her gently.

When Rosie returned and held the teacup in front of her, she accepted the foul brew and sipped.

"Better?" Sterling asked.

The crowd must be recording, she thought, envisioning her Twitter feed tomorrow. The thought made her gag. Well, that and the Super Perk. But she nodded. She did feel better.

"Michael, tonight let's make her take short breathers throughout the investigation instead of letting her careen from one place to the next. You know, like athletes pace themselves."

"Do you honestly think we haven't attempted to make her do that? Every. Time."

"Maybe I just have the right touch." Sterling began to massage her temples.

"I'm recovered," she insisted, leaning away from his fingers. The dizziness his warm touch sent shivering through her was more than she could handle in her present state. "All better."

"I assume you got something?" Michael crouched in front of her. "Did you connect with someone?"

"Not some*one*. Some*thing*. The piano."

Stan swooped in close to catch the information she shared in a tight shot.

"The piano talked to you?" Sterling asked.

There was the skepticism. But she didn't mind. He'd given her the perfect opportunity to explain on camera.

"Not talked, per se, but I could feel its history. As Elise described, the piano experienced illness and death wherever it went. And then I saw the young couple."

"So you imagined the previous owners as detailed by Elise and then imagined a young couple from the descriptions you've heard during the investigation."

"I saw them. It was the same young man I saw playing the piano the other night and then the young woman from your room. I know it's them. I'm more certain than ever that they are involved in this somehow. I need one of them to talk to me. I need to connect."

The onlookers began to buzz with excitement. She caught snatches of whispered conversations.

" . . . get to see a ghost?"

" . . . so cool if she can . . . "

"Dang it! My battery is getting low."

"How are you going to lure them?" Michael asked. "Do you know enough about them?"

Normally if she needed help connecting to a spirit, she used information gleaned from the investigation to attract it. Surrounding herself with favorite things from life often did the trick. "Not really. We know they liked playing piano."

"So play the piano," Sterling suggested.

"Clever idea, but I can't play."

He joined her on the piano bench, bumping her hip with his to nudge her over. His fingers skimmed the keys as he ran through a few scales and then struck several chords. "Out of tune, but I've heard worse. What did your ghost play? *Für Elise?*"

The crowd oohed and aahed listening to him coax the elegant classical piece from the instrument. She was pretty sure she heard Kerry and Suzie clap and giggle with delight.

He's good. Really good.

"I didn't know you play piano," she said as casually as possible while her fans doubted out loud that, "Jason can do that."

"One of my many talents." He pierced her with a hypno-gaze that was surely lifted from his stage act. "I only reveal my tricks slowly."

He hadn't missed a note while gazing at her.

That's it. I'm Googling him. No more springing surprises on me.

Her skin began to crackle, hairs standing on end. Something restless in the spirit realm shifted. She rested a hand on Sterling's arm. "Keep playing. No matter what."

"Got it," he confirmed, then called to the crowd. "I am now taking requests. I can play anything you'd like to hear, anything at all, as long as it's *Für Elise.*"

A ghost tour, led by none other than Lorenzo, wandered from the staircase into the lobby, eyes wide with curiosity, still brimming with excitement from the tour. The already-present onlookers quickly filled them in and answered questions.

"She's going into a trance!"

"I can't believe we're here for this."

"Think we'll see a ghost?"

Murmurs and mumbles accompanied gasps through the new cluster of people.

She left one hand resting on Sterling's arm and clutched her quartz with the other. "If you can keep them quiet, that would help."

"Ladies and gentlemen," he addressed the crowd. "For our next trick, Ms. Wantland will"—she felt him shrug—"conjure a ghost. We must have . . . complete silence."

Lorenzo instructed his group, "Everyone remember I demonstrated how to silence your personal EMF devices? Please do so now to allow our visiting paranormal investigators silence and enjoy watching your devices light up as ghosts move about us."

She spotted Rosie edging over to Lorenzo, who put an arm around her and tugged her close. Annoyance flared briefly, but she pushed it aside. Not the time to worry. Anxiety only clouded her abilities.

Someone in the audience intoned a drum roll.

Sterling played on as he spoke. "While I appreciate a good drumroll as much as the next guy, that's actually the opposite of silence. That's noise."

She caught a glimpse of his furrowed brow as she took a deep breath and closed her eyes.

Focusing all her attention and energy on her uppermost chakra, she encouraged it to spin and grow until it bathed her in its warm white light.

Nothing answered her invitation. She sunk deeper into

herself, detaching her psyche from the world around her and pressing further into the spirit realm.

Sterling's *Für Elise* sounded distant, as though he played in a cave, not directly beside her.

She set her lighthouse beacon twirling, seeking out Nathan or any spirit who could lead her to him.

Something to her left nudged her. She turned to find a fresh-faced young man sitting on the bench beside her. Hands in front of him, he mimicked Sterling's movements precisely. He bent his head, smiling as only someone young and completely in love smiles.

In the space beside him, Sarah materialized, slowly, almost hesitantly it seemed to Kimberly, as if fearful to show herself. She stood beside the piano, fervent attention fixed on Nathan's playing. Enraptured, she swayed slightly to the music, setting her floor-length dress swinging to the notes. Nathan stood, hands raised as if to caress her cheeks, then stopped. He looked around, distracted apparently by the crowd.

His hands dropped to his sides, Sarah forgotten. His head swiveled to face Kimberly, his gaze locking on hers. She watched in horror as his features melted, decayed, until the only flesh that remained clung in putrid pieces from his skull.

He threw his head back and roared, a guttural howl giving voice to utter rage. Nathan snapped his attention back to Sarah.

Sarah's spirit cringed and cried out before fading to nothing.

"Sarah!" Nathan's ghost wailed. He made eye contact with Kimberly once more, promising, "Revenge," before he shot like a rocket through the ceiling.

CHAPTER FIFTY

KIMBERLY SLUMPED SIDEWAYS, falling out of her trance.

Sterling encircled her with his arms before she slid to the floor. "I know you said to keep playing, but I couldn't let you fall."

Gasps from her crowd of onlookers preceded anxious voices.

"Is she okay?"

"Did anyone record any orbs or other celestial images?"

"What happened?"

Rosie descended on her. "Here. Drink this."

Her assistant tipped tea into her mouth. She managed several swallows.

Rosie dabbed eucalyptus oil on her temples and earlobes. "Sterling, if she can sit up, rub this lemon oil into her hands like before."

Sterling shifted on the bench so he sat behind her, his legs straddling her. Even in her weakened state, she felt his orange chakra flare with interest as he drew her close. She fit quite nicely, she noticed, as he leaned her back against his chest. "Give me the oil."

Helpless to move, grateful to retain consciousness, she nestled closer and gave herself up to his hands caressing hers.

The tenderness with which he handled her melted some of the frostiness she attempted to use as a barrier. Letting people get too close only resulted in heartache. But oh, his hands felt so good against her skin. How could someone be so strong yet so gentle?

Michael squatted in front of her. "What happened this time? Did you get something good?"

She took another swallow of tea and breathed in lemon and eucalyptus. "I connected. I saw them. It's him. The young man playing the piano sat beside me but then morphed into the angry vengeful spirit when Sarah arrived. I knew they were somehow tied together but I had no idea they were different manifestations of the same spirit."

"You're certain? This is our ghost?"

"Yes. Completely certain. Nathan the laundry boy has become a fury in the afterlife. Something drives him to murderous rage in a quest for revenge."

"So what next?"

"He raced off after Sarah. She's in danger. We need to intervene." Pushing herself into a sitting position, she tested her strength.

"I thought you said they were a happy couple in love," Michael said. "And the diary entries confirmed that. Why would he want revenge?"

She glanced at Rosie, who raised a knowing eyebrow.

"Do we have to spell this out Michael?" Her stylist rocked back on her heels. "What would make a smitten young man so furious that he would threaten his girlfriend?"

"His *pregnant* girlfriend," Kimberly added.

Michael's eyes widened as the pieces clicked. "She cheated on him."

"This has turned into a soap opera," Sterling commented. Vibrations as he spoke rumbled through his chest and against her back. "It's a good story if nothing else."

"Do you really think he was angry enough to kill her?" Michael asked. "Perhaps he even pushed her off the balcony?"

"I couldn't tell in the vision who grappled with her on the balcony or even if they intended to push her over the edge. Whoever he was, he burned with rage, like Nathan's spirit burns now. We have to help her."

She stood—wobbly and woozy, but she stood.

"Let's recharge," Rosie said. "A quick Reiki session should do it."

As much as she hated to lose precious time, she needed more energy or she wouldn't get far. She stretched out on the floor. "No wonder Sarah's spirit is restless. Her murderer is back haunting her."

Rosie knelt beside her and placed chakra stones on her forehead, throat, sternum, stomach, abdomen, and pelvis. She clasped her hands and grew completely still.

Kimberly watched Rosie lower her hands over her body. Her assistant did not make contact but rather concentrated on sending energy to her chakras and anywhere she needed to heal.

She felt heat radiate through her abdomen, then her torso as Rosie moved from one chakra center to the next.

Sterling watched with an eyebrow cocked, one corner of his mouth curled up in bemusement. Only when Rosie frowned did his expression change, morphing into concern. "Something wrong?"

"Only if you plan on making a move in the next few days. She's ovulating. So have protection on hand, just in case."

"Rosie!" Her indignant cry overlapped with Sterling's choke of surprise. "I would thank you not to broadcast my personal information to the jam-packed lobby!"

"I spoke to you in confidence, Rosie." Sterling's tone conveyed true betrayal.

She whipped her head to face him, sending chakra stones tumbling. "Rosie is *my* confidante. What did you tell her?"

"It doesn't matter," he mumbled. "Can you finish 'recharging' so we can move along? Sounds like you're ready to invent the rest of the fabrication so we can wrap tonight. I totally support that. I'm tired of this place."

Rosie returned to the Reiki treatment, realigning, unclogging, and energizing her chakras. Finally, she smoothed the energy field around Kimberly. "There. I topped you off by transferring some of my own energy to you. If you feel a bit giddy and buzzed, that's why."

Kimberly stood. The crowd clapped. She stretched and flexed her fingers.

"All better?" Kerry called.

"I feel great, Rosie. You're awesome," she told her assistant.

Sterling nudged her. "Tell *them*."

She turned to her fans and raised both hands in the air. "I feel great! Rosie is awesome!"

The clustered onlookers cheered.

"The crew went ahead to scout out what's going on up on three," Michael said. "Let's go catch up."

"Well played," Sterling whispered to her, then addressed the crowd. "Upstairs to the third floor!"

"I don't really want them to follow us," she said.

"Yes, you do. Trust me."

"I don't think I can stop them anyway." She noted the crowd at least maintained a distance while they all climbed the staircase.

As she rounded the third floor, heading toward the psych ward, a presence pulled at her highly charged senses. Her hair crackled and her skin prickled. She paused, closed her eyes, and sought the source. Fury, anger, and confusion consumed her.

"It's Nathan," she murmured.

Sterling noticed and turned. "You okay?"

"He's here."

She veered away from the psych ward and followed the manifestation in silence until it stopped in front of Rosie and Elise's room. "He's searching for Sarah. Maybe this was her room when she lived here. Isn't this the room witnesses see the girl fall from?"

"Yes!" Rosie said. "He must be returning to the scene of his crime."

"What's he doing?" Michael asked.

"He's standing at the door. I'm going to try to engage him." She approached the door where Nathan's ghost hovered. "She isn't here, Nathan. You're scaring her. You must calm down."

"Careful, Kimmy. Don't rile him up too much."

"I'm not trying to rile him up. I want him to calm down so we can help him cross over." She moved closer. "Please, listen to me. I know Sarah hurt you during life, but it's time to forgive her. Calm down and let me help you."

The spirit turned to face her, his face contorting into rage. He rushed at her, blasting past. She ran to follow.

Stan swung his camera to focus on her location. She hoped the recording caught evidence of something. If not a shadow, perhaps a burst of static or a ripple across the screen could offer substantiated proof of a presence. Not that Sterling would consider a blip, a shadow, or static proof of anything except technical difficulties or lighting malfunctions. He didn't even believe in orbs, for crying out loud. Too bad the ghost didn't scratch him. Three long, inexplicable scrapes appearing down his arm would surely—

Wait a minute. All the victims have been female. Maybe—

"Kimmy!" Jason struggled to penetrate the crowd in the hall. "Excuse me. I need . . . could you please let me by?"

"Oh, joy," Sterling muttered, loudly enough she was certain he intended her to hear. "Mr. Potato Head. He's clipped on some cozy casual today. Cuz, you know, it's all good. Whatevs. No big thang. What a douche."

She opted not to chastise Sterling, rather irritated with Jason's interruption.

Jason emerged from the crowd, wriggling through like a salmon swimming upstream. "Hey. Can we talk?"

"I'm in the middle of an investigation and just had a breakthrough. Now is not a good time."

"But I want to apologize for earlier."

"She said not now," Sterling interrupted, his tone gruff and protective as it had been with the heckler. "Get lost."

She saw TJ move to intercede as well but Michael threw out an arm to block him. The look in his eyes and the half smile said it all. *Story gold.*

Not about to stand around for a pissing contest, she turned and attempted to push past them.

A hand smacked against her back, throwing her off balance, right into the bannister, which struck her mid-thigh. The momentum threw her forward. She threw her arms out, grasping wildly for anything to stop her.

She lost her balance.

"Kimmy!" Jason, still trailing her, gasped.

Numerous screams from her crowd of fans barely pierced her thoughts.

She twisted away from the dizzying stairwell and managed to turn around, but couldn't grab the low railing. Sitting on the bannister, she teetered, clawing at the air around her. She reached forward, sure someone would catch her. She watched Jason stand motionless, eyes wide, as she tipped backward over the railing. She felt herself losing to gravity, fumbled with the bannister, scrabbling to hold on. Gravity coaxed her further, winning the battle. "Jason!" she gasped. "Help me!"

She tipped further and glanced down, three floors yawning beneath her to the basement level. She wouldn't survive. Would she join other ghosts who had perished in the hotel stairwell? Or would she move on? And would her mother welcome her to the next existence, as she sometimes dreamed she would?

Rosie screamed. "Someone help!"

She heard scuffling and shouting. She lost the fight, pitched backward over the bannister, still fighting for a grip on something. Gravity pulled like a hungry beast.

Two strong hands gripped her forearms. "I have her!" Sterling yelled.

Relief suffused her until she realized that though he'd stopped her descent over the cavernous space, he struggled to heave her back over the edge. He pulled, but the angle was odd and she could offer nothing from her helpless perch. She caught a glimpse of young Nathan's ghost, leaned over the edge, reaching for her.

Sterling twisted to yell over his shoulder. "A little help here? Jason! I can't . . . can you please—"

Nathan's hazy features conveyed fear and concern. His translucent hands reached out, grabbing for her.

"I'm here!" Michael appeared in her limited vision. "Kimmy, don't look down. Focus on me."

More hands reached across the bannister, reminding her momentarily of the ghosts clawing and plucking at her, begging for her help. This time, the hands offered survival. She barely breathed, watching the cluster of faces, terror visible in every eye. They pulled and heaved until the combined strength of her crew rocked her back over the bannister to safety. She lost sight of Nathan.

Sterling crushed her in a hug as she burst into tears.

"Thank you," she whispered. "I thought that was it. Thought I was falling for sure and—"

He hushed her before she could voice the concern. "I will always catch you. You'll never fall as long as I'm around." He squeezed her tighter. "You have to stop scaring me like that, though. I'm not sure how much more my heart can take."

Jason appeared beside Sterling. "Kimmy, I'm so sorry. I don't know what happened. I just froze up. I can't believe I—"

"Don't worry about it," Sterling said. "I've got her." He held an arm out to block Jason as Rosie dove for a hug.

Her stylist's mascara had streaked long black lines down her cheeks. "Don't you ever, ever do that again! What would I do without you and this show?"

"I'll remember you said that." She took a deep breath, still slightly incredulous she was alive and well and not lying on the basement floor of the stairwell. "And I don't intend to go anywhere."

Sterling eased her into Rosie's arms.

Stan rested his camera on the ground, wiping at his eyes. "I, uh, don't know how much we got on tape. Most of it up until you fell. I set the camera on the ground and hoped we'd get something. I had to make sure you didn't fall."

"Thank you, Stan. For once I don't care what we recorded. I'm just relieved to be alive."

"So what happened?" Sterling asked. "How did you lose your balance? If you tell me Jason bumped you—"

"No. I don't know where he was when this happened. It was the ghost. Nathan. He became distraught and worked up. Except I thought I saw him after I fell and he didn't look angry. He looked . . . concerned. Scared even."

"Ghosts can't . . . ghosts are not real, first of all. But even people who believe in them agree they aren't . . . I mean, they're transparent and not solid. Not something that can hurt you."

"This one is remarkably powerful. Fueled by hate and revenge. We're not dealing with a typical ghost. Although I think I'm still missing something. If he wanted me to fall and be hurt, he should've looked delighted to see me toppling over the railing. He looked like he wanted to help."

A stinging pain in her arm drew her attention. Three long, open wounds ran down her forearm, identical to the other injuries. She held her arm out to Sterling.

Sterling inspected her injury. "Someone must've scraped up your arm trying to drag you back over the railing."

Rosie grabbed the affected arm. "Oh, no. No, no, no. This is the ghost. Look."

She and Rosie placed their arms side by side. The wounds were identical.

"He really wants you gone, doesn't he?" Michael asked. "He pushed you over. He's hurt your arm. He is bent on revenge."

"I don't think he meant to hurt me. I think the scratches were unintentional. Accidental. Maybe . . . maybe I've interpreted this incorrectly. I need Sarah to come back and tell me what happened to her. But he's scaring her away."

"No more tonight," Sterling said. "You need a break and a little recovery time. Michael?"

"Definitely. Everyone, let's call it for tonight. You may continue on your own or go calm down and rest. Kimmy is okay. We will pick back up tomorrow."

"No way am I stopping," she insisted. "I won't. I refuse."

Sterling opened his mouth to argue.

"I appreciate the concern but we are too close and this ghost is too hot. I need to figure out what I'm missing."

Elise rounded the stairs, flushed and panting. "Ms. Wantland! I know what happened!"

Finally, the break she needed to end this tonight. She hoped.

CHAPTER FIFTY-ONE

"Elise!" Kimberly called, relieved to see her researcher return. "I thought we had it figured out. I thought Nathan was angry with Sarah for cheating on him. Now I'm not so sure."

"No," Elise said. "He didn't even know she was pregnant. The very last diary entry went on for pages and pages. The girl was distraught by what she'd seen and never wrote in the diary again. She must have hidden it, scared to be involved as a witness."

"A witness to what?"

"Sarah's death."

"You mean she saw it? She knew what happened but remained silent?"

Sterling held up a hand. "Look, Kimberly had a very traumatic experience and we called the investigation for the night. She needs to rest now."

"I can't rest when we're so close. And Elise has the answer literally in her hands."

"Michael?"

"Sterling, I can't control her. Nor can I walk away when Elise is standing here with the answer to a decades-old mystery."

Kimberly rested a hand on Sterling. "I'm okay. Promise. Stan, let's roll. Record this. Tell us what you discovered, Elise."

"In the weeks leading up to the night of Sarah's death, the girl wrote in her diary about the budding romance a number of times. Here's an example. 'Nathan can play piano and has taken to playing for Sarah. Her favorite is *Für Elise*. He may be only a laundry boy, but he is elegant and cultured and clearly raised well. I can understand Sarah being smitten with him and confess a bit of envy. I fear she may be completely swept away. I urged caution, but she confided that she snuck Nathan to her room in the laundry basket two nights ago. She insists her parents will come to accept him once they meet him and see how good he is to her. And hinted that perhaps if she was with child, they would have no choice but to allow the match.'"

"Because parents love when their children defy them," Sterling murmured.

Elise turned a page in her notebook. "Nothing about Sarah for a few weeks, then a new development. 'I would not wish to be in Sarah's shoes for anything in the world. The dean's son, Richard, has taken a liking to Sarah and is making unwanted advances on her. She rebuked him in no uncertain terms, but he is spoiled and perhaps has never been told no before. Sarah says he came to her room last night and when she wouldn't open the door, he unlocked it and let himself in! He must have taken his father's key. He attempted to force a kiss, but she screamed and he left, vowing to return. I told her she can come to my room at night to hide from him. We both fear being caught, and Sarah believes the dean will not act against his son or even believe her if she reports the boy's transgressions.'"

Michael drew a hand across his brow. "Whew. Sterling was right. This does sound like it was lifted right out of a soap opera."

"And this girl's room is the one Sterling is staying in now, isn't it?"

Sterling scowled. "You can't possibly know that."

"The girl described looking out over the gardens from her

room. Plus you've seen Sarah at night. And she hid in the girl's room to avoid the dean's creepy son."

"Lots of rooms look out over the gardens."

Rosie shook her head. "That poor girl. What can you do when no one believes you or defends you? If this happened today, it would be on Twitter with other MeToo stories. I'd like to think things have changed but, have they really?"

"At least people might listen and believe her now," Michael said. "What happened next?"

"There are a few brief references to Sarah and her woes over the next few weeks. Sarah strongly suspected she was pregnant, for one thing. Then the final entry. The night of the incident. The girl wrote, 'Sarah did not come to supper this evening nor did she join us for any evening activities. Fearing she was once again sick with her new pregnancy, I went to her room to check on her before retiring to my own. I discovered Richard at her door, fumbling with the lock and trying to force his way in. I ran to the laundry room to get Nathan, thinking how fortunate he was there. Little did I know how greatly I would regret my actions before this night was done. When we arrived, Sarah fought with Richard, struggling to get out of his grasp. She stood on the balcony, and I can only assume she had retreated there in her attempts to evade him. Sarah spurned him yet again with a slap to the face. Nathan cried out and raced to her side. Richard became so angry he shoved her. Sarah lost her balance, and as we watched, tipped over the railing. Nathan tried to catch her but alas. I confess I turned my head, as I could not bear to see. Nathan raced downstairs. I had crept to the balcony and watched in horror. Richard joined Nathan at her side and realized the result of his actions. Nathan cried out in agony and struck Richard. They fought until Richard knocked Nathan down, where he fell against a sharp rock. I watched in silence as Richard dragged him to the nearby woods. He returned some time later covered in dirt. I can only assume he buried the evidence of his murder. Sarah's body he left alone to be discovered. I dare not speak out against the dean's son for fear he will murder me next. One who will kill twice would not bat an eye at a third murder to cover his deeds.' That's the end of the diary."

"That's it?" TJ asked. "Didn't anyone notice the laundry boy was gone? And nothing happened to this douche Richard? He got away with it?"

"Nathan's family had turned him out on his own. They didn't know anything had happened to him. Richard may never have told the truth to anyone."

Rosie sniffed. "And the one witness was too scared to come forward. This is horrible. I can't stand it."

Kimberly nodded. "It's Richard he wants. No wonder he's so angry in the after life. His beloved was killed in front of him and then he was murdered."

"And the murderer never faced justice! Now I want revenge," TJ said. "Can we find out what happened to the jerk?"

She felt a tug on her psyche. Turning, she found Nathan's spirit in his young form, barely more than a boy, as he was when he passed violently, wrenching his spiritual self from the physical. The anguish of those final moments remained clearly on his face. Her heart melted as it always did when she encountered a miserable entity trapped in a limbo of aching pain. He didn't intend to hurt anyone. He was lost and confused and imprisoned.

Holding a hand out to the spirit, she offered an end to the suffering. "I know it isn't fair. I know it hurts. You've wandered too long this way. Let me help you."

"What's happening, Kimmy?"

"Nathan is here with me. He has calmed down. I'm going to try to help him cross over. Keep the cameras on me."

But as she reached out to attempt to connect and guide him to the next plane of existence, Nathan shot out a hand and clamped it over her wrist.

She drew in a breath, startled by the sudden chill his touch sent through her body. Immediately, she connected with him, with no effort on her part. Nathan badly wanted to share something.

"He wants to connect," she managed to say before she sunk too far into her trance-like state to communicate. She also reached for Sterling and clasped his hand, hoping he would remember—or someone would remind him—not to let go. The last thing she felt was an arm whip around her waist, firmly holding her upright.

Leaving the hotel and her crew behind, she allowed herself to be drawn into Nathan's thoughts. She saw his memories, felt his emotions, and relived his past as he shared his last living moments.

Nathan watched his darling Sarah struggle with the dean's son. The spoiled worthless young man had never worked a day in his life. How dare he force himself on sweet Sarah? He pushed past Juliette and raced to Sarah as she slapped Richard. While he watched, Richard shook Sarah violently and shoved her backwards against the balcony railing.

Nathan's memories slowed as he watched Sarah hit the balcony railing and tip backwards, upper body dangling over nothing. He lunged past Richard, poor Sarah's hands pinwheeling as she sought something to grab to stop her descent. Her feet lifted from the floor. He threw a hand out, catching Sarah by the arm as she dropped over the balcony. Her momentum was too great. Gravity fought for her. He dug his fingers into her arm. *Please. Please, no. Let me save her.* His fingernails raked down her arm as she stared up at him, fear and disbelief in her eyes. He leaned dangerously far over the railing himself, hoping to grab her with his second hand. She sucked in a breath and appeared to want to tell him something. His fingertips grazed hers. She slipped away, plummeting to the ground below. He heard the soft thud her body made on impact.

Squeezing his eyes, fighting a scream that threatened to roar from his throat, he turned and sprinted from the room, tore down the staircase two at a time and out the back door. Her crumpled body lay motionless. He gathered her in his arms. Her head lolled, eyes lifeless. She was gone. Just like that. Gone. His plan to marry her and spend his life with her came to naught. Because of one man. One selfish, uncaring spoiled brat took her away and stole his dreams. He threw back his head and wailed his anguish into the evening air.

Richard squatted beside him. "You really think she was going to marry you? Hoped her family money would get you out of the washing room, laundry boy? You never had a chance."

Nathan lowered Sarah to the ground and pounced at Richard. "I'll kill you for this!"

Kimberly felt the raw rage coursing through Nathan as his fist connected with Richard's jaw, cheek, nose, each blow worse than the one before it. Richard, taken by surprise, recovered and scrambled to his feet. He landed several punches, the pain exploding through Nathan's face nothing compared to the devastating loss of his lovely Sarah and their future together. *For a spoiled Daddy's boy, he can fight.*

"You thought playing the piano would make her yours?" Richard taunted him. "Her father would only approve of a suitor from a moneyed family, you fool. Too bad you were born poor."

Rage blinded Nathan. He struck with no thought. Richard ducked, avoiding his fists, caught him by the collar, and threw him to the ground.

Everything went black.

Kimberly sucked in a breath. She opened her eyes to find Rosie and Michael watching her closely. Sterling clutched her hand in a death grip, face pale.

"I didn't let go," he told her. "But I don't think I can handle this passing out thing."

"Kimmy? What happened? Did Nathan cross over?"

"No. He wanted to show me what happened that day. When he and Sarah died." She shivered. "It was awful. He grabbed her arm as she fell. I think he's been scratching women's arms because it's one of the last things that he remembers before he died. He's grieving the loss of Sarah and remembers their happy moments together. But he's also consumed with rage and desire for revenge. He's caught between two versions of himself."

"How do we help him?" Michael asked.

"He has to come to terms with his anger and hatred in order to cross to the next existence. Otherwise he will continue in this purgatory of sorts, roaming the hotel, searching for Richard, hungry for revenge that he can never have. Missing a life he can never have."

"You're sure Richard isn't here somewhere?" TJ asked. "I wouldn't mind seeing that little twerp pay for his actions."

"If he was," she said, "I think Nathan would have already found him. It seems highly unlikely the dean's son would remain here. The dean isn't here. When the school closed they probably moved elsewhere and I assume Richard went on to live a normal life."

"That boils my blood," Rosie said. "So unfair."

"We don't know what kind of life he led or if he perhaps came to regret what he'd done. Perhaps he did ultimately feel remorse. For that matter, we don't know where he's living out his after life. He didn't necessarily get away with it entirely. But Nathan is our concern now."

As if drawn to his name, Nathan materialized beside her, his outline dim and diffuse after the energy he expended connecting with her. She understood completely. Having shared her energy with him during the session, she no longer brimmed with it herself. No giddy buzz.

She saw Sarah hovering in the hallway, in her white nightgown, hair twisted and tied in curling cloths. As before, she seemed hesitant to come closer, unsure what to do.

As if Nathan felt her presence, the ghost turned. At the sight of her, he morphed into the vengeful, decaying version of himself.

"Nathan, no, don't!" Kimberly tried to stop him.

He cried out in agony. Sarah looked as though she wanted to cry before dissipating.

Nathan raced to where she had stood. He turned back to Kimberly. His glare bore into her. "Revenge," he promised and disappeared.

"He has to get that under control," she muttered.

"What's happening?" Michael asked.

"I got something!" Kerry called from the crowd. "Look, Suzie! It's the same ghost that we saw before. The one that scratched you!"

She heard other onlookers claiming to have captured images and orbs. Others watched and admired Kerry's recording.

Alarms sounded.

She looked around. "What is that? KIIs? EMF sensors?"

"Both," Stan said. "We're seeing a significant amount of static and orbs on the sta-cams. Looks like your psych ward patients are restless tonight. And I think they want your attention."

CHAPTER FIFTY-TWO

THE CREW CONGREGATED near the entry to the wing of Crescent Hotel once dubbed the psych ward, where patients in the most pain were locked away to die in agony. They switched off the alarming equipment and reviewed recent recordings.

"Ms. Wantland," TJ said. "The girl is back. The one in the mirror. Look."

"I see her," she said.

The young woman's image remained frozen in the center of the mirror, head hanging as if exhaustion dragged her down. The wall around the mirror pulsed and throbbed, outlines of hands stretching the physical barrier, perhaps an indication of their desire to break through the spiritual realm.

A blast of icy air enveloped Kimberly. She drew in a breath and shook violently.

"Temperature plummeting," Elise said.

"I feel a chill," someone in the crowd confirmed.

"Amazing what the power of suggestion can do," Sterling said.

The girl in the mirror jerked her head up and locked her gaze with Kimberly. *Help me*, she mouthed. *Help me*. The girl held out a hand, face contorted in pain, then collapsed back into her catatonic state.

"She's asking for my help."

"Kimmy," Michael cautioned, "you cannot release these spirits."

"I have to, Michael. You can't feel their pain or see her agony. I will not leave anyone like this."

"But Ms. Reddick said—"

"I know what I said." Ms. Reddick emerged from the crowd. "Let her do what she needs to do. And, Kimberly, if anyone is miserable or trapped here, well, I wouldn't want that. So . . . so go ahead and let him go."

She nodded once. "I understand."

Holding out a hand to the mirror, she coaxed the spirits toward her. With luck, the intrigue of freely-offered energy would lure them to her. Would her beating heart be enough enticement?

The young woman's head snapped up again. This time when she reached out, her wispy form floated free of the mirror and clasped Kimberly's hand.

"I have her, TJ." Kimberly spoke through chattering teeth. "I have her. She's ready and eager to go."

The pulsing walls bent, then snapped back into place, releasing more ghosts from confinement. They all floated to her, grasping, pulling, wanting.

"Too much," she muttered as her psychic energy drained. The ghosts couldn't understand but she was no help to them if they drained her completely.

Sterling rushed to her side, attempting to hold her up, probably fearful she would pass out. "What the—She's ice cold. What's the opposite of a fever and how do we treat it?"

Everyone seemed to shout at once, all of them pelting Sterling with some form of, "Leave her alone."

"She's helping the patients transition," Michael explained. "Don't disrupt."

She focused all her energy near a corner of the hallway, not far from the mirror. The air around her crackled, the sharp tang of ozone thick. Opening a passage between this world and the next took a lot of energy. She preferred spirits find their own way. But with so many lost souls pleading with her for guidance and assistance, she was willing to provide it.

Nothing happened.

Her teeth chattered. "Michael, I can't transition them. Too weak. Too many of them."

"Sweetie, you know we can't risk the SEEPS. We're eating through batteries as it is trying to keep the cameras going."

"The spirits are too strong already. I'm not sure what to do."

Ms. Theodora dropped through the ceiling and descended to their level like a ghostly Mary Poppins, sans umbrella.

"Spectral burst near Ms. Wantland. Possibly originated from the ceiling," TJ said.

"Ms. Theodora," she told him. Her voice sounded off, almost distant.

"Kimmy, you still good?" Michael called.

"She is clearly having another episode," Sterling answered. "She is not good."

The concerns of onlookers in the crowd broke through her trance-like state.

"Did anyone else just record a huge blue light up at the ceiling?"

"I'm ... too cold ... to work my phone."

"I'm cold too! Thought I just had the shivers."

"I'm out of here. I thought this was all faked. I can't handle this."

Kimberly, virtually unable to move, watched Ms. Theodora drift closer. The ghost nurse extended a hand and rested it on her forehead. Immediate relief flowed over her. The chill relaxed its paralyzing grip. Her teeth stopped chattering. The nurse pointed to the corner where Kimberly had attempted a transitional portal to bridge to the next world.

"Ms. Theodora wants to help. She's going to serve as a conduit and bridge the divide. I need more energy though. I'm not strong enough to power it."

"Yes!" Kerry's voice rose above the general hubbub of the crowd. "Our time has come, Suzie. Kimberly Wantland needs us!"

Kerry and Suzie pressed through the crowd. They stood behind her and placed their hands on her shoulders. "Come on everyone! Join hands! We can send our energy to Kimberly to help open the portal."

Kimberly opened her mouth to turn down the offer of assistance, but then thought better of it. "That . . . actually might work."

More fans tentatively approached, gathered around her, and rested their hands on her, or on someone else in direct contact with her.

A warm current flowed through her. She grasped her crystal. "I think this is working. Please, everyone join in. Help me send the ghosts on their way. Share your energy with me and Ms. Theodora."

She heard Sterling sigh nearby. "Look at my little padawan. She's learning how to play to the crowd. Should you be burning dandelions or something, Rosie? Wouldn't that add to the effect?"

"You mean sage?" Rosie asked. "Are you out of your mind? That would expel all the spirits from the area."

"That's what she's pretending to do, right? Exorcise spirits?"

"No! She's helping them find their way to the light. To the next world."

TJ scoffed. "Dude, you need to study. That is some basic stuff right there."

She wished briefly she was back in her semi-catatonic state and didn't have to listen. She took a deep breath. "Everyone, focus on that corner. Send all your energy. Imagine it flowing through your arms and out your fingertips."

Ms. Theodora seemed to be giving instructions to the other ghosts. All of them released their grip on her—all except the young woman, who continued clutching her hand. No more energy drained from her but the energy of those around her continued to pour through. The ghostly nurse's image amplified as the increased energy reached her. Appearing nearly as corporeal as a living person, Ms. Theodora extended her arm toward the corner again.

A faint blue line formed midair, stretching apart the space between the planes of existence until a bright blue cavern, brilliant white at the core, blazed open.

Ms. Theodora gestured to the waiting ghosts. She took them by the hand, one by one as they approached the open door, most with trepidation, and stood by them as they crossed through. One by one they left their agony behind, moving on to the next world.

The young woman with a tumor continued to clutch Kimberly's hand and hold back while Ms. Theodora gestured for patient after patient. When no one else remained, Kimberly gently disengaged her hand and held it out to Theodora, who had cared for her so long ago. Sensing contrition on Theodora's part and fear from the young woman, Kimberly encouraged them both.

"It's okay. Theodora wants to help you. She always wanted to help you. Let her make it up to you now by helping you translocate to the next world. A whole new existence awaits you. Pain free."

The young woman took Theodora's hand and allowed her nurse from long ago to guide her toward the passageway. As she stood in the flickering, blazing glow of the unknown, the young woman turned back for a final look at this world. The lines illness and suffering had etched into her face were gone, replaced with relief, her visage young and pain-free once more. The woman seemed to sigh in relief. She waved to Kimberly and disappeared into the light.

Sarah appeared beside her. The sad, wistful image looked around.

She wants Nathan.

Kimberly closed her eyes and sent out as much of a beacon as she could muster, hoping he would respond.

The temperature dropped another degree. Nathan materialized in his younger form.

"It's time, Nathan," she called. "Time to let go. You'll be so much happier. Let the anger go so you can cross to the next world."

Sarah spoke his name but only set him off further—he roared and morphed into the angry, decaying spirit. Sarah dimmed almost into non-existence, eyeing the flickering blue portal.

Kimberly knew she couldn't hold the fragile window open much longer. Eventually, all the energy would be exhausted.

"Nathan. Revenge never helps. It's making your spirit ugly and scaring away the woman you love. Let go of the anger and revenge so you can be with her." She saw him struggle, his face fighting to return to the gentle, loving young man at his core.

Sarah rested a hand on his arm.

The angry spirit roared, pain contorting his face. "He stole you from me. Destroyed everything. Killed you, killed me. We were to be married. We would have had a life together. I want revenge. I want him to suffer."

Sarah stood taller, unbowed by his anger this time. "Yes. He deserves to suffer for what he did. But instead, you are suffering. You cannot reach him now. What's done is done. If you insist on seeking revenge, you will be required to go to a place I'm not going. And I am going now, Nathan. I am tired. So tired. I have waited and waited, hoping you would return to me someday. But look how you've returned."

"It isn't fair. I want him to know how he hurt us. What he stole from us."

"Then you will suffer for eternity. Without me. Or you can

let go and find peace. And we can spend forever together. With our little girl."

Nathan shook violently, melting back into his younger self. "Our what?"

"Our daughter. I never got to tell you. I waited in my room for you. I planned to tell you that night. I was expecting our child when I died." A bundle appeared in her arms. "Look how beautiful she is."

Nathan leaned over and brushed a finger across the baby's face. "She's ours?"

"Choose love, Nathan. Come with me. We didn't get our time here. But I will spend my eternity with you and our daughter."

Kimberly sensed Nathan's struggle. *Come on. Make the right decision.*

"I have a daughter?" Nathan shook his head again. Would the knowledge only further inflame him?

Sarah extended her hand. "Please, Nathan. Come with me. It's time for us to be together."

Nathan stared at her hand. He looked around the hotel before turning to look back at Kimberly. "I'm so sorry. Tell everyone I hurt that I'm sorry. I . . . I'm going with them."

Her energy ebbed as relief flowed through her. The portal flickered. "I will. Hurry. Go now. I'm completely drained. Your window is closing."

He nodded then joined Sarah, seemingly transfixed by the infant. He took her hand, and the two of them turned and crossed through the portal.

She watched their outlines disappear. A huge weight lifted from her shoulders, knowing so many found peace tonight. *This is what it's all about. Nights like tonight make all the sacrifices worth it.*

She saw the image of an older man from the corner of her eye. When she turned to see who remained, he tapped his nose and pointed to her with a smile. *Who? What?*

She collapsed on the floor. Before everything went black, Ms. Theodora bent low and whispered, "They are all well. Now you can go home."

CHAPTER FIFTY-THREE

KIMBERLY SAT ALONE in her trailer nursing a lukewarm cup of coffee, which was not helping her headache. She should be jubilant. Despite all the complications and interfering spirits and self-doubt, she had helped resolve Nathan's desire for revenge and cleared the hotel for Ms. Reddick. And had an extra bit of good news for the sweet older woman. But a persistent tug of disappointment wouldn't leave her alone. Wrap day always seemed to be shrouded in gloom for her. Closing a chapter held a bittersweet note. Kind of like reaching the end of a really good book. The satisfaction of resolution was tinged with the knowledge that it was over. No more. Until the next one, of course.

Plus, Rosie had not confirmed if she intended to remain with the show. Rosie normally hovered at her side, anticipating her every need. Where was she? In the trailer making a wrap-day tea to comfort her? Reminding her they would start a new case next week? Teasing her about how hot Sterling was and making her believe a guy like that, who had no interest in the paranormal and wanted everything explained away, could truly have feelings for a psychic? No.

She suspected her stylist/assistant/best friend was with Lorenzo. Darned Lorenzo. Why did he have to be so polite and caring and treat Rosie well? If he was a typical jerk, she could trash him and feel okay about pushing Rosie to walk away. She wanted Rosie to be happy above all else. And if the show no longer made her completely happy, if she needed a man to sweep her off her feet and make Eureka Springs her home to be happy, then they would all have to accept it. Somehow. And yet her absence stung.

Speaking of typical jerk, the whole Jason thing still hung over her. Maybe he would simply leave and that would be the end of it. If she'd had any lingering concerns about making a mistake not taking him back, last night decided it. The way he'd stood there and watched as she dangled over the stairwell, courting death, stunned her. He hadn't done a thing. Sure, everyone responded differently to fear and traumatic situations. But she needed someone who sprang to action and could be relied upon to keep his head in an emergency.

Like Sterling. Her stomach quivered at the thought of him diving to her aid. She felt safe and trusted him when he told her he would never let her fall. She could believe him. Her ears strained for the sound of her trailer door swinging open. She'd become accustomed to him bounding in unannounced, teasing grin on his face, masculine scent filling the space.

She'd expected him to join her for coffee this morning. And didn't want to admit how disappointed his nonappearance left her. *I wish I'd asked him to take me to that café he told me about*, she thought as she sipped at a mug she'd brewed from the machine he gifted her.

She'd also received a call from Angela, her house sitter, alerting her to an increase in activity at her home. Angela swore she'd woken to the scent of "lavender and something else" in the night and thought she might have heard a woman's voice again. Angela knew something of the house's history, and Kimberly knew Sterling would argue her house sitter invented or imagined occurrences that would support what Kimberly expected and hoped to hear about.

But I never told Angela about my mother's perfume. Lavender and freesia.

She needed more time in the house. Even if she couldn't bring in equipment for a full-blown investigation, if she could spend more time there and really focus on the house, surely she could determine once and for all if her mother remained in the dwelling. A night or two here and there wasn't enough.

Someone knocked on the door. She jumped. Was Sterling finally listening to her and knocking instead of barging in? She smoothed her hair and adjusted her blouse. And silently cursed Rosie for not being there to do her makeup. *Oh, well. He's seen me with and he's seen me without.*

She opened the door.

Jason.

Disappointment dropped like a stone in her stomach.

"Hey," he said, eyeing her closely. "Have you been crying?"

"What? No." Irritation at the insult reminded her how oblivious he could be to others' feelings. *Definitely not a fellow sensitive.* "I'm completely drained from the investigation. Surely you remember how much they impacted me and how it often takes days to recover."

He shrugged. "I don't remember you looking like this. Can I come in?"

Tell him no! Her head knew best but her heart still thought it over.

He must have seen the hesitation. "I won't be long."

She stepped back and allowed him in. "Just for a moment."

He glanced around the trailer. "Nice. This is really nice. Much better than using our bathroom to get ready, huh? All the counter space is yours."

The reminder of the time they lived together twisted her stomach into knots. "Jason, I—"

"I came by to tell you I can't do this."

Wait, what? That was her line. *He* can't do this? *He's the one who showed up unexpectedly and asked for a second chance.* Her mouth opened and closed as she attempted to think of something clever and biting in reply. "You can't what?" *Good job, mouth.*

"I'm really sorry. Not to sound cliché but it's me, not you. You're successful. You're as smart and sweet as ever. But I can't handle all the publicity. It's really getting to me. Maybe if your fans embraced me like they do Sterling instead of eviscerating me every time I get near you. Or maybe if I could feel like I was more important to you than the show."

His hang dog expression, clearly intended to guilt her into feeling sorry for him, didn't fool her for a moment. A quick reading of his spectrum confirmed he was being manipulative and self-serving. His heart chakra and throat chakra gave off no energy—no friendship, no love, no true desire to communicate.

His desired outcome wasn't compromise or reconciliation. He wanted things his way. Unless she capitulated and gave him exactly what he wanted, nothing would change. And he genuinely seemed to think he had a chance at winning her over.

Knowing nothing she wanted to say to him would accomplish anything good, she remained silent.

He raised his eyebrows, presumably attempting to prompt her into replying.

She crossed her arms and maintained silence.

He squirmed, clearly uncomfortable with this reaction. When she still said nothing, his brow furrowed. With a shrug, he said, "Well, goodbye, I guess."

He walked to the door but turned back as if to give her one last chance.

To grovel? No, thanks. What a drama king.

The door flew open to reveal a scowling Sterling.

"He's leaving, Sterling. Please don't block the way."

Sterling stepped aside and swept his arm in an arc, gesturing down the stairs. He lifted his phone and snapped a picture of Jason's back before joining her in the trailer. "What was that?"

"He came here to dump me. Again." The words caught in her throat, and she fought the tears that threatened to spill from her eyes. Though she knew she'd done the right thing not letting that toxic mess back into her life, getting dumped still hurt. She swiped at her cheeks. "Damn it. I can't believe he did it again."

"Give me your phone," Sterling said, an edge to his voice and fire in his eyes.

Not exactly the response she expected. Too startled to ask why, she complied.

His fingers flew over his own phone screen, then he switched to hers.

"How did you unlock—"

"Magician never reveals his secrets," he mumbled, engrossed in her phone.

He had pulled up her Twitter account, loaded the photo he'd taken of Jason walking away, and was composing a tweet. A smile spread across his face as he typed.

Just showed him the door. He never looked better. Goodbye and good riddance.

She sucked in a breath when he posted. "But I didn't—"

"Were you dating him? Did you take him back?"

"No!"

"Did you imply you might date him in the future?"

"Absolutely not."

"Exactly. So why are you standing here misty-eyed thinking he dumped you? You're Kimberly freakin' Wantland. Nobody dumps you. Especially not Mr. Potato Head, a loser you weren't dating. As your media specialist, I've taken control of the situation before he posts some fabricated nonsense. Your fans didn't like him anyway. Look. There's your proof."

She kept her phone silenced at all times, but she could see the Twitter notifications ticking steadily upwards. In less than a minute, they numbered over a hundred.

She hazarded a glance at a few. Lots of hearts and heart-eyed emoji faces. A few people echoed the post with varying forms of "good riddance!" Someone, presumably a hotel guest, had added a photo from last night as she dangled above the stairwell, barely clinging to the bannister. Jason stood in the background doing nothing while Sterling dove to grab her, probably saving her life. The photographer had added graphics to the photo—the word LOSER with an arrow pointing to Jason and HERO with an arrow pointing to Sterling.

She shivered at the image of herself, horrified by how close she had come to a terrifying fate. The look on Sterling's face as he fought gravity, refusing to let her go, said it all.

"Anything negative?" he asked.

She shook her head and raised her eyes to meet his gaze. Her heart pounded. She knew what she intended to do and wasn't going to stop herself.

Sterling shifted from one foot to the other. "What? What does that look mean? Did I do something wrong?"

She crossed to him. "Wrong? You saved my life." She felt his orange chakra flare.

"Well, I'm sure someone would have—"

She threw herself against him, wrapped her arms around him, and flooded him with all the positive energy she could gather.

He gasped. And then he curled his arms around her. "Yes. Definitely. I saved you. Frankly, I'm not sure how you survived before I joined the show."

She radiated energy until her already-depleted reserve emptied. But she didn't break off the embrace. Leaning against his chest, his fingertips gently stroking her back, she reveled in the warmth, confident that he would support and help her. Even if it was only to guard his own job security, she would take it. "I wanted to show you how grateful I am. This is the best way I know how."

His chest rumbled against her cheek. "Message received. Not understood. But received. I had convinced myself I imagined this feeling that night in the laundry room. How do you do it? I feel electric. Not bad like a shock, but . . . charged up. It's nice. Except I don't know how you're doing it."

"I told you before, you wouldn't believe me if I told you.

Maybe some day you'll believe." Warm and safe in his arms, she took a chance of asking him the question that niggled at the back of her mind. "Did you save me to make sure you wouldn't be out of a job again?"

He leaned back, lifting her face and forcing eye contact. "You can't possibly mean that."

"I can't tell. You talk so much about media and publicity and promotion and making sure the show does well."

"And that's a bad thing?"

"Of course not."

"I like to think I've dropped some pretty solid hints about the desire to be close partners at least. But a guy can only hint so much before his feelings start to get hurt."

"Some of us aren't very good with hints."

"Besides, you've stated in no uncertain terms how you feel about relationships. Repeatedly."

"They complicate things. I stand by that."

"I've heard that when you're with the right person, it's more an acclimatization than a complication. Some people even go so far as to say that having the right person in your life can actually improve things."

The intensity of his gaze captivated her. His pulsating orange chakra radiated desire, compounding her quickening awareness of his body. She couldn't remember ever responding to a man this way. His husky voice, musky scent, and raging chakras tantalized and inflamed her own desire. Her lower chakras throbbed and spun in response.

He tightened his embrace and leaned forward.

She watched his mouth approach, the anticipation of his lips on hers driving all other thoughts away.

The trailer door opened.

"Sorry I'm so late, girl. I—"

She turned just in time to see Rosie's jaw drop and wondered which of them looked guiltier.

Rosie backed away, feeling for the door behind her. "Oh my

gosh, I'm so sorry. Now I wish I'd been even later. Worst timing ever. Pretend I was never here. I wasn't here. I saw nothing."

Sterling laughed. And kept his arms around her waist. "We're all adults and I have no secrets. Heck, snap a picture and post it. Pretend you walked in on something more than a hug. Possibly the hottest, most incredible hug ever. But a hug."

Rosie looked to Kimberly for guidance. "Can you salvage the moment?"

Michael burst into the trailer. "Are we wrapping today or what? What's the—Oh. Oh. Oh. Sorry." He stared at the ceiling, then the floor, then the door. "Maybe it's time to add a lock to that door?"

"I'd settle for a sign on the handle that says 'Go away,'" Kimberly said. "Come on, Rosie. The cameras await and I need makeup."

"Actually, I had something to tell, Kimberly. Or show you, I guess," Sterling said.

Rosie lifted an eyebrow. "If he's showing you something, you need some privacy. Makeup can wait."

"Not what I'm showing her, Rosie. I'm old-fashioned enough that I prefer a first kiss before I start whipping things out."

"Sterling!" She wriggled out of his arms, her face flushing.

Michael wiped a hand across his forehead. "Whew. It's getting warm in here. Maybe don't rub the single guy's nose in it, huh?"

"He really is the complete package," Rosie said. "You're so lucky."

"Wait a minute. What about Lorenzo?"

Rosie shrugged. "I told him I really like him and could see myself settling down with him here in Eureka Springs."

Her stomach dropped. Things were going so well. Surely Rosie wouldn't pull the rug out from under her.

"Eventually," Rosie said. "But not yet. I can't imagine leaving the show. Or you guys."

Michael's head whipped back and forth between them. "Excuse me? Kimmy? Rosie leaving?"

"Lorenzo asked her to stay."

"And you didn't bother telling me about that?"

"I couldn't bring myself to entertain the thought it might actually happen." The morning roller coaster of emotions sent tears of happiness streaking her cheeks. She hugged Rosie, squeezing as though she would never let go. "I told you the show doesn't go on without you."

Michael blanched. "Sorry, sweetie, but I beg to differ. We would find a new stylist for you. The show would have to go on no matter how much we missed Rosie."

"See?" Rosie said. "And then I'd go to jail cuz I would have to kill that bitch. So this is for the best."

"Jeez," Sterling said. "Jealous much?"

Rosie gave him the look. "Do you know me at all?"

He cleared his throat. "Well, I hope my news doesn't pale in comparison."

"Oh, right," Kimberly said, drying her eyes. "What did you want to tell me? Or show me?"

He handed her a piece of paper.

She read it. Read it again. Still unconvinced, she read it a third time. "I don't . . . Is this what I think it is?"

Sterling nodded. "Legal and binding. Drawn up by my attorney friend."

Her eyes brimmed with tears yet again.

"Kimmy? What is it?"

"Sterling apparently convinced my Aunt Dolly to let me investigate my house!"

Michael's eyes looked like they might pop out of the sockets. "What? But she's been so adamant."

"I know that better than anyone."

Michael rushed to her side and took the document. He shook his head as he read it. "I don't believe this."

Sterling beamed. "And you'll notice the language is such that your aunt relinquishes all claims and influences on the home. Everything. For the record, the attorney agreed that once you bought the home, enforcing the no-investigation clause would have been difficult."

She opened her mouth to refute the belief, but he held up a hand.

"But he also understands that you wouldn't want the bad press a family feud would result in. This document now renders all previous clauses in the will and home contract null and void."

She threw herself into his arms a second time. "But how? How did you sway her?"

He rubbed the back of his neck. "I promised her I would be trying to prove the house isn't haunted. You may not like it, but my skepticism worked in our favor."

"*Our* favor?" She liked the sound of that.

"Hey, happy cohost, happy life. Right? It may not rhyme, but—"

"But it's headed in the right direction," Rosie said.

Michael squinted at the document. "Do we have caveats in this fine print?"

"No. The contract is clear. You may do what you like with the house. But I did make a promise I'd be there to refute your claims of paranormal activity. And I'm a man of my word."

"But you do that anyway. That's what you do on my show."

A Cheshire cat smile spread across his face, a devilish gleam in his eyes. "I know."

"It will be a regular investigation!" A giggle erupted from her. A giggle. When did she start giggling? "Michael! Guess what our season finale will be!"

"I hate to be a Debbie Downer, but the crew and Ms. Reddick are waiting. Rosie, I see you trying to sneak out. Get some makeup on these two and let's wrap. Then they can have the rest of the day alone."

"I'll do their makeup. But then we're leaving them alone for five minutes before we start the wrap."

CHAPTER FIFTY-FOUR

KIMBERLY SKIPPED up the front steps and into the hotel lobby. The crew had arranged a couch beside the piano at her request. The bright, vibrant lobby would make a better wrap location than the dark dreariness of the laundry room where they'd started. Let her fans see her basking in the sparkling sunlight, glowing in her glory. Looking around the lobby, she noticed others orienting to face her and faces returning her beaming smile. Her chakras must be radiating her overwhelming positive energy, flooding the room with good vibes.

Selma Reddick already perched on the edge of the sofa cushion, leaning heavily on her cane. A pall of concern seemed to weigh her down. At the sight of Kimberly, however, the older woman's slumped back straightened.

"You look like you have good news," Ms. Reddick said as Kimberly settled in beside her.

"I do." She squeezed Ms. Reddick's hand.

Rosie clipped a mike to her blouse. "I intended to press for all the juicy details of your alone time with Sterling, but your face says it all, girl."

She shook her head and wished she could stop blushing.

"Stop. Lipstick doesn't lie and you know it. Do you see so much as a smudge?"

"Seriously? You wasted that alone time?"

"I didn't say that. We had a nice talk."

Rosie grimaced. "Ick. Too boring. You need to give the shippers something to talk about."

Ms. Reddick offered a sly smile and tapped the side of her nose. "You and Sterling? I thought I sensed something there."

"It's not a thing. Yet. I don't know. But we have arrived at the conclusion that we make good partners and are on the same page in acknowledging friendship and perhaps being open to something more at a future date."

Rosie gave her the look and pressed her fingers to her temples. "That was way too many words to say you like someone. You gave me a headache."

"I agree with Rosie," Ms. Reddick said. "I think I like Sterling's approach a bit more." The older woman turned her phone, open to Twitter of all things.

She felt her flush spread further across her face and creep down her neck. "Et tù, Ms. Reddick? Seriously, when did Twitter become such a thing?"

Sterling had posted a photograph of them and captioned it: *Hands off, guys. She's all mine.*

"He will do anything for a little attention," she said, rolling her eyes. Though she tried hard to feign annoyance, she couldn't hide from herself. The butterflies dancing in her stomach, her increased heart rate, and the warm and fuzzy buzzing coursing through her body wouldn't allow her to deny how pleased she was to have the attention of Sterling Wakefield.

Movement at the front door drew her attention. Sterling paused in the sun rays at the entrance, clad in his usual black denim and black shirt. Rosie had convinced him to trade up from a T-shirt to a collared button up. He'd left it unbuttoned enough to expose a little skin. He raked his fingers through his tousled hair, scanning the lobby. Her pulse pounded at the sight of him, but the smile that lit his face when he caught sight of her melted her heart.

Ms. Reddick patted her hand. "You know, after the accident that took my husband away, all I could think about was how unfair life is. And I truly believed I had no right to be happy. How could I find happiness when my husband was gone? If he's not here to see the flowers bloom, how could I enjoy the gardens? One night, I woke up to the smell of roses in my flat upstairs. It wasn't a whiff, mind you. The scent filled the entire space. Now, I know your Sterling would say I dreamed it, but I believe my husband came to let me know I *should* enjoy the flowers and everything else. I believe he wanted to tell me it's okay to be happy."

Kimberly clutched the woman's hand, blinking back tears. How many times had she smelled lavender and freesia growing up?

"And now," Ms. Reddick continued, "I'm telling you, whatever or whoever you're missing and longing to see again, no matter how much guilt you might feel about the loss, it's okay to be happy."

"Oh, don't make me cry. My makeup will run." She hugged Ms. Reddick. "Thank you."

Rosie pressed a tissue into her hand. "Blot, don't wipe. I have powder if you need it."

Kimberly nodded at Rosie, then whispered to Ms. Reddick. "He's here. You're right about that. I saw him last night."

Ms. Reddick's eyes widened. "My husband?"

"I'm certain. He tapped the side of his nose, like you do."

"Yes! That's him. I knew it. I knew he stayed close by. How did he look?"

"Happy. He smiled. He nodded. And he definitely opted to stay. He could have crossed through the portal, but he didn't so we can be sure he isn't trapped or miserable. I believe he wants to stay here with you until you're ready to cross."

Ms. Reddick took the tissue from her hand and dabbed at

her own eyes. "We always wanted to do everything together. I'm so glad he's okay. And I'm glad to know he'll be waiting for me when my time comes. Thank you so much."

Sterling stood in front of the couch. "You making our client cry, Kimberly? Whoa. You're crying too? What happened in the five minutes I wasn't with you?"

"They're happy tears, you goose," she said. "Sit down there on the other side of Ms. Reddick."

"Goose?" he said, wrinkling his nose. "I guess I've been called worse."

Rosie swooped in to clip a mike to his collar. "You look divine. That shirt really shows off that trim waist and your biceps. Nice."

He grinned at the praise and glanced at Kimberly, perhaps hoping she was equally impressed.

Michael cleared his throat. "Are you ready to do this, Kimmy? Er, Kimberly? Sweetie, I'm sorry I forgot Jason gave you that nickname. I've called you that since college and frankly I didn't associate it with him. Be honest with me. What do you want me to call you?"

"Michael, I can honestly say I am over Jason. I've made my peace and I'm glad we went our separate ways. Seeing him again this week helped with that at least. And frankly, you've called me Kimmy longer than he did. It's turned into your special name for me."

Michael fanned his face. "Now you're making me cry."

"She's okay with Kimmy!" someone from the crowd of onlookers called.

"Nope! That's only for Michael. No one else!"

She may be okay with it, but she still didn't love it.

Sterling raised his voice. "I thought we were wrapping this show." He caught her gaze and gave her a thumbs up.

Butterflies flitted through her stomach yet again and her cheeks flushed. She wished her abilities gave her the power to control her reactions.

She's all mine.

"Yes, here we go. Kimmy? Ready?"

She faced Stan's camera as Michael counted her in. After summarizing the pertinent findings of the investigation, she extended her hand to Ms. Reddick. "Thank you so much for allowing us to stay here at your beautiful hotel. Don't hesitate to reach out if you have any further problems."

"Thank you, Kimberly, for helping with our problem. And for easing my mind." Ms. Reddick tapped the side of her nose.

"And cut," Michael called. "That was quick and to the point. Let's get a shot of you two in front of the hotel as our episode closing image."

TJ intercepted her as she moved through the lobby. "Ms. Wantland? Can I show you something?"

"Right now? In the middle of wrap?"

"Please?"

"Okay. Sure. What is it?"

He pulled a laptop from his backpack and brought up a video. "It's just an idea I had and you can say no. Remember how Sterling wanted to reshoot the opening sequence?"

"Actually I had forgotten about that." Letting Sterling in, allowing him to be part of her show and her brand, meant she would have to make some concessions. *Easier said than done.* Did she want him in the opening sequence? What was next? *The Wantland/Wakefield Files?*

TJ pushed his glasses back up his nose. "Okay, your face tells me you don't love the idea. And I was totally against it at first, too. But I do kinda agree that if he's staying permanently, it would be nice to at least acknowledge him in the opening sequence. Right? I mean, Dr. Who gets a new opening every time the Doctor regenerates. You've had the same one for three years running. Don't want to get stale."

Stale sounded too much like "old," "has-been," and "yesterday's news." She couldn't have that. "A new opening might be exactly what we need for a new season. Let's see."

TJ moved the mouse and played the video.

Her voice began as always. "Dark figures." TJ had changed the clip that accompanied the vocal track to a piece of footage of The Dark from the Williams' home investigation last season.

Sterling's voice spoke the next line. "Flickering lights." A segment from the Crescent Hotel laundry room while the washer and dryer lights flipped on and off played alongside his words.

"Moving objects." Her original recording again, with a bit of footage from a previous investigation where they captured a woman's toiletries shifting on her vanity.

Sterling took the next line, "Noises in the night," now coupled with the EVP, "Get out!" captured last season.

Her concerned voice intoned, "The feeling something isn't quite right," as she comforted Sterling in the laundry room while the angry manifestation of Nathan's spirit antagonized him.

"Is it your imagination?" Sterling spoke this line from a Confidential Corner, his arms crossed, a knowing look on his face.

"Or something reaching out from beyond?" The ghost of the young woman in the mirror filled the frame to her words.

"I'm Kimberly Wantland." This line and visual segment remained exactly the same as the first opening credits sequence. She stood in front of their headquarters in Albuquerque while a graphic of her name swooped into the screen and landed at the bottom of the frame.

"I'm Sterling Wakefield." TJ had spliced in audio and video that mimicked hers, complete with his name on the screen.

"And these are *The Wantland Files*." Her young camera operator had isolated a bit of recording that captured both her and Sterling in the shot, peering thoughtfully at something that had piqued their interest.

The Wantland Files logo materialized over the last image.

TJ tried to apologize before the video faded. "I know no one asked me to do this and I know I'm just a camera guy. And I know you didn't really want a new opening sequence. But I thought maybe if you had a mock-up, you'd see it could be a good change. It's still the same show. It just has Sterling now. But if you hate it—"

"I love it."

"Really?"

"You are more skilled than I realized. This is very good."

TJ blushed and pushed one finger against the bridge of his glasses, sliding them back into place. "I was only messing around. I've been making videos since I was a kid."

"Messing around? It's great. Let's get it to production so they can include it with this season opener. Michael, have you seen the new opening sequence?"

"Yes, sweetie. Waiting to loop in RandMeier until I got the green light from you."

She gave him a thumbs up. "It's awesome."

"Then we run with it. Let's get this last shot in the can. I think I see a hot bubble bath in my future tonight. I need a relaxing evening before we hit the road."

Marcus answered the phone as she passed the desk. His eyes widened. "Ms. Wantland? It's for you." He held the phone out to her. "It's a call from Ms. Theodora's room."

She accepted the receiver and pressed it to her ear. "Hello?"

Static crackled and hissed. But she heard a female voice say, "Thank you," before the line went dead, replaced by a dial tone.

She gave the phone back to Marcus. "I don't think she will call again."

Marcus breathed a sigh of relief. "Thank you, Ms. Wantland. I'm so glad you believed us and took care of the ghosts."

She shook his hand one last time. Gratitude like his kept her getting up every morning and staying up all night. "I'm glad I could help."

The crew had already moved outside to gauge lighting and set up for the final shoot. Sterling fell into step beside her. "Another satisfied customer."

"Yes. It feels really good to help. I wish someone had believed me when I was younger."

"Ghosts or not, there is no denying people feel better after meeting you. The older couple you met with at the cave are all over the news and posting online. You saved that woman's life. She went to the doctor and is lucky she did. You did that."

"Her mother's spirit told me."

"Whatever happened, you took the time to sit with her, to console her. And convince her to seek treatment. I'm impressed. You have a huge heart."

She flushed. Of course Sterling would be online watching for anything to do with her or the show. She hadn't seen it and appreciated he shared the news with her. "I only intended to put her mind at ease. This was an extreme case. But thank you."

"You're okay with the changes TJ and I made to the opening?"

"I like it."

"But you're okay changing things?"

"I changed things the moment I asked you to join me. The changes weren't exactly what I expected, but that's on me. I'll work on being less rigid and protective. I know you only want what's best for the show."

He touched her arm. "I want to be what you expected. I may not believe in ghosts, but I'll always have your back. I mean that."

Michael called instructions to them. "Come down off the steps, please. We're losing you in shadow. Good. Now angle away from each other. You don't have to be back-to-back, but maybe shoulder-to-shoulder. That's it. No, you can't both cross your arms. Sterling, maybe hands on hips. Yes. Good. And five, four, three . . ."

She turned to Stan's camera. "Crescent Hotel, American's most haunted hotel, proved to be a serious challenge. The location teems with activity and singling out one entity among the bunch wasn't easy. But we did it, and I'm delighted even Sterling experienced some things he couldn't quite explain."

Sterling chuckled. "I'm not ready to admit I saw ghosts, but this was a fantastic investigation, rich with history. I'm glad for the opportunity to stay in this beautiful part of the country and learn a little history. And I'm glad I was here to catch Kimberly."

She smiled at him, glad he was here and grateful he caught her. "We helped transition some ghosts and eased Ms. Reddick's mind in the process. All in all, a great experience. Join us next time for more *Wantland Files*."

"And cut," Michael yelled. "That's a wrap. Everyone relax and rest so we can do it all over again."

Sterling turned to her, eyes bright. "Where to next?"

ACKNOWLEDGMENTS

Crescent Hotel is a stunning hotel in beautiful Eureka Springs, Arkansas. I fell in love with both the hotel and the town my first visit. Norman Baker actually owned Crescent Hotel and used it as a cancer treatment center as described in the book. Though I included actual locations, referenced historical information, and incorporated some elements of the real ghost lore, I took great artistic liberties with my story and no character in the book should be confused with a real person (or ghost). This mystery and reimagining of what could happen is entirely the product of my imagination. My thanks to hotel owner Elise Roenigk for allowing me to set my story in her fabulous hotel. I knew I had to bring my characters to Crescent and am pleased she gave her blessing.

The Grotto really exists on Center Street in Eureka Springs. The owners are delightful and I highly recommend enjoying dinner there if at all possible.

Mud Street Café on Main Street Eureka Springs makes the best coffee and pastries. The cinnamon rolls are heavenly and highly recommended.

Thank you Betty Ridge, Rick Johnson, and Sean Callahan for your feedback on the manuscript.

Thank you to my cover designers Maria and Victoria at BeauteBooks.

And, as always, thank you Bill.

SIGN UP FOR MORE

Did you enjoy *The Haunting of Crescent Hotel*? If so, please leave a review wherever you purchase books.

Sign up for my newsletter to be the first to know of upcoming releases, chances for contests, and to receive previews and insider information http://www.larabernhardt.com/contact

I'd love to hear about YOUR supernatural encounters! Feel free to reach out and share!

MORE BY ADMISSION PRESS

ADMISSION PRESS

Looking for your next great read?
Visit www.admissionpress.com

ABOUT THE AUTHOR

Lara Bernhardt is a Pushcart-nominated writer, editor, and audiobook narrator. She is Editor-in-Chief of Balkan Press and also publishes a literary magazine, *Conclave*. Twice a finalist for the Oklahoma Book Award for Best Fiction, she writes supernatural suspense and women's fiction. You can follow her on Amazon and on all the socials @larawells1 on Twitter and @larabern10 on Facebook, BookBub, and Instagram.

ALSO BY LARA BERNHARDT

The Wantland Files series
The Wantland Files
Ghosts of Guthrie

Women's Fiction
Shadow of the Taj

Made in the USA
Coppell, TX
28 December 2021